BEAUFORT

Ron Leshem, born in 1976, is a native of Ramat Gan, near Tel Aviv. His novel *Beaufort* won the Sapir Prize – Israel's top literary award – for 2006, as well as the Yitzhak Sadeh Prize for military literature. In 2002 he became deputy editor of Maariv newspaper and in 2006 joined the Channel Two television station as deputy director in charge of programming and special projects. *Beaufort* is his first novel.

Evan Fallenberg is a US-born writer, translator and teacher living in Israel. He is the author of the novel *Light Fell*.

'Ron Leshem has succeeded in creating an entire world, simply through language'
David Grossman

'This gripping first novel describes . . . a country increasingly weary of endless war and strained by differences between hawks and doves . . . By turns, it is tragic, funny, mordant, irate, shocking, and poignant . . . A must read'
Booklist

'A radical anti-war novel; a universal reflection about fear and defeat . . . The novel has a documentary power which is difficult to evade . . . It is not a war novel but a novel about retreat and a petition for the message that defeat can be much more strengthening than any victory bought with blood'
Der Spiegel

'Scenarios unfold, funny, chilling and unrelenting . . . Leshem never slackens his pace'
San Francisco Chronicle

'Skilfully sketches the alternating terror and tedium of war'
The Economist

'The novel plays with language in several ways . . . It is also a critique of the language of war and the comfortable platitudes fed to the civilians at home'
Times Literary Supplement

'In pungent and rhythmic writing, Leshem depicts a society which feels morally as well as physically besieged.'

Le Figaro

'A gripping, viscerally powerful tale ... An alternately grim and blackly comic war/coming-of-age novel'

Kirkus Reviews

'An important novel ... This is a picture of war from a soldier's point of view. Its language is crude, the body count rises, and yet the tenderness of the bonds among the men is extraordinary'

Library Journal

'In this gritty first novel ... a certain vulnerable charm ... pulls the reader through'

New York Times Book Review

'Gritty ... the anxiety and fear are palpable throughout Leshem's vivid novel – you can practically feel the shells explode'

Publishers Weekly

RON LESHEM

Beaufort

TRANSLATED FROM THE HEBREW BY
Evan Fallenberg

VINTAGE BOOKS
London

Published by Vintage 2009

2 4 6 8 10 9 7 5 3 1

Copyright © Ron Leshem 2005
English translation copyright © Evan Fallenberg, 2007

Ron Leshem has asserted his right under the Copyright, Designs
and Patents Act 1988 to be identified as the author of this work

First published with the title *Beaufort* in 2005 by
Kinneret, Zmora-Bitan, Divir – Publishing House Ltd.

First published in Great Britain in 2008 by Harvill Secker

Vintage
Random House, 20 Vauxhall Bridge Road
London, SW1V 2SA

www.vintage-books.co.uk

Addresses for companies within The Random House Group Limited
can be found at: www.randomhouse.co.uk/offices.htm

The Random House Group Limited Reg. No. 954009

The book has been selected to receive financial assistance
from English PEN's Writers in Translation programme supported
by Bloomberg

A CIP catalogue record for this book
is available from the British Library

ISBN 9780099516729

The Random House Group Limited supports The Forest Stewardship
Council (FSC), the leading international forest certification
organisation. All our titles that are printed on Greenpeace approved
FSC certified paper carry the FSC logo. Our paper procurement
policy can be found at www.rbooks.co.uk/environment

Printed and bound in Great Britain by
CPI Cox & Wyman, Reading RG1 8EX

BEAUFORT

PROLOGUE

What He Can't Do Any More

Yonatan can't see us growing ugly any more. 'We'll never be as handsome as we are today,' he'd say, and I'd ask if that was meant to make us feel better, because it didn't.

What? Are you completely out of it? How could you not know this game? There's no way you don't know it. It's called 'What he can't do any more' and it's what everyone plays when a friend is killed. You toss his name into the air and whoever's there at the time has to come up with something he can't do any more. Sometimes it goes on for hours. On the playing field, in the middle of a penalty kick. Or late at night, for no good reason, you wake everyone up about half a minute after they've dropped off to sleep. Or you're at home, working on your girlfriend, not thinking about us at all, and the last thing in the world you want is to play the game, well BAM! the phone rings and it's us on the line. 'Yonatan can't . . .' we say, and you have to – everyone has to – reel off some association, that's the rule, and you can't repeat what's already been said. Here's what I'm talking about:

Yonatan can't take his little brother to the cinema any more. Yonatan can't watch Hapoel bring home the cup any more. Yonatan can't listen to Zion Golan's latest CD any more. He can't see Tom with the ugliest slut in Nahariya any more, and after he laughed at all of us, that little Mongoloid. He'll never know how fucking bad it is when you can't get it up. He'll never know how great it is when your mother's proud of you for getting accepted by a college. Even a community college. He won't be at his grandfather's funeral, he won't know if his sister gets married, he won't take a piss with us from the highest peak in South America, he won't ski in

Chacaltaya, he won't screw the hottest Peruvian chick in Casa Fistuk.

Yonatan can't know any more the feeling of renting a flat with his girlfriend. Yonatan can't know any more what it is to go shopping with her to Castro's and come out with the entire new winter collection, or to head out to the Roladin Bakery in the middle of the night, when it's raining, because all of a sudden she wants a doughnut, and anyway you're a jerk, you never knew how to say no to her. And here I am thinking how lucky I am that I've already had the chance once to run out for doughnuts in the rain.

He'll never cheat on her. He'll never know what it's like to fuck the living daylights out of the sexiest girl in the country, some whore from Haifa who lures you into a one night stand, before you understand, too late, that it wasn't worth it, and the love of your life has left you. He'll never know how much that hurts. And he'll never know what it's like to sit on the grass with a child that's his very own, telling him stories about how we were larger than life in those ambushes in Lebanon. How we pulled off some magnificent stuff up there. He'll never tell him. There are so many things Yonatan can't do any more.

Yonatan won't know what song they played at his grave when he died: *Shir Hamaalot*, a psalm done Middle Eastern-style. It became his song. Everyone killed has a song played at his funeral, that stays with his friends for ever. For months you listen and never get sick of it.

Yonatan will never know how River the medic cried over his body, how he couldn't calm down, how he fell apart, to pieces. Wailed like a baby. Yonatan'll never know how Furman and I spent a whole day in the trenches and down the slopes looking for his missing head. When the missile hit the guard post his head blew off and rolled down to the Litani River. We didn't want to believe that it had rolled all the way down, to the river, but that's exactly what happened, and in the end we gave up. Nothing we could do about it. I leaned over in that heavy smoke and grabbed his body with both hands, a body with no head. He'll never know. How the fire kept on burning all around us and we kept shooting and shooting and shooting in every possible direction, as though that would make us feel better. How shattered everyone was. The day before, we'd danced the waltz in our freezing dugout. We lit candles, we were happy. And then it ended. He'll never ever know.

Yonatan can't sniff that sweet sweat mixed with the faint smell of shampoo during a long night of wild sex and cuddling, like during the week we all had when we left Lebanon, when everything ended. Yonatan will never even know that we left Lebanon.

A lot of people have lost a lot of people since we lost Yonatan. We've lost others since then too, because another war broke out and everything became more savage. And indifferent, too. And who's got enough time on his hands to deal with what happened back then? When that new war broke out we lost Barnoy. Then another eleven guys. Then, when the dead reached 920 and it looked like it was all over, we lost Koka's brother, who'd followed in his footsteps and enlisted with us. We've made love a thousand times since then, it's not like we haven't, and we've laughed a thousand times. We moved on to other places, we escaped and came back, we remembered. But quietly. We've all imagined how we'll return to the fortress, to our mountain. There'll be a hotel there, maybe. Or a place for lovers to sit. Or maybe it will be deserted. There'll be peace. And I will lead her along the paths, we'll walk hand in hand. 'Here, baby, this is exactly where it happened.' And, stone by stone, I'll show her. She might even ask if that's the whole story. 'How can that be the whole story? What made you cry so much, it's so beautiful and peaceful here, so green, and quiet. This is the place where you broke down?'

Try to imagine what it's like when they stick you high up on a mountain cliff, higher up than the roof of the Azrieli Building. How could you not have a breathtaking view? You see wide expanses of green countryside chequered with patches of brown and red, snowy mountains, frothing rivers, narrow, winding, deserted European-style roads. And there's the sweetest wind. Zitlawi used to say that air like this should be bottled and sold to rich people on the north side of Tel Aviv. Christ, what quality. It's so fucking pastoral you could cut the calm with a knife. Our sunsets, too, they're the most beautiful on the planet, and the sunrises are even more beautiful, glimmering serenity from the roof of the world. Bring a girl or two here when the sky is orange and you've got it made. And dawn, an amazing cocktail of deep blue and turquoise and wine red and thin strips of pink, like an oil painting. And the deep wadi that twists away from the big rock we're sitting on. Try to explain how this could be the place where you broke down.

But from that night I remember the lights of Kiryat Shmona on the Israeli side of the border receding on the horizon, and each man's heart beating – I swear it, I can hear them – as we make our way up to the top that very first time. It's getting colder by the minute. There's not a living soul around except for us, barely a village in our zone. The convoy crawls along, gets swallowed up in a thick fog, we can't see more than a hundred yards ahead. Tanks are spread out along the road to provide cover for us. From a slit near the roof of the Safari I try to work out how far along we've come, silently poring over the map which outlines danger spots and racing through an abbreviated battle history, whispering because no talking is allowed. Where will the evil erupt from? I have the urge to shout to the commanding officer that we've gone too far, but I bite my lip and remain silent. From this moment on nobody can tell me any more 'You haven't got a clue what Lebanon is, wait'll you get there.' I'm here, finally, that's what's important. A long line, heavy traffic: a supply Safari, a personnel Safari, a fuel Safari, behind these an ordance truck with a big crane, an Abir truck carrying a doctor and a medic, another personnel Safari, the commander's Hummer, the lieutenant's Hummer, and an electronic equipment Hummer. Oshri asks if I've brought my lucky under-wear with me. I gesture to him that I'm wearing them. After all, our good fortune depends on my lucky underwear. They're on, even if that means thirty-two days without washing them.

And I remember how the gate of the outpost opens to let us in, how our Safari comes to a halt inside a cloud of dust. Everyone grabs hold of whatever's lying around – bags, equipment, your own or someone else's – and runs like hell inside. The commanders curse under their breath – 'Out of the vehicles, run, get a move on!' – and people go down, people come up, you're not allowed to stand still, you have to go for shelter. As the parking area fills up with dozens of soldiers, the enemy fires salvoes of mortar shells. And I can't see anything, don't recognize anyone around me, I grab hold of the shirt of some soldier I don't know and get pulled along after him. I'm thrown into a crowded maze, with thick concrete on all sides, long passageways with no visible end or beginning, rooms leading to steep dead-end stairways, culs-de-sac, and then a collection of larger rooms lit up in red, with low ceilings and stretchers. Thirty seconds later I'm already in one of the bomb shelters, a long and narrow alcove, a kind of underground cavern with concave walls covered in rusting metal and cramped three-tiered bunk beds hanging by heavy iron chains from the ceiling.

WELCOME TO DOWN TOWN someone has carved over the doorway, and inside the air is stuffy, suffocating, the stench of sweat overwhelms you again and again, in waves. This pit, called 'the submarine', is where my entire life will take place from now on. I consider a quick trip to the toilet. A seasoned sergeant tells me to follow the blue light to the end of the hall and turn right, but, he informs me, I'll need a flak jacket [battle vest] and a helmet. I decide to hold on. What's the matter, is there a war on or something? I'm not ready to go up in smoke right here and now.

Back then it seemed like it was light years away, but it was just thirty, forty feet to the three green toilets with a graffitied welcome – I CAME, I SAW, I CONQUERED. JULIUS CAESAR – and an official sign commanding users DO NOT LEAVE PIECES OF SHIT ON THE TOILET SEAT so there was never any chance of forgetting where you were.

And next morning, with the first sunrise, as the view of Lebanon spreads out before us like an endless green ocean, Furman, our commanding officer, makes his opening address, which he has undoubtedly been rehearsing for weeks, maybe months, or maybe it has been handed down through the generations: 'Welcome. If there is a heaven, this is what it looks like, and if there is a hell, this is how it feels. The Beaufort outpost.'

Once, Lila asked me, what exactly was Beaufort? And I realized how difficult it is to describe. You have to have been there to understand, and even then that's not enough. Because Beaufort is a lot of things. Like any military outpost, Beaufort is backgammon, Turkish coffee and cheese toasts. You play backgammon for cheese toasts, whoever loses makes them for everyone – killer cheese toasts with pesto. When things are really boring, you play poker for cigarettes. Beaufort is living without a single second of privacy, long weeks with the squad, one bed pushed up against the next, the ability to pick out the smell from each man's boots in your sleep. With your eyes closed, and at any given moment, it's being able to name the guy who farted by the smell alone. This is how true friendship is measured. Beaufort is lying to your mother on the phone so she won't worry. You always say, 'Everything's fine, I've just had a shower and I'm going to bed,' when in fact you haven't showered for twenty-one days, the water in the tanks has been used up, and in a minute you're going up for guard duty. And not just guard duty, but guarding the scariest position there is. When she asks when you're coming home you answer in code. 'Mum, you know the name of the neighbour's dog? I get out of here on the day that begins with the same letter.' What's most important is to keep Hezbollah from listening in and working out when to bomb your convoy. You really want to tell her you love her, that you miss her, but you can't, because your entire squad is there. If you say that, you'll give them ammunition for months, they'll tear you apart with humiliation. And then there's the worst situation of all: in the middle of a conversation with your mother, the mortar shells start raining down on the outpost. She hears an explosion and then the line goes dead. She's over there shaking, certain her boy has been killed, she waits on the balcony for a visit from the army bereavement team. You can't stop thinking about her, feeling sorry for her, but it might be days before the phone line to the command post back in Israel can be reconnected. Worry. That was why I preferred not to call at all. I told my mother I'd been transferred to a base right on the border, near the fence, Lebanon-lite, not deep in at all – definitely not deep in Lebanon – so that she'd sleep at night. Gut feeling, you ask? She knew the truth the whole time, even if she didn't admit it till now.

Beaufort is the South Lebanon Army, the SLA, local Christians, a mad bunch of Phalangists. Cigarettes in their mouths all day long. Smelly, wild, funny. They come in every morning at eight o'clock and we put a guard on them. They build, renovate whatever's been destroyed by the air raids, do what they're told. They're not allowed inside the secure area, not even permitted near the dining room.

Beaufort is guard duty. Sixteen hours a day. How do you stay sane after thousands of dead hours? We're all fucked up in different ways, but do me a favour and don't choke it during guard duty. 'Choke it' is our way of saying 'jerk off'. And some of the boys choke it; they choke it big time. You won't believe this, but a lot of people get really turned on by our green jungle atmosphere. I'm not joking. Nature is romantic, sensual. You would lose control, too. And it's not only nature that turns us on. The Sayas Network, at 67 MHz, used for open transmissions between the outposts, can also give you a hard-on sometimes. It's not an official network – it got its underground nickname from a radio broadcaster who specializes in melancholy late night monologues – but everyone knows about it because everyone, overwhelmed by boredom at one time or another, tunes the dial to Sayas, the boys' favourite, where they can talk bullshit all night long and melt at the sound of the female voices. Because the girls from the command post are on the other end, back in the war room, hot as fire, no air-conditioning, no boys, no reason not to unbutton their shirts a little, let off some steam. They sprawl across their chairs – I'd bet on it – stretching, spreading their legs, dripping hormones, dying for someone to make them laugh, flirt with them, make a little date for when they're back in Israel. Why not? Give them what they really need. Sure, honey, I've got lots of weapons. I got my short-barrelled M-16 flat top, a real beauty. And my Glock, a fantastic pistol. And I also have . . . my personal weapon. Measure it? You want me to? No problem, sure, I'm happy to measure it for you . . . actually I've forgotten how long it is, apologies, honey. That's the way you talk, making it up as you go along, turning yourself on, and they giggle, toying and teasing on that very thin border, one step over the line, one step back, and you're dying to believe that maybe, at the end of the night, when all the other men have dropped out, the girls are left alone, poor things, stuck with having to satisfy one another. What, you don't think so? A little touching, great stuff, nobody's ever died of it. But don't get your hopes up: the sweeter her voice over the airwaves, the more of a dog she is. I take full responsibility for that statement, I've been disappointed often enough in my life. A high squeaky voice, on the other hand, means you might want to invest a little time, because she's got huge tits. That's a fact, I'm not messing you around.

Beaufort is going out on seventy-two-hour ambushes with a huge supply of beef jerky in your knapsack. You can't believe how much of that stuff you can eat in three days. Beef jerky with chocolate and beef jerky with strawberry jam. And how you can talk and talk without saying anything. Pretty soon you reach the point where you know everything about everyone. Who did what, when, with who, why, in what position and what he was thinking about while he was doing it. I can tell you about their parents, their brothers and sisters, their not-so-close friends, their darkest perversions. There's a lot of time alone, too, when you're fed up with all that talking. You think about yourself, your home. You wonder if your mother is hanging out the washing right now, or maybe she's watching Dudu Topaz on television. Lila's probably in the shower. I'm fantasizing. Or maybe she's cheating on me. Freezing cold – we call it 'cold enough for foxes' up here, ice cube cold, the nose is frozen and the extremities numb. The feet have been numb for ages. Fingers, too. That's Beaufort. You have chilblains all over but your belly is burning hot, dripping sweat even. At these times everyone starts thinking about some wanker drinking coffee on Sheinkin Street in Tel Aviv. And here I fucking am, smelling like diesel oil, sweating with fear, lying in the middle of nowhere, and nobody's going to help me if I die. It won't interest the bloke in that café on Sheinkin Street, when I'm blown to pieces a few minutes from now. He'll keep sipping from his mug, probably at the very moment it happens he'll tell a joke and everyone will pretend to laugh and then he'll go home and screw his girlfriend, he won't even turn on the news, and as far as he is concerned, nothing will have happened this evening. Because it really doesn't affect him: for him, it's business as usual. He drives to his desk job at army headquarters each morning in the car that Daddy bought him, finishes the army every afternoon at four o'clock, and drinks coffee with whipped cream all the time. Blond hair, five o'clock shadow, pretty ugly. Hate him? Of course, it helps sometimes. Hatred is an excellent antidote to boredom.

Beaufort is Oshri. He rolls over in my direction, lies next to me, chews my ear off in whispers. Every time. Just before darkness fades and we're almost done with an ambush, he has an attack. 'Tell me, Erez, please, man: how did I wind up here?' he asks. 'What am I doing here dressed up like a bush? Why do I paint my face? What am I, a child? Am I in Crusader fortress, you fucking bastard? What is this, are we living in the Bible? Am I some sort of retard, pissing in bottles? What am I doing here in sub-zero temperatures, in the snow, waiting to knock off an Arab who decides to climb out of bed at three o'clock in the morning? Does this make sense to you? And then going back to that stinking rat hole I sleep in at the outpost? Does that seem logical? Tell me, have you seen where I sleep? It isn't good for me here, really not good. Grown-ups shouldn't have to live like this, wallowing in black mud mixed with snow each night. It's a fucking nightmare. Too much of a nightmare for me. Open your eyes. People have been dying on this mountain for a thousand years, isn't it about time to give up? I swear, it doesn't make sense that Beaufort exists. I'm telling you, there's no such place and we're all stuck in this hell for no good reason. It's a mistake. All over the world you can phone wherever you want in seconds. I'm the only person who can't! Six minutes from here by air some sexy bitch is walking along the high street in a g-string, and her only worry is whether to buy the mandarin orange, ginger and green tea extract shampoo or the jasmine, rose and orchid extract one, that's enriched with pure scented oils. "For that extra shiny softness" my arse. Big fucking dilemma. God, give me that kind of dilemma any day. Fuckers, all of them. And in Tel Aviv someone's pushing a girl's legs apart, they're doing it standing up in the toilets of a nightclub. And what about New York? Think about New York. Bright, noisy, everyone living the high life. The best fucking life. How am I supposed to hang on in this torture – tell me – with all the rules they make up for us every day? New laws. It's enough, you've turned me into a fucking nutcase totally and completely freaked out. I'm an arsehole for agreeing to be here at all, there's no explanation for it. Why don't I ask myself what I'm doing here? Do I ever ask myself that? Is my self-esteem so low that I need to play along with this pathetic game of yours? Enough. I swear, I've had enough.'

He goads me, tries to reach new heights of absurdity, astonishing himself, while I crack up laughing, hysterical, but inside so the boys won't see. I take care to hold it in. I know in a minute or two the fellow will sober up. I know him. Everything will look normal again, logical. He chose to be here, and he has good reasons for it, the best, and he'll remember them. He loves the mountain, it's good for him. And I'm good for him, too. And he's the best for me, we're the best together. He's my soulmate, my lucky charm, my best friend since our first cigarette at the induction centre.

Friend? No, brother! My brother, who knows what's good for me better than I ever will. He says, 'Erez, draw a black sheep for me,' and I draw him a whole flock. He says, 'Erez, give me a hug, you jerk,' and I climb into bed with him, squash his tiny frame against the wall, fall asleep holding him. He says, 'Erez,' and I know it's for life.

And sometimes Beaufort is a night ambush. Even then we bring the beef jerky. Of course we do! One night, simple, like that one back in December 1997. I'm still a squad sergeant, and I'm lying under a thorny bush just as dawn is breaking, lost in thought. Calm. Like I'm drugged. That calm. And my whole being is dying to run down that steep, rocky slope, run to the edge of our cliff and leap off. An incredible dive from the peak to the sweet mountain waters in the deep valley below, into the abyss, a long, whistling plunge that thunders in my ears. I am dying to dip into those waters, to float on my back, be swept away by the current into the blue stream, lie in the shade of the soft, bold, wild vegetation that crowds around the water and snakes after it like a dream jungle. Then, to warm up, lying like barefoot nature children on the rocks: naked, turned on, carefree. Dying to smoke a joint, get stoned, laze around, cuddle. Oshri says you can hear the splash of the water down below if you listen hard, but the closer you are the more forbidding and dangerous it is. It won't happen. Beaufort is a cage of ugliness right at the centre of heaven. You move a small, hesitant, camouflaged foot outside our iron gate, groping, sniffing, then you retreat inside our little enclave again. If I could only fly along the rivers and over the mountains, I would be home already.

'Cheetah to Deputy One. Testing transmission.'

'Roger, affirmative,' I respond into the two-way radio. 'Functioning.' I return to my long silence.

Bleary eyes, mountain air, a brown and green desert, orchards and gardens, small stone buildings in turquoise and orange, olive groves. Everything is spread out before us. The evil coastal towns, too, soon to awaken. Are you dozing off? Dozing off? Not on your life! Your mother's dozing. Hey, did you see that? You spot that? Is it what I think it is? Yeah, yeah. Are they armed? Yes, absolutely. Armed.

'Cheetah, this is Deputy One,' I report. 'We've got three scumbags north of the Virlist road.' Oshri's got one in his sights, Chaki another and Bendori the third. They've entered killing range, they've got packs on their backs, it can't be anything else.

'Deputy One to Cheetah, marksmen on targets,' I inform them, then I ask, 'Do I have confirmation?' I wait.

'Deputy One this is Cheetah. Negative, repeat: negative. No confirmation, Deputy One.'

'Cheetah, this is Deputy One, we've got them covered. Awaiting confirmation.'

'No confirmation, Deputy One. Negative, repeat: no confirmation for action.'

'But they're moving forward. Fast. We shouldn't lose them. We've got them in our sights.'

'Negative, Deputy One.'

Negative? Why negative, you fucking arseholes! Does it make sense to you that I should lie here like a fucking poofter and miss an opportunity like this? Does it really? No it doesn't. 'Squad, on my count. Four, three, two, one, fire. Twenty-one, twenty-two, fire. Prepare to attack.'

'Commander Cheetah to Deputy One, do not fire your weapons! No confirmation, stay in position.'

'Squad, prepare to attack.'

'Erez, you lunatic! Stay where you are. That's an order! Erez, you're in violation of an order!'

'Squad, attack!'

2

But anyway, my name is really Liraz. In basic training, at the very first roll call, the platoon commander ran through the names and when he got to mine he stopped. He didn't like it, my name. 'Wait, wait. What's that?' he asked. 'What kind of a name is that? Liraz? That's a girl's name. From now on you're Erez, like the cedars of Lebanon. Congratulations.' Erez. And that's who I am today.

Was there ever anything I wanted more than to lead – on my own, as commander – a squad of fighters to the top of Beaufort? You can be sure there wasn't. But when I came back from officers' academy I discovered that no one intended to make my dream come true. My company commander said I was too testy, hot-tempered, aggressive, impulsive. That maybe on paper I was an excellent fighter who always sought opportunities to connect with the enemy and demonstrated courage, but that I was also a shit-head. Testy people, he told me, can't lead combat squads. True, I once had attacked a military policeman. The little prick caught me with mud on my boots. I told him, 'You arsehole, I'm on my way back from thirty-five days in Lebanon, I haven't showered for weeks, and at six this morning we suddenly got clearance and my commanding officer shouts, "Run, Erez, get out of here now or you're stuck for another week." So what's the story, are you going to fuck with me over a pair of muddy boots?' But this bloke, he didn't give a shit. He made a complaint about me. But that's not the whole story. That wanker knows me from the neighbourhood, back in Afula. I said to him, 'Gonen, you're pretty full of yourself, aren't you? You put a uniform on and became a big shot, eh? You know what? I'm going to be generous with you. Take your report, rip it up and get out of here now. We'll forget about the whole thing.' But he didn't take the hint, and he fucked me over. I gave him forty-eight hours to let the earth swallow him up and then I beat the living daylights out of him. Till today, to tell the truth, I haven't got over the disgrace of it: a guy from Afula making a complaint about a fellow Afulan.

OK, it's also true that I was tried for wilful desecration of military property when I was a platoon sergeant. I threw a two-way radio at somebody, along with a few other small objects. And when someone mentioned my sister Vicky, I would lose control. Lots of things made me lose control. I even got sent to jail for insubordination after that ambush business, after they shouted 'Do not fire your weapons! No confirmation, you lunatic!' OK, it was a long time ago, but turn me into a training officer? There was no way I was going to deal with paper targets, no way I would agree to train soldiers to shoot without learning the hard way, through my own experience, what it felt like to lead them at the front. For weeks I stuck to the company commander like a leech. I begged, went berserk, shouted, cried, refused jobs. I even asked to be discharged from the brigade. They'd never seen anyone so fired up before. But they didn't budge. Until the hand of fate intervened and one of the officers left when his father died. The position of squadron leader opened up without warning, and I filled it. In actual fact I became squadron leader on probation and under a magnifying glass.

At the time, the boys were on a survival navigation course at the brigade's training base. I showed up there one morning without the insignia on my uniform and observed, the thirteen of them. I didn't introduce myself, I didn't approach them. They didn't have the slightest clue that I was their new commanding officer. For several weeks I spied on them, eavesdropped, heard things. Heard things and grew alarmed. For example, I heard Emilio shout at Bayliss, 'What were you touching my bag for?' Just like that, word for word. Was the situation that bad? This is a squad, you loser. Who asks questions like that? Everyone touches everyone's bags, that's the whole idea. Being part of a squad means stealing Zitlawi's crisps, taking underwear from River's bag, nicking socks from Spitzer – because his are the cleanest, everyone knows his mother uses fabric softener. Being a squad means that you run to the shower, take off your towel and get swatted on your arse. The weather's cold enough to freeze the balls off a brass monkey and you're dying to get under the nice hot water, but you're pushed out, they're slapping you around from every direction, and you thank God you have friends like these.

But not these boys. I'd been handed a frigid bunch, not a drop of group spirit in them. They weren't connected to one another, they didn't put their all into what they were doing, they looked sloppy, and they had rifle/shooting skills that'd embarrass female officers in the Romanian army. I got rid of their sergeant on the very first day, a thickset arsehole, too Ashkenazi. I replaced him with Oshri. When I spoke to them for the first time, I told them to forget the rules. You don't make a fighter ready for Lebanon with six hours of sleep, an hour each for breakfast, lunch and dinner and an hour of rest after every three in the sun. That's training for company clerks, a bunch of girls. I brought them down to three hours of light sleep a day, made them do all-nighters more often than not. When I found a mess in one of the rooms I moved them out to sleep in tents. When I overheard Itamar shouting at his mother over the phone – 'OK, Mum, shut your mouth!' – I ordered that there would be no more phone calls. Anyone caught with a mobile phone would be kicked out. To put it simply, I was on their arses day and night, and I made them eat shit. Tons of it. They did push-ups on their fists on hot gravel until they bled. 'Like you're in jail,' I told them. 'Like you're prisoners of war. You can shout, but nobody's going to rescue you. Or you can just open your legs and enjoy yourselves.' After a few days you could start to see a spark in their eyes, the first signs of a common denominator. Not just any common denominator but the most toxic of them all: hatred. They hated my guts, all of them, to the very last man.

Well, maybe there was one exception. River, the medic. It started during a week of complicated field exercises. The soldiers crawled, trampled down thorn bushes, moved boulders, took out their aggression on nature. The usual stuff. When they were scratched from head to toe and Bayliss was dripping blood from his mouth I gave one last and final order: At nine o'clock from where I'm standing, 250 feet from here, see that green tree? Bring it down! Within seconds they had scaled it, stormed it, were jumping on it, tearing at it, ripping away, a battalion of elephants assisted by a commando unit of rodents. Look at this, I said to Oshri, they're actually taking the thing down. But before I could wipe the smile off my face I caught sight of River off to the left, leaning on a rock, glaring at me. I was contemplating what punishment his unexplained loitering called for when River suddenly approached me – River, the quietest, most disciplined soldier of them all – and said without faltering, 'This wasn't necessary. You should stop them.' I swallowed. I felt so stupid. What had I turned into? A few seconds passed before I muttered that he was right. From that day on I made River work harder than all of them. I ripped into him, I shredded his soul, I wanted to turn him into a fighting machine. Under me he became a stallion, every vein in his body throbbing. At night, when the squad tucked into junk food and Coke and then a deep sleep, I would leave him outside for medical training and physical fitness sessions that sometimes lasted hours. At two in the morning he would join me for a run around the base with Itamar slung over his back playing the wounded soldier. Itamar, who's built like a tank, like a D9 bulldozer. A human refrigerator. Even in hailstorms we went out. I turned him into a two-way radio and made him run from commander to commander, delivering wake-up calls and messages. In the end, when he was almost broken, I gave him five minutes to recharge his batteries by leaning on an electricity pole. It's not easy being the favourite soldier of the squad commander. River didn't bat an eye, didn't complain. One day, when I finally let him go back to his tent, I allowed myself to tell him that I was happy with him. I think I said something stupid like 'It would be an honour to be a wounded soldier in your care.' He said nothing, just gave me that famous penetrating glare of his and I knew –

don't ask me how, it can't be explained – that he was happy with me, too. There's no making sense of that.

My big brother Guy once told me that to be a squad commander is to love. Thirteen fragile soldiers are placed in your hands, you call them 'the boys', you drag them in their nappies on a long, long journey through a dense forest of breaking points, and the whole time you pray that nothing bad will happen to them. You worry about them, he told me, not about yourself, and when one of your soldiers tells you that his uncle died of a heart attack and you see the pain in his eyes, you hurt too, deep down inside. The truth is, I wanted to suffer from that kind of sick love. I swear, I really tried. But it didn't work for me. Sometimes I felt disrespect for them, sometimes even a revulsion. Sometimes anger, and every once in a great while a little satisfaction. But most of the time I simply didn't feel at all. For a long time River was the only exception.

I wanted to love Emilio, for instance. He came to Israel from Argentina without his parents, only with his twin sister, left all his friends and family on another planet just to enlist in the IDF. Wasn't he worthy of respect? Of course he was. But how can you not be driven insane by a soldier who vomits non-stop, like a coffee machine gone berserk? On treks, during runs, when he's shouted at. And what about Tom? The bloke's on a trip: he's got red eyes, sees snails flying in the air, people spaced out, drifting, Muslims going wild in Mecca, he has no idea where he is, just goes with the flow, floats, he's stunned, in shock, connected to nothing. And Spitzer? Too relaxed. Itamar: too fat. Bayliss, too religious and self-righteous. Boaz is too enthusiastic, Eldad too vain, he's certain that all the girls are after him. He's disgusting, a spoiled Tel Aviv rich kid, an intellectual pretending he's down to earth, one of the boys; but I know he's a fake. And Pinchuk? Juvenile. Sleeps curled up with a teddy bear he calls Yaron, thinks that's really cool. Too easily offended. And Barnoy's a bleeding heart and Zion's thick as a plank and Koka's just plain boring. And we're actually on our way to war

– as pompous as that sounds – and how am I, as squad commander, supposed to love this group of weaklings and whiners that aren't capable of comprehending what's about to happen to them? Two months at the training base seemed like an eternity.

3

And most of all, I wanted to love Zitlawi. How could you not love him? Zitlawi is warm and funny and happy. He can charm the pants off anyone. You'll never hear him complain. Zitlawi's a good friend – the best – and that's something I admire. I had a lot of reasons to love Zitlawi, I know, but with all my best efforts and the best will in the world, it didn't work, because Zitlawi is an insolent soldier, without an iota of discipline, no respect for his commanding officers, and too scatter-brained, vague, the kind of bloke who leaves his gun in the most irresponsible places possible. If you don't tie his hands and feet to his body he'll lose them in a matter of seconds. And that drives me nuts.

The truth is that Zitlawi is a real arse, a jerk with a cigarette behind his ear and a way of talking that makes everything sound like a string of swear words, even when it isn't (though it usually is). A whole new language took root with us thanks to him, imported from all the different corps and brigades. He was the first to introduce new swear words, and not just swear words; he developed and introduced expressions and pearls of wisdom that spread through the entire northern zone in a matter of days. The IDF dictionary was issuing new volumes every month, thanks to him.

To 'ram,' for example. In our language it means sleep deeply. The full term is 'to pillow-ram'. It can be conjugated, too: pillow-rammer, pillow-ramming, pillow-rammed. A 'rusher' is a quick snog with a girl. A 'double-rusher' is a small rusher. A double can happen between two guys, but not a rusher. An 'owl' is a guy who walks around with his cock in his hand, choking it, jerking off all the time. A 'terror dick,' is someone that gets non-stop hard-ons, morning, noon and night, out of control. During kitchen duty, watching *Schindler's List*. 'Scud five' is a huge dick.

A 'ticket-taker' is a bloke who sleeps with all the girls. 'Tevye the Milkman' also sleeps with all the girls, but he's a nerd with glasses. A 'fortune teller' is a girl who puts out (when you're with her you're 'fortunate' because she 'tells' you to screw her. See also: 'ear-hole virgin' and 'boiler heater'). Then there's a 'mezuzah', a girl that everyone kisses, and a 'pringle': once she's open, everyone wants a taste. A 'magic marker' is a girl that gives blow jobs. 'Get it on with a suck-baby' means go fuck yourself. A sexy tourist is called a 'foreign fuck', 'ironing board' is flat-chested, 'mosquito-bitten' is a girl cursed with small breasts.

A 'hummus' is a dumb soldier. A 'flip-flop' is someone thick-headed, a 'schnitzel' is even more thickheaded, and an 'aubergine' is as thick as you can get. A thickheaded girl is called a 'booma'. A flatterer is a 'tangerine-peeler', a soldier with no friends. A 'Herzl' is a fighter who talks too much about the future, the name comes from the man who predicted the founding of the State of Israel. 'Zionist' is another nickname for a blabbermouth, or someone who sticks his nose into everyone's business. '*Kapod*' is a nickname for Sepharadim, '*hardor*' for Ashkenazim and 'journalist' for Ashkenazim who tell lies. Zitlawi calls everyone a fox, a shark, a hammer, a sleaze. A 'panther' is a fox that Zitlawi particularly likes. A 'pink panther' is a gay fox.

A 'flamer' is a homo. A 'momo' is a homo, too. There are lots of ways to call someone gay: arse-checker, for example, and zipper-reader, and doorpost-wiggler. Bed-shaker, wall-scratcher, umbrella-opener, pot-opener, soap-dropper. Sheet-ripper, faucet-stealer, tile-chewer, tree-hugger, sink-gripper, ball-grabber, pickle-dicer, shoelace-tier, tea-stirrer, thing-sucker, banana-straightener, horse-whisperer, pillow-biter, feather-cougher. A homo is a bloke who cries at movies, disappoints his parents, rides a bike without a seat.

He's a suckler, a limper, a bend-overer, an excavator, a nailer. A champagne-boy is a homo, too, and so's a sharpener, a flautist, a scout leader, a g-string-wearer, a closet-lover, a sitting-pisser, an exhaust pipe, a bugler. 'Omo' is homo. 'Sensitive' is homo. In fact, say anything but 'homo', because it's not nice to swear. And lesbian? Don't say that, either. 'Carpet-muncher' is OK, you can use that.

'Strawberry-pisser' is someone who's scared. An 'orange soda' is someone scared shitless. 'Toast' is a burnt-out soldier. A 'draft dodger in uniform' is a soldier with a desk job somewhere near his home. 'Fox-brained' is a code name for someone fucked up by drugs and 'rabbit' for a light user. 'Enchanted garden' is a hash den. When Zitlawi says, 'I'm tripping, don't bother me,' nobody comes near him.

A 'potato-crisp wetter' is a miser, someone who doesn't want you to hear him munching. A 'marble-shitter' is a monster, a weird soldier, a loner, so ugly he looks like he hasn't really evolved. A 'sprinkler' is a bragger; the female version's a 'Nile perch'. A 'futt' is a fat slut. A fox-scarer. A mud pie. A 'kebab' is a fat guy. So's a 'sumo', someone so big he blocks the view. A male soldier who sits around doing nothing is called a 'semen-squanderer' while the female version is 'wasting labour pains'. A 'yam-peeler' is someone lazy. A 'rivet-pisser' is someone who gets too excited about things. 'Siamese cat' is a spoiled brat. '*Chakhna*' means smelly and '*karkhana*', someone messed up with drugs. A 'chocolate situation' is one where nobody's happy and a 'honey situation' is one where everyone is. And to Zitlawi I was a 'pinscher', someone who barks all the time but isn't really dangerous, just a moaner. That's what he thought of me. Sometimes he also called me 'gremlin' behind my back, meaning someone with a nice face but whose soul is dark and evil. Zitlawi himself was known as 'Psalms', someone with a saying for everything.

'*Jakha*' is a personal favour. Do a *jakha* for me, will you? *Jakha* me. He's *jakhad* and so forth, ad infinitum. To 'drum' is to stir coffee. Turkish coffee, or Beaufort instant, with halva and walnut oil. Zitlawi would spend hours, days, with the finjan and the thermos. If he had his way he would thump all the boys and bounce all the girls in bed. And there wasn't a single girl he wouldn't mince, fry, spear or devour, the horny bastard. No holds barred, no choosiness if you believed what came out of his mouth along with all the drool.

And then there's the worst curse of all: May your prayer be nicked from the crack in the Wailing Wall where you stuffed it.

Zitlawi's most frequent saying: 'Are you making fun of the way I talk?' uttered in a defensive tone. That's what he would ask, with a killer look, when one of the boys pointed out a mistake to him, corrected his Hebrew, or, worst of all, dared to smile – which happened all the time. He was violent, but gentle, too, like when he forbade the boys from squashing the monster-like grasshoppers that hovered near the lights at the outpost. He had this tape he would listen to, the collected songs of Hana Harman. Once I asked him where she was from, that singer, and he was really offended. 'Hana Harman is not a she,' he told me, 'he's a he.' And not just any old singer but an Arab singer. One of the good Arabs.

We had our first head-on collision on the day I took over command of the squad, on the afternoon of the hottest day in history. The boys stood facing me in rows of three on the parade ground, pretty frightened, dripping with sweat, waiting to receive their first orders. They were wearing sunglasses on the order of the brigade medical officer – all of them except Zitlawi, who stood there watching me with smiling eyes. When I asked him where his glasses were, he said, 'What do I need sunglasses for? My mother told me I shouldn't hide my beautiful eyes.' He got his first punishment there and then, and then another that night in the tent camp, when he was caught after lights-out organizing 'The Prettiest Hoicker Contest', a spitting competition. From then on he never stopped getting punished. When I first interviewed him he gave nothing away. He answered briefly and dodged direct questions. He was a smart-arse. The only thing I learned was that he came from Tiberias, had three brothers, and liked to listen to Yehuda Poliker's music while getting a blow job. There was nothing beyond this in his files from the adjutant at HQ or the soldiers' welfare officers. Nor did I expect there would be. Three weeks of insubordination went by before I discovered the tip of the iceberg.

It happened when Oshri took the initiative, pulling Zitlawi out of bed at three in the morning without my permission and dragging him out on a walking tour of the cypress forest just south of the eucalyptus grove near us, with a canteen filled with hot tea. For the first ten minutes, as they walked outside the base, Oshri didn't utter a word, making Zitlawi fill the gap with his usual bullshit. He tried to guess the meaning of this hike, he swore, talked a little about the squad and mostly about himself, all in an effort to hide the fact that – simply put – he was terrified. When they came to a clearing in the forest, Oshri sat at one of the three rickety picnic tables that had been placed on the dirt. He waited a few seconds for the rebel to break down and sit across from him, then he asked, 'Zitlawi, what's your story?' Yeah, what *was* his fucking story, what was happening with the boy, what was the cause of all this self-destructive behaviour? He played dumb, claimed this was what made him happy, he was used to entertaining people and if someone had a problem with it they should toss him out of the army. He wouldn't appeal if he was kicked out, he wouldn't rat to the press about the abuse or bullying or non-compliance with HQ orders, they had nothing to worry about, he would keep quiet. Oshri pulled two thin Indian cigarettes out of a wrinkled pink paper bag, little ones made of dried eucalyptus leaves. He lit them both. Zitlawi sniffed the sweet, spicy scent that filled the air – or was the smell in fact bitter, kind of hard to define, the odour of a campfire? 'Why not?' he said. 'But isn't there any boof, as long as we're at it?' Oshri didn't even know what boof was. A little cube of hash, Zitlawi explained. Everyone has a stoner friend who keeps some *boof* in the little condom pocket of his jeans for emergencies, don't they? Something nice for the boys to share at the right moment. Oshri kept silent, lay back on the damp wooden bench of the picnic table and let the stars hypnotize him. And he smoked. He has a face that always looks hypnotized, narrow and dark and closed, with tiny ears, only his lips are big and thick, and he's all peace and serenity, a rascal who seems to know that everything will work out so there's nothing to fear. Zitlawi remained standing, watching him from above. 'What do you want to hear?' he asked. 'That the crazy boy has unique qualities of his own? That he's special, different, like the children in special needs classes?' Oshri didn't answer. 'And what about you?' Zitlawi asked. 'What's your story, Mr Sergeant?' Oshri focused on the halo around the moon and didn't even bother to look at him. Then Zitlawi lay down on the table. They smoked three cigarettes, one after the other. It wasn't until the third that they spoke again, and then Oshri took the initiative, again, kind of forced. 'You got anybody to fix me up with?' he asked. He told him he didn't have a girlfriend – here, something about himself – and in fact had never had one, because before he fell in love they always, every time, told him there was no chance, and now, in the army, the situation was even worse, there wasn't even anybody to look at, and it had been bothering him for some time now, everyone was screwing right and left and he wasn't. Oshri finished talking and prepared for an attack, for a nasty comment. Zitlawi took a Snickers bar out of the pocket of his uniform and broke it in two. 'Sir!' he said as he offered Oshri the bigger of the two pieces. 'Now that's actually a subject I know something about. We'll work something out for you, you can count on me.' He said this with total seriousness, tone of voice, with compassion even. And this really was a matter Zitlawi knew something about, because girls of every kind threw themselves at him, finding him sexy, if not particularly good-looking. His face was coarse and his body massive, the manliest soldier in the company. And he was funny. Girls love funny guys, especially during sex when you're getting turned on and talking, it gives them a huge orgasm. Then Oshri let his head drop back over the edge of the bench and said, 'What's going to happen?' Bingo.

That was an excellent question, right on time. Even if it had been thrown out unintentionally, Zitlawi grabbed hold of it and used it to open a window on himself. His mother was a fortune teller, he told Oshri. A real one though, a member of the union, with diplomas and certificates and everything. The kind who knew how to answer questions like 'What's going to happen?' She studied Kabbalah and read coffee grounds, palms, tea leaves and oil and tarot cards. She could interpret dreams and do astrology charts and undo curses. She could make a former lover come back, get rid of the evil eye, help with fertility and family matters, and fears and anxieties and low self-esteem, too, and help couples to communicate. She handed out charms for good luck and for failing businesses, she was an expert in numerology, she solved marital and financial troubles. She gave courses, appeared at hen parties and at events in private homes. In short, she brought happiness to people. The only thing she didn't do was crystal-ball gazing. When people asked 'What's going to happen?' she answered, in detail, and she was never wrong. And ever since she had accurately predicted the results of the elections in Tiberias she'd become famous all over the north, and visits to her had to be booked at least two months in advance. Her name was Aliza, but people called her Solange, that was her professional name, and at home you weren't allowed to use the term 'fortune teller'. Instead she was a spiritual adviser, that's what it was being called in those last few seconds before the new millennium.

It took a moment for Oshri to realize that Zitlawi wasn't pulling his leg. He was serious. He really had a fortune teller for a mother, which is to say, a psychotic with an audience. But that wasn't the end of the story. 'The truth is,' Zitlawi continued, 'even with her success in the elections, these past few months, things aren't good at home. My father spends money in places he shouldn't, and it gets harder every day to talk sense to him. He's not an easy man. And my mother's got cancer. Bad, even. It started with a cough and then she was spitting up blood and had trouble breathing, and then they found a tumour, two inches in diameter, in the top of her left lung. They took it out but that didn't help because the cancer cells got into her bloodstream and now they're everywhere. In the liver, the bones. All of a sudden it's life-threatening, even if the doctors aren't saying so. They're trying to get us to be optimistic. Strong. But who's going to take care of my three brothers? There's Samson – we call him Sammy. He's only six. And Roy's ten, and Eli – Eliko – he's finishing high school next year. Who's going to take care of them?'

There, it had come out. The next morning Oshri told me. Together we went to our unit's welfare worker and for a couple of days we tried, the whole senior staff, to convince Zitlawi to leave. We told him he had to serve near home, but he wouldn't listen. We asked him again and again to go home to his mother. After all, the squad might spend weeks and weeks up at Beaufort, even months, and she needed him. What would happen if he wasn't there to say goodbye? So Zitlawi want back and paid a visit to Rabbi Pitusi in the Poriah neighbourhood of Tiberias, presented the dilemma to him, explained what he felt in his heart and asked for his blessing for his decision to stay at Beaufort. And the rabbi gave his blessing. Maybe it was an escape for Zitlawi, it's hard to know. But ever since that night in the cypress forest he's been one of us, and that's what counts. As for me, I search for sadness in his eyes every time I look at him, make an effort to locate a single glum twitch of muscles. But there's nothing. I haven't found it because he's smiling this never-quit smile, and there's no telling if good intentions lie behind it, or bad.

4

February 1999. Here's the picture at thirty-nine minutes to darkness, five hours to departure for the target: River, stark naked, gasping for breath after a maniacal run, comes to a halt in the watermelon patch behind Rabbi Elifaz's abandoned cowshed and tries to convince a startled young religious girl to lend him her bicycle. He fires off rounds of confused explanations, something about an ATV (All Terrain Vehicle) that took off with everyone's uniforms, apparently in the direction of the fields. The uniforms aren't even the worst of it: the sun is setting and they have to reach Ha'egel immediately. The girl, who has never heard of the Ha'egel, has never seen this River before, has never laid eyes on a dick and most of all doesn't understand what this whole mess has to do with the sun setting, loans him her bicycle at once. That is to say, she doesn't really loan it to him, she just doesn't protest. And him, that little owl, he doesn't get anything from her – not her name, not her phone number, not a little kiss, just a long silence and a bicycle. He nabs it and takes off.

Half a mile away as the crow flies, at the entrance to a grove of pear trees, Zitlawi and the ATV are sunk deep in mud. He grabs hold of the pile of uniforms and underwear and climbs the highest eucalyptus tree. Utterly infantile, Zitlawi just doesn't know when to quit. After all, the goal had already been achieved: a first-rate clip for the end-of-training film starring River, Emilio and Bayliss. Fantastic landscape, a wide road in the Golan Heights along which they run naked, waving their arms like wounded animals, swearing like Palestinian policemen, and pleading with Zitlawi for their lost honour. Emilio even cried a little, the tosser. And everything captured on film; what more could you ask for? But now the time has come to climb down from the tree, rescue the ATV, wipe the embarrassment from River's red face, return the bicycle to the blonde girl, hook up with the others left shivering and naked back at the Bajurya pool – it's February, remember – pick up Spitzer and the camera, get back to Bayliss's village, Nov, and hope that his father Menahem will take them over to Ha'egel, the Armoured Corps base from where they monitor convoy movements. Otherwise it would be curtains.

Truth be told, Emilio had had his doubts from the start. Back at the barbecue they were having in the yard of the house at Nov he'd remarked that it was unlike Zitlawi to be so eager to pass up on the opportunity to sit around and eat and do absolutely nothing. And for what? Nothing more than a boring old puddle of winter rainwater next to a main road? And what was suddenly so important about stripping naked? And what the fuck made them risk being really, really late on the most critical day of their military service? It was a lost cause, though: Emilio's worn-out whining – which every man in the squad had learned to tune out ages ago – didn't stand a chance against Zitlawi's powers of persuasion. Even Bayliss, who since he was still in nappies had been explaining to guests that the Bajurya was not fit for swimming in – too shallow, home to otters, salamanders, rats and black cockroaches – even he plunged headlong into the trap.

The chances of me hearing the details of this incident were slight. I gave this motley crew their punishment without even waiting to hear the whole story. I refused to hear it. With a record like theirs, being eighty minutes late justified being shut up in the outpost for forty-nine days, in other words, a two week extension to the thirty-five days they were already scheduled for on their first tour of duty in Lebanon. Apart from Emilio, who always appeared to be on the verge of tears, nobody was surprised. Zitlawi even muttered something about it having been worth it. They had a special mood for moments like these, a sort of detached desperation, and they were already quite used to receiving punishments.

I wouldn't have known about the business at Bajurya if it hadn't been for the girl who got mixed up in it all. Not just any girl, but a sixteen year old student at the girls' religious school in Nov, an innocent lamb with bells, really gorgeous if you believe what they say. Her name – Hodaya – Zitlawi extracted with enormous effort when they returned the bike. Other than that they knew nothing about her, only that a real, live, sexy encounter with a religious girl wouldn't easily be forgotten in our unit, but would pursue its victim up and down the front lines of Lebanon. All the way up to Beirut, stories of Corporal Naor River's escapade would be told in exaggerated and embellished terms. It would've been one thing if a religious girl had fallen into the hands of Zitlawi or Spitzer, or anyone else for that matter. But River? Well that could only have been a gift from God. He was the baddest boy of them all, the one that drew the most fire, the one who'd been working on his abdominals since sixth grade, and his suntan, too, and he was horny like a fifteen year old virgin. And shy like you can't believe, the shyest of all when a girl was around. It could only end badly.

It was a Monday evening when we gathered on the white-top, the asphalt courtyard at Ha'egel where convoys are prepared for dispatch to enemy territory. I was just waiting for the sun to finish its business and for the curtain to rise on a new winter at Beaufort. Back in Israel I really missed the pungent smell of it, of green nature and thick vegetation and crisp air, of grease and Lysol and gunpowder and sweat, and all of it together. I'm not joking, I really missed it. And I missed the old boys, the veterans, in the company too: Twina aka Tuti and Tiran aka Kuti, Bodnik the rat and Neufeld the flea and Pizov, who we called Poza, and the triplets – the good, the bad and the stuffed – Lubeck, Ezroni and Boaron. We pounce on each other, hug like always and wait for the first appearance of the youngsters, my boys. They're so happy, the old boys, and why not? When you're part of a sergeants' squad, Beaufort becomes a sleep research institute, lots of snoozing hours every day, all day, entire days, with little breaks in between for heroic operations. No distress, no assignments, no floor-mopping. It's no wonder that the boys at Beaufort spend a large part of their time plotting mutinies and composing official complaints – 'on the grounds of unfair distribution of workload', my arse – but it's also no wonder that they bury those complaints and calm down when they realize that one day, not too far off, they, too, will be old hands. So why take on the best friends of the commanding officer? Not a healthy idea.

This is the time when the veterans feign indifference. The cooks, the sentinels, the Signal Corps soldiers – all the Beaufort regulars go out of their way to be nonchalant in wholesale quantities. Everything's fine, it's no big deal. The new boys can barely contain their excitement, they're counting the seconds; and I know that feeling. They're dying for action, certain that the whole of Hezbollah is peeing its pants, of course they are, and if you ask them they'll tell you that Nasrallah's vacation is over, because this killer company is on its way to take over the front, to make war, to get rid of the homos currently manning the outpost.

We sat waiting off to one side, huddled on a mound of sand. A Yasur helicopter crossed the red sky and disappeared over the border. We might be making the return trip in one of those, Oshri said, on a stretcher or under a grey army blanket. He winked, and I silenced him with a hard slap on the neck, so he'd keep quiet, keep cool. The white-top was in a hollow, hidden from Lebanese observation points to conceal from terrorists when convoys were being prepared for entry into their territory. A small, sputtering generator spat a cloud of diesel into the air, mixing with exhaust fumes so that the air was choked with a salty stench. The white-top was unlit, and as darkness fell the only light came from the headlights of the Safari trucks parked all around. A small booklet produced by the IDF, which describes what time the moon will rise each day of the month and with what illumination it will shine, determines the movement of the convoys. When the sky is light they stay put. By order. But that night a late moonrise meant clogged roads and long lines of trucks filled with soldiers and supplies and equipment would be crossing the border in both directions. And by the time the moon was high in the sky, at two a.m., the roads would be clear again.

Another three hours and twenty minutes to go until that clutch would be put in gear. We lined up in threes in the courtyard, fighting against an icy wind. Names, ID numbers, seating positions in vehicles were carefully recorded. If something happened they'd know immediately which one of us was gone. Oshri moved from soldier to soldier, writing in thick black marker on the back of his hand his 'iron number'. It would remain there for days and days, creating negative associations. It was known as the 'death number', and that's what it was, but it was the only way of making sure that during moments of panic nobody forgot his place and that we'd know quickly who was missing. The veteran soldiers were arguing over numbers. Seven, for example, was a number nobody was willing to take.

I gathered my squad around for some last minute pointers and to give them a speech I'd had written in my head for months. What sounds today like an embarrassing mix of Zionism and kitsch was, back then, absolutely true and straight from the heart, I swear: 'We may not be an elite commando unit,' I told them. 'Not even the naval commandos. We don't run around with shiny insignia and we're not yet allowed to remove the elastic from our trouser cuffs and we don't spend our army service in state-of-the-art training facilities run by the American army. There are no heroes here, and we're not looking for heroes. But we do the hardest work there is in the IDF, and that's something to be proud of. I don't know if this evening, on the way here, you had a chance to look around you. You would have seen children having fun in playgrounds in the northern kibbutzim, and on the high street of Kiryat Shmona you'd have seen women licking chocolate pancakes with banana and sprinkles and window-shopping for silk dressing gowns. The skies are quiet there, and not a single terrorist can get near the border fence. And why is that? It's because of the war we're on our way to, together, tonight. People like to forget what went on here twenty years ago, right in this very place. They also like to forget what could happen if the IDF didn't do its job: Katyusha rockets, border infiltrations, terrorist cells slaughtering whole families: that's the alternative.

'It's there,' I told them, 'in the middle of a no man's land teeming with murderous beasts, I want you to keep this goal in mind all the time. Look at your watches,' I said. 'From this moment on I want you to forget everything you knew till now, wipe away all the bullshit. Your lives are going to run according to a different script. From now on you stop calling me 'Platoon leader, sir.' Now I'm Erez, and it's for good reason. I'm not going to be any less strict with you – on the contrary, from this moment there will be no concessions – but from this moment, and this is the difference, we're completely dependent on one another. It's a matter of life and death. I want to trust you people, so don't disappoint me. That's all. Now, iron numbers, count off!'

After that there was silence. The battalion commander of Ha'egel, the man who would lead the convoy, stood looking at our row. 'You're playing with fire for the first time today,' he said. And just at that very moment, only then, did the Bayliss family truck come to a screeching halt outside the main gate. I was already hoping they wouldn't show up at all, but that band of jokers, in wrinkled uniforms splotched with mud, were here to cause me the biggest embarrassment of my life. It was clear that I would have to murder them. In my worst nightmare I couldn't have imagined such an unprofessional, humiliating start to our first time at the front. The lieutenant colonel stared at me and said nothing. He waited for one long moment, then continued his briefing.

'You still have no idea where you're going,' he said. 'I'm warning you now that on this trip, every little thing, even lighting up your watch, could have tragic consequences.'

The boys listened intently, they were absorbing every word, and still it seemed to me that they couldn't really take it all in. A forty minute journey was all that separated us from the outpost, but the convoy briefing was an order to head out to battle. 'I'm going to review situations and responses,' he told them. 'I'll explain them like you're retarded children so there will be no questions left in your mind.

'First situation: missiles. How will you know if the convoy's being fired at by missiles? You'll see a flying torch headed our way, an orange-red dot floating through the air, or a blinding flash followed by a whizzing sound. If it's a Sagger missile you'll hear the clatter of a motor, too. When we're on our way, each Safari will post a missile sentinel at the opening at the back. If the sentinel sees something, he gets on the open radio and shouts, "Missiles! Missiles!" If he sees them on the right he shouts, "Missiles, right!" and if they're on the left he shouts, "Missiles, left!" The driver will stop immediately and all of you will get out of the vehicle on the same side that the missiles are coming from. Why? Because the shrapnel will fly to the opposite side. Now, imagine a situation where all of you jump off the vehicles in the middle of nowhere and Hezbollah manages to abduct a soldier. What do you do? To prepare for this, in a few minutes you're going to divide into pairs. Each pair will stay together and guard the other's arse. Fighters, I'm expecting you to take responsibility for those boys who don't have adequate training. If we find ourselves with a cook running around alone in the middle of Lebanon, the bereavement team back in Israel can set out for his parents' house. And one more important comment, men: we're moving out today in old Safari trucks, as you can see for yourselves. The drivers' doors are blocked off from the inside with protective panels and can only be opened from the outside. So in the event of an emergency, whoever's sitting in the front passenger seat has to run around to the driver's side and help him out of the vehicle. Don't forget anyone, please.

'Next situation: mortar shells. First man who hears a champagne cork popping shouts, "Launch! Launch!" Mortar shells never come alone, it could be seventy at one go. The vehicles will come to a halt, each pair will jump down and run as far as possible from the others. Do not stand near one another, create distance between yourselves. Otherwise, we'll lose an entire squad thanks to one lousy shell. What do you do after that? Wait. Just stay where you are until the barrage lets up. Is that clear?

'Third situation: "Code Hannibal". If you've been abducted, what do you do? As far as the abducted soldier himself is concerned, struggle as hard as you can, pop buttons off and let them drop on the ground so we have a trail. The rest of you must try to stop the terrorists at any cost. If they're making off with a soldier and there's no other choice, you shoot. I repeat: you shoot. The abducted soldier as well. An abduction is worse than death. I hope you people understand that.

'Fourth situation: an explosives charge, either a landmine or a roadside bomb. The vehicles stop, you stay inside and wait. An intervention force, which I will name in just a few minutes, handles the rescue, scans the area to make sure we're not talking about a wider range of charges that might be awaiting us. Those on the team will stretch white marking tape around the area of the charge. Explosives at the head of the convoy is most common. In this situation, apart from the vehicle that's been hit, everyone travels backwards. If the explosives hit the middle of the convoy, then the vehicles in front move forward and the ones behind move backwards. If the damage is at the back of the convoy, everyone moves forward. It might be a situation where we hit a charge and seconds later we're attacked by mortar shells, all according to plan. Be prepared.

'Fifth situation: we find ourselves in a field of explosive charges, they're going off one after the other in every direction, and at the very same moment, BAM! – we're attacked by armed Hezbollah guerillas, face to face. What do you do? Attack the terrorists, or freeze, terrified that they're going to set off additional charges hidden in the bushes and along the road? Listen, and listen carefully, I don't want any misunderstandings here, no fuck-ups, no messes, and this is an iron rule: explosive charge or not, you people go on the offensive. A face-to-face encounter trumps everything, even under attack of mortar shells, or missiles, or aliens from Mars. It's saved. Engaging them, not letting them get away, is our highest priority. Is that clear? Be ready, because when the intervention team is engaging in hand-to-hand combat or rescuing the convoy, the terrorists will try to pump rounds into the last Safari with twenty soldiers stuffed inside who can't see a thing and can't shoot. That's why it's the responsibility of the sentinel on each Safari to man the back opening of the vehicle and watch what's happening.

'That's all for situations and responses. From this moment on I want your helmets on your heads, cartridges locked in to your weapons, and nobody sleeping along the way. The motto for everything I've just said is simple: If something happens we want to minimize the damage. I'm not hiding anything from you, there's no way to ensure no harm will come to this convoy, but if you use your brains the damage can be contained. Drivers, be aware: we're moving slowly, the roads are slippery, don't forget to turn off all lights and headlights the minute we've passed the three mile mark. The rest of the trip will be made using night-vision equipment. Keep maximum distance between each Safari and the next, but don't lose each other. If there's someone here who forgot to leave his mobile phone at home, go now to your bag and separate the battery from the phone. In fifteen minutes, everyone is to be in place and ready to move out. Good luck.'

And that was all. At that moment everything fell silent, the shouting stopped. Tasks were carried out with the volume turned right down, and they were technical and precise. The soldiers closed themselves off from one another, preoccupied with trying to digest the battalion commander's briefing, and somewhat frightened. I could see it in their eyes as they went over the procedures, picturing dangers. There were so many confusing commands they had to remember from that moment. Then it was the time for a few drills – explosives drill, face-to-face-encounter drill, missile drill – so we jumped in and out until the battalion commander was satisfied. Minutes later everyone was crammed into the back of the Safari, packed in and silent, waiting. Once, this truck would have been carrying eggs, or chickens to the slaughter, but now, done over in olive and looking like it had been saddled with a huge safe, it transported soldiers into enemy territory.

There were long hours of waiting ahead before we would receive the order to move out. If a sentinel in Taibe or Marjayoun or the

Dlaat outpost noticed suspicious movement on the roads then everything would be frozen, or if a soldier at Beaufort imagined he saw a wild boar through his binoculars, we'd be delayed by thirty minutes at the very least. A whole day, even, if an alert was issued about some large explosive charge or if some doubt was raised about whether the electronic warning devices that accompanied the convoy were in proper working order. The order to abort could come even in the last few seconds, with all of us already in the vehicles and waiting at the border gate. They don't take chances with a mission like this, instead they'll send the soldiers to spend the night in comfortable beds at the Soldiers' Hotel in Kiryat Shmona. The big celebrations that take place when this happens, when we storm the hotel, come at a price: it's hard to describe how bad the feeling is at Beaufort when soldiers who were due to go home discover that the convoy has been cancelled.

That evening, as we waited at the border gate, it seemed that everything was in order. The intelligence officer gathered all the squad commanders and read them an update. 'Nothing special to report this evening,' he said. 'Alert 012, on Hezbollah intentions to carry out an attack on a convoy on the Nikras road, is still operative. We'll wait for final clearance and then we'll move out.' The last minutes. The bolt is removed. This was the first time I had earned the right to mount the Safari as a commander, in the front seat, to observe the trip from the passenger's seat and not one of the narrow slits in the sides at the back of the vehicle. Our night-vision equipment coloured the world in stark shades of green and black. 'Tapuz stations, confirm. Over and out.'

'Diesel, in order.'

'Kfir, in order.'

'Puma, in order.'

'Venus, waiting for confirmation.'

'Venus, in order.'

The driver, a reservist, lit a last cigarette, but I let fly with an angry order. 'Put it out,' I demanded. He tried to make a case for another half minute, what was the big deal? I grabbed his hand, yanked the cigarette away from him, stubbed it out on the dashboard and threw it out the window. From that moment on we didn't exchange a word. A long silence. Nights in the north always make you feel this loneliness; here, I can feel it now. Then from the radio we heard 'Mission confirmed', and it happened.

On the first leg of the journey you hit fifty-five m.p.h., that's what the regulations state. After that you crawl along, barely at twenty. The endless trip takes you through climbs, descents, twists. This is the tensest time of my life. I go over past threats, recall a sixteen year old Lebanese boy waiting for an IDF convoy with a bomb strapped to his body. The soldiers were suspicious, even fired warning shots in the air, and then suddenly the boy saluted. They stopped shooting. Seconds later he blew himself up, just a few yards from the convoy. So think about where it's going to come from and how you'll respond. I think about Bayliss, who's positioned as missile sentinel at the back of the Safari, completely exposed, surely shivering from cold and looking for the first time at this view, of a landscape like Switzerland. You can't miss the thin halo of pale blue light floating above Beaufort, carried high in the middle of the sky in the centre of the black forest ahead. And how beautiful the ancient fortress that stands next to the outpost is in the moonlight. I wonder how long it will be before I can make out the huge flag flying on the top of our hill.

'Get the fuck out! Everything out, out!' Always the same huge ruckus in the parking area. Soldiers jumping down, stepping on each other, everyone throwing bags about. Where are the sleeping bags? The personal bags? Everyone's thinking about his own stuff, worried something will get left behind on one of the trucks and wind up making its way back to Israel with the outgoing troops. As for me, I run this way and back. 'Oshri, count them now!' Their eyes are glazed, each is lost in his own thoughts, trying to take in as much as possible. They have no idea what to do. They sit down on the floor of the secure area and wait.

The boys in the company we are replacing weren't willing to put on their dress fatigues or clear out their rooms or beds in advance. They insisted on waiting for the moment that our convoy was visible to the naked eye from the guard positions as it climbed the hill. It's bad luck to pack in advance. And when they did pack it was done like a hurricane, in total madness that left behind destruction: a dismantled outpost in chaos.

When I went down to the submarine to get myself settled in, Oshri was already there, sprawled across the rusty iron bed. A tropical island scene hung just above his pillow, stuck with scotch tape to the metal walls of the stifling pit we lived in, along with a lone, sketchy coconut tree and a floating raft carrying a small black man with a cup and a straw, bobbing on the waves of a green sea. A countdown chart, too, showing the number of days we had left at Beaufort. When the hell had he found the time to hang it all? The chart, with eighty-eight days just begging to be wiped out, had been inaugurated a few hours earlier with an X over the first day. Yes, eighty-eight. That's less than ninety, that's three months minus one day, Oshri announced as he lay on his back, the lazy arse. As I polished my boots I asked him what was so terrible about being with me. 'Are you some sort of attention seeker?' he asked by way of response, his soft, round Yemenite face beaming. 'You've got to give me advance warning for questions like that.' He wouldn't stay on, I knew that. Even if I begged and pleaded he wouldn't postpone his discharge, his mind was already there, on the outside. As for me, just the thought of the replacements that could land on me – some pale-faced jerk of a platoon sergeant, for example, who might show up here, or a homo, even, who knows – could drive me bonkers. 'Where would they find you one like that?' Oshri would ask every time the subject came up, trying to calm me down. 'Sergeants are wild bastards, there's one everywhere you look. Don't worry, they'll send you someone lousy, like me.' And I would answer that I could rely on Furman; just to fuck me up he'd bring in a female sergeant.

Now Oshri sank into his sleeping bag, rolled up inside his faded green sheet printed with a fake, subversive Middle Eastern version of the Care Bears. He's leaving me, that little bastard. Just like that, while we're at the front, he'll go off and start a different life. I was even angry – somewhere deep inside I felt betrayed. In the name of our friendship, in the name of our mission, in the name of the knowledge that at the end of the day we had it good up here, and we were good here, really, really good and professional, better than we'd be anywhere else. I didn't know how I would pass the time up there on the hill and in the infiltration operations and training exercises without Oshri. He's the only one who understands me. When my engine stalls he revs me up again. When I'm on fire he cools me down. When I'm cold he's the only one who knows how to warm my soul and when I'm hot he takes care to stop me one minute before my tantrum lands me in military prison. Only Oshri knows how to let me know when I'm being a jerk, when I'm shooting my month off, out of control. He knows how to throw it right back at me without pissing me off or hurting my feelings. He says, 'Report to me for a heart-to-heart,' and I know I've been an arsehole. He's modest, an introvert, warm. He's the only person who knows everything about me and still – it's hard to believe – loves me. And I know everything about him, too. Only me. About the tattoo on his right arm, for example, which is always covered with a patch to hide the shame. It was supposed to have been a gesture to a Japanese tourist he met in Eilat. Her name was Mika but the tattoo read 'Mike'. I'd warned him in advance but Oshri, drunk, only noticed in the morning. When he exercised in the gym in a white t-shirt everyone would shout at him, 'Come on, take that stupid thing off,' trying to draw him out, get him to expose himself. 'What's he hiding?' they would ask, pressing me for information. But I never sold him out. And I never told anybody that the little Yemenite has a cat at home. He looks like the type who'd have a scary attack dog – an Amstaff or Rottweiler at the very least. Not a Chihuahua or a cat. And yet it turns out that he goes home and pets a little creature with a moustache, the kind women like. And he's really strong-willed. Disciplined. A good boy. Doesn't touch drugs, hasn't ever even tried them. I have friends in my neighbourhood whose faces should be on Colombian postage stamps. By the age of fourteen they were minor dope smokers, making up all kinds of stories and telling me, 'It develops your brain, this stuff. It's been proven!' By fifteen they'd got me used to sprinting off whenever a squad car drove up, and by sixteen they were spending nights in the police cells. I had no idea where they were by the time we were seventeen. But until we lost touch they were in trouble again and again, and I was their pet nerd. Hard to believe, but in our neighbourhood gang, it was me who was known as the good boy. Then along comes Oshri and steals my crown. Next to him I'm a criminal. But soon he'll be gone. He says he'll email me, but I don't even have a computer. And if I did, how exactly could I send my thoughts, let off steam, get advice? So who am I left with? Lila. Other than her, I'm all alone. But she can't understand the things that happen to me, it's not possible. She can't understand anything about the army. How could she? 'Start writing her letters,' Oshri advised me. 'But only positive ones.'

I was thirteen when I visited Lila's house in the rich neighbourhood on the other side of Afula for the first time. Her father said to her, 'You're going to marry this boy.' Just like that, in front of me, in front of the aunts, ugly cows from the south who were drinking coffee in the living room. Lila nearly fainted with embarrassment. 'Listen to what I'm telling you. I see how you look at him and I know it's for life,' he insisted. And who would believe it, but we're still together, not going anywhere, and it really is for life. Before my first tour of duty in Lebanon I thought I would keep the truth from her. I made something up about a nice, quiet posting near the border, near a farming village. At the last minute I realized the truth was preferable, because if I lied and then something happened to me, God forbid, it would catch her by surprise, explode in her face, and that would be much harder for her. I'd seen girlfriends whose lives had caved in on them suddenly, in one swoop, without warning. So I told her, 'Look, there's a chance I'll get killed. That's the way it is in Lebanon. There's no plastering over the truth, no sense in lying to you about this.' With the sincerest words I knew I told her it was better for her to be prepared. She asked why I was going, and I answered that it was an enormous challenge for me, that was why I wanted to be there. On the last night, before I crossed the border, we did it twice. When I was completely spent, she put my dog tags around my neck and slipped a little note inside the cloth pouch they were kept in. She made me promise not to read it until the day of my release from the army. And I promised. But what if I die without knowing what it says? I'm often tempted to peek, because the feeling of having missed something will turn heaven into hell if I go up there without knowing what she wrote. But so far, I haven't looked. Sometimes, when I'm bored, I nearly give in, but then I close my eyes and see her lying on my bed in purple knickers (perhaps even a g-string), slowly stroking her breasts, her head hanging back over the bed and her hair falling to the floor, until I'm dying to run my hands through her hair and over her hot belly, her soft skin, smooth as a baby's, and like a magnet to continue down, to sneak in under the cloth and squeeze, to feel how wet it is there because of me, and to hope that in a few more seconds she'll be begging to feel me there. I think about her trembling, and that's how I forget about that little piece of paper . . .

Furman, the company commander, appeared suddenly in the doorway. 'Come,' he said, all aggression. Last time we crossed paths, he and I, was on the couch in his office during my squad's basic training. Just us, face to face, sitting there until the middle of the night trying to dismantle the landmines we'd laid between us, each trying to back down from the heavy artillery we'd been aiming at one another, to call a ceasefire, at least for a few weeks. 'Turning over a new leaf,' he'd said. 'It's only temporary,' I'd answered. 'For the sake of the soldiers,' he'd said. 'For the sake of the mission,' I'd countered. And eventually a ceasefire was in place. He hates my guts, which is fine, legitimate, not everyone has to love everyone else. They stuck him with me, that's clear, he took me because he had no choice, he was forced into it, but now we're at the front, our first time together, and everyone has to be a little mature about this, since I'm part of the senior staff. So now, at two-thirty in the morning, Furman was dragging me out for another round of couples therapy. We went out into the darkness like we were doing a sector briefing. Which I suppose in a way it was. At first anyway – the warm-up exercises – there was plenty to brief on, because the next day I had to pass on the battalion positions and the call signals and landmarks to my squad and the others as well, as duty officer.

'The Ali Taher mountain range battalion oversees six outposts, remember? Beaufort and Dlaat belong to the IDF while Brosh, Gamba, Hadar and Valencia belong to the SLA, our Christian partners. We watch out for each other's arses, take care of over-lapping zones. By air we're six or seven miles from the Israeli border at Metullah, our elevation is 2,460 feet above sea level, and we're responsible for Marjayoun and the Litani River, which means this place for years has been the eyes of Israel in southern Lebanon and one of the most strategically important points in the Israeli control of the entire northern region. Before we raised the flag here in June 1982, the Palestinians were bombarding northern Galilee from Beaufort. Here, you must keep alert, down over there are tobacco factories, past them is the town of Nabatiye, then Tibnit and Arb Salim and Jabel Zafi just beyond.' Furman described what lay before us at lightning speed and I stood there tense and confused, seeing nothing, absorbing nothing. 'The region is practically un-populated,' he continued, 'and on principle citizens don't just walk around the sector, certainly not at night. If somebody approaches you can be sure he's no innocent, so he's dead on the spot.'

'Automatically,' I answered. 'No hesitation.'

'I don't remember it being so quiet here,' I muttered, and Furman reminded me that at Beaufort there's no shouting, no loud talking, lights off, no light-coloured clothes. 'You'll get used to it again,' he said. 'A hundred soldiers are stationed here: Armoured Corps, Ordnance Corps, Signal Corps, medics and of course us, the infantry, who usually total about seventy guns. The outpost sits on less than two acres of land. Under normal circumstances we man four guard positions: White, Red, Blue and Green. But when there's fog or we're on high alert we set up additional posts. Apart from soldiers manning the guard positions, no one goes out in daylight, no one goes out under the night sky, no one dares step out from under that ten foot thick cement overhang. We live in darkness. Even the toilets are more or less off limits now. The architect who designed the toilets and showers separated them from the living quarters and guard posts. They say he was fucking drunk. Or maybe he just wanted to keep the germs and disease and stench away from our small, airtight main building – a matter of hygiene. We've found a reasonable solution to the problem: we pee into empty plastic bottles and allow trips to the toilets only for getting rid of the heavy loads, and during quiet interludes. As for the heavy loads, they have been reduced here to record lows and require the permission of an officer or one of the men on war room duty.'

'During the time I served here,' I said, 'we sat on the loo first thing in the morning and read the paper for as long as we wanted.'

'Things are different here now,' he said. 'Next: Dawn Alert. Remember what that is?'

Yes, I remember. It's part of standard procedures. You wake up in a good mood, like you've had a morning fuck. Every morning, between five a.m. and six-thirty, the entire outpost is on its feet, high alert, fully equipped. These are the danger hours: Hezbollah loves the glow of sunrise, it's the ideal time for attacking the outpost, the kind of attack that starts with combined hellfire: RPGs, grenades, mortar shells, light artillery, everything all at once in an intense opening onslaught, then the foot soldiers follow, trying to storm the place, wipe us out. All the recent attacks on the outpost have taken place in the dawn hours, when there's still no light, but the night-vision equipment is no longer effective, when everything's in this sort of in-between state and it's hard for us to pinpoint where they're shooting from and it's hard for us to return their fire and it's hard for us to function because it's hard to stay on your feet at those hours. And the fighters are *milfed*.

I tried to break the ice by asking Furman where the hell that word – *milfed, milfered, milfistic*, in all its permutations – had come from. We were suddenly hearing it in every second sentence in the army. 'Jesus, what a fucking stupid word,' I said, laughing. 'Who's the twat who made it up?'

'It's an abbreviation,' he said without hesitation, 'for "military fatigue."'

'Wow, Furman, I am impressed. With that kind of general knowledge I'd have made a bundle on TV ages ago,' I said. 'You know, on *Bible Quiz*, or we could set you up with a hostess from *Wheel of Fortune*.' Furman gave me a long, drawn-out, fucked-off look. All right, so it wasn't funny, I admit it. I looked like a jerk. But try to be polite, you fucking prick. Smile, I thought, so I don't stand here like a complete tosser. I'd wound up as frozen as the ice I was trying to break.

'Early wake-up, Erez, which means being completely awake during these critical hours, not just pretending to open your eyes, not a bunch of worn-out soldiers who are sloppily organized' – he took us right back to the matter at hand in that patronizing, sour tone of his that hits me in the spleen like a fist – 'and it will be your responsibility to make sure that everyone absorbs this way down deep in their consciousness,' he said. At another time this snub might have provoked me into losing my cool. But not tonight.

We fell silent, and all around us was the sharp hush that existed out there, a numbing silence that is familiar only to those who have had the privilege of standing high above the thick ring of clouds on that isolated, barren peak at an hour when even the birds are in their sleeping bags, enjoying their El Al business class eye masks. There is no silence like it in all of Israel.

Winter was the season of swampy mud, and Furman and I crossed the maze of open and covered trenches, dragging our feet from guard post to guard post, replacing the air in our lungs that we'd brought from home with this new air that was as pure as laughing gas, and left frozen droplets of water on your tongue and in your mouth when you drew a whistling breath. It's addictive, so invigorating. When you're dying to be angry you can't, when your body wants to be tense you're relaxed. A kind of nirvana. I waited for Furman to be the first to squeeze the trigger, break the silence.

'You know that you make one single mistake and you're out of here, don't you?' he said as we passed the tank facing the main gate, just before the final turn that would bring us back to the building.

'Don't get your hopes up, there's not going to be a mistake,' I replied.

'This posting is beyond your capabilities, Erez, you're not equipped for this. Everyone here knows you well enough to know you're going to mess it up. It's just a matter of time,' he said.

'What's your problem?' I asked, angry now. 'Do you think I don't know you did everything in your power to keep me from promotion? I actually do know. And now you're probably putting in overtime in front of the mirror practising your "I told you so" speech for Amos and the brigade commander. So you'd better start getting used to this idea: you're going to be disappointed. I'm not leaving.'

'I don't know what kind of fairy tale world you're living in,' Furman said, 'but I can tell you that I plan to be completely professional with you, as professional and businesslike as possible. I'm just warning you that all that will end with your first fuck-up. It's up to you. You're welcome to surprise me.'

'You're afraid I'll surprise you, that's the problem. Amos put me here because he knows the truth, he knows I can bring in operational results, not just sit back and take the blows all the time. That I can inject some courage into those boys and pursue encounters with terrorists. That I'll send a few of those arseholes to Israel in black bags, like we did back in the glory days of this place.'

It was the first time I'd seen the king of cool turn red, and even the cold air and the quiet couldn't calm him down. He pushed me hard in the chest against the tank. 'You've got the wrong idea altogether,' he said. 'Nobody wants terrorists from you, nobody wants assassinations, nobody wants confrontations with the enemy. You have only one mission: you came up here with thirteen soldiers and I want you to leave here with thirteen soldiers without a scratch on them. That's all.'

'What are you trying to tell me?' I asked.

'I'm trying to tell you that I know your record,' he said, 'and you haven't changed or matured by even a single day since doing time in jail for disobeying orders. Believe me,' he continued, 'and Amos and the brigade commander and the head of Northern Command and the chief of general staff and God Himself will tell you exactly what I'm about to: the IDF is not looking for complications now, and certainly not the kind that are the initiative of a gung-ho officer playing war games. Just keep cool.'

In those days I loved to say that a white-bread commander like Furman could never have come from the units I'd passed through, that the blond in his hair had seeped into his skull and messed up the clearheadedness required for tactical planning, so that his mouth fired off whole salvoes of statements of fear without shame. Captain Ofir Furman had come to us from the pampered commando babes, and this was enough for me, at the time, to explain all our problems. Months of training under him had signalled to me that this tour of duty would be filled with friction. I'd known all this, but now that we'd come to the heart of it for the first time it was clear that the situation was much worse than I'd thought. Furman was going to try and turn me into a pot plant. And he was making a big mistake. His irritating and threatening tone was still echoing in my mind as he walked away towards the company leaving me lagging a few steps behind, as I tried to digest it all.

At three a.m. we all jammed into the briefing room for our welcome speech. Furman supplied us with ninety minutes' worth of theory, maps, exercises and combat standing orders. Everyone dozed off. Then the boys were sent off to sleep, but when you finally get a chance to sleep is when you're most awake, because of the fear, you're trying to piece together what you're supposed to do if a barrage of mortar rains down on you suddenly, and if the whole mess starts up right when you're dozing. Even God can't help you then, when your head's spinning. You're tossed into your pint-sized quarters where the bunks are stacked three high, with so little space between them that there's no real room for you to move around. You can't sit on them, you can only lie down. They sway, they creak, when somebody climbs on them they all rock and nearly break. The boys were too tired to argue over who was going to get which bed, but Spitzer dared to ask if they were allowed to undress. Oshri laughed. 'What a stupid question. It's going to be a long time before you can take off your uniform, mate. All right, that's enough, shut your mouths and your eyes.' It's really hard to sleep in the infantry quarters, deep inside the building, where you can hear radio static and people dragging heavy things down the halls and running and shouting, and in the kitchen nearby pots are being hurled to the floor, and there's the clanging of metal as squads return from overnight ambushes at dawn and raid the dining room for a lavish meal. All these sounds jumble up in your head. In the submarine where we sleep – the officers and veterans – the light is very dim because the lightbulbs have been scribbled over with red or blue markers to minimize the halo of light that flickers over the outpost. But where the boys sleep, in the inner rooms, the light is on all the time, it's really strong, blinding, and it produces unnatural colours, it's very psychedelic. Staring directly into the bulbs mesmerizes you for a few minutes, until you feel dizzy and want to puke. Now, the boys crawled into their sleeping bags in stunned desperation, then thirty minutes later the loudspeakers announced wake-up. Dawn Alert. Everyone tumbled out of the barracks for ninety minutes, during which they sat dumbstruck and nodding off on chairs made of broken wood and rusting metal at the entrance to the security area, waiting for the hourglass to set them free. Everyone was sitting except for my youngsters, who I told to stand, with full gear on their backs, facing the green and white sign on the western wall that proclaimed our mission statement. THE AIM: TO DEFEND ISRAEL'S NORTHERN BORDER, FROM MOUNT DOV IN THE EAST TO ROSH HANIKRA IN THE WEST. Flags were draped across the walls, and the boys' faces were serious as they absorbed the place, the outpost, the situation. They were excited. Only Zitlawi's eyes drifted north to another place, filled with girls posing nude or in bikinis.

5

When you're young, Beaufort is a big, bustling diner where you're not even the Arab guy who chops vegetables; you're the migrant worker who scrubs away the scum of oil splattered on the utensils, the plates, the stainless steel. And guard duty? An hour and a half at a time followed by three hours of 'rest', then another ninety minutes, over and over again for the entire day. 'Rest' means back into the kitchen, and, for a little variety, outpost chores. The company sergeant major takes you every once in a while to pour diesel fuel into the generator, which stands at the remotest edge of the outpost, so that if the fuel tanks are hit by mortar shells we won't be blasted into the sky. When he takes you for a walk you're elated, you take a stolen glance at the world, say hello to the tanks, kick stones down the path, and it's all a real pleasure – except that you come back splattered with oil, aware that there may be two weeks between you and your next shower.

The Beaufort kitchen was unlike any kitchen you'll find in the IDF today, mainly because it had no running water. The washing of dishes took place in laundry tubs, one with soap for scrubbing and the other for rinsing. There were no hoses. Twice a week, on Mondays and Thursdays, a water truck driven by an SLA guy made its way up to us, equipped with iron chains and a coded lock that prevented the water tank it carried from being broken into along the way. At the entrance to Beaufort, the outpost doctor would remove the lock and check the water quality with a special poison-testing kit. The lack of water also regulated showering, so that a single shower was allocated to every soldier for each period of two-and-a-half to three weeks, subject, of course, to the frequency of mortar attack warnings. At least the food at Beaufort was excellent, better than any soldier could dream up in his fevered imagination. On that, everyone was agreed. The very best rations in the entire IDF were sent to Beaufort; everything that Chili, our cook, could possibly think of to ask for was provided by the army caterers back in Israel. They sent every kind of cheese – hard cheese, feta, Swiss, Roquefort, mozzarella – and banana-flavoured milk and non-dairy cream and all kinds of puddings in all the best flavours, and French mustard and fantastic salads and schnitzel and Lebanese kebab and carton loads of oven chips and first-class spreads. Real gourmet meals. We had everything except for chicken. Chicken was never sent to Beaufort because it spoils too quickly. No more than twenty soldiers would show up for breakfast and about forty for lunch (the sergeants were sleeping then), but every evening, when the sun went down, the outpost went into party mode. Nobody missed the massive, meat-based meals that were the centrepiece of our days, around which everything turned. For the boys it was also the cause of their nightmares: the Great Wall of dishes piled up for washing on the floor of the back kitchen. A mere three soldiers on kitchen duty were meant to tackle the whole lot, struggling right through until morning. But even before the first meal, River and Bayliss had held a vote (at my command) that determined that all the soldiers in our squad would lend a hand each night to the three on duty. If they worked together like a well-oiled machine, I explained, they would be quick to discover new methods for washing and drying and storing the copious quantities of pots and cutlery.

On their very first day of kitchen duty under Chili they really messed up. That's what happens when you don't know the legend or the man. They gathered around the dishwashing tubs for a training session after breakfast had been put away, and Zitlawi opened his mouth. He started talking and didn't notice that Chili was listening.

'What do you mean you didn't get an erection?' Zitlawi asked, attacking River. 'How could you not get an erection? That's not possible. Are you taking the piss? Please tell me you're talking bullshit. What are you, a homo? That's fine, sweetheart, really, I don't have a problem with that, just let us know so we can set you up with a great job in the air force. All kinds of perks there. But listen to your old mate for a minute: where I come from, when some sweet little sixteen year old checks out your M16, it guides itself into the firing position of an Iraqi scud missile. And no cold weather or birds or cows or ATVs should have fucked up your sensors. You would have tarnished the reputation of the entire company, brother. I hope you understand the enormity of your fuck-up.'

'She wasn't my type', River said. 'With me these things are very specific.' The squad demanded specifics. 'First of all, she has to be athletic,' he announced without hesitation, 'plus, creamy skin is a must, ditto green or blue eyes. South American origin, long, flowing, curly, hair, the right sized tits. She's got to love sports and hiking, and if she isn't mad about the beach then she's out of the running. She should have the name of a real quality babe, something like Avishag, let's say.' Over the scrubbing tub Zitlawi demanded more detail about the tits. 'Be professional about this. Give us a bra size.'

River, who was already red-faced and hunched under the squad's expectant gaze politely refused. If you ask me, he had already realized that Hodaya was simmering somewhere inside him and that he would go out looking for her, whether or not he might succeed. Oshri and I laughed quietly, because there's no such thing as a babe whose name begins with an 'H', every old-timer knows that. Any girl whose name begins with an 'H' – or any vowel sound, for that matter – can not be really gorgeous. Ever. A tested truth. No Avishag, no Hodaya. I don't even need to see the objects of this boy's fantasies to know I'm right. Babes are Sharon Stone, Sigal Simchon. Too bad for the fellow, he's going to take a bad fall.

'Tell me, Bayliss,' Zitlawi said, shifting his attention. 'Sixteen year old religious girls: what do they know about the facts of life? No, really, I'm asking. I'm serious. It's an important question, don't you think? Philosophical. Psychological. Ideological. Does someone teach them the things that are worth knowing? Does someone, let's say, spread their legs gently and make nice with them? Because the truth is, I stood there facing that holy virgin of yours in that cowshed and I felt real compassion for her, because I knew how much good I could do her. How I could set that girl on fire. But she'll never get the chance.'

This is where they tripped up. Chili is not the kind of guy to ignore a paedophilic monologue. He's got a gentle soul, and morals. He's religiously traditional. When someone messes around with the sanctity of women he sees red. He came over, restrained, to check on their work, see how they were doing. He spotted a grain of rice on an orange plastic cup, and inflicted an inhuman punishment on them: the bleaching of all the kitchen's utensils, which would take an entire day, right up until the loudspeakers announced Dawn Alert again.

While this was going on, Oshri and I took them out in threes for a tour of the guard posts, their first look around in daylight. They dashed from the entrance of the security area to Green, the northern post, the most isolated and distant of the four. They wore helmets and flak jackets topped with warm coats and gloves, not yet accustomed to the cold. They peered into what was about to become their lives, into the enormous ancient fortress – known as The Rock – and at the tattered and dusty flag flying at the top of the pole, the rips and tears of which are clearly visible from below. You don't replace a flag that bears a history, a certain pride and honour, I told them.

As it moves from the breathtaking fortress to the ugly outpost alongside, the eye catches, off to the left, a low whitewashed wall with a metal plaque chained to it. The date on the plaque has faded, the text is missing in places, but the last line is deeply engraved: THE BEAUFORT WAS CAPTURED BY THE SOLDIERS AND COMMANDERS OF THE GOLANI RECONNAISSANCE UNIT. THE BATTLE TOOK THE LIVES OF GONI HARNICK, YOSSI ELIEL, GIL BEN-AKIVA, RAZ GUTERMAN, YARON ZAMIR, AVIKAM SHERF. WHERE DO YOU FIND MEN LIKE THE ONE WHO WAS AS A WEEPING WILLOW, AND LIKE AN ANCIENT FORTRESS, AT THE END OF HIS ROAD? Those boys had a real literary streak back then, in the eighties. I showed my squad the key targets. The closet populated settlement, a mere six hundred and fifty feet down the hill, was Arnoun. The new Arnoun was a village of about one hundred buildings, well paved and fairly progressive. To its right was the old, abandoned Arnoun, which had been a stronghold for terrorists until the IDF removed them. The constant presence of terrorists at the foot of Beaufort, where the access road to our outpost split off from the main road, was intolerable. According to the intelligence, an old woman was the only person left now, living alone behind the heavy concrete barriers blocking the entrance to visitors.

From Green you can see everything. Yukhmur is in plain view, straight ahead. A little to its left is the Nikras road, which connects all the outposts, from Dlaat to Beaufort to Gamba and beyond. Green was made up of three guard posts, two of which were protected by domes and concrete roofs with the aim of minimizing damage from mortar attack. I told them honestly that there was no way of surviving a direct hit. The visibility from inside the fortified position was limited, providing clear observation for only about thirty feet, not much more, so during daylight it was necessary to post a man outside as well. One soldier was inside while the other stood outside. Outside the guard posts the concrete barriers protected only the lower body; the body was exposed from the chest up. What more was there to know? At each guard post there was a MAG heavy machine-gun, always loaded and ready to fire. Behind each were two emergency fortified shelters so that the soldiers could take cover if need be.

We continued our tour. It was pitch black in the trenches and they were lined with long fluorescent strips in orange, yellow and green to keep the men from stumbling. Outside, everything was camouflaged in an olive colour, with the occasional black netting, and there were endless stairs, everything hidden from view by walls of sandbags. A big old shipping container that sat in the parking area, riddled with holes from shrapnel, was our storeroom. Once upon a time they played football here, in the carefree eighties, and sunbathed lying on the front of a tank in their underwear. These days we stayed in uniform even in our sleeping bags.

We reached Red, the eastern guard post that commanded a view of the rest of the outpost and of the access road. There's a 60 mm mortar shell there, two covered guard posts and an exposed position for escape under attack. White, our southern post, is closer to deserted Arnoun. It has one manned covered post and two exposed posts that are usually not in use. The field of vision is limited here and only marginally effective; mainly you can see the Litani River, but if Hezbollah tried to attack on foot it would probably come from here because White is where the hill is least steep. From here you can see Manzurieh, an SLA outpost with batteries of cannons. Israel, too: you can see Metullah, and Kiryat Shmona.

After that I introduced them to the guys from the Intelligence, the soldiers who listen around the clock to static that comes from the screen of a broken computer. Every once in a while you hear a click and they say, 'There, a car just drove down the road,' or 'There, a car is braking.' Work that one out. I suppose it helps, maybe when there's fog, but those boys, what can I say? Have pity on them. They work and sleep round the clock in that same little room with those grating metallic noises and yelps and brakes and chirps. After two years at Beaufort is there any chance of them being anything but utterly insane? They did seem strange to us, cut off, new immigrants with glasses the size of television screens.

We continued our tour. The wild chirping and the soft whisper of the radio accompanied us the whole way, and from time to time the rumble of armoured personnel carriers shook the earth. 'So, River,' I asked, 'what have you got to say?'

'Exotic,' he answered. 'Fucking exotic.'

By the time the sun rose on the next day they were deep into the silent, grinding boredom that is outpost routine, from guard duty to kitchen duty to maintenance duty. They would gather up the piss bottles and spent shells from the guard posts, which after a night of guard duty looked like the remains of a Fourth World War. They would polish the MAG machine-guns, and if we were lucky and the skies were quiet, they were also sent on lightning missions to disinfect the toilets – three toilets for one hundred men equals a nuclear holocaust; they make the public restrooms at the Rafiah border crossing into Gaza look like the King David Hotel. They'd sweep and wash down the secure area again and again in a futile attempt to keep at bay the clinging mud that the men brought back with them to the linoleum floors and concrete court-yard. 'Where have they dumped us?' I heard Bayliss asking in despair. 'This was supposed to be a war, they promised us war, and it turns out there isn't one. Not even a feeling of danger. Yeah, I know, we came in on that scary convoy, but that was it. Since then it's been nothing but talk, and if you ask the sergeants when there's no officer around, they'll tell you that the stated threats are completely detached from reality. All we are doing is hard labour. Donkey work. Where's the real thing?'

6

On our sixth night on the hill, Mickey Bayliss stopped wearing his *kippa*. He waited for me to leave the submarine and went in to inform Oshri. Next he went to tell the boys, who were already buried deep in their sleeping bags. He made his announcement, picked up his flak jacket and went off to guard duty. The squad was paralysed, that's the only way to describe it. It seemed completely illogical. No one spoke. When he returned they were waiting for him, awake and curious, and they bombarded him with questions: which sins had he already committed and which were still in the planning stages? And with whom? Zitlawi offered hearty congratulations to the new member of the jerk off club, to the league of the heavy abusers. Spitzer promised to fix him up with his first secular girl, Emilio described in great detail the juicy slab of pork he would season and grill for him. Truth is, we love surprises, but not a single fake smile managed to cover up the inexplicable feeling of sadness that pervaded the barracks just then. I knew it wasn't easy to stay religious, to keep the commandments, in our squad. I'd seen it often enough: good guys cutting corners. On the Sabbath, smoking a cigarette they claimed had been lit by someone else. On a holy day, keeping one eye on the television they insisted had been turned on by someone else. In the end, they're even watching porn videos. And when Dave from the war room, a bearded redhead with the black *kippa* of the seriously religious, ran around like a mad thing, desperately hunting for enough men to form a quorum for prayer, they'd avoid him. All of them but Bayliss. Bayliss never once missed morning prayers, afternoon prayers, evening prayers. He talked about the obligation, the calling, the 'personal fortitude'. He was no fanatic, not bigoted or blind to other opinions and lifestyles, but we all saw him as a star of the religious Zionist world, our hope and pride. And here he was suddenly looking us straight in the eye and telling us he'd decided to take a break. Maybe for a year, he said, maybe ten, maybe for his whole life. He no longer had the spiritual willpower, didn't feel strong enough, wasn't worthy of representing us. And if he wasn't worthy, then there was no need for him to continue wearing a *kippa*. On the contrary, he said he would be putting the religious Zionists to shame if he kept it on.

The knitted *kippa* guys of the religious Zionist camp had become the backbone of our brigade – in fact, of all the Infantry brigades. They were the best fighters and were growing in numbers and strength. They were a new generation, not like their settler fathers, not like anything that the state religious schools had produced in the past. Ours were a different breed: no more ragged parkas or tattered sandals; no longer the heavy beards of diaspora Jews. They'd done away with a look that set them apart and now they looked the same as us. They dressed like us and wore their hair like us, they talked like us, liked the same films, the same music. They knew how to party like the best of us. They didn't even always have a *kippa* on their heads. They were determined not to be prejudiced against, told that they weren't good enough, or didn't keep the commandments strictly enough to call themselves card carrying members of the religious Zionist club. They like to say that maybe one day they'll mend their ways and study and wear their *kippas* again. They call themselves 'pocket-*kippa* boys' and some of them screw as many girls as we do. Really, I swear it, this generation actually fucks, because they know how to bend their religious obligations since those rules are no longer the centre of their lives. But when it comes to loving the Land of Israel, patriotism, to sacrifice, even to friendship, they're the best, the most 'religious' of us all, and often the most extreme. With body-building, too, nobody can compete with their enthusiasm and determination to succeed. These guys are achievers, go-getters, they dream of a *kippa*-wearing chief of staff and they believe they'll win over the people of Israel through battle and sacrifice. They've already filled the ranks of the battalions, the reconnaissance units, officer training. Just before enlisting they prepare answers to all the questions. Tools. When a secular friend on duty with them says, 'Prove to me that there's a God,' or in bed, during late night talks, if he comes up with something really tricky like 'What possible reason is there for me not to jerk off?' these guys will never be tongue-tied. Sometimes it seemed as though to be one of them, part of that perfect world, was the sexiest thing possible; those boys were the army's most popular brand name. I'd been handed a mainly secular squad, which was rare, unusual, but I had Bayliss. And Bayliss was one of their leaders, ethical and strong-willed, the poster child, the one everyone everywhere knew and loved, the one who knew everything about everyone like only a religious person with aunts and uncles and cousins in every settlement and outpost can know, and still hang on to his principles. When he announced that he'd decided to stop wearing his *kippa*, it wasn't really the *kippa* that bothered us. It was the way Bayliss had decided to give it up, just like that, when all around us the religious soldiers were doing so well, putting forward such a solid front.

I joined him at his guard post at midnight. He was surprised, even a bit taken aback, and didn't say hello. I asked him why he'd removed the *kippa* but he just muttered a dejected 'That's that.' I hung around, waiting for him to speak. Bayliss didn't utter a word. So I hunted for words that would break the ice. 'So,' I asked, 'what happened? All of a sudden there's no God?'

'It's all over,' he answered. He explained that he'd had enough, that he was wasted in terms of being a religious person. I kept asking again and again what he meant by wasted, but he didn't respond. I tried pissing him off, I asked him what his parents would say, what kind of an example this would set for all those soldiers who looked up to him. A few long minutes passed before he finally began to talk.

Bayliss told me he hadn't met any secular people until he was fourteen. He encountered them for the first time when Rabbi Schwarz arranged to take the children in his village, Nov, to a demonstration in Rabin Square in Tel Aviv, which was called the Kings of Israel Square back then. Another demonstration followed that one, and then another. The struggle against the Israeli withdrawal from the Golan Heights punctured the first hole in his well-insulated bubble. In a little religious village like theirs there was no chance some secular girl would walk across the grass waving temptation before your eyes. Everyone you know, everyone you've ever met in your short life, is part of the world of faith. The girls study in a girls' school in Tiberias, the boys in a religious boarding school. At six a.m. they are already at prayer, then they study religious subjects until midday and secular subjects like computers and literature in the afternoon. At six in the evening they start up with the faith lessons again, before finishing the day with the Talmud. No movies, no going to the cinema, there was no television at the *yeshiva*. Cigarettes were forbidden, buses only came twice a week and the only pub (not for people under twenty) served the same stuff for the same price, year after year. There was a once-yearly visit to Tel Aviv with your parents. And above all in school there was politics, where you wouldn't find a single leftist. He remembered, before Prime Minister Rabin was assassinated, wishing time and again for exactly that to happen. It was in their thoughts, and when it took place few tears were shed. When they were told to send a representative from the village to the funeral they were hard-pressed to find a volunteer. Was this a result of the attitude of the state religious schools? Maybe, but Rabin had broken his promises, Bayliss told me.

'We weren't superhuman,' he said, 'just human. A little more restrained, but living with all the same urges, jerking off, everyone jerks off, if not at thirteen like the secular kids then three years later. And just like other sixteen year old boys, we talked about girls. But we didn't say, "I screwed her," or "I touched her breasts."

'I've never in my life talked about a woman's breasts,' he was careful to tell me. But there are other ways of saying things. Instead of 'I turned her on,' they'd say, 'I had some business with her,' and everyone knew what that meant. And when some rude bloke asked, 'How far did the business go?' and you answered 'far' or 'a little' or 'almost all the way', the most important thing was not to be specific. They'd made up a language of their own, and they would switch letters to hide swear words, like 'trick' instead of 'prick', or a 'son of a witch'. To this very day they still say 'loobs' instead of 'boobs' in Bayliss's village. It's a matter of holiness. They didn't have sex education in the schools, still don't. Bayliss met his first girlfriend thanks to a mix-up with telephone numbers. A completely secular girl. They nearly had sex on their first date. It was when he was sixteen, on the *Lag BaOmer* holiday. She was from the south – Kiryat Gat – and he was from way up in the Golan Heights. His parents thought he was at boarding school. He snuck out of school at one in the afternoon and hitchhiked to Kiryat Gat, arriving at six. She was waiting for him in her room. They went to the beach. She asked if he'd already done stuff and he said he had, tried to play it cool. But he didn't know where to touch her, what to do; he didn't even know how to kiss her, so how in hell was he supposed to know how to take her bra off? How could he know he was supposed to take it off? She dropped hints, he got it wrong. What a jerk he was! They sat talking for a while. She moved in on him with her hands. In his wildest dreams he'd never imagined anything like this, hadn't gone looking for it, it just came to him suddenly from heaven. They stayed together, really turned on, all night. At two a.m. she asked him if he had a condom. He didn't know what she was talking about. He'd heard the word on TV but he didn't really know what it was. And he certainly didn't have one. On the way home he realized his life as he'd known it was shattering. He'd done what he'd done and the sky hadn't fallen. He'd even enjoyed himself.

It was back then that all his doubts began. By mid morning he was back at school, late for a class given by Rabbi Uri, who'd been raised as secular, on a kibbutz, but who had become religious and was now a teacher. During the break he locked himself in the toilets with his best friend and told him he'd had some business. Business? his friend asked. They weren't supposed to touch girls, let alone screw them – doing that would put his whole life in danger. But even there, in the heartland of the religious Zionist faithful, a bloke who travelled all the way to the city to do business with a girl was a stud, a superstar. And anyone who began to open up to the secular world got hooked and became anxious to learn more about it, desperate for a taste of what lay beyond the forbidden mountain. Bayliss would sneak out – his parents thought he was at boarding school, at school they thought he was at home – and sometimes he would take his friend and they would tear up the city. Their classes on faith didn't fortify them, he started sleeping in and missing the morning prayers. Three weeks later he hitch-hiked south again. On the way he stopped at a chemist, at her urging. He took off his *kippa* at her front door. If he was going to have sex without getting married, if he was going to desecrate God's name, then at least it should be without the *kippa* on his head. It was crucial not to represent religious Zionism in a bad light. That's the way they are, Bayliss explained to me: if they're going to vandalize a bus stop or spray graffiti on the walls of a school or break into a football field, they'll take their *kippas* off first. It's an important statement.

So there he was, and the girl said, 'I'm going to have a shower. Want to join me?' Nothing came out of his mouth for a full five minutes, then he joined her. They only had three condoms, but they managed. It was a wild Sabbath for them both, his first time. And outside, the rivers kept on flowing at their pace. Meanwhile, back in Nov, Haim, his neighbour, had been going out with Tzurit for three years. He'd call her sweetheart sometimes and maybe even declare his love for her, but he didn't dare touch her. And if his hand brushed against her shoulder, by accident, he'd apologize immediately: 'Sorry, I didn't mean to!' In the late spring the boys would swim in their underwear at a local reservoir during breaks. When their rabbi came looking for them they would duck under the water and stay there for a minute or more. Then, after a cow entered the water and couldn't get out, slowly sinking and then drowning, they stopped going there out of fear. But there, at the edge of the water, Bayliss also smoked for the first time and had his first look at a *Playboy* magazine that was keeping the entire class occupied, passed from hand to hand.

He'd thought that in the army he would mend his ways, leave behind the foolishness. But the army, according to Bayliss, was even worse. In spite of his account of a lust-filled adolescence, it was the army that was ruining religious boys, exposing them to temptation and placing them in an impossible situation. 'I don't feel like pretending any more,' he said. 'At home, safe in my environment, I could handle it. But here, what options do I have? I could try to become more religious, improve myself, be less despicable, strengthen my resolve. But I don't have the spiritual fortitude to spend time doing it, work out what's really happening to me. I can't even get up for prayers in the morning. Any secular person would look at me now and see a disgrace and he'd hold the religious world in contempt because of me. I take my hat off to anyone who can survive his army service as a religious person. Not me, I'm not strong enough, not up to the challenge. I set myself a mission and failed.'

'And what about God?' I asked.

'I don't know,' he answered. 'Maybe there's such a thing as personal providence. I'm not sure. Who knows?'

Over the next few months, on furloughs home, he would put the *kippa* back on as the bus climbed towards the Golan Heights. In Nov, he continued to attend prayer services, living in two worlds. No one there would guess that Menahem Bayliss's son was no longer religious, that he'd broken ranks. He had one very religious, very observant sister who had completed her national service for religious women and was now studying at the nation's Orthodox university, Bar Ilan. Another sister had been living for years in a West Bank settlement. He, too, was well thought of, a nice young man who said hello in the street, and the locals were convinced he'd go far. He couldn't break the soul and spirit and image of his family just for a few more hours of sleep on Saturday mornings. So his father could continue to believe that his son was one of them while his mother, who knew the truth, could believe with all her heart that this was only a passing phase.

When a guard from the next shift came to replace Bayliss, I walked him back to the secure area. I searched his face for emotion but he appeared unmoved.

I brought a boiling cup of black coffee with three sugars to Oshri, in bed. 'What's the matter, don't you love me any more, you shithead?' I asked, trying to draw fire. 'Truth is,' he said, 'if you'd grow a pair of big tits I'd marry you. Really.' Oshri was right, of course. How could you not marry someone who brings you coffee like this, the best in southern Lebanon? 'So, what'll it take, brother?' I continued, acting like the child that I am. 'A sex change operation? And what if I come out as ugly as a dog? What then? I'll be left with nothing.' He made another X on his wall chart as though he'd been waiting all day to do it, so he could make my eyes burn. Couldn't he have waited till I wasn't around? I winced. 'Oh come on, are you going to start moaning to me about it again?' he asked. 'We'll warm up the girls for you in Colombia. What's wrong with that? You should thank me.'

At seven in the morning, when the boys were mopping the floors, Furman called me in for an officers' meeting, and took us through the intelligence reports. He said there was a good chance something was going to happen, that we shouldn't be fooled by the quiet. Hezbollah had taken up positions in a ring around the tobacco factories, putting them in a strong position to fire rockets and mortar shells at us. We leaned over the aerial photo of the Ali Taher mountain range as Furman drew a red circle on the shiny laminate and outlined how in the past forty-eight hours five enemy supply trucks had been spotted arriving at the site and unloading large wooden crates. Next he read an encrypted message from Command Intelligence, something about weaponry being sent by Tehran to Hezbollah via Damascus. The two things were perhaps connected, he said. I asked why we weren't bombing the position. After all, we knew they were there. Furman ignored me, didn't even glance at me, and continued his briefing, mentioning Wadi Zirin, which had been quiet in the past few days.

'Was that a stupid question?' I persisted. 'Tell me if that was a stupid question, because I don't think it was. I'm trying to understand the logic of sitting here like morons in the outpost while Hezbollah are gaining a stronghold.'

When Command tell us to attack,' Furman responded, 'we'll attack.'

'Why the hell aren't we at least recommending it?' I asked.

'Hey, Erez,' Furman said, mocking me, 'you're even more useful than I'd thought! Until I'm asked to attend a cabinet meeting, do me a favour and stick to your job.' My job, at that time, was to prepare my squad for their first operational mission: a one night ambush on the access road. Yes, and it sounded pretty depressing and futile – lying like a fossil in the bushes just sixty or seventy feet from the gate of the outpost – but that was our mission. 'Really, I'm very sorry we're not sending you to set up ambushes in Beirut,' Furman continued, his voice filled with contempt. 'In the meantime you'll have to make do with the menial task of preventing terrorists from getting near the outpost.'

It wasn't even a real ambush, just what's known as a 'patrol'. Fifteen boys hiding along the edges of a winding stretch of the path that runs up to Beaufort, a blind spot to the guard posts above. From seven in the evening until four-thirty in the morning you pray for a terrorist to leave the comfort of his warm bed on a winter's night and make an heroic attempt to break through, driving away your boredom. In the past, Hezbollah had managed to come within ten yards or so of the outpost and plant landmines. If our access road were mined we'd be cut off for days without food or fuel, and one of our vehicles might be blown sky high. And of course the outpost would be in danger of being stormed. For two years now the enemy had tried repeatedly to raid Beaufort and get inside the fortress, mow down a few soldiers and plant a yellow flag while a TV crew from Al-Manar captured the victory on film, to be used for boosting morale, of course.

A patrol on the access road reduces the chance of just such a fiasco because it gives us the advantage of surprise. Reduces, but doesn't remove it; on a foggy night even a whole cluster of ambushes wouldn't save us. On thick grey nights like those, a terrorist with balls could come in through the gate, sleep with us in the submarine, wake up in the morning before the rest of the outpost and kill everyone before going back home, happy and content, with one of Chili's schnitzels and a carton of chocolate milk in his hand. When there's thick fog everything shuts down. You can't see two feet in front of you. The guards shake in their boots when they hear the sound of martens and weasels running around in the undergrowth. Is that an animal or a bearded terrorist about to slit your throat from behind? You're welcome to guess. In this kind of situation you hold on tightly to your MAG, tenser than ever, but there's nothing you can do. And there are lots of foggy nights on this mountain. So why the hell do we let ourselves sit around waiting for this evil to come and get us, instead of striking first and taking out the threat in advance with an attack on the hideout where they're polishing their swords and preparing to storm us?

Straight after the briefing I gathered the squad for a talk about the ambush that night. I made them line up near the medical bay where the stretchers were always ready. I had to be tough with them, I didn't have a choice. 'The terrorists are watching us,' I told them. 'They're checking out every IDF outpost, one by one, weighing up which is the best to hit. If they sense that we're in a muddle they'll attack. If, on the other hand, they can see we're completely prepared and in shape, they'll go for it somewhere else. The Hezbollah men are no fools, they want to make it home safely, too. So they'll always take on the units whose combat readiness is weak. Even weeds on dirt embankments are a sign that things aren't in order, and could put us right in their sights. It's a matter of life and death.' I decreed that wearing gloves was prohibited in spite of the miserable cold since, I explained, gloves made it hard to squeeze the trigger, lengthened reaction time and hampered accuracy. True, the other squads were allowed to keep warm at night, but that wouldn't pass muster with me; my squad would have to get used to the cold. After that I gave them a schedule for the gym (practically a closet, in fact, with exercise bicycles gathering dust, five barbells and a treadmill that the company had won on the brigade sports day). Only my squad used the gym, maybe because sports gear was forbidden from use at the outpost and exercising in uniform was a particularly stinky affair, made worse by the fact that the chances of a shower afterwards were almost nil. I also made it clear that there was no using the toilets without my permission, even if that meant waking me up. I had to know where every one of them was at all times. As for the one phone at the outpost – an ancient, black, faulty army telephone – I let them use it between seven and eight p.m. only, a time when the long queue made getting a turn virtually impossible. The entire battalion fought over that one wretched line, with conversations from other outposts and operations rooms crossing lines and messing up the connection. And if by some miracle you managed to work your way up to the receiver, you'd get jabbed from behind and people would gesture at their watches. Two conversations, one with your mother and one with your girlfriend? Are you out of your mind? That's out of the question! You have to make a choice. Long personal calls from Beaufort were only possible in the dead of night, say, when you came off guard duty. Everyone did that; only my squad was forbidden. 'How am I supposed to keep in touch with my girlfriend?' Zitlawi asked me. 'First get yourself a girlfriend,' I told him, 'and then we'll teach you how to write letters.' And to finish up, I gave them another test: What's 'Caesar?' Caesar is the code name for the outpost. And what's 'Two?' 'Three' means operations in Israel, but what the hell is 'Two?' And where's the 'Dump?' And what's the code name for the observation post in Marjayoun? Wake up! 'Emilio, what's the code name for Manzurieh?'

'Milano,' he answered.

'Congratulations,' I said, 'you've just used up your whole quota of stupidity for our time at the front! I'm adding another week to your first tour.'

'Are you out of your mind?' Zitlawi let fly, and he was given an extra week as well. Altogether, including the punishment they'd received over the saga of their late arrival, those two wouldn't be seeing home for fifty-six days.

7

Potato crisps make noise. Pretzels make noise. Chocolate *Kif Kef* bars don't, provided that you take off the wrapper first. Wrappers make noise. So does sucking sweets. When you're preparing to go out on an ambush you give a lot of thought to the food that goes out with you. In enemy territory a bag of *Ruffles* could cost you your life. Make a rustling noise and you're exposed. Hezbollah is listening. Drop a wrapper and expect to be bombarded.

Just before zero-hour you enter the kitchen and organize provisions. The IDF provides a portion of beef jerky and chocolate bars – the good kind, *Elite* chocolate with nuts, the one with the red cow on the wrapper, so you feel like they're really investing in you. There are bread rolls, too, which you squeeze and knead until they're about as thick and compressed as a broomstick so that they take up as little room in your bag as possible. You fill them with sliced cheese and jam, an Ethiopian dish that has caught on in the infantry over the last few years. Then you add a large helping of gummy bears and chocolate covered wafers that you've brought from home. And of course there are the losers who pack dates and raisins (dominant mothers, I guess, or troubled childhoods). All this you shove into your treat pack, cramming in everything you can. Within twenty minutes it's all one big sticky mess. Bits of beef jerky stuck to chocolate, chocolate stuck to gummy bears. Tastes like shit, but everybody is hooked on it.

The treat pack is a brilliant invention, part of every soldier's equipment. It's basically a lunch bag made out of khaki-coloured corduroy that's been attached to your backpack or flak jacket, and it's specially designed for ambushes. You can run, jump, roll on the ground and that treat pack won't make a sound. It won't fall off, either. Only don't forget, no wrappers inside.

At ninety minutes to sunset, Oshri instructs the squad to start preparing. They take off their army boots and smear them with oil to waterproof them, then they pile on the heavy clothes: long underwear, Thermax trousers and shirts, combat uniform, a layer of fleece-lined clothes, and to top it all off, a storm suit and flak jacket. They wear nomex gloves and three pairs of heavy socks, one on top of the other, and a pair of overboots, too. On their heads they wear a Madonna set, a black cloth headband with a microphone and earpiece. Each soldier puts eight full magazines into his backpack along with two hand grenades, two torches (one standard, one red) and a fluorescent stick light. You add a probe too, which is a long, sharp rod for testing suspicious objects: with it you can strike a stone to make sure it isn't a fake one made from fibreglass and manufactured in Iran, its hollow insides concealing a deadly landmine. And four heat packs, which can reach a temperature of about 50°C (just don't let them touch your skin). A compass, too, and night-vision equipment and a pair of binoculars. And the treat pack, of course. Every item that goes out with a soldier on a mission like this, even the piss bottle and the canteen and the helmet, are roped to the side of the backpack to ensure that nothing will be left behind or fall when it's time to retreat. Oshri adds spare radios and replacement batteries. River slips in a shit pack, an airtight bag that fits in your helmet and is designed for taking a dump while in enemy territory. When the bag is full, the squad seals it carefully and brings it back to the outpost for proper burial. If we leave our droppings out there, in the places the IDF has selected for ambushes, we'll expose our hiding places to the terrorists. If we're talking about an overnight ambush it's fair to demand that a sane and healthy soldier hold it in, and anyway, when we go out for a day or more we take 'Stop-It' pills, which make us constipated for at least seventy-two hours. Don't try it. Release, when it finally comes, rips you to shreds. And yet, in spite of it all, there's never been a single ambush that some soldier didn't stink up. We have to be prepared.

The boys pop off one by one for a final shit while Bayliss mans the sewing machine, knocking up a few last treat packs for those who don't have them. River checks everyone's veins, prodding them and trying to commit them to memory, forcing himself to believe he'll be able to administer an IV with his eyes closed, in the dark, if need be. Then he takes everyone's temperature. 'They promised us a rectal thermometer,' Zitlawi complains, to which Oshri replies that everyone should keep his perversions to himself. Truth is, the cold spell that hit Beaufort in the winter of 1998 and led to the hospitalization of a group of soldiers gave birth to a whole folklore in the company about rectal virginity. A 'virgin' is someone who hasn't been rectally penetrated. By a thermometer, that is. I'm one of them, luckily: after all my years in the field I still haven't lost my virginity. But Oshri, boy did he lose his. One winter, he and I were out on an ambush, both still as soldiers, and our commanding officer passed around an oral thermometer. When it came to Oshri's turn, the thermometer read 35ºC. That got the medic worried, and he made it clear that the poor fucker had no choice but to open up his arse for a more accurate check. Those were the orders, no way around it. Oshri stubbornly refused, claimed he wasn't capable of removing eight layers of clothing in the freezing cold. But the officer and the medic insisted. In the end, he gave in. At first he tried administering it himself, kept at it for a while. When that didn't work the medic lost patience, grabbed him, spread his cheeks and shoved it in in one go. If it had been a thin thermometer – a revolutionary development now found in the kit of every medic serving in the cold – we would have forgotten about it a long time ago. But that night, with the thickest rod of glass you'll find in any medic's kit, that little jerk's screams could be heard all the way to Damascus. And there we were, surrounding him, watching him writhe in pain and laughing our heads off. Oshri likes to tell us how at first it was scary and agonizing but after a while it was relaxing, addictive, even pleasurable. I can only think how lucky it is that my boys haven't heard this particular battle story yet. If they had, they'd never stop winding him up about it. What's certain is that they wouldn't treat him with respect or take orders from him.

Twenty-five minutes until we move out. When the packs are filled, tradition has it that the squad takes advantage of a few spare minutes for some quick bargaining: 'You got any extra heat packs? Give me two and you'll get a gummy bear.' 'What, all you've got is cherry flavour? Here, take grape.' Oshri is always the last one to get ready leaving it till the squad is lined up to go. They've all got short-barrel M16s hanging from their shoulders with the new laser targeters that make it easy to shoot from the hip. 'Let's go,' Oshri announces. 'Equipment lists.' 'Equipment lists, equipment lists,' they repeat after him. This means they check each other's flak jackets, their packs, make sure nothing's been forgotten, and that everything's been recorded in the log that stays behind, at the outpost. If we get blown up they'll know in the war room and the storeroom exactly what is missing, what sensitive equipment could have fallen into enemy hands. After that each soldier steps on to the digital scales with all his equipment on his back and his flak jacket and gun in order to make sure that nobody's over the weight limit, and the data recorded in a chart. Another chart. Each backpack weighs anywhere from sixty-five to eighty-five pounds, a soldier's flak jacket is another forty-five, and when you add surveillance equipment and extra weaponry – for the snipers, for example – sometimes a soldier has to carry a load of 150 pounds on his back for the entire duration of an ambush. While Oshri is getting the boys ready, I'm in the briefing room, staring at an aerial photograph, trying to absorb the details of the operation. You have to memorize the terrain: at which outcrop I cut to the right, next to which boulder I head left, where gaps may open up between the soldiers, where it's safest to make contact with the outpost, when we can stop for the first time and where exactly each man will position himself. Amos, the battalion commander, is talking to me on the red phone, the hotline from the war room back in Israel. 'Don't panic, but tonight you're coming under fire,' he says, dropping his bomb.

'What does that mean, Amos?'

'Don't ask me, I have no idea. We have intelligence that Hezbollah are on their way. I don't know when, I don't know how many of them, but it looks like you'll finally get to meet the terrorist cell that's been operating in the area recently.'

'How can you tell me this a minute before we move out?' I ask. 'And without detailed information?'

'Focus, Erez. Once you're out there you've got to remember we're here for our country. Everything you've gone through up to now has been preparation for this moment. So the time has come for you to do your best and show us what you boys are made of. Good luck.'

Where the fuck was he pulling these clichés from? Battalion commanders don't talk like that. Not during operations, anyway, maybe at funerals. While I'm still trying to make sense of what he's said, Oshri walks in. I cast around looking for the right words to tell him tonight's the night, but he beats me to it. 'I don't think we should go out tonight,' he says, which is unlike him, and surprises me. 'The moon's ninety-eight per cent full, it's too dangerous. Like daylight. They'll see us all the way to Beirut.' I chuckle. If our own General Spineless, little Furman, is finally sending us on a mission, who are we to refuse? Trust me, there's no danger at all. 'Come on, mate,' I say, 'we're already ten minutes behind schedule, let's give them a rousing commanding officer's speech and get the hell out of here.' Oshri stands there for a few long seconds, looking at me while I stare back at him. I put my hands around his neck and say, 'What's wrong, little girl? Are you afraid?' 'I'm not afraid,' he answers, and I can see he realizes it's too late to back down now, there's no way out. I open the door and push him out. 'Let me paint your face so we can get going before you start falling apart in here,' I say. In the courtyard Emilio has pulled out a video camera. 'Come on,' he says, 'show Mummy what nice warm clothes you're wearing, make her happy.' 'Too bad, sweetheart, filming us like that before an ambush. You're not giving us much of a chance,' Zitlawi tells him. He tries to block the lens with his large paws. 'We're fried now, anyone you filmed is toast. It'll be all over the papers tomorrow.' But River steps in. 'Cut out all that superstitious crap,' he shouts, furious. 'We'll head out, knock off a couple of terrorists with pleasure, confirm they're dead, and drink Champagne for dessert. It'll be great.' Bayliss joins in. 'God willing,' he says, sounding old-fashioned, 'everything will be fine.'

Now it's time to get their adrenalin pumping, scare some life into them. And how do you get soldiers worked up? By putting the pressure on, spooking them, that's the tactic. In most cases, a man in a state of panic is a man who reacts faster, so there's nothing for it but to mess with their minds a little. Oshri and I join them outside, where a mug of coffee is waiting for us, according to procedure. When the air is swimming with tension and your stomach's filled with butterflies, you need no less than five-and-a-half spoonfuls of Turkish coffee mixed with a single spoonful of sugar. The coffee we drank that night was the bitterest I've ever tasted in my life. Everyone fell silent as I started to speak. 'Boys, it's going to happen. Tonight we'll come under fire. This time it's for real, not just a hunch of mine, not a prediction based on intelligence we've received, but a definite encounter. And if that isn't enough, Hezbollah isn't our only enemy in this ambush but also the complete, ball-busting cold waiting for us out there. You boys know the job, you're familiar with the procedure, make sure you follow the rules when we march, don't pull any sharp moves, flow with the land-scape. We're going to be walking slowly, in complete silence. Your night-vision equipment stays on at all times. Does everyone remember the shelters we set up in case of emergency? Emilio, have you got the hydrogen balloon catheters in your left pocket? OK. Once we're in place we take turns on guard duty. If someone spots suspicious figures, the kind walking in columns with large packs on their backs, you whisper 'Sighted' and then we wait until they're within shooting range, we count four, three, two, one, fire just as we've done in training. If someone's hit he'll feel a sudden strong gushing through his body. Don't panic. Shout 'I've been hit!', then wait patiently. Tonight you're not only holding your own life in your hands but those of another seventy soldiers at Beaufort and, no less important, the prestige of the entire company. I'm counting on you.'

They paint each other's faces, squeezing two thick lines of black and green from tubes of camouflage paint. Your skin itches like mad and you break out afterwards. You start at the neck, and then spread it around in circles. They try to make sure there's not a single spot of shiny white skin that will expose them to a Shi'ite sniper. Emilio! You're shining! What's this pathetic cover-up of yours? Are we going on an ambush in Sweden? Squeeze that tube, get some paint on you! Just before we cock our weapons and slip out the gate I tell them they've got six minutes, time for a last cigarette – that's part of the procedure. They light whatever there is as long as it's not 'Light'. (No one would dare bring 'light' cigar-ettes to Beaufort.) The last fag ceremony is a hangover from the glory days, back when the IDF had the upper hand, when the festive tradition before every ambush was a group shower with wild music, lots of slapping under the water, shouting in unison 'Piss towards the drains!' followed by that last cigarette. In those days, Beaufort soldiers left for an ambush with big hair and a well-combed forelock, a look that would go down well in a Tel Aviv nightclub. It's only in the last few years that everyone here has started to look dusty and grey.

Now it's time for a few laughs, pre-ambush laughs. I am friendlier towards the boys than usual, trying ease the tension a little, let them joke about me, call me 'midget'. 'Do you still wear boys' sizes?' they tease. 'You look like a child inside that storm suit.'

'Yeah, I'm a midget with spiky hair,' I answer. 'That's why they say I look like a fashion model.' They relax a bit, start punching each other. Then the moment arrives. 'OK, girls, we've got to move out,' Oshri announces. They raise their guns. 'Three, two, one, cock your weapons!' They ready their guns in one single, co-ordinated action so that anyone listening in from outside the outpost can't count how many of us there are. 'Iron numbers, count off,' he says in a whisper. One, two, three, up to fifteen. I'm number fifteen. We're off.

It's freezing and raining, but I am so hot. My foot sinks into stinking mud – disgusting black mud, Lebanese mud – and I struggle to lift it out, again and again. I'm sticky all over. And my equipment is dragging me down. The point we're heading for is only about 650 feet outside the gate but it's hidden from the outpost by a bend in the road and you can't see it from the guard posts up above. Our mission: a patrol, an overnight ambush. The goals: to repel terrorist attacks, prevent Hezbollah from approaching the outpost, foil attempts at placing explosives in our sector, lie in wait for the enemy at a place he's not expecting us. The short march takes forty minutes when you're trying to make your way along an overgrown path that may be littered with explosives. Your movements are delicate and gentle, the kind that are indiscernible from a distance. If someone slips and falls he'll not only split his head open or break his arm; he'll expose us all. I march at the front with

Zitlawi at my side carrying an IMI Negev light machine-gun, the rest of the boys following. We're a long, silent column, twenty yards separating one man from the next, and we stop each time we see something suspicious, then we kneel (in order to lower our shadows) and look around before continuing. Everything is hushed. Peaceful and tense. We're moving along smoothly, at a good pace. I approach the target spot, signal to everyone to stop, and check for the enemy with my night-vision equipment. I move forward with only Zitlawi and his Negev and make a thorough sweep before everyone else joins us. We've set up ambushes here in the past so there's a chance the spot's been discovered and booby-trapped. Maybe somebody's lying there in the bushes, about to pop up and pump a round of ammunition into us. If we draw fire at least the whole squad won't be mowed down. The others take cover at a distance. At each ambush you're careful not to trample the undergrowth so next time you can check if it's been disturbed, if an unwanted guest has paid a visit. I check to see if the access paths to the spot have been exposed, if someone has cut back branches or made a way through from another direction. I check the earth – maybe it's been dug up – taking mental pictures of every stone. I move ahead on my own. Is there anything suspicious? This goes on for fifteen minutes, some of the scariest goddamned moments of my life, and I think to myself, Shit, just don't let anything explode now, because I feel completely alone, I miss the sound of my soldiers' breathing. Those fourteen boys won't let you die, I whisper to myself, there's no chance they're going to let you die, and if you don't believe that then what have you got in life? If I get killed it'll be alone, at a moment like this, so better the bomb should blow up in another ten minutes when River's with me. He'll revive me.

When I'm sure that everything's OK I signal behind me with my hands like a bird. That's how they know the coast is clear, they can approach. And they do, with blind faith. They live under the illusion that I would never lead them into a place where they'd get blown up. I'm surprised by the way they follow me without asking any questions. They're such children, true innocents, they don't understand that I'm their age, just a year older, that's all. I get told off by my mother, ask my father to borrow the car, I'm just a little more experienced than these boys but not much. Now, they form a banana-shaped line and begin to observe Wadi Zirin and the road that leads to Beaufort. Congratulations, we're in, we've made it. Now all we have to do is wait for the enemy to arrive.

'The Silence' is what we call the first ten minutes of an ambush, during which no one dares cough, breathe, scratch or even think. Even the equipment stays on the soldiers during The Silence. Dropped your weapon? Leave it there, don't pick it up, whatever you do, don't make any more noise. If a terrorist is hiding out in your spot, let him be the first to make a noise; let him make an incautious movement that will expose him. These are the most critical moments of them all. Sometimes, because of a gut feeling, The Silence stretches to twenty minutes; this time I drag it out to thirty. I want to be absolutely certain there's no one here. And then I whisper, 'Basic manoeuvres,' which they pass on from one to the other: 'Basic manoeuvres, basic manoeuvres.' This means they remove their helmets, placing them carefully on their backs. They rearrange their packs, lie mattresses on the ground and, if thirsty, they put the tube that runs from their canteens into their mouths. Spitzer and Koka attach missile launchers to their weapons. Zitlawi adds ammunition to his Negev machine-gun. Bayliss loads a bullet into his M24 sniper rifle and locks the bolt, giving him five bullets in the magazine and one in the chamber. Emilio is responsible for the surveillance equipment we use while on the move, which he now places in his pack, taking out a thermal imaging system, a small screen on a tripod that enables surveillance at a distance of two to three miles. Since he is weaponless he remains near me. For night vision we use the Aquila weapon sight, which magnifies everything to three times larger than actual size, and a device we call the 'one-eyed rabbit'. I am at the centre of the banana, my gun at my shoulder. Oshri has his back to me facing the less exposed side. Zion is in charge of the boys to my left, Eldad of the boys to my right. Boaz is the signaller, Tom the sniper, River the medic, of course, Itamar and Pinchuk the lookouts along with Barnoy, watching behind us and to the sides. Now it's OK to talk, preferable even, so they don't fall asleep on me. When you think someone is drifting off, the procedure is to pinch him, slap him, punch him even. Jab him with an elbow, a blow to the head, whatever it takes to keep the boy awake. As a squad commander I dish out blows liberally, of course, really smack them around. And then I say, innocently, 'Oh, sorry, I thought you were sleeping.' They actually like it. I hear someone whisper 'Vicky' in the background. They're talking about my sister again. 'There's no way you guys would actually dare . . .' I say, to which River responds in a low voice, 'No, no, she's no one you know. He's talking about some whore.' Everyone laughs. They know I can't get up now and take him on. So I go along with it, for their sake, to entertain them. That's how it is: when you're out there the most difficult task of all is keeping occupied. During the first few hours you talk, just chat. Zion tells us about how it's uncomfortable for him to screw Eldad's sister when Eldad's asleep in the next room. He stayed at the family home once and he and Eldad's sister clicked and they've been a couple ever since. And so there's Eldad, inside a bush in the middle of Lebanon, listening to stories about someone fucking his sister in great detail, how his friend hammers her, fucks her in the arse even – and there's nothing he can do about it. What could he do, punch the bloke? He whispers, 'Zion, enough.' Zion says, 'What? Your sister's really great. I want everyone to know. Come on, let me tell Zitlawi.' The boys are listening, chuckling quietly. No one has to act grown up out here, we're all made of the same stuff. When we've finished talking about screwing, the conversation turns to plans for the future. After all, this guerrilla camp will come to an end one day. On the face of it we're really, really close – until we start talking about life outside the army and then it's clear that we are such different people that it's not to be believed. Then, in the middle of the night, things get really surreal. I tell them about this friend of mine from one of the West Bank settlements who used to fantasize about making the Arabs disappear. Neatly, simply. Just get his hands on them and make them go away. This was his dream. He would get carried away describing it in lurid detail, exactly how he'd carry it out, trying to convince the boys in our squad it was a feasible plan, easy even. Stop some Arab in the street, get him into the car, bury him somewhere and leave no trace. Once he told me about a friend from the same settlement who thinks the same way he does, who was prepared to do it with him, to go all the way. I said, 'Jesus, you are one stupid fuck. Pass the gummy bears, will you? All this talk of yours is wasting good eating time.' After that there was quiet and we ate rolls with hummus and pastrami. I wonder if he ever carried out his fantasy.

We are supposed to stay here until thirty minutes before sunrise. We have to complete the trek back to the outpost while the sky is still dark; if we fuck it up and it starts getting light we'll be forced to stay here for an entire day, and that is truly fucked. I call over to Oshri in the coded slang we've established as a way of referring to what's around us. So, for example, the goat path on the horizon that looks like the Hebrew letter *lamed* we call 'Lila', which naturally leads to all kinds of digressions: 'When are we going to open Lila up, man?' 'I recommended to Furman that we bring in reinforcements and push that baby wide open, go all the way, but he says she's not ready yet, too dry.' Those are the kinds of things that fly around in an ambush. And so, while I'm pretending to be engrossed in studying the code map which is dangling by a piece of string from my backpack, they're slagging off Emilio's grandmother, and saying that River is allergic to condoms, that he starts sneezing like crazy every time he . . . and how religious blokes fuck like rabbits and how our own apostate rabbi, Bayliss, has the most gorgeous little sister. These boys are mad about religious girls. Zitlawi wants to know why Spitzer hasn't introduced his Russian girlfriend to them, and how it is that Spitzer got fixed up with a

Russian, of all people, because Russian girls like the sleazy men, the arseholes, and the arseholes like Russian girls and Spitzer's a good little white boy, as good and white as they come. Is it possible that he's embarrassed by her? The squad needs to know.

'Is she a *bliad* Russian, mate?' Zitlawi asks.

Spitzer has no idea what Zitlawi means by a '*bliad* Russian'. 'You know,' Zitlawi persists, 'a *bliad* Russian, the kind with a heavy accent, like those Russian men who get pissed on vodka and then *bliad* becomes every other word that comes out of their mouths. Don't take it hard, mate, those girls have their good points: they moan like hell and they take you ballroom dancing.' The thirsty audience laps up every word of it. 'It's like the blacks in America,' Zitlawi continues, 'just like the ones in the movies who can't stop saying "you know" all the time. Or the arseholes right here in Israel who keep saying "*k'ilu*" even when they don't mean "like". How could you not know any *bliad* Russians? Of course you do. But between you and me,' Zitlawi tells Spitzer, 'why not go for some upper class Russian chick from the north side of Moscow?'

'No,' Spitzer answers, 'she's not a *bliad* Russian.' His puppy eyes register hurt.

'Aw, come off it,' Zitlawi whispers, 'you're just a jerk, getting all emotional. I should take a plastic hammer to your brain. I was just asking, as a friend. Why do you take me seriously?' And he throws a stone at him.

'I answered you,' Spitzer says. 'She's not a *bliad* Russian and she's not keen on sleazy men.' He tells us she wants to meet the squad after all the stories she's heard, she's fascinated by Beaufort, but he's not willing to take the risk. The boys could cost him his relationship. 'She's sensitive,' he explains. 'She came to Israel on her own, think about what kind of courage that takes. She's a volunteer at Kibbutz Kinneret, works in the fields. She talks about studying medicine and I have no doubt she'll do it.' Zitlawi is busy downing a chocolate bar, and still trying to figure out why Russian girls like swarthy men, because it's common knowledge that

Moroccans have little pricks. Iraqis have big ones, he says, but the Moroccans – tiny. But shapely. Tiny but shapely. Now he's on a roll, and even though someone says, 'Damn, the remote's not working,' as if they're trying to turn the TV off, which is like saying, 'Time for a commercial break,' which is like saying, 'Enough,' or 'Shut your mouth,' or 'Change the subject.' But he is oblivious to them.

I stifle a smile, while Oshri, as usual, is in shock. He's always in shock when we're out in the field, and the conversation takes a turn for the surreal. He brings his face close, intending, like usual, to whisper in my ear, but this time I beat him to it. 'Aren't you going to miss all this shit?' I ask him quietly, but Zitlawi overhears me, and demands to know to where the honourable sergeant will be making his escape. 'Ladies,' Oshri announces, 'in the near future you will find me sprawled drunk and stoned on some nudist beach in South America.' Suddenly there is a dull sound from far off, a kind of a pop, really strong. It's a missile being fired. 'Helmets on!' I shout, making it clear that the fun is over. They're startled and drop their food on the ground. A few seconds later there are two gigantic explosions about a hundred yards away from us, each a huge flash and then a mushroom cloud. Now it's OK to shout because we're exposed. We're under fire. I call into the radio: 'Cheetah, this is One. Squad under attack.' I shout, 'Provide cover!' hoping that the outpost will dispatch tanks and artillery quickly to the source of the fire, that they'll launch combat helicopters and anything else they've got. Now there are more and more explosions, it doesn't let up. Pits open up around us, craters, there are fires burning in every direction, I see red – one minute light, one minute dark. They seem to be firing from the village of Mazraat Al-Hamra, from below the abandoned farm there, about four or five miles away. These are rockets, not mortar shells. They are falling very close to each other so you can't escape them. Not far from where we are, near the bend in the access road up to Beaufort, there are some huge slabs of concrete we call *dabeshim*, which we can shelter behind. I shout, 'Retreat!' to get us out of there. 'My crew in twos!' I holler, and they are supposed to get to safety in small groups not too close to each other. I run first, then they follow, three pairs in all. Then Oshri shouts, 'Forget crews, everyone run *now!*' and the rest of them charge, all in a group. Oshri remains there for another twenty seconds or so, checking that no sensitive equipment has been left behind. I reach the *dabeshim*. Two huge explosions shake the earth, cracking it open. I've never heard anything so loud, or seen so blinding a light. A ton of mud flies at me, covers me. Twenty yards away a fire is raging. During a split second of silence between explosions I hear the siren up at the outpost, which means they're getting into their flak jackets and helmets and cocking their weapons and loading stretchers and pretty soon a team will be on their way to pull us out of this. After all, they can see what's happening on the surveillance equipment. But eight of my squad haven't reached me yet, goddamn it, I can't even see them. Oshri and the boys, where are they? Another explosion. It's right on top of them, for sure, and here I am, helpless, telling myself they may all be dead. I'm already picturing it, that's it, it's all over, I'm going to be picking up eight dead bodies. What did we do in our training exercises? Should we wait for the bombing to stop? Should I run over there now, dodging the bombs and hoping my luck holds out? I start racing through their names like I'm taking stock – who's over there, who isn't, maybe they're wounded, writhing in pain. And Oshri! Shit. Oshri. I love that boy so much, I've got to run back there right now, fuck the training exercises. The air is thick with smoke. I don't know how long – maybe seconds, maybe minutes, maybe longer – I'm alone, a little boy's thoughts filling my mind, just waiting for something to happen, something to keep me busy. The waiting is killing me. And then I hear this long shriek and I can see them running for their lives, and they are alive, emerging from the wall of smoke. 'Lie down behind the concrete!' I shout. 'Hang on tight to each other!' The boys lie down close together, burrowing down, their hands cupped over their ears. Oshri and I lie down too, on top of them, crosswise, on their heads. They're shaking, God, how they're shaking. 'Everyone here?' I ask. They're not even capable of talking, they're paralysed. 'Snap out of it!' I yell. But they're silent. Then suddenly everything is quiet, except for the sound of the bonfires all around us, and our own heavy breathing. The silence grows and grows, even the radio isn't chirping, and all around the night returns and we can feel the icy air cooling the sweat on our faces. We are tense. No one talks. Silence. Then suddenly the silence ends, all at once. Another huge barrage of Katyusha rockets, and I mean huge. They're falling ten yards away from us. I hear them whistling and say to myself, that's it, what are the chances of them not falling on us this time, finishing us off? BOOM! BOOM! BOOM! They're getting closer, they're falling on the bend in the road. I can't breathe, can't do anything but lie there and hope to God we don't get hit. Between explosions I hear the boys screaming from behind the *dabeshim*, their voices ragged. 'Let's get out of here now!' I see River and Oshri hanging on to each other, hiding inside each other, River trying to dig himself right into the ground. Even if he manages to cover himself in dirt it won't help if a shell falls on him. I call request after request into the radio for them to provide cover, but nothing happens. There's no one on the other end. The explosions are now suddenly behind us as well, at our backs. I take a gamble and shout to everyone to move to the other side of the *dabeshim*. The rockets keep on falling, four at each launch. Amos is suddenly talking to me on the secure radio. 'Everything OK, One?' he asks. Before I can answer there are four more explosions. The *dabeshim* have taken a direct hit and half the wall breaks off and falls right above us, smashing my secure radio, breaking the antenna. Our connection is cut off. We've still got the open radio line but if we use it Hezbollah will be listening in. If we say 'Squad under fire' they'll understand they are firing exactly in the right spot and they won't stop until we're dust.

Oshri says, 'Let's evacuate to the outpost.' I say, 'No.' He argues with me, gets hysterical. 'You're wrong!' He's never questioned my authority before. 'We've got to get out of here,' he screams. 'We're dead if we don't get out now!' I'm considering it, and if so, where to. Back to the outpost, or is it better to run down to the home of the collaborator a quarter of a mile below us? The path leading there seems less exposed, fewer rockets have fallen there. In the end, I give in. 'Get on the open radio and have them send a Nakpadon.' A Nakpadon is a huge Israeli-made tank that's perfect for rescue missions because it has no turret; every part of it closes inward, nothing's exposed to attack. 'Cheetah, this is Deputy One,' Oshri shouts into the radio. 'Requesting a Nakpadon for evacuation.'

'Deputy One, this is Cheetah,' Furman answers. 'Good to hear you! Give us a report.'

'Requesting a Nakpadon for evacuation,' Oshri answers, insistent.

'Negative. That's negative.'

Oshri and I look at one another. Negative? What is that motherfucker talking about? Negative? Do they have any idea what our situation is? 'Deputy to Cheetah, Number One is next to me, asks me to relay request for immediate evacuation.'

'There's no way to send anything out to you right now. Hold tight.'

'Too dangerous, Cheetah,' Oshri pleads.

'Get off the radio, Deputy. You'll have to manage without it for a while.'

Oshri takes it in, gives up. Through the smoke that separates us I try – unsuccessfully – to see if he's in shock or wounded, what exactly is going on with him. Maybe he's simply afraid. The rockets are still falling, minutes are passing – who knows how many? – and Furman asks again for a report. 'Everything in order, Deputy One?' Oshri doesn't answer. 'Is everything in order, Deputy One?'

'Answer them calmly,' I tell him. 'Say everything's in order.'

'I can't,' he says.

'Is everything in order, Deputy One?' they ask again from the war room.

I shout, 'Oshri, tell them that everything's OK, now, and that we're back from the line of fire. Hezbollah's listening in on this, damn it, tell them we're no longer under fire!'

His hands shaking, he answers. 'Roger, affirmative, everything in order. We're out of the line of fire.'

After thirty seconds or so we can feel the missiles gradually moving away from us towards the outpost. Maybe the terrorists have come to the conclusion that they're firing in the wrong place. My soldiers' weapons are still shaking, they're banging against the rocks. 'What, you're not going to get scared on me, are you?' I ask Zitlawi, who's underneath me. 'Don't get emotional now.' I only want them to move, I think, to laugh. I've got to find a way to keep them busy in the meantime. The situation is getting worse.

Just then, when it seems it's all over, the radio crackles with a cry from the war room: 'Enemy approaching White!' Which means a Hezbollah terrorist cell is approaching on foot, trying to infiltrate the guard post on the northern side of Beaufort. Suddenly it becomes clear that the rocket fire was intended to draw our attention away while a cell crept in. The soldiers at the outpost open fire with shells and anti-tank missiles and machine-guns. It's called Firebox, when all the guard posts fire in every direction without discretion, surrounding the mountain with a deadly ring. The only place they're not firing is at us, behind the *dabeshim*. Again, long, terrifying minutes pass. I'm lying under concrete with fourteen people in the middle of nowhere and no one is communicating with me and I have no idea what's happening. There's an inferno all around us, tanks are firing non-stop, rocket tails and flares are slicing through the skies over our heads, it's clear something dangerous is going down. Oshri is holding River's head, forcing him to lift his gaze and watch the glowing rockets, it's Independence

Day up in the sky. But he insists on sticking to the earth. Emilio asks if the outpost is in danger, Zitlawi wonders if they've forgotten about us, and we simply wait.

Long months will pass before River writes the following lines about that night (I read them years later, which is to say only recently): 'Lying there, I was most of all curious. Curious to know whether I would get out alive or not, if I'd survive, if the next bomb would blow off my leg or my whole body, if shrapnel would pierce my hand or crush me completely. Curious to know if it would hurt. The tension kills you in these situations, gets into your blood. It's the uncertainty. As far as I'm concerned, let it happen now, whatever it is, just so I know what it's going to be. That's what I was thinking. At those moments you don't think about home, or your parents, you only think about whether you're going to live or not and you pray that something you've been trained to handle will happen, that a terrorist will come along, that fighting will begin, because you have no tools to cope with the present situation. You pray to God, to Allah, even to Mohammed or Jesus, or all of them together, because there's no way of describing how scary it is when everything closes in around you, making your heart pound at a rate of four hundred beats to the minute and there's nowhere to run. That night, for the first time, I felt death. I heard the bombs whistling close by, and the rockets, and I watched them up there, saw them explode near me and I told myself as far as I'm concerned, it's all over for me. Fear, they try to reassure you, is just part of the preparation; when you set out on your mission it fades. When they open fire on you it disappears completely. Well, it turns out that isn't quite true. Try to imagine your very first bungee jump, multiply that by a hundred or a thousand, then cut the rope and you'll begin to know the feeling.

'As for me, ever since that ambush I don't feel good at night. Even today in fact, I don't like nighttime. Because after that experience my heart skipped a beat when night fell at the outpost.

My eyes would hunt for flashes and launches. I'd close them and see explosions. Even today sometimes, especially when I'm outside the city, I suddenly get hit by the smell of the night at the bend in the road below Beaufort and the pounding of my heart reminds me what I felt like back then. I become tense and less sure of myself. But those were also the moments of our first memories together, the black humour, the pride. And sometimes, when it's really quiet and someone asks, "You boys remember the rockets?" we all answer, "Shit yes, do we ever," because on that night, for the first time, I understood where I was. We would never again ask where that war was that everyone was talking about.'

That's what River wrote.

It was the first time we lay together under fire. Three terrorists were killed that night outside the outpost, and it was only after they were hit that things started to quiet down a little. Furman came on the radio. 'Start to evacuate,' he ordered. 'Back to the outpost in pairs,' I called out, and we all began to run up the steep slope pulling one another along. We were our own rescue team. In the video footage of our arrival, which is in the Lebanon War Archives in the army base at Elyakim, you see us, pale, each one of us whiter than the next, coming in with glazed looks on our faces and collapsing. We didn't even disarm our weapons. As we entered, everyone stood around clapping wildly. They told us they were certain for a while that we were all dead. Finished. From the surveillance cameras in the war room they'd seen the heavy clouds of smoke over our heads. In the footage, you can hear Furman saying, 'Prepare eight stretchers, we've got eight "poppies".' Eight bodies. They say there was crying in the halls.

In the middle of all the madness and joy I tried to count my soldiers, face by face, to make sure everyone had made it back. But it was impossible. They were mixed in with groups of soldiers, all hugging. That's the way it is: after the pressure the tears flow even though you're not exactly crying, and you kiss everything that moves. I held Oshri in my arms and wouldn't let go. I kept thinking how good it was to have him with me. Then Furman showed up. 'That's the last time in your life,' he whispered, 'that you give your soldiers an order to improve their positions *en masse*. You do it in pairs or by crew. Were you sleeping when they taught you that at the officers' academy? You were crowded together, Erez, one rocket would've taken out the whole bunch of you.' What? A few seconds passed before I was able to respond. 'What are you talking about?' I asked. 'What crews? The bombs were dropping right on our position. If the eight men who got out of there last hadn't run out together, they'd be dead right now.' Furman ignored my answer, turned his back on me and started to walk away. 'Why didn't you evacuate us?' I shouted after him. But he kept walking, getting further away. 'You were sure I had eight poppies, that's why you didn't come to get us!' I hollered. That made him stop. He asked me to see him in his office.

'Screw the office, you tell me why you didn't come to rescue us. What the hell were you people thinking?'

'It wasn't the right thing to do tactically. It would have caused more casualties.'

I felt a volcano rising inside me, boiling and bubbling, which in another second was going to erupt. I could almost have pointed my gun at him, right there in front of all the men at the outpost, who were watching us, stunned. I tried biting my lips but it didn't work. 'Do you get it?' I asked him. 'Do you get what you did? You sent us out there without knowing if you'd be able to rescue us, if you had the balls to do it! Isn't the safety of the men our highest principle, our supreme goal? Bringing your soldiers back, wounded, at any price? Do you have any idea what kind of hits we were taking out there?' He didn't say a word. His face was red but he stood there like he didn't care, which made me even angrier. 'And why did you send us out in ninety-eight per cent moonlight?' I continued. 'Hezbollah could've seen us with a plain old pair of binoculars.'

'Erez, what's important now is that your soldiers are scared shitless. You're taking them out there again tonight to rip that fear out of them. Get yourselves organized.'

'Definitely not. No. Not a chance we're going out there now.'

'Yes, you are. And I don't want any arguments about it.'

I pushed him backwards, against a wall. Everyone held their breath. I shouted that he'd better forget the idea, that I wasn't taking them back out there. If he wanted to he could send another squad. 'Is that the way you're going to be?' he said in a cold and mocking tone. 'You want to go back to being a private? What are you, a new recruit who thinks he can get whatever he wants? No problem, go ahead and refuse to follow an order. Don't go out. I'll go out in your place. With your squad.'

'How can you talk to me like that, Furman? Moments ago I was nearly killed. You people forget where you are.'

'So what do you want?'

'For my soldiers not to go out tonight.'

We didn't go out that night. Furman consulted with the powers that be back in Israel and decided to leave us alone, which I knew would cost me buckets of sweat in the near future. I went to the public phone and dialled. Lila didn't answer. 'Hi, where are you? You're probably sleeping, so I won't disturb you. I just wanted to tell you that I'm fine, because you might hear something on the radio. Things got a little wild up here. But don't worry. I'll try to catch you again soon.'

Sometime before daybreak the squad met in the dining room and sat around a table filled with treats, the fantastic meal that awaits fighters after every return from an ambush or operation. Little cartons of banana milkshake, biscuits and pastries, schnitzel and French fries, exactly in that order. It's called an 'operational spread'. I wasn't there. I sat thinking alone in the briefing room, trying to recall it all, and asking myself whether I'd passed the test, if I'd been brave enough, if I'd been a disappointment. Zitlawi came to find me. 'You coming for coffee in the security room?' he asked. My soldiers had never asked me to join them for coffee before.

Now they were sitting next to me, talking with me; suddenly there was a kind of a click between us, something that said, 'We've accepted you, brother, you're one of us. OK, it'll take a little while to get used to this, but you're one of us.' A lot of things changed after the night of that ambush. Even me. Until that night I couldn't give a fuck if, let's say, Zion's girl was cheating on him. Now it mattered a lot, because I cared about him. I depended on him and he depended on me. I knew I'd been shitty with them, and they hated me for it. Now everything had shifted, priorities and all that. 'No, thanks, some other time,' I told Zitlawi that night. 'There's something I have to do.' I was a little embarrassed, ashamed, but the only thing that would calm me down was some solo time with Oshri. We lay on our beds not saying anything. I thought, What exactly am I supposed to be feeling right now? Relief? Maybe fear? Maybe it should be hitting me how close we'd come? Or that I should love them more than I already do? Could it be that apart from anger, plain old anger, I'm not feeling anything? Maybe because I was so confused. 'They were shaking,' I told Oshri. 'Shaking and quivering. I don't want to think what would have been if we'd had to go on the offensive out there, engage in hand-to-hand combat.'

'What, and you and I weren't shaking?' Oshri asked.

I didn't answer. He hesitated for a moment, then said he was certain the squad would have been fine in combat, it was the feeling of helplessness and the indecision and the lack of opportunity to react that had affected their courage. Lying there in the foetal position in the dirt, no enemy in sight, no way of putting a face to him – that was the problem. We'd been taught to fight, hadn't we? If there'd been anyone to attack they would have charged with us, every last man. 'How can you be so sure?' I asked. 'I don't know,' he responded. 'I can sense it.'

So much research has been done, by the IDF and other armies, in an attempt at unravelling that mystery: What is it that makes a man rise up and charge? What causes him to stand exposed and face the fire rather than remain behind a rock, protected and comfortable? It's so involuntary, so illogical, so unnatural. Our survival instinct is supposed to be stronger than anything, right? And still we rise up, when the time comes, we switch on the autopilot without thinking about it, we take the chance and we charge, risking everything. Studies show that friendship is the driving force, along with social pressure. Yes, the fear of being humiliated before your friends is bigger than the fear of death. 'These people and this country,' I would chant whenever I was asked why. I've always known I would be the first to charge. But maybe I just love action.

We stopped talking, fell silent. 'I'm sorry,' Oshri said suddenly. I should have answered, What, are you mad? and then leaned over his bed, held his hand, stroked his face and said, My friend, you are a loser. What's there to be sorry about? You were a god out there, brother, you saved their lives. What? The argument? Forget about it, it's all bullshit, you *need* to argue with me in those situations. The truth is, you were right. But I said nothing. I thought I saw him gazing at his countdown chart, but I said nothing. That seemed best.

8

Days passed. Storms of mortar shells fell on Beaufort at night. We called it 'purple rain'. It was a kind of concert that started with the loudspeakers suddenly announcing, 'Launch! Launch!' and then there'd be a second or two of silent tension, sometimes three, when we'd all freeze in place and wait. And then a terrifying, shattering explosion. Two, sometimes. The earth would shake, things moved around in the room. The loudspeaker announced, 'Hit! Hit!' and then there'd be another 'Launch! Launch!' and another salvo. More explosions. Launches and explosions. Sometimes it lasted for long minutes, dozens of thundering booms one after another, and then the noise of hits. The more time passed, the more the warnings would begin to sound drowsy, jaded and serene, like the beat of a soundtrack. The floor would vibrate, the walls would groan, but inside the outpost we remained calm, particularly when the attacks began. These were little breaks from everyday life, when our daily routine – maintenance jobs, running around, arguments – would stop, and we would grab an easy chair or, whenever possible, throw ourselves on our beds, shut our eyes, and listen to the sound, thriving on it, enjoying it. BOOM! BOOM! BOOM! Shattered slabs of concrete rained down in every direction. Antennae were smashed, the reservoirs took direct hits and sprayed water everywhere, turning the parking area into a sea of mud. Those who did continue doing chores slackened their pace, keeping time with the rhythm of the explosions and even adding their own musical accompaniment. The symphony of our routine, which was composed there, plays in my head to this very day. Spitzer pounding bread rolls with a meat hammer before an ambush, rolling them out to the thickness of a broom handle, squishing them one after the other, his own assembly line. Chili ladling dollops of soft cheese on to creamed potatoes, keeping time, too, as he added fried onions to each one. BOOM! BOOM! Hit! hit! Bayliss scrubbing his face in a circular motion with a rag and laundry detergent, no running water to be had, trying to remove the last of the camouflage paint. Launch! Launch! to the strains of the music from *The Lion King*, which we loved to watch, as it jerked and skipped on the fuzzy screen of a small TV. And those corny Israeli films we could watch over and over again. And horror movies and trips to outer space and Bruce Willis storming terrorists who'd taken over a building; we lay there reciting every line again and again. BOOM! BOOM! And the chirping of the radios and the bobbin whirring on the sewing machine, and the sipping of tea, and the stirring of coffee and a quick round of dramatic pounding on the *darbuka* drums. BOOM! While Dave from the war room, who wants us to believe he's a celebrity hair stylist, shaves everyone's heads with the electric razor. And the boys making phone calls home. And Chili calling us to dinner: 'Come and get it, soldiers! Come and get it, Vets!' – as he bangs a metal spoon on a large pot. And the footsteps in the halls, and the flag fluttering high above the fortress. It's keeping time too, with the wind. Launch, launch, hit, hit. And the morning prayer service of a quorum of men at sunrise. BOOM! Everything keeps time. It was during the times of silence, when we weren't under a rain of rockets, that I would tense up.

If I described all this to Lila, what would she say? I didn't try to tell her what it was like. If I had, she would think I was exaggerating, that's for sure. And even if she didn't think I was exaggerating, there's no chance she would understand. My fault, not hers. How can words make it real? Anyway, is it really important to me for her to know, for her to be a little afraid? Would fear like this – the fear of losing me – make her love stronger? Or weaker? Would I still feel the animal passion of her kiss when I return to Israel, when she's waiting for me by the door and pounces, sniffing my body all over and never letting up, as if she wants to suck every drop from me, as if it might be her last chance? Maybe if she understood, she'd put her guard up, distance herself, a stubborn inner voice would shriek at her from within: 'You jerk, don't stick with him, don't devote yourself to him, you'll only get hurt.' And it really would hurt her. Maybe she'd start to get on my nerves, if she was afraid, maybe she'd give me an ultimatum about getting out, leaving the army. When I'm calm, I think it's better for me to keep my mouth shut.

Each time an attack began I'd imagine her: just back from a trek, say, where she rode a gushing waterfall into a natural pool, giggling, screaming, singing, telling stories about each and every plant, everybody touching her, hugging her. Her shirt is wet, stretched out, torn, her bra shows through. Maybe she was wearing a bikini, a blue and red one, and now, in her room, she's taken it off and she's naked with her friends, and now she is falling asleep for long seconds under the shower. I can hear that shallow breathing of hers, which I love. A steaming flow of water caresses her, her eyes are clouded, there's steam everywhere. At the field school where she's doing her military service, each new group of soldiers stays for a week. High school students are sent out there, in large numbers, and her job is to take them out on treks. They get really turned on by the sense of freedom, I know that feeling. Running around in their underwear all night between rooms, a beer in their hands, cigarettes behind their ears. They lie on the grass getting high and then look around for somewhere hot and wet to stick their hormones. They're happy. And how does she handle it? Does she lose control sometimes? Let's say she's wet right now, maybe even a bit drunk. What would I be willing for her to do? Maybe, for the sake of argument, it wouldn't bother me if she let a girl-friend undress her, stroke her a little, maybe even kiss her. If she closed her eyes and thought about me while it was happening, while one of those nymphomaniac lesbians who serve in the field schools turned her on, rubbed her nipples and her soft belly, maybe I would go along with it. Not one of those lesbos would miss an opportunity to tempt her into mutual masturbation, at the very least. Would that bother me? In fact it would, absolutely. Very much. I'm getting angry just thinking about it. I've got to work out with her what she does and what she almost does and what she wants to do and how she resists temptation. But there's no chance we'd talk openly about something like that, even after all the time we've been together. It's really cheap and whorish, to hold a conversation like that with your girlfriend, and while I'm cheap and whorish, she's not. She's true quality, a lot smarter than me. We're like heaven and earth. It doesn't matter how many times she tells me she loves me, that it's the real thing, that I can let my guard down. She'll say it, and I'll even believe her, and I'll still keep trying to impress her, I'll think eight times about every stupid word before I let it out of my mouth. I am utterly childish compared with her. She's already grown up, a real woman. 'Why do you love me, baby?' I'm dying to ask her when we're pressed up against one another. 'After all, I'm a complete arsehole, a fucked-up little jerk. You could find so many men better than me.' But I don't ask her, I'm afraid of putting ideas in her head. She's mature, but she's pure and innocent too, looks at life with a naïvety that makes me furious. She believes in everyone's goodwill, never listens to me when I warn her not to trust people. God, how I love her. And the rockets keep falling. And Bitter, my dog, is probably relaxing right now on the windowsill of the room he and I share, looking out into the darkened park where a few losers are finishing off their night with a last cigarette before heading to their beds. His white belly is on the sill and his black legs are dangling out the window, and I know he's missing me. He's waiting for me to join him, behind the curtain, where I'll light a cigarette. The wind strokes my chest and Bitter licks my face for a few seconds. He'll look to the left and I will, too. He'll look to the right, and I'll do the same. He'll wag his tail. When his tail stands up straight, what does it mean? Is he turned on? In the end he'll get bored first and make for the bed. He'll signal me to join him. When he was a puppy I liked to put him on my stomach, all curled up, right on the muscles around my navel. He'd climb up towards my heart, sit right on my chest and fall asleep there. I would push him back down to my stomach and he'd inch up again and fall asleep. He'd do it again and again, he only wanted my heart, to fall asleep to my heartbeat like a baby with its mother. His love for me was unconditional.

And still the mortar shells are falling, they're bombarding us for whole nights on end and my eyes are red, burning with fatigue. The boys are in the next room, Spitzer is sprawled on his belly playing a small electric organ. He sings, 'Over by Marjayoun I became a buffoon,' and then together they mangle a few popular songs. When they get to 'Chava Alberstein' I've had enough. It's sacrilegious to make fun of Memorial Day songs. I get up from my bed and kick their door. 'What's an organ doing at Beaufort? Next thing you'll be bringing me the Afula Junior Singers,' I shout at them. Another hit, another launch. I go back to my bed. They try to sleep, I can hear them falling silent. Only Zitlawi is his usual energetic self, he's trying to find someone to pester. He jumps into Spitzer's bed, smashes up against him. 'It's because I love you,' he says by way of apology. 'Forget trying to sleep now. I'm going to help you make a film, *The Guide for Spitzer's Russian Girlfriend*. Great idea, no? I mean, she hasn't got a clue, right? About war, I mean. And you can't tell her in words, that's for sure. So why don't we prepare something fucking great and real for her so she doesn't miss all the action?' Spitzer loves the idea. That human aquarium doesn't know how to conceal his smile when he gets excited about something, and really, it is a good idea, even I have to admit it. What's wrong with a little romance? They wait for a quiet moment, for the explosions to let up, and when the sun is high in the sky and the only bombs on the soundtrack are the dull echoes of explosions coming from every direction – a typical Lebanese afternoon – they go on duty together to the White guard post with Emilio's Argentine video camera. Against Emilio's will, because he is certain it will end badly. But what can he do? Moan a little, like usual. Spitzer stands inside the walled trench, the view of Lebanon behind him, tense and uncomfortable, ready to inaugurate the guide. Zitlawi takes a few steps back to get a good angle, presses the red button then zooms in for a close-up in order to capture the little of Spitzer that peeps out from between his flak jacket and his helmet, barely a pair of eyes and a mouth.

'From here we are able to keep watch over Nabatiye, which is actually a city. Over there is Tibnit, then Arb Salim and Jabel Zafi,' Spitzer announces to the camera stiffly, barely even pointing out the places he is talking about. 'Whoa, whoa,' Zitlawi says, stopping him. 'Do you really think that's what you want to send her? What are you, totally fucked? It's terrible, brother. This isn't the fucking news. Put a little emotion into it.' He places the camera on top one of the sandbags lining the trench, sets it on automatic and joins Spitzer inside the frame, slinging his arm over his shoulders. 'Shit, what's her name?' he asks in a whisper. 'I've forgotten. Is it Nicole?'

'Nicole, you idiot? It's Lana.'

'OK, Lana, baby,' Zitlawi says, 'our little Spitzer is making a video for you so you won't miss anything that's going on. As you can see, we're stuck here in the shit while you're probably screwing some bloke at a beach on the Sea of Galilee, sucking lemonade up a straw, maybe cheating on Spitzer with a surfer boy with gel in his hair, a cool guy who thinks he's something special, a suntanned stud in a pair of flip-flops, the arsehole. But we love you, you sweet thing, we're crazy about you, so here it is, *A Guide for Lana*, take one. Fun stuff, specials, goodies, the bodies of dead terrorists. We're going to make a world war for you! Just get the Vaseline ready, this is going to hurt.'

Launch, launch. Purple rain.

9

When exactly did it happen? I swore I'd never forget the date, but suddenly now I can't remember. A total disgrace. Seems to me it was the eve of Holocaust Remembrance Day that Ziv was killed. Five days before his discharge. He'd already bought a ticket to South America, he had a girlfriend, owned a car – a VW Beetle he'd purchased two months earlier; the good life. He'd promised everyone that this would be his last trip into Lebanon. He called me 'Chong.' which is army slang for someone really green, a new recruit. I would say to him, 'Shut your mouth.'

On the night he arrived at Beaufort, Ziv sat across from me at the Sabbath evening meal. He held out his hand and said, 'Nice to meet you, I'm Ziv Farran.' I didn't even reply. I was waiting for Dave, the guy from the war room, to finish collecting the prayer books before I started eating. There was a holy Ark of the Covenant, housing the Torah scrolls, in the corner of the dining room. It was army green and made of metal so thin that it dented if you kicked it. Layers of paint applied over the years had thickened the Ark, and rust covered its small metal legs. It was unsteady, it wobbled, and was propped up by pieces of cardboard that would dissolve after ten or twelve floor moppings. Next to it stood another, shorter, supply cabinet in which were stored dozens of prayer books, all banged up and stained. On Friday afternoons Dave would pull them out and place them on the wooden table covered in light blue formica which, to us, looked new and was reserved for special occasions, the cleanest there was at the outpost. You weren't allowed to eat on it, so of course sitting on it or standing on it or jumping on it or playing ping pong on it or flipping it on its back and using it to skate across the wet floor were all totally out of the question. Dave made sure of that. He was still religious and respectful, even though his ultra-Orthodox family and community had disowned him for joining the army, it was regarded as a stain on them. Beaufort had become his home. When the Sabbath started, the dining room was transformed into a synagogue. Around thirty soldiers would sing and mumble the prayers, but quickly, making it up as they went along, because the rest of us – the wild beasts – were queued up outside for the royal feast, the one we spent the whole week waiting for, salivating. We never managed to hold out till the end of the service. We'd lose patience way before it ended and we'd burst into the room shouting, 'People are hungry here, that's enough wailing!' And there, on the tables, we'd find food that the army pencil pushers could only dream about: steaks, hamburgers, fish, *bourekas*, five-star cakes. A real fucking restaurant.

But by that *Shabbat* when Ziv arrived the storerooms were empty. Chili's fridges, too. We had a light meal that night, on little plates. Creamed potatoes and homemade *matbucha*, and a tomato salad seasoned with onions and egg. And our famous test – soft white cheese with fried onions and a sauce that's spicy as fire – the

97

company speciality, the ultimate measure of stamina; he who didn't survive this dish (and sometimes even officers failed) wasn't ready to take part in an ambush against Hezbollah. But there was no meat that night. When all of us burst into the room to put an end to the prayers, I dragged Oshri quickly over to our usual seats, trying to make sure none of the white-bread guests that had landed at the outpost that evening would breach custom and mess up our seating arrangements. It didn't help. Before we'd had a chance to pour hot tea into our blue plastic cups and signal to the guys from the Ordnance Corps or the Signal Corps or Army Administration or the kennels to come and sit with us to fill up our table, Ziv appeared and sat right across from me. That pretty boy looked as if he'd been parachuted in from some commercial for low calorie sour cream. He was one of these TV soldiers with a pair of the most Italian sunglasses you've ever seen in your life and a perfect, even tan, the kind you can only get from a sun bed. Real fighters don't glow like that, and what was that happy expression doing smeared across his face? What the fuck! If that little white boy knew anything about bomb disposal, I'd cut off my dick, I was thinking. 'Am I imagining it or is that gel in Mr Sunshine's hair, right here in the middle of the Beaufort?' I asked Oshir, out loud. 'That's some styling job,' Oshri answered. Ziv was smiling, but then he hadn't stopped smiling from the minute he'd arrived on the hill. He asked if I'd heard the rumour that he and I would be going out on an operation together. The word 'Negative' was on the tip of my tongue but just then Amos, the battalion commander, came over to update us and it turned out Ziv was right. We'd be going out together, me and Ziv, on command. I was to stick close by him – that's what had been decided – introduce him to the sector, entertain him, then lead him and my squad inside, to the target. He'd be the commander for bomb disposal while I'd be the commander of the squad who were to provide support. Was that clear? I nodded, not giving a damn.

It had all started just over a week earlier, when a large supply convoy was supposed to make the climb to Beaufort. On a normal day we made do with surveillance and patrolling, circling the outpost on foot in the morning fog looking for any unusual markings, but on that morning, with a convoy due, we wanted to be certain that the roads leading to us were safe and clear. I took the squad out to open the road, as it's called, which for generations of Beaufort soldiers has been the most despised job there is. It's a slow and exhausting march along the four mile hilly path that leads from the outpost, crosses the bend in the road up to the outpost, enters the village of Arnoun, winds through country lanes, draws near the Dlaat outpost and reaches the Parah landing strip, an abandoned airfield on the way to Manzurieh. We always gave a woman's name to a road opening mission and this time it was Hodaya who got the honours. We're on our way to open up Hodaya, Oshri announced, and gave Bayliss the job of wire searcher. The wire searcher walks next to the tracker at the head of the column looking for tripwires, the kind that when stepped on set off explosions that send you to heaven so fast you don't even have time for the Hear O Israel prayer. All the others were strung out in a line behind us wearing heavy ceramic flak jackets. Several of the boys were carrying dozens of pounds of electronic equipment on their backs with long antennae sticking out above them. They were panting and sweating like pigs, trying to carry out the mission with precision, a mission that's supposed to be an ongoing series of quick glances in search of suspicious signs, but which very quickly turns into the dragging of feet coupled with a closed-off and exhausted look. Anyway, there is a certain logic to this procedure: during a road opening the fighters march at a distance from each other, either alone or in pairs – the fewer together, the better. Better to expose a long, broken line of foot soldiers like this one to a potential threat than endanger a convoy of Safari jeeps crammed with soldiers. And of course you've got trackers along while you're marching. We liked to believe back then that trackers, all native Arabic speakers, had an innate ability to locate every landmine buried along the way.

We followed after them feeling assured, full of admiration, trying to deny the obvious: that our confidence in them was a load of bullshit, since even with all the skill and experience and genes that had been honed over thousands of years on this land, no man would find a single thing in the kind of undergrowth we were marching through. You could have hidden a tank right there in the bushes that surrounded us and we wouldn't have seen it. Really, God's honest truth. But apparently the commanders actually knew that very well, since high alert intelligence warnings were piling up, and they preferred to keep our road closed. On those occasions they would bring in the gigantic D9 bulldozers, the ones as big as three storey buildings, a real fortress on wheels. Driven by SLA men, they were manoeuvred back and forth over the roads. Huge numbers of mines and explosives hit them, yet they came out of every attack without a scratch.

That morning, as we set out to open Hodaya, we couldn't have guessed how short the mission would be. We'd barely gone 400 yards, we'd passed the bend in the road and joined the Virlist road when suddenly, a few steps away from us there was an explosion. We shouted, 'Bomb!' and we all froze in our tracks, waiting for an assessment of the damage and the rear rescue exercise. It was the most fatal mix there was: a Claymore mine filled with explosives and fortified with bits of metal and nails. It had been activated by an infrared sensor triggered by movement. It was well hidden in a fibreglass rock. Everything necessary to bring disaster to our troops was there. However, the Shi'ite fool who, I admit, was deserving of praise for having slipped on to a closed military road under the noses of the guards above, had made two embarrassing mistakes: he had placed the explosive device face down so that it pointed at the ground, and he had forgotten one of the wires most crucial to connecting the whole apparatus. The explosion was weak, almost unnoticeable – a kind of fireworks. No flames, no columns of smoke, not a single scratch or scrape sustained by the troops. And still, since this was the first explosion any squad in our company had encountered in fifteen months, it was only natural that there would be quite an uproar back at the outpost. Real excitement, a day or two of heroic stories and the royal treatment for everyone involved. We actually thought like that back then, looked forward to the royal treatment. But was it likely that a terrorist had worked his long way up the hill, nearly to the top, and made do with placing a single Claymore mine? That's it? The whole shebang? He hadn't set traps still waiting for us on the road? What were the chances? Very low. That's experience talking. So, that morning, right after the incident, it was decided to seal off the road to all traffic, on foot or otherwise. No one coming in or going out, no mail, no packages filled with snacks from home, no supply convoys and no SLA soldiers to come to the outpost to fix the damage from nightly purple rain attacks. Until it could be determined that no other explosive devices had been placed in the vicinity, we were cut off.

The days crawled by, the storerooms emptied out. There was no more meat, no more schnitzel or beef jerky, and everything in the canteen fridge had disappeared. We were waiting for a D9 bulldozer to plough the road and absorb any explosions, but Command had a more creative idea. On Friday afternoon, just before sunset, a Bell 206 helicopter landed at the outpost. Amos jumped out of it into a sandstorm, followed by three shiny, perfumed fighters from the bomb disposal unit. We stood facing them, Oshri and me, just by the outpost fence. Together we stood watching the new guests. It was Ziv we spotted first. 'Looks like we've got ourselves a few more arrogant bastards,' I said. 'That's just what we're missing around here.' From there we went to the Sabbath evening meal when Ziv held out his hand and said, 'Nice to meet you, I'm Ziv Farran,' with crinkly, shining eyes. That fair hair, the thick, red lips. I didn't even bother answering. I made do with a quick, feeble handshake that made it clear how little patience I had for being friendly, and looked away. That's when Amos came over to pair us up. We'd be going out on an operation together, him and me, a two-headed command.

I don't think I really understood, even then, the logic behind their decision. They called it an 'Admiral Procedure'. We would lead a squad on foot into the crater left by the explosion on the Virlist road, in order to investigate it (what did that mean, anyway, to investigate a crater?) and patrol the area for the purpose of locating and neutralizing any additional explosives. It all sounded too dangerous. Bizarre. What about the D9 bulldozers, what had happened to them? This was a classic job for the bulldozers. But there you had it, Command had decided, and apparently it was important to investigate the pit, the explosive device, to gather intelligence, so these soldiers who looked like they'd stepped out of an American movie came to join us, with their shiny black parachute bags and hi-tech flak jackets and electronic equipment and folders, and their styled hair. They stood out in our dusty human landscape, leaving no doubt that they had no connection at all to us, to our brigade. And yet suddenly we were assigned to be together. I nodded.

I had a good excuse for the long silence that followed: Spitzer and Zitlawi took advantage of the quiet and began playing two old and partially destringed guitars some kibbutz had donated to Beaufort back in the eighties. They moved from one generation to the next, right up to the most recent songs. Spitzer played, Zitlawi thumped the wooden guitar, and the whole room joined in for the singing of 'Flowers in the Gun Barrel and Girls in the Turret'. Everyone was beating time on the tables and singing with amazing precision, even the most recent verses about the sunshine over Gaza and Rafiah, which suddenly seemed about the most relevant thing in the world. Before I heard him singing I would have sworn that Zitlawi had never even heard such fancy, flowery language in his life. Amos seemed to be pretty pleased at this excitement and sense of togetherness. In the spirit of Moshe Dayan in a military parade, he scrutinized us all from the head table. He and Furman whispered to each other, seemingly happy and content. Ziv swallowed some of the cheese with the deadly fried onion and survived it in style. Didn't give a single sign of suffering. I signalled my surprise to Oshri. Chili entered with cups of chocolate mousse, one per pair. That was one great Sabbath evening meal we had out there.

When it was over I was summoned to a meeting in Furman's office. Before I'd even shut the door behind me, Amos pulled the trigger. 'You never learn, do you?' he asked. He waited for me to answer. I really was surprised. What? What had I done? Finally it dawned on me: the argument we'd had on the night of the attack on our ambush. I was in shock. How could a senior officer like Amos listen to the whining of a company commander? Were we meant to now discuss Furman and his wounded honour, instead of talking about what was really important, like who should be crucified for the operational and moral failure that had occurred as we lay there, drawing fire, and no rescue team was organized to save us? Since when had the IDF stopped considering the rescue of wounded soldiers to be of supreme value? They'd abandoned us out there. But Amos insisted on opening with his own agenda, or rather, with Furman's. He sank deep into Furman's torn, black, imitation-leather armchair. Furman was sitting on a small wooden chair on the other side of the desk, hunched into himself. I quickly took a chair for myself and sat down, pulling myself as close as possible to Amos. This wasn't a court martial.

'Yes, it's true,' I said, 'sure as shit true. I lost my temper, which is why I shouted at Furman in front of everyone. But I had good reason to, because how the fuck could I be expected to endanger the lives of my soldiers on enemy soil? They've been living since that night with the feeling that they don't have support. I swear it, they tell themselves that nobody's watching over them, that they can't trust anyone.'

Furman butted in. 'That's what I'm talking about. That's exactly what I'm talking about. I can't command the outpost like this.'

I was about to attack him but Amos – impatient, kind of bored – cut us off. He had no intention of listening to the details and his ride home could already be heard in the distance, circling and preparing to land.

'One more outburst like that, Erez,' he said in a deep voice that was nearly a whisper, 'and you'll land up back in prison. But this time it'll be for a long stretch.'

He stood up, grabbed his weapon and left. I bit my lip and followed him out without a word. All I cared about was not being left alone with Furman. For some strange reason, at that painful and humiliating moment, I felt a kind of relief. Was that what a reprimand sounded like? In fact it seemed more like an attempt at projecting forgiveness, like he was just going through the motions in order to keep Furman happy while at the same time subtly signalling that on a personal, moral level he could understand what it was that had set me on fire. My company commander, on the other hand, did not want me at the outpost; that was perfectly clear. As far as he was concerned it would be better for me to be dismissed. What was keeping me there, at Beaufort, was the fact that the brigade apparently had no one readily available they could replace me with. And maybe also because Amos believed in me, seemed to understand that while I still had much to improve in myself – especially my impulsiveness – I was a devoted player with good intentions, a decent fighter who might grow into a decent commander. Better than Furman, that's for sure.

At about 10 p.m., I went off to the showers. Many officers preferred to give up that pleasure completely – sometimes they wouldn't shower for four weeks at a time, so they wouldn't be caught with their pants down if the outpost suddenly came under attack. I tried to manage once every two and a half weeks. That Sabbath I took a chance because it really was calm. There was a special scent to that peace and quiet, hard to explain, and when it surfaced in the Lebanese air you filled up with tranquillity and the tension eased. I sensed it that evening, so I went to rinse the dust off for a few moments (the water level in the tanks was low, you had to keep from getting carried away). That brief moment in time was worth everything. First, the cloth that has been strangling your body is removed: the shirts that have been sticking to you are taken off, the socks. A winter wind strokes your skin, it's orgasmic. You die from happiness, even if you're frozen to the bone. Your naked feet turn into blocks of ice when they touch the ground. You take a few seconds longer to perform each action, the point is to steal a few moments while naked. You shiver, your whole being is drugged with cold and you're about to be drugged with heat. You step under the boiling hot water (hoping there will be no hitches). Your diaphragm fills up with steam. Holy shit, what luxury.

But then Ziv appeared. He burst in, stripped, jumped under the water. During these few seconds, when I lose touch with reality under the water, I need total quiet. It's part of the ritual. No one may speak to me. That's what I'm accustomed to and everyone can go fuck themselves. It's my escape, my refuge, my only private fortress. I shut my eyes and think of nothing. I'm hollow. Just don't mess with me now, I whispered to myself. Let him save his energy for the upcoming evening in the submarine, for the rowdy late night snack. Shit, anything but right now.

'I was warned in advance not to bother you,' he said.

'Hmmmm,' I answered, in despair.

'People talk, you know.'

'OK, what have your girlfriends been telling you about me?' I asked him, full of scorn.

And then, without a moment of hesitation, Ziv whips out the Abu-Jabai episode. 'The battalion commander shouted to you five times over the radio: "Erez, no confirmation." But you wouldn't listen. Landed in jail for that, didn't you, big guy? You see, I'm up to date.'

'So, we're going to play *This Is Your Life?*' I answered. I shut off the water and went to get dressed. My peaceful moment was ruined. I considered explaining that while it was true that I'd gone to prison for disobeying an order, I'd also received positive feedback, praise for engaging in combat. Mixed messages, that's the way it worked in this army. All the officers had patted me on the shoulder and whispered that I'd done well. But I kept quiet. 'In the officers' academy I learned about you,' Ziv said, laughing. 'Would you believe it? The young criminal.' I wondered whether it was good or bad – probably more good than bad – that my incident was being discussed at officer training. I had nothing to be ashamed of, I'd been a sergeant back then, when I'd fired without permission, and in the meantime I'd become an officer myself, which said something. I got dressed. On the bench, next to my decrepit toiletries kit, which had been in Lebanon with both of my brothers before me and had seen combat, was Ziv's, which looked like it belonged to a battalion commander. Draped over it was a white, shortsleeved t-shirt. I thought I was seeing things. It couldn't be, couldn't be true, but there it was, in big blue and red letters printed right on the shirt: OUT OF LEBANON IN PEACE. I swear it, the motto of the Four Mothers movement plastered on his shirt. That band of females, those hysterical women who stir up trouble at intersections, wailing and moaning and threatening to wear us all down. Trying to convince anyone willing to listen that we, the fighters, are nothing but cannon fodder for a meaningless war, expendable tools. And the IDF, they claim, is blind and deaf, inciting us to war, sending young men into the crossfire. We are those young men.

Try to imagine the feeling. In those days you'd make your way home after a six week tour, and it was like that damned Lebanon was chasing after you. It was everywhere: on the radio, on television, in the street. Talk, talk, talk, no end to it. A whole country full of people who know fuck all about the army, but they know better than anyone what needs to be done. At least they think they do. And then along come the commentators: get out, stay in, escalate, soften, change, leave it, left, right – each one of them smarter than the next, each one of them adding his own contribution to boosting the enemy's morale, to his honour, to the wide smile you'd see on Nasrallah's face on TV. And helpless mothers who can't sleep at night, and people worried about their friends, and frightened girls in love: only Lebanon, all day long. They'd stir up doubts, when all you wanted was a little peace and quiet. I'd learned a long time before that there was no chance of finding any peace and quiet when you went home. You came down from the snowy mountain, from our bubble, cut off from the world and floating somewhere up there above the clouds and the chatter, and you'd land on muddy ground, where you'd find a wounded, confused nation of blabbermouths. The Four Mothers shrieked and everyone listened. That's how it is in Israel, and I can understand why. But up at Beaufort? You arsehole! Stirring up doubts up here? Spreading defeatist mottos and political messages? We don't need any cracks right now, anything that's going to affect the boys, take their minds off the goal, break the supreme concentration you need when you go out on a mission. Cracks like those endanger your faith, the willingness to give your all to this place. Up at Beaufort we'd succeeded, for the time being, in keeping out of the debates raging back in Israel. And the boys? Thank God they were fired up, full of morale, hoping for encounters with the enemy, eager for action, as many ambushes as possible and for as long as possible. They wanted to return to Israel with Xs on their weapons, an X for each terrorist they'd downed. We were fighters; that's what we had enlisted to be. We'd chosen to be at the outpost, surrounded by the best friends you can ever have, partners in everything. Friendships that need no interpretation. Telling a soldier at Beaufort that he was not needed was certainly not a healthy idea, and certainly wouldn't motivate anybody. It was a lie, too. A complete and total lie. Anyone who didn't understand that, anyone who didn't see that the alternative was dead children all along the northern border, was a fool.

That was the first time I'd seen – in Lebanon, at Beaufort – evidence of the war that was raging at home and should have stayed there. I debated whether to say something. You know that feeling where you're so stunned that you can't think what to say? Well, that's how it was. 'What's bothering you?' I asked, restrained.

'Don't know,' he answered. 'I'm curious, I suppose, that's all.' He still hadn't sensed my anger.

'Here's a piece of free advice, you fucking faggot. If you don't want this entire outpost to fuck your tiny arse to shreds you'd better not play the PEACE NOW activist up here.'

Silence followed. For the first time his smile disappeared and his eyes lost their light. In a single moment the structure of his face had shifted, was one big grimace. I'd hit home. I glared into his eyes for a few seconds, then took my toiletries and left. He didn't move.

Late that night I went back to him. I'm not sure why. It was out of character. But I went to see him. I told myself we needed to show our professionalism, our maturity, because we had a mission to lead. A complicated one. And when you're leading an operation together – soldiers, that is – there's got to be communication between you, chemistry even. We didn't have the privilege of fighting among ourselves. Maybe that was the reason for the sharp change in his expression in the showers, which was now etched in my brain and making me so uncomfortable. He'd looked despondent. He was pretty much alone up here. I tried to remember the tone of my voice, how deadly I'd sounded. Had I shouted? Or did I just come across as nasty? I couldn't remember. I tortured myself over this for about two hours while Oshri slept facing me and I was alone with myself, thinking, lying wide awake and scrunched up, uncovered. I was wondering if I should make a report stating that we had an extreme left activist at the outpost who was unfit to command. Why should I even agree to go into the field with him? After that, the temporary insanity wore off and I realised that I wouldn't be able to fall asleep without talking to him. I gave in. Maybe it had something to do with Amos's reprimand, or maybe it was just plain old curiosity. I went to the room where the guests slept and I leaned over him. He lay there dozing, maybe even actually sleeping. I shook him gently awake and asked him as calmly as possible if he wanted to join me for a tour of the outpost. Let him learn, why not? It took him a few seconds to restart himself, gain composure, then he grinned like a little boy and sat up. He looked happy, like we'd just made up. Perhaps he was a good man after all, someone who liked people. Strange, I thought, that he didn't despise me. He didn't look at me like some fucked up loser from Afula who liked to play with guns, someone too immature to comprehend that the leftists had the answers. Maybe he even respected me. Because here he was, happy that I was holding out my hand to him, and even after I'd spoken so harshly, he still wanted to connect with me. Surprising. We went out into the darkness together.

We walked along without exchanging a word. It was so quiet. Only the wind whistling, and every two or three minutes a short series of dull explosions from a faraway outpost. The yellow flames and the orange mushroom clouds looked tiny on the horizon. Up above was a thick carpet of thousands of glowing stars. That's how it was at Beaufort: the darker it was on the ground, the brighter it was in the sky. When we got close to the Red guard post, Ziv stopped me with a touch to the shoulder. He said it was amazing here, and he left his hand there a few seconds longer, holding me gently. I told him that the explosive devices were thought to be coming from a slope near the Musicali road. He asked from where Hezbollah would be able to observe us when we were out there on our mission. Mainly from Arnoun, I said, pointing out the village. Then more silence, as we stood gazing at the flickering lights coming from the border, off in the distance. He asked if I'd been offended by that business with the Abu-Jabai cell. 'Don't flatter yourself,' I said.

He announced that he only had a week to go in uniform until his discharge. Wow, I said, some finale you arranged for yourself up here. After that he was leaving for South America. 'Don't you want to join me?' he asked.

'Are you trying to pick me up?'

'Don't worry,' he said, 'I come equipped with a girlfriend.'

He asked where I lived. Afula, I told him. He told me he was from Holon. Holon? I was surprised, I'd expected something fancier.

'We're going to have a barbecue in my back yard, you and me, after we get this road open,' he announced.

'You don't give up, do you?' I said with a smile.

We continued our stroll. He talked about his speciality, explosives. He told me how at the beginning of the explosives war, nine years earlier, the terrorists were primarily using wireless systems detonated from a distance by laser, or infrared, or ultra-something, all with the most advanced technology available, thanks to the Iranians. The more advanced their methods became, the more the IDF advanced, providing solutions and creating electronic warfare equipment and learning to locate and neutralize. But then the terrorists caught on and suddenly went back to their roots, to the most primitive means and most ancient methods. These simpler devices were more difficult to detect, the biggest problem being metal tripwires buried in the dirt. All this green earth is covered in dozens of such traps: explosive devices and landmines. The cat and mouse game is lost from the start, because there is no way of catching up with the enemy. The whole area is one big inferno. Years might pass and still we would have no chance of roaming around in this jungle freely. A pity. So we'd have to jet off to South America, maybe South Africa, to the rainforests.

'I have to have Oshri on this operation with me,' I told him. 'I don't move an inch without him.' He nodded. I said, 'I'm bringing two marksmen, one guy with a Negev light machine-gun, one Nakpadon driver.' We argued over the need for one more tracker, one more medic. Silence again. That's how we walked around, breaking the ice. Somewhere near the Green guard post I remembered the t-shirt, even felt angry about it for a minute. It really was a disgrace, what was he – a total jerk? But I held off. I reminded myself to stay focused, not to break down barriers, but it was impossible not to break down barriers with Ziv. He was so determined, with those warm hands and that smile of his and that winking, charming tone that left you no chance of staying pissed off at him for any length of time. So the barriers fell. God knows how that happened, but the more time we spent together during those six days, the closer we got. We stood at the guard posts together, we learned the landmarks together, agreed on codes, pored over old aerial photographs, briefed the squad, conducted exercises, dress rehearsals. Ziv wanted to know everything, rummage through everything, do everything. We put the boys through every surprise imaginable: Wounded soldier at the back of the squad! Wounded soldier at the middle of the squad! Wounded soldier at the front of the squad! For three nights we had them running around the outpost so they'd be totally calibrated for this operation. In the end, I think, we felt pretty ready.

Every morning before sunrise he would come to the submarine and sit on the knapsacks near me, on the floor, and keep me from sleeping. He would get me laughing, talking about life, trying to decide whether he should study history, whether his girlfriend would wait for him to come back from the big trip he was planning. He loved trekking more than anything. He couldn't understand how I wasn't familiar with a certain cave back in Israel, and promised to take me in his white VW to the sea, where we'd sit in his special spot on the white rocks, drink until the middle of the night and whistle songs. He told me he'd take me to Puerto Rico, too, to fish. And the Amazon. We'd fly there. It was a must. How could I not have heard of the Amazon? He laughed at me. Peru, Ecuador, those places were just for me, he said. To lie on a beach with *ayahuasca*, well yes, it really did sound great. But what exactly was *ayahuasca*? A drink made from a holy plant that makes you hallucinate. Hallucinations? Not for me, I told him. But those rainforests, with a shiny red and yellow toucan sitting on your shoulder and a blue-green butterfly fluttering nearby and drunken swans crossing clear blue rivers? That sounded great. Why not? I think he'd watched too many hours of *National Geographic*. Why was that clown always going on about those rainforests? I didn't miss them here in Israel – not the forests or the rain. But talking like that is how we passed the time. And Ziv would photograph us together in every position and every situation, and he would hug me and smack me hard in the head. And imitate me. And teach me how to act like a snooty barman – well, he tried anyway, but of course there was no alcohol to be found at the outpost. He told me he had a secret hiding place for booze back at his base. What a jerk I was. I'm trying to remember. We played cards – Speed and Whist – betting on beers. He lost. By the third night he'd already moved his sleeping bag to our room and by the fourth, his knapsack. He'd say to me, 'Shut your mouth, Chong.' And I'd say, 'OK Granddad, get a move on, put those false teeth in place.' Zitlawi would show up and join in, give Ziv language lessons. 'A "*bourekas*-grinder" is an officer who doesn't have a clue what to do in a war,' Zitlawi explained. '"*Souvlaki*" is an officer who comes up to Beaufort just to waste some of our high-quality food. "Butt-tasty" is gourmet food. When someone farts we say "Saddam is coming for a visit." "Wetting the edge" means fucking, the same as "flipping a girl's grapefruits". A "piercer" is a new name for a babe. A "bambi" is a childish soldier, a "*jaalul*" is an irritating one. "Safari" is when we act like crazy kids on a field trip. "Self-conflicted" is a soldier with complexes, a "family terrorist attack" is when your extended family arrives for a visit when you've just come back from Lebanon and you need a little peace and quiet, you're dying for sleep. "They turned over your chair" means you've been screwed, like when they send you to carry out an operation in Lebanon a week before your discharge.'

Ziv and I pretended to be totally serious, listening, arguing, finally kicking the boy out of the submarine, with a hug – 'Come on Zitlawi, mate, curtail your presence, take a running leap into the wall, turn the wheel, go find some pickles' – and then we'd burst out laughing. We'd spend hours horsing around like that. And then we'd 're-route' together: that is, return to routine. Sleep. Get some shut-eye.

I don't know why I liked Ziv so much, but there was something about him that attracted me. Maybe it was the fact that he was the big man among the bomb disposal boys. The other two called him Number One: that was his nickname and the definition of his job. Two and Three revered him. He'd actually started out training to be a pilot, then he was top of the new recruits for the Engineering Corps commando unit. Good-looking, athletic but not too muscular. Modest. Hyperactive, too, always on the move, always wanting to wrestle with me, giving me massages. It sounds stupid, but I hadn't ever had an Ashkenazi friend until then. Until him. He would laugh at everything I said, give me this great look, didn't make fun of me even when I said something stupid. He wasn't patronizing.

We spent the last night talking. Just the usual bullshit, mostly about my Lila. Oshri was always saying I was weak in the romance department. Ziv seemed like a professor of romance, so I asked him for an original idea for our sixth anniversary (we celebrated from the first kiss). I had to come up with something significant this time, something sensitive, otherwise it'd be all over for me with her. And there wasn't much time to prepare, barely a month. 'Do you know anything about hotels?' I asked him. He laughed at me. 'Hotels are passé,' he explained. 'Have you heard of the Vanishing Valley?' When I shrugged he repeated it, excited now, 'Yes, the Vanishing Valley.' No, I hadn't heard of it. He ripped out a page from a military notebook and handed it to me, along with a pen. Golden desert, a purple-black volcanic mountain, red horizon, red sea, big blue stars, and a silence that would quiet your soul. I wrote it all down, the road to Eilat, the ancient camel track near Uziah. Down to the palms at Racham. Craters there, a narrow crevice, a stream. We would spread out our sleeping bags at Mitzpeh Amram, facing the Bay of Eilat and a sea of boulders, above the waterfalls and the canyon and the coloured stones sculpted into strange shapes by the wind and rain, and there we would sleep. That was the Vanishing Valley. Even quieter than Beaufort. The next morning we would tackle the Sahara dunes of the Kasui riverbed and the cliffs and dirt paths at Maaleh Shaharut, and we'd climb Mount Argaman and stand on the edge of the abyss. 'It's paradise,' Ziv said. 'Bring ropes for rock climbing.' I wrote everything down. She loves trekking, my little girl. What a man: I would surprise her.

I asked him if I could make one request. 'Shoot,' he said. 'That t-shirt of yours,' I said, 'the white one from those Arab-lovers: don't go out wearing it tomorrow. It'll bring us bad luck. It'll make me lose my concentration. Take it off and I'll keep it for you until you're out of here. A favour I'm asking, for your bro.' He laughed, told me I was sick in the head, and agreed. He took off his shirt and threw it to me.

A few hours earlier we had gathered in Furman's office for a final briefing, to present deployment for this so-called Admiral Procedure. It was a discussion of situations and responses that deteriorated into haggling, proof that not a single one of the officers knew what he was supposed to be doing. I go that way, you move over there, no, wait, you go that way, nobody's over there. We changed the plans at least ten times until I was completely confused. Ziv's Number Three suddenly insisted on being Number Two, and Number Two claimed he was qualified to be Number One so they should give him the chance because Ziv was being discharged anyway. They couldn't agree about where we should march – on the road, near the road, maybe as far as possible from the road. And where we would stand and wait – on the path or in the undergrowth? Nothing was agreed upon. Ziv was afraid of the road because it was a target. I was afraid of the undergrowth at the side of the road, at that time filled with chest-high bushes (later they would be chopped down). The trackers were of the same opinion as me. And then there was the matter of how to approach the crater where the Claymore had detonated. It was decided we would first send a dog in. When he returned we would move out and circle the pit, 360 degrees – a half circle from the south side, then a half circle from the north. If we came across another device we would shoot a rocket at it, blow it up. And where would we situate the Nakpadon, that huge tank which was perfect for rescue missions? Should it wait for us in the area below the crater, or should we leave it parked above, behind us? I presented the security plan and Furman asked questions. After that we reviewed the alerts listed in the intelligence reports and the tracker expressed his reservations; Furman deflected them. For some reason, nothing seemed clear. Then an argument broke out between Ziv and me about how we would move: he demanded to march first, followed by Number Two and then a medic with a stretcher. I refused. Why send a medic up front? A medic had to be as far back as possible, that was the IDF way. Medics don't come near the action, they need to be protected in case they're needed in an emergency. Ziv insisted that the medic be close. I gave in. 'Behind Number Three is the closest I'm willing to allow him,' I said.

When the briefing had ended Ziv went up to River. 'You're the medic, right?' he asked. 'Nice to meet you, Farran,' River replied. They chatted, and then Ziv got to the point: 'I want to explain to you what happens if I get hit,' he said. He lifted his flak jacket, a special number created by the Engineering Corps with a ceramic coating and lots of pockets containing explosive materials. 'If I get hit,' Ziv explained, 'you'll have to open all the Velcro bands and the snaps and then cut the flak jacket and get it off me. Do it as fast as possible, and get it as far away from the squad as you can. It could blow up and then the whole squad would vaporize.' That's how he said it, brief and to the point. River said OK, no problem, open, cut, remove, toss. We parted. Number Three, a redhead, went with Bayliss to the Nakpadon to install an electronic scrambler that helps prevent charges from exploding. One of the green lights that was supposed to indicate if the scrambler was working wouldn't go on. They asked an officer from the Signal Corps about it, but he said there was no way of knowing whether it was functioning. 'There's never any indication whether those instruments are working or not. Maybe it's just the light that's burnt out.' Ziv, in the meantime, had gone back up to Red for a last look around. Alone.

In theory, we were prepared. But something still didn't feel right. That's how the night ended, even before it began.

Emilio, film me a minute, bro. Come on, come here a second. What are you making such a fuss about? Come on brother, film me. Is it filming? Good. Excellent. Come in for a close-up. Nice. Hello? Army Radio? Razi Barkai's morning programme? Good, yes, good morning, Razi. How are you? This is Zitlawi speaking. So here we are – we feel like we're securing the northern border. In fact, I want to tell all the people of this country that we're here for them, at any cost, keeping them safe. Believe me people, the most important thing to us is that you can sleep at night. The fact is, Razi, you're dealing with a bunch of sharks here, that's what we are. Each one of us a killer. Even Emilio the nerd. So what if he looks totally white bread? He's actually real combat material. You want to know what combat is, just look at him. The bloke's never afraid, he doesn't act like an Ashkenazi at all. Come on you jerk, what's bothering you? If you cover up the lens I'll kick you hard, so calm down. Shall we continue? Very good, my man. Yes, Razi, the boy is one hell of an assassin, and it's all for you people. Mmmmm, yes, it's true, we keep narghiles at the guard posts. Sure, why not? You've got to have a little fun, there's no choice. But we want you all to feel safe, to keep on enjoying yourselves all the time. Sorry, I've got to run, Channel Two is waiting to talk to me. Yeah, the *Good Morning, Israel* programme.

Still filming, bro? OK, back to *A Guide for Lana, Spitzer's Russian Girlfriend*. Take two. Hey, Lana, sweetheart: travel log, it's two o'clock in the morning now. See my face? Look close. This is the face of a person who's forgotten what home looks like. After fifty-six days in this dump he was supposed to go home to see his mother, had his bag on his back waiting for the convoy, and then all of a sudden they say there isn't one. Cancelled. Now he's stuck here for another couple of days, maybe a week. Or two. And our officer, Erez, has completely lost it. I'm sick of the guy, I've had it up to here with him. He makes us eat shit the whole day long, you have no idea: hell on earth, a nightmare. Barks at us constantly. I don't know how we ended up with this prick. My grandmother would say, 'If you go through a little hell now you'll enjoy heaven that much more.' So here we are, preparing for the enjoyment. Working our arses off on guard duty and kitchen duty all day long. You think the soldiers in the top commando units have to do kitchen duty? Of course they don't! Their food's catered. Come, come with us for a minute, sweetheart, we'll show you our toilets. It's a bit of a walk, but no big deal, right? You see? Without a doubt the most exclusive model there is. Nasrallah's wife would be happy to come and take a dump here, you can be sure of that. A fucking nuclear holocaust. Let's keep going. This is the door to the outpost. If it falls on your foot, you die. Left here. Have patience, please. Go with the flow. This is our war room. Meet Dave. Brother, tell us about the work of the boys in the war room. Don't worry, mate, this has been approved by the army censor's office. Our friend Mofaz himself gave his permission. Let it roll. The outpost is divided into three parts: Carmel One, Carmel Two, Carmel Three. If the outpost is hit it's my job to alert everyone to go on the attack. Wow, Davey, thank you. We learned a lot. Hey, here's Bayliss, down on the floor talking on the phone. Isn't he cute? Let's sneak up behind him, eavesdrop a little. Hey, Mum, how are you? Dangerous? Of course not! Believe me, Ma, it's like summer camp here. If something happens to me up here it'll be from boredom, so don't worry. How's Dad? OK, enough, this Bayliss is fucking boring! We'll continue our tour. Here we are, back in the room again. You see, sweetheart? Here's Spitzer, your little bunny rabbit, like a blob on the mattress, sleeping, the little angel. Angel? What angel? A devil! But just so you know, he's faithful to you all the way. No hanky-panky, even though the place is full of gorgeous girls. And if anyone tries to say something bad about you – you know, like 'that Russky', that sort of thing – Spitzer whomps him, beats the shit out of him on the spot. Hey look, the boy's waking up. Good morning, sweetie. What a beautiful smile! Say something to your whore. Talk to her. What do you mean, you don't want to? What? What's wrong with you? Hey, no violence. Keep cool.

That's how the night ended, and at five a.m. we got up as usual, spent an hour and a half on the equipment, prepared for an attack on the outpost. After that I went back to sleep. At seven-thirty Furman slapped me awake. 'Get up on the double,' he said. 'What are you doing sleeping on the day of an Admiral Procedure?' I went to the briefing room, half asleep. Ziv was already there, working at full throttle on the preparation. A quick, final briefing to tie up loose ends. I went back to the submarine to get the equipment. Ziv's t-shirt was rolled up on a corner of my bed and I threw it behind a small cabinet so we'd all forget about it. I didn't want the boys to catch sight of it. We were off.

Oshri climbed on to the Nakpadon. Bayliss was driving. River was with me on foot and Emilio was serving as sentinel, on the lookout for rocket launches from the direction of Nabatiye and Tibnit. It was just an arse-saving job; you'd never spot a launch from a mile and a half away. You'd really only notice it as it fell on you. Zitlawi was marching with us too, carrying on his back the portable electronic scrambler – the kind that fries your balls – with Spitzer, Boaz and Tom serving as the security force. Then there was the dog-handler, and Ziv, and two of his men providing cover. We were all completely silent. About a hundred yards before the pit I signalled to everyone to go down on one knee. With two fingers I indicated to Ziv that he should look straight ahead, that's where the pit was.

We started to send the dog ahead, send the dog ahead, send the dog ahead – three times. Dogs don't get what you want from them on the first try. They don't always know what to look for or what to find. He didn't really get close to the pit, came back too quick, wasn't concentrating. It wasn't working. So, according to plan, we carried out a comprehensive search, circled the place to determine whether the terrorists had beaten a path in through the undergrowth, and which route they'd chosen to booby-trap the target. We unrolled white marking tape as we walked so we'd know where we'd been. It was hot and sticky. The sun had come up too fast. It took us half an hour to complete the first half-circle.

Oshri peered out from the Nakpadon, which had stopped along the road, past the bend. He shouted, 'River, River, come get the stretcher.' River didn't think twice and began to run through the field. I shouted like I've never shouted in my life: 'Don't move! No! Don't move!' River stopped, came back. He trusts Oshri and me without giving it a thought, it amazes me. The stretcher remained on the Nakpadon. I looked down, saw Oshri standing up, exposed, the top half of his body sticking out of the vehicle. 'Get back inside!' I shouted at him, too.

An argument broke out over how to continue. The tracker insisted he couldn't lead us through the bushes, it wasn't safe; we'd have to move forward on the road. But the bomb disposal team protested in unison that the road was the least safe option. In the end it was decided to stay close to the road but not on it, pressed up against the *dabeshim*, on the dirt road that runs the length of the curve. My soldiers positioned themselves behind the *dabeshim* and maintained surveillance. Ziv began descending the slope. 'Bring me the medic and the signal operator, I'm going into the crater,' he said. I told him to forget that idea. 'None of my boys are moving,' I told him. 'I'll come with you.' I would be his medic and his signal operator. That pissed Ziv off. 'You're going to be surprised to hear this,' he said, 'but the medic and the signal operator come with me. That's what was decided up at the outpost.' But I refused. I can't say exactly why, but I did. I felt like I couldn't rely on anyone. I didn't want to involve my men because something didn't feel right. Another argument. 'We're exposed – they can see us from here,' I said in the end. 'You either take me or I'm climbing inside the Nakpadon and leaving with my soldiers.' He gave in and we formed a line. Ziv was first, I was a few yards behind him, then his two men and the tracker. 'Just so you know,' Ziv said, already moving towards the pit, 'this is not according to procedure. You're not supposed to be in charge here, you're supposed to be providing back-up.' He took another few steps forward, maybe ten, no more than that, and I was behind him. He turned his head back towards me and said, 'My friend, keep your distance,' with that broad smile of his. He was always so quick to cool down and make up. 'My friend, keep your distance.' That's what he said, and I answered, 'Get on with it, you big baby.'

And suddenly, an explosion. A huge boom. Ziv fell. Clouds of earth and mud and dust covered us in waves. Everything stopped, fell silent. That's according to procedure: you freeze in place. The explosion made my ears ring. Everything was muffled.

When Ziv fell I could still hear his voice echoing in the air: 'My friend, keep your distance.' He lifted himself on his side for a moment, then fell again. Black smoke began to swallow us up and I lost sight of him. A second passed, maybe two or three, and Ziv's men ran towards the pit, ignoring what had been discussed in the briefing and in complete contempt of procedure. 'Stop, stop!' I shrieked. Who knew how many more mines were lying in wait for us out there? Ten? Maybe more? Someone had his eye on us, maybe in Arnoun, and was pressing the button, making sure we were wiped out one by one. The two of them looked at me for a moment, then continued. They didn't care. They disappeared into a screen of dust, completely out of sight. 'Cheetah, One here. We found a present! A present! One flower down, the rest intact. Start rescue.' Silence. I waited for something to happen. I radioed again. 'Head of Admiral took a hit. I repeat, head of Admiral took a hit. Unclear how bad. Requesting helicopter for rescue. Requesting helicopter for rescue. Over and out.' A few more seconds passed, then I heard Ziv's men shouting: 'Medic, medic, come quick!' That was forbidden, too, according to our training. You have to drag the wounded soldier back. But they were shouting and River went running – occupational instincts. 'Stop! Stop, River!' I shouted. When he didn't, I began to run, too. Where was Ziv? Where was he? I couldn't see anything because of all the smoke. I never thought for a second that he was dead, the possibility didn't even cross my mind. I didn't know anything, didn't think anything, didn't take anything in.

River found him lying in the thick smoke. He bent down, tried rousing him. Was he conscious? No. He asked Number Two to take Ziv's helmet off and Number Three to strip his clothes. They opened his flak jacket, ripped open his shirt. They didn't cry. River checked his breathing. There was none. None of this was supposed to be carried out in the vicinity of the explosion, but that's what they did. It seemed too complicated to move him. River tried resuscitating him, tried forcing air into his body, without success. We could hear fluid blocking his windpipe. Ziv was perfectly whole, all his limbs attached, but his neck was swollen, bulging, and blood was streaming from his nose, his ears and especially his mouth. Blood was pouring from every orifice. He was covered in bits of shrapnel, his eyes were wide open and red. And all around was the smell of burning plastic. It was hard to breathe. 'River,' I said, 'what's going on?' He didn't answer me, just kept on trying to resuscitate Ziv. I asked again and again: What's going on? What's going on? What's going on? He said nothing. I shouted, 'Tell me what's happening to him!' and I pulled River's face in my direction. It was covered in blood. He said, 'Nothing.' Nothing what? Nothing what! River kept trying with all his strength, drained fluid, huge quantities of blood from Ziv's mouth. It kept coming. Come on, we've got to get some air in there. But the blood didn't stop flowing. I could hear myself shouting: 'How long is this going to take? Get him breathing, for God's sake get him breathing, I'll do anything, anything! I'll stop smoking, just let him breathe.' Then River started going mad, pounding with all his strength on Ziv's body in desperation. It went on for ever. And there's Ziv, lying in a pair of short, dark underpants, wasted. River knew he was gone, the blast had killed him, all his internal organs and his blood vessels had imploded like a diver whose lungs have shrivelled and then along comes a little pressurization and he's done for. But out in the field there's no pronouncing someone dead. That can only be done by the outpost doctor. I looked behind me, the smoke was beginning to clear. I could see how my soldiers were starting to lose it. I shouted, 'Emilio, look at me now! Everyone, look at me!' I knew I had to remain in their line of vision; if they didn't see me for a minute they'd go mental. 'Don't panic,' Furman said over the radio. Don't panic, you arsehole? He gave us instructions designed to ensure we'd make it back up to the outpost without incident.

I remember how the minutes passed and Ziv was lying there, unconscious, not breathing, his body limp as rubber, his head bloated, hot all over from the pooling blood, and there I was, standing next to him, waiting, feeling so alone while the thoughts got all mixed up in my head: one part of me was thinking about what needed to be done, like reporting to the outpost, having them aim artillery, requesting that the doctor be put on standby, talking to the soldiers about what needed to be done. And the other part wasn't thinking at all. It was trying to think about what I needed to think about, but nothing was happening.

Bayliss started the engine of the Nakpadon, backed towards us, and stopped thirty yards away. The entire chassis of the tank was full of holes. It was supposed to be a secure vehicle, the Nakpadon, but it had been pummelled with so much shrapnel that some of it had got stuck in the chassis and some had actually penetrated the engine. Oshri and Bayliss brought out the stretcher. Number Two and Number Three helped River load Ziv on to it and then we repositioned ourselves, moving him for further treatment to the foot of the Nakpadon. Still dangerous, but less so. River tried resuscitating him again, a last effort. Tried removing fluids again, too. It's called 'logging', when you turn the wounded soldier gingerly on to his side, careful not to break his neck – in these situations gentle treatment is really important so the head and the body move together – then you stick a finger in and clear the mouth. River even succeeded, managed to get some air in for a second and Ziv's chest inflated for a breath or two. But that's all. We refused to accept that it was over, but every push on his chest brought up more blood. Fuck, let's get him up to the outpost, to the doctor. In a couple of seconds we had the stretcher hoisted on to the Nakpadon, and River climbed on, too. Bayliss, at the wheel, was trying to navigate, but the periscope was damaged and of course there are no windows so he was forced to drive without seeing where he was going. He was just hoping not to plunge into the crater. Oshri peered out of the slit at the top and guided him the best he could – a little to the left, a little to the right. At the outer gate of the base they hit something and nearly ran over three men doing maintenance. River, in the meantime, was like a robot in the belly of the Nakpadon, caring for Ziv even though there was nothing for him to take care of because there were no external injuries. He tried giving Ziv an infusion. Why? He wasn't breathing, had no pulse. Why try to give him an infusion? I ran like a madman on the road, alongside the vehicle.

We reached the outpost. Oshri took charge of unloading. A few soldiers came out to help, grabbed hold of the stretcher and ran it inside to the doctor and the two medics waiting for his arrival. River dragged in after them. They started intubation, which is when you insert a tube that's attached to an oxygen pump down the throat, almost all the way to the lungs. The tube went in easy the first time. That's lucky, because sometimes it goes crooked and punctures the oesophagus.

'Doctor, doctor, his throat is all bloated. Full of blood. Don't miss!' River was shouting, getting in their way. I tried to get close, too, but the medics forced us out, pushed us backwards. After that they kept themselves busy, taking care of an injury to Ziv's leg, something small and unimportant that nobody had noticed. They wrapped an elastic bandage around it. Furman crowded the squad into the briefing room so they wouldn't see what was happening.

The doctor pronounced Ziv dead. Oshri started to cry. I ripped the Madonna set with the microphone and ear piece off my head and entered the room. I went to the farthest corner, stood against the wall, alone, while they leaned over the body.

River stepped aside, too, went to the dining room on his own, leaned backwards over the blue table reserved for Sabbath, took off his vest and his equipment. He stood there taking air in. I went up to him and said, 'It'll be OK. You performed well. It'll be OK.' I wanted him to talk to me. The door was open a little, and through that chink we watched as they placed a wool blanket over Ziv. The doctor shut his eyes and then they covered his head, too. They lifted the stretcher, carried him to the storeroom until the rescue helicopter could come from Israel. River fell apart. It happened in a second, just burst out of him. All his reservoirs started flowing, he cried like a baby, then he attacked some furniture: picked up a chair and hurled it at the wall, upended a table. I stood facing him, trying to decide what to say. His face was covered in blood. His hands, too. He took a long look at them, absorbing what had happened to him in the past few hours. 'They did everything they could, River,' I said, putting my hand on his shoulder. 'You did. The doctor did. He's dead. There's nothing we can do about it.' He cried even harder. 'I have to take a shower,' he shrieked, 'I've got to shower!' I asked him to wait a bit, till things had calmed down some. We were still on alert. 'I don't give a fuck,' he shouted. 'I need a shower!' I took hold of him, grabbed his waist, sat him down. He was furious at the whole world: at Hezbollah, at the IDF, at God. 'What is this? What are we doing here? What is this fucking bullshit?' He went wild, soaked with tears. 'Fuck everyone! Give me one good reason why he died. For what?' Those few minutes, when River collapsed in my arms, I remember only in a kind of fog. I know I said all kinds of things to him, trying to get him to calm down. But I didn't cry. I waited for him to get hold of himself, let it all out. I sat on the floor next to him with my back to the wall. All the images ran through my mind. And the smell of gunpowder. And Ziv, may he rest in peace. I could see him starting down towards the bend in the road and then disappearing all of a sudden, falling. And the explosion, I kept feeling it again and again, seeing black. And how I'd run towards it. And the first sight of him, wounded, covered in blood. I was going over it all. How we'd cared for him, how we'd functioned, what I'd done right and what I hadn't. Everything was racing through my mind. The stretcher, the wool blanket. And what a dead man looks like – the blank look, like something is missing. River cried while I sat thinking.

Even when he calmed down we remained silent, for a long time, I don't know how long. 'My first injured soldier,' he said finally. I didn't know how to answer that. 'The first time I take care of a wounded soldier, and he dies. I made mistakes, you saw for yourself.'

'Listen to me,' I said, resolutely. 'Ziv was gone from the first minute.'

River started to cry again, this time quietly, subdued, but at length. Then he lay down on the floor and curled up. 'You were great, River,' I said. 'You didn't go into shock, not even for a minute.' I moved over to him, grabbed hold of his neck, pulled him close. 'It'll be OK,' I reassured him. 'We'll look out for one another. You're here, I'm here. It'll be OK.' He lowered his gaze. I asked him, 'Do you trust me?' I brought my face down close to him. 'Do you trust me?' I persisted. 'I want you to tell me if you trust me.' He looked up at me again. And that's when it happened. 'I'm ready to die for you,' he said. He was right there in front of me, as close as can be, and he said, 'I'm ready to die for you.' Just like that, straight at me. What a thing to say: 'I'm ready to die for you.' How can you answer that? Any answer gets dwarfed, becomes meaningless. I thought about saying that I'd be prepared to die for him in the next life, but that would've sounded stupid. So what do you do in a situation like this? Just give a hug, a kiss, say, 'I love you.' What a disgrace that I can't remember the date. His eyes were wet, sparkling, they pierced my soul. Suddenly he was a little boy lying there in front of me. I put the palms of my hands on his cheeks and stroked him. We were so weak and resigned when Ziv fell, but now my strength was returning. We crushed each other in a long embrace, then I stood up, extended my hand to him and pulled him over to the water buckets so he could clean himself up.

He asked permission to go back to Israel to attend the funeral, but I declined. I told him it wasn't possible, but that we would sent him home in the near future. I couldn't let him get away from us, from the squad, from me; after such a traumatic event the best thing for him would be to get back to routine.

We left the dining room. River was locked deep inside himself. Eveyone watched him, a few tried talking to him, but River ignored them, kept silent. He went into the submarine and lay down on his bed. The boys were on edge, in shock – every last one of them – but River had lost Ziv from his own hands. He pulled a box of goodies sent to him by friends back in Israel from under his bed and told the guys to help themselves, he wasn't capable of touching any of it. I went to rest, too. On the way I saw Number Two and Number Three sitting in a dark corner of the security area near a row of open stretchers – drained, dead tired, sobbing, broken. I'd never seen tears at Beaufort before, not until that day. And they looked so alone and out of their element there, in our place. I didn't look directly at them, just checked them out from the corner of my eye. I didn't know what to say. Nothing could be done. All the while the knowledge that the body lay nearby, in the storeroom, permeated the air.

That night, Ziv's body was covered with a second blanket, he was wrapped up according to procedure, and the Kaddish prayer for the dead was recited. I was asked to carry the stretcher. I stood twenty yards from the helicopter pad, one hand on the body, the other on my weapon. Ziv's bag was on my back. We waited. For a moment I uncovered his face, I had this strong urge to see it one last time. I gazed at him. Who says that death has no face? A

Yasur helicopter landed and we ran forward against the wind into the dust, inside the darkness. We loaded the body into the helicopter while a few high-ranking officers got out of the other side, here for an update on the situation. They didn't even notice Ziv as we loaded him in, they marched ahead without even a passing glance at the blanket, or at us. I tossed the bag inside the helicopter. ZIV FARRAN, IDF# 5154182, BOMB DISPOSAL SQUAD: it was all written there. Dave handed me his flak jacket and helmet. There was a hole in it made by a big piece of shrapnel from the Claymore mine. I handed them up to the pilot. Thirty seconds later he was in the air. I stood in place, watching Ziv grow distant until he disappeared into the horizon. In the background, mortars fired by the terrorists in every sector reinforced the feeling that something was happening. I went back to Oshri. He was lying on his bed staring at the television screen intermittently broadcasting from Hezbollah's *Al-Manar* station. 'Look at the Jews,' they were singing in broken Hebrew with a Shi'ite accent. 'The Jews are in deep mourning. The Jews have a big problem. They love life, those Jews. We, on the other hand, love death. We love death, that's why we'll win.' A man impersonating Prime Minister Ehud Barak walked into a room set up to look like the Tel Aviv office of the IDF chief of staff but painted in colours from the flags of Arab states. He shouted, 'What is this fear in the ranks of our soldiers? Why are they running away? What is this madness, this pressure? Why aren't our soldiers prepared to serve in Lebanon?' The screen showed rows of coffins, our own. Real footage from different military cemeteries. We watched in silence. Every once in a while the ground shook. 'This is the valley of death here, not a security zone,' Oshri said. Everyone was in a poetic mood. I handed him a rubbish bag and asked him to go around and collect all the uniforms and equipment that had been spattered with blood. River's gun, too – I went to the junior soldiers' submarine to get it, for a thorough cleaning. I found Spitzer dozing there, his head on Zitlawi's chest and his arms around him. Zitlawi was staring at a naked bulb. But

River wasn't there. I raced to the dining room, the briefing room, checked the line for the telephone in the hall, which was now filled with stretchers. I looked everywhere for him. Outside, too. I went to the showers, the connecting trenches, the guard posts: from White to Blue to Red. On the way up to Green I saw his skinny shadow. He was crouched there by a steep stairway, frozen, his face turned towards the fortress. He was holding something, one of our tattered prayer books. This soldier was reacting badly. I was worried. 'What are you doing?' I asked him. 'I don't know,' he answered. He was looking for the right words, I guess. 'You should say the Thanksgiving blessing if anything,' I told him. 'I don't know it,' he said. I pulled the prayer book out of his hands, closed it and put it on top of one of the sandbags nearby. OK, my friend, let's do it together,' I said. 'Repeat after me: *'Blessed are You, God, King of the Universe, who bestows good things upon the guilty, who has bestowed every goodness upon me. Amen. May He who has bestowed goodness upon you continue to bestow every goodness upon you for ever.'*

That's what I recited, the prayer for someone who's been saved from disaster and the response of those listening, and he repeated it, at first quietly, a kind of mumble, and then out loud, almost shouting. I asked him, 'Has anyone ever told you that you look like Marco from that TV programme about the boy who goes off in search of his mother for the whole summer holiday? You look like him. Same face.' He smiled, and sang part of the theme song. 'When we were children,' he said, 'my grandfather would take us to synagogue. He's religious, my grandfather. Son of a rabbi. But I haven't set foot inside a synagogue since my Bar Mitzvah. I'm a real infidel, a pork-eater and all that.' I told him that my parents are observant, but like him I've grown away from it. 'So what's this all about?' I asked him. 'Death? Is that what's going to make us change our ways? Suddenly we'll become believers? Come on, man, it doesn't make sense. It's childish.'

'We did not take that bomb seriously,' he said. 'Not at all. The same way we behave with mortar shells and rockets. We laugh, we sing, we whistle, everything's a big joke. And then they attack, bombs explode in our faces and suddenly a soldier dies for no good reason right in my arms.'

'Yes,' I said, 'but what does that mean?'

'That maybe we should be a little afraid,' River answered.

'No,' I said. 'We don't have that luxury. That's the privilege of people who aren't here to be afraid and to ask theoretical questions. To be afraid you have to think too much, you have to be a regular citizen, not a soldier.' He nodded.

That evening, at the Reichan outpost not far from us, eight paratroopers were wounded. 'Moderately': they lost arms, legs, eyes. But no one counts the wounded. Only the dead are counted.

The next day, as the sun set and the Sabbath began – exactly one week since Ziv had arrived – it became clear that even the people furthest from religion at the outpost were discovering their spiritual side. Everyone came with makeshift *kippas*, everyone suddenly knew how to pray – or at least pretended to. Even the most blatantly secular soldiers, the ones who couldn't stay away from Chili's fridge during the day of Yom Kippur fasting, seemed to feel a need to say thank you for having survived the week. Each in his own way, at his own pace, in actions he'd brought from home. You could hear the singing from every corner of Beaufort, and the 'Amens' that came in waves. Only the guards on duty were absent from the service. And Bayliss.

You go on, that's the way it is. No shortcuts, no special treatment. No therapists, no mind-fucking. Nights, I would stay awake, going from guard post to guard post, walking around and listening. I looked into their eyes, each of them, to make sure they were getting back to routine. I would test River from time to time to make sure the bloke wasn't turning into a six-pack. 'Six-pack' is our code word for someone deeply fucked up, someone with a screw loose. I'd say, 'River, Ziv will never . . .' and he would fill in the blank, what it was he wouldn't be able to do any more. It was a kind of test, a sanity test. The crazier the answer, the healthier the player was – and the less you needed to worry about him. Ziv won't be able to sing 'A Sea of Cornstalks' any more in the middle of a ploughed wheat field during a training exercise using live ammo. Ziv won't be able to tattoo a portrait of Hanan Ashrawi on his arse any more. Come on, bitch, let's see you mess with the boys. Ziv won't be able to get turned on by the Spring 1967 Delta underwear catalogue any more and he'll never eat a flower or drink a leaf and he'll never say, 'Tomorrow it'll all be over.'

But River still blamed himself. He barely opened his mouth. He was shell-shocked, withdrawn. He couldn't shake the idea that Ziv had been alive after the explosion, that some other treatment would have saved his life. I shouted at him. 'Forget about that, you jerk. He was dead.' But River wouldn't listen. 'You've been through a trauma,' I would say to him. 'You held someone in your hands and he died, and there are consequences to that. You've got to rest, relax. After all, we've agreed: we're together to the end.' On the third night, when I thought he'd calmed down, River caught hold of me during one of my tours of the guard posts. He said, angrily, 'Erez, I just wanted you to know that when I asked what the fuck we're doing here, I really meant it.' That's the pain talking, I thought. I didn't pay too much attention to it, but I played along with him. 'You have your doubts about our mission here, River?' I asked. 'Don't the towns and villages along our northern border interest you any more?' But River didn't even take a breath or miss a beat before he replied. 'It has nothing to do with the northern border. We're looking out for our own arses, that's all. We sit up here at Beaufort, disconnected from every-thing, drawing rockets and mortar shells and explosive devices, endangering our lives, just so we can continue sitting at Beaufort. That's the entire mission. What a shitty feeling. What on earth were we doing in that fucked up operation? All we wanted to do was open up that fucking road, the road that leads back and forth to Israel, nothing more than that. You tell me, Erez, as an officer. What are we doing here?'

'What do you prefer?' I recited. 'For Hezbollah to move freely right up to the fence and settle in there? You're talking bullshit, River. If we weren't here, if we didn't have a string of outposts deep in Lebanese territory, the enemy would be pushed up against the border fence with their weapons drawn, ready to shoot at Metullah and Nurit and Manara.'

How could you argue with that? River didn't even try. He tucked his tail between his legs and went back inside. I hoped he'd just lost it for a moment, that was all. He was blaming himself, which was understandable. Me too. For months I blamed myself. After all, I was the commander of the squad when Ziv fell. Even if Ziv was senior to me and on his way out of the army in another few days, he was no guerrilla fighter, and not at home on the roads of this sector. It was my responsibility to keep him safe, my responsibility to locate the dangers in advance, even to have refused point blank to set out on the mission. We should never have gone out in those circumstances! And how the hell had Hezbollah managed to place that mine anyway, just a few feet from the bend in the road? My boys had watched that spot all night. Could they have snuck that device in under their noses? Under the noses of my own soldiers? Had one of them fallen asleep on duty? And why hadn't the scrambler disabled the mechanism? Why hadn't it even beeped a warning?

When River returned to the submarine he found the boys crowded around a helmet filled with tiny pieces of paper with a name written on each. It was a lottery to determine who would be the next to be killed, Zitlawi explained. He asked Emilio to draw, but he refused. Spitzer did, too. In the end Zitlawi drew out a slip of paper. River's name was on it. A low grumble rose from the group gathered there, but River didn't react. He squeezed past them to his bed and lay down with his face to the wall. He didn't utter a word until lunchtime. Bayliss kicked the helmet, sent it flying and shouted that they'd all lost their minds, that it wasn't funny, and then he went to lie down, too. They all lay down and shut their eyes.

The following Monday it was decided to send us home for a visit. This was an impossible mission, given that the roads were still closed to traffic and the air force was refusing to send in helicopters due to a security alert. And yet, it was clear that there was no way the squad could be kept at the outpost any longer. I'd had an eye on my soldiers, and knew that they were worn out, finished, and missing home terribly. For some of them – the ones who'd been given extra time at Beaufort as a punishment when we'd first arrived – this should have been their first furlough, and even that had come after a long delay. Twenty-two days earlier, River, Bayliss and Spitzer had been packed, their knapsacks on their backs, when their convoy was cancelled at the last minute – as usual, thanks to Intelligence – as were two more the following week. Time dragged on and the three stayed in their same smelly underpants and filthy mood for another week. On 28 March they were certain that this was it, they were on their way home. Zitlawi and Emilio were supposed to leave with them, having completed their record-breaking punishment. But bad luck had it that twelve hours before they were due to set out a landmine exploded for the first time on the Virlist road and the roads were sealed off. Another week and two days passed, a real siege, and then Ziv came with Number Two and the redhead and six more days crawled by, and then Ziv was killed. They needed to get home, these boys.

When I told them they were heading home on Monday they didn't believe me. They refused to prepare or get their equipment together – it was a kind of superstition. Nobody knew how we were supposed to get back to Israel. Then in the afternoon a cryptic message was received by the war room. The message was called 'Exodus' and the mission was to leave the outpost on foot – not in vehicles or helicopters – by the White guard post at the back of Beaufort, marching in a line through the undergrowth that covered that steep and rocky slope, on a path that had never before been used. From there, we'd have a long trek through village fields to the Parah landing strip, and from there another three miles along a winding dirt road. Then, at an improvised parking area, just as we arrived, Safari vehicles would come out of nowhere, perfectly timed, and take us to the border. This would be the first and only time we would carry out this plan. Hezbollah, they believed, would be caught totally by surprise. They probably wouldn't even know it had happened. A line of soldiers did not glow in the dark, didn't go back and forth like a convoy of trucks or helicopters. And even if they did catch sight of troops marching in the dark, they wouldn't have time to strike a serious blow. Still, when the rumour about Exodus spread around the outpost, there wasn't a single person who believed it was real. It was insane, marching like that through a battle zone with cooks and soldiers from the Signal Corps and the Ordnance Corps. Between you and me, those guys are pencil pushers. We kept saying there was no way, we laughed, and still it happened. At two o'clock in the morning we found ourselves in the middle of an olive grove at the edge of the hill.

It's freezing cold, but your belly's burning up as usual, drops of sweat are trickling down your forehead and cheeks. Your legs are tired from crossing wadis, slopes, stone walls, wire fences – it feels never-ending. After falling a couple of times you realize you shouldn't step on the white rocks. And like always, you can hear the dull sound of shooting in the distance, pinching the frozen silence. Your fear vanishes as you start moving; if we come under fire it will disappear completely. At two thirty a.m. the roosters of Arnoun begin their loud crowing. Dogs, too, suddenly start barking. Could it be that they smell us? Are the residents here able to sleep through the noise? Or are they awake already? In the distance, you glimpse a dark green fluorescent light coming from a mosque in the midst of a cluster of weak lights of a village. A few more minutes pass and we are sucked into a little forest, no more than a grove of trees. A few yards away we encounter a bonfire between the trees, the smell of smoke thick in the air. What the hell is some Arab doing barbecuing at three in the morning? Emilio moans that this is too dangerous, utter insanity. 'Who would dare come near us, my friend?' Zitlawi whispers. 'Believe me, when I'm surrounded by all these shitheads from our squad I feel safer than I do at home.' I stop, tap Oshri on the shoulder and say under my breath, 'Number Two, distance yourself from the next soldier and keep quiet. Pass it on.' Oshri runs to River, the next in line. 'Three,' he says, 'distance yourself. Pass it on.' We walk carefully, we lower our shadows, we can't see three feet ahead. Suddenly the calls of the muezzin pierce the air. *Muhammad rasul Allah, Muhammad rasul Allah*, comes the cry again and again in that thick, coarse voice. Gradually, other voices join his from different directions. I order everyone to drink, and they take sips from the tubes coming out of their packs. Every once in a while we see a suspicious movement and everyone goes down on one knee. Oshri and I check to see that the coast is clear and then we signal to them that it's OK to continue. As a gesture to the non-combat guys, we stop occasionally for a rest. You fall backwards all at once, lose your balance, fall on your pack, which stops you – it's the best feeling for a fighter, that letting go. You let your heavy pack hit the ground, but quietly. It feels like falling on to a soft king-sized bed with satin sheets. You lie there staring up at the sky. The moon mesmerizes you. I hear River whispering to Bayliss, mentioning – on his own initiative for the first time – the girl from Nov, Bayliss's village. He pretends not to remember her name. Says he just wanted to know if she was OK, that she wasn't traumatized – my arse – because what happened to her wasn't very nice. He is mumbling, confused. 'Do you know her?' he asks. 'Not really. She's at boarding school,' Bayliss answers. He tells River that's where the problem girls are sent, the ones who didn't cope with school. The good girls are sent to school in Tiberias. But if River is interested he can fix him up with someone from the girls' *yeshiva*. They are eighteen to twenty-three years old, more suitable. And legal. The only problem is the *kippa*. After all, these are traditional girls. River cuts him off, reassures him he isn't interested, he only wanted to know about the girl's welfare, was feeling a little guilty – nothing more than that. 'But what do you mean by "problem girls?"' No, Bayliss tells him sharply, these are not sluts. River decides to let it go. We pass along the message to start moving again and the rest period comes to an end. Your gaze drops once again from the moon to reality: the ground. That's the way it is, you're booted out of your dream and you're surprised to find you're still there in the middle of this other-worldly green-black darkness, in a landscape that surprises you.

A house, straight ahead of us. I don't remember there being a house along the route. There wasn't one in the aerial photos or on the maps. Candlelight flickers in the kitchen window. We pass by crouched down, moving very quietly, praying that no one will go to the fridge for a midnight snack. I steal a glance inside, and think about how normal life goes on here, there's a pleasant family dining table and a rocking chair in the living room, and the drawings of a small child on the fridge. Where is the TV? Interesting. Four o'clock in the morning and the wind has kicked up, the temperature has dropped, piercing your bones; there is no way not to shiver, your teeth chatter. Finally, we reach the meeting point, where the Safaris pick us up. Our shivering turns to goosebumps of excitement. Israel is drawing closer, along with a feeling of relief that this insane thing is ending without incident. By the time the border gate opens and we cross through, and bolt from the vehicles on the white-top at Ha'egel base, we can see the first light in the sky. Take in a deep breath of air, I gesture to River. Look at the sky and calm yourself. There's nothing like entering Israel at that hour, when everyone's waking up along with you, a new day. They have no idea where you're coming from and no clue what you've been through. Milk trucks unload their wares at Itzik Zagouri's grocery in Kiryat Shmona and the bakery puts out its first tray of croissants and the paperboys deliver their newspapers and the roosters are having a field day – Jewish roosters, kosher ones – and people are out jogging, waving hello to you. It's a different planet. Such sweet moments, like from a movie, and at first glance everything seems so innocent. Just a village filled with calm people smiling at one another, unaware of what's happening a few feet away from their lives, right under their noses. We cross their main street like zombies, after being up all night, covered in dust. We don't talk. We try to recover, reduce the level of adrenalin, adjust to this new environment. And then we have to part. Bye, bro, take care of yourself, man. That's all, just a short, quiet goodbye then each soldier heads in a different direction. How weird it is in those first moments, even scary, to be without them, to walk completely alone, among people you don't know. You feel so strange. You're sorry you didn't hug a few of those before parting. But it would be stupid to run back now just for that. And soon you'll be in your own, small bed, back to being a spoiled mama's boy between coloured sheets. Life up at Beaufort will seem unreal, like a bad dream. But part of you will wait, tense, to get back into uniform and up there again, if only to satisfy your curiosity, to verify that it really happened, that it exists, that you're not hallucinating.

For the boys, too, this sudden switch to being alone isn't simple. That's a fact. River and Zitlawi decided, completely spontaneously, to join Bayliss for a two-day trip around the Golan Heights before returning home to their parents. They'd have a week-long holiday at home, they said, and their good friends from high school would only be back from their army bases on the weekend, if at all. So Bayliss asked his father, Menahem, to pick them up, and the three of them stood waiting for him at the petrol station near the shopping mall. Oshri caught a ride with an Armoured Corps officer heading towards Tel Aviv, while I had been summoned to a debriefing in the office of the commander of Northern Command about what had happened to Ziv during the Admiral Procedure. All of a sudden I wasn't so eager to get out of uniform. On the contrary, I felt glad to have the excuse to wear it a little longer, to keep myself busy in the brief moment before home would smack me in the face and I would turn into one giant ball of sleep, ramming my pillow sixteen straight hours a day if they'd only let me. Israel makes a person tired.

I walked through a deserted public garden just before reaching the central bus station. A little Pekinese followed me, wouldn't leave me alone. The last thing I needed was the smell of a strange dog on me. That would drive Bitter crazy. He'd feel betrayed, it's only natural. He's all alone without me, he'll never learn to keep himself busy without me. I knew I should find a public phone and call Lila, so she'd know I was on my way. I wondered if her commanding officers would let her off, and how fast it would happen. Today? Tomorrow? I hoped I wouldn't sit rotting at home without her until Friday. The uncertainty was maddening. What if they didn't let her go? Who are they anyway, the bunch of eager arseholes, nothing more than a pack of tour guides at a field school. All at once the truest, strongest longing you could ever imagine settled on me. I spend weeks trying to feel like I miss her but I manage without her just fine. Fantasize about her a little, sometimes when my dick is hard, but no more than that. And here I am suddenly, without warning, almost in tears from all this thinking about her. Really, truly, it's like my heart is going to explode, I'm dying to smell her neck. I want her to hold me, stroke my ears, put her hand on my hair, rake it with her fingernails. I want to lie naked with her – no covers – and stare off into space, listen to the music of Rami Kleinstein or Arik Einstein. Put some strawberries, bananas and milk into the blender, make her a smoothie. Take Bitter for a walk in the park. I say out loud: 'If I don't get to look at her today I'll go mad: I really will.' Engines are revving in the bus station, first runs of the day. Nothing's been renovated since the seventies: the rusted red and white poles, the awnings, the *bourekas* stand. Eccentric old people talk to themselves. I buy a phone card, go to the public phone. No answer. How come there's nobody in the room this early in the morning? Maybe they're off on a trek? And what'll I do if it's a long one, a few days? I catch a bus to Safed.

The debriefing only began at three o'clock in the afternoon. They had plenty of time at Northern Command. In the meantime I wasted a day sitting on the benches at the base, enjoying the view towards the Hula Valley and the neatly pressed desk jockeys running through the flowerbeds and lying on the grass to sunbathe and watch the girls. I didn't know a soul. A secretary caught sight of me, and came out with a newspaper. It was two days old, she said. I flipped through it. There was a gigantic photo of Number Two throwing himself on the grave at Ziv's funeral. And one of Ziv, from his army ID. And another of him with his girlfriend on holiday in Greece. She was a real beauty. There was an article that was supposed to be an investigation into the event, splashed over two pages, all of it total bullshit. So much crap was written in that newspaper that I was in pain, I swear; I could have murdered the reporter. I thought about Ziv's family: if they'd read it, and believed it, what would they think of us? It said we'd left him untreated for four hours. That we hadn't managed to get him back to the outpost, that he'd suffered in agony for hours until his soul finally expired. By the time he'd reached the outpost, the article said, it was too late. What would happen if River read this now? A disgrace. Every fifteen minutes or so I tried to call Lila. Her room was deserted. A little before one o'clock I settled down under a tree near the commander's office and dozed until a long row of army vehicles filled up the parking area and woke me up. The head honchos had arrived.

They all grabbed places around the conference table in the office: the brigadier general himself, the brigade commanders, the vice-brigade commanders, the regiment commander, the heads of the commando units. Northern Command Debriefing Number 105. Re: Detonation of Claymore Mine During Admiral Procedure. Operation in Sector: 91st Division, Hiram Territorial Brigade, Ali

Taher Mountain Range Battalion – Beaufort. Results: One IDF casualty. In turn, each man present explained why he bore no responsibility. The first said, 'I approved the procedure because I thought Hanan had spoken with Ehud.' Then Hanan said, 'I gave my approval because I understood that the commander of the bomb disposal unit had talked to someone.' That's the way it went, one after another. I couldn't keep up. I stood up and said I didn't understand what we were doing there, because if they wanted to point the finger at me then they should go ahead and do it and save everyone time. I mean, who could they really blame? The dog's nose? The tracker's eyes? The batteries in the scrambler? The brigadier general motioned to me to calm down. 'We're not looking to blame anyone. We just want to know what happened,' he said, trying to sound paternal. I answered that if that was the case then the right questions were not, in my opinion, being asked. Then, when I realized that it was stupid to argue with them, I shut my mouth. It was all too much, too big, for me. The brigadier general asked me to outline what had occurred. I told him in two sentences or less and fell silent again. I sat myself behind one of the officers and hid there. I'm just a nothing of a second lieutenant, I shouldn't even have been there at all. The brigade commander gave a summary of the main errors and failures and requested that a bomb-dismantling robot be used in future outpost operations. The officers from the Engineering Corps explained that robots couldn't manoeuvre in that mountainous area. And then the brigadier general summed up. 'Our basic assumption,' he said, 'is that explosive devices are going to continue to be our main threat. Some forty of them have been placed in the vicinity of our outposts recently. We must treat the entire length of the access road leading to Beaufort as an area under suspicion to be traversed only when there is no other option and only after the procedure for opening roads has been carried out, with a tracker and dog at the lead. Concurrently, our offensive assault activity in the Ali Taher mountain range sector is insufficient. We need to plan operations that will bring greater damage to the terrorist cells that are placing the explosive devices. The necessary manpower and battle equipment will be requisitioned according to need.'

The IDF never again carried out the Admiral Procedure in Lebanon. Ziv was its last casualty.

I got up and left, couldn't hold out to the end. At the gate of the base I hitched a ride down to Rosh Pina. There was soft music in the car and I looked out the window, motionless as if dozing, but inside I was in a kind of delirium, shaking, counting the seconds, barely breathing. I was trying to plan my time so that it wouldn't get away from me in the blink of an eye. I was afraid I'd find myself too quickly back inside a Safari crossing the border. I thought how I should visit Ziv's parents one evening, to tell them the truth about what had happened, so they wouldn't believe all those lies. I wanted to visit them, I swear. But I didn't. Mainly I was afraid. I was sure his family, his friends, would blame me. What would I tell his mother? That I had been the head of security on the operation? That mine was the last ugly face Ziv saw before he fell? That I was the last person to look at his face before we loaded the body into the helicopter? I didn't visit them. Not then and not on the first anniversary of his death. I read in the paper that his grandmother died ten days after he was killed. She'd refused to eat or drink. Said she didn't want to live in a country where grandmothers bury their grandchildren. Those were tough, sad words, but kind of clichéd. We've heard them so many times that we don't get too upset by them. And his mother told reporters that she'd begged him not to go into Lebanon again, and he would always answer, 'What do you want from me? You brought me up to think big, and not just about myself, didn't you?' That's what she said. It turned out that his parents had been active in the Four Mothers organization from the time it was established, and his older brother, who'd served years earlier in Lebanon, had started a protest movement of army reservists who served in combat units: 'Bring My Brother Back from Lebanon' they called themselves. That was even before he'd lost Ziv. I really did want to meet them, to explain. And every day I'd tell myself that I had to do it, but I never did. Never visited the family, never visited the grave.

When I got home that Tuesday after the debriefing, I told my parents about it. They were very calm, asked a few questions, took an interest, but only briefly. Twenty minutes later we sat down to eat, we went on with our lives. I decided not to tell Lila, or my friends, either. I preferred to forget.

By this time Bayliss, River and Zitlawi had already finished a long round of showers and huge meals at Bayliss's house in Nov. They put a couple of mattresses on the floor in Bayliss's cramped bedroom, sealed off the small porch window and tried to make themselves sleep. It took a while for them to realize it wasn't going to happen. Their bodies wouldn't let them waste the first few hours of their furlough, especially when they were together. Even after an exhausting night's journey without a minute of sleep they had too much energy. They sat in their boxer shorts and t-shirts on the front porch overlooking Menahem's horse ranch. It was fairly cool out, but there was a feeling of spring in the air that had to be enjoyed. Zitlawi tried to catch and mount a colt. He even fell a few times from the back of an old horse named Jehoshaphat. After that he lay in the hammock, challenging himself to get it to swing to new heights. Rivka, Bayliss's mother, poured them apple juice, served strawberry cake with whipped cream. His younger siblings brought a football and dragged River on to a makeshift playing field, where River wrestled with them in the sand. Bayliss, wearing the *kippa* he'd donned while they waited for his father to pick them up in Kiryat Shmona, pored over maps, trying to come up with a trek on a remote path for them to attempt the following morning. It was a calm and peaceful scene, until Zitlawi spotted a girl riding a bicycle on the lane leading from the synagogue, with long, straight, fair hair. Was it her? A few seconds later he'd jumped on to a small blue bicycle that belonged to one of the children and raced after her. He dashed off without saying a word.

It took a couple of minutes until River, who'd been busy playing football, guessed what was happening. He saw Hodaya, with a small knapsack on her back, disappearing behind a row of trees that lead out of the village. He felt a pain in his stomach, a fist, at seeing her, and seeing that arse chasing after her. It killed him. Bayliss caught sight of River staring at the spot where they'd vanished, while the children tried pulling him back to the game, and went over to him. 'Believe me, she is one fucked-up girl,' he said. It didn't help. 'Ignore Zitlawi, that maniac,' Bayliss told him. 'And ignore her, too. You've only laid eyes on her for two minutes. What's got into you?' When River failed to deny that something was up, Bayliss realized the situation was serious. Zitlawi, in the meantime, had nearly managed to catch up to Hodaya. By the Bajurya pool he left the road and turned on to a path that led to Rabbi Elifaz's abandoned cowshed, exactly where he'd seen her before. He whistled to her. She ignored him. When he caught up with her, rode alongside her, she turned her gaze to him for the first time and kept on riding. She was in fucking good shape, even he was starting to pant. 'You know, we haven't been in Israel since that last time you saw us,' he told her. She ignored him. 'We came back from Lebanon today. Will you allow me to apologize? I can explain the whole thing,' he said. She still hadn't said a word. She picked up the pace, as if she was trying to compete with him, prove herself. But to Zitlawi's surprise, she didn't seem frightened, not at all. At least that's what Zitlawi claimed. When they reached the field behind the cowshed she braked and got off her bicycle, took a large pad of white drawing paper, a pencil box containing crayons and a small blanket from her knapsack, while he stood watching her. From time to time he'd toss out a question, ask something about her without getting an answer, try to get her to co-operate. 'What's wrong? Are you mad?' he asked in the end, with the tone of someone who's lost patience. 'It really seems like you're mad.'

'You think so?' she answered. 'I just like quiet when I'm drawing. I didn't come out here to chat.'

'OK, I'll shut up,' he replied, happy that at least he'd got an answer. He was taken aback by her self-confidence. After all, she was only a girl of sixteen. Where did she learn to talk like that, he wondered. He smiled to himself.

She lay on the blanket, on her stomach, with the pad on the dirt in front of her. Zitlawi sat on a rock nearby, not daring to get too close. But he wasn't going to give up. He was enjoying the challenge too much. He could see a thick book and two sandwiches in a plastic bag peeking out of Hodaya's knapsack. She wasn't drawing. After fifteen minutes the page was still blank. All she did was scan the surrounding trees, and the distant cliff, and the bored cows, with slow glances. Sometimes she would turn over on to her back and gaze up at the clouds, mesmerized, then flip on to her stomach once again. Zitlawi, restless, searched desperately for some new way to get the conversation going. The lines he used in the clubs wouldn't help with this little girl. He couldn't call her by the pet names he used for the others, he'd never manage to break the ice that way. He couldn't even ask her why she wasn't drawing. It might offend her, he thought, make her even more distant. So he kept silent, waiting until he could find something to say or until she caved in first. When he told us about it afterwards he couldn't remember how long it had taken, but finally she spoke. 'Is that friend of yours all right?' she asked. 'Did he get over it?'

'Who? River?' Zitlawi answered. 'The guy you saw naked?'

She nodded. He shrugged it off, tried to explain that with them, the secular boys, it was no big deal getting caught naked. It meant nothing, he said, happened all the time, nobody even got embarrassed. She had nothing to worry about, River had forgotten all about it in a matter of hours, maybe even minutes. But they'd felt really bad about her, because they'd worried that she'd been traumatized by it. He said he was sure she'd been scared. If she were only secular, she'd understand how much fun it was to be so free, naked. But because she was a religious girl they'd been worried.

By this point, Zitlawi's prick was already in launch position – you can be sure of that – it was fucking with his mind and making him talk dirty. He calls it 'eight inches of steel wrapped in hot flesh'. He prayed for some response, just a tiny bit of encouragement from her. But she kept quiet. 'Tell the truth, Hodaya, don't you get the urge to go running naked in the fields here sometimes?' he asked her, crossing boundaries without flinching. 'It's so peaceful here, and private.' Did he really see a little smile play on her thin lips, or was this his warped imagination? There's no way of knowing. Still, she said nothing. His heart was bursting from the tension. In his mind she'd already taken off the thin, dark red sweater that was wrapped around her long, graceful neck. And her black skirt. She was standing there in front of him in her bra and knickers. He would have killed to know what kind of knickers she was wearing under her clothes. What kind of knickers did religious girls wear, anyway? 'Am I right?' he asked, still trying to lead her on. 'Boy, do you talk a lot of nonsense,' she answered. What? Nonsense? What are you talking about? He wanted to know which aspect of his nonsense she was referring to. He wouldn't let up. 'What do you mean, nonsense? Tell me.' She smiled – this time it was definitely a smile, absolutely – and turned on her back. He took a deep breath and then tossed a grenade. 'Should I prove it to you?' he asked. 'If you think I'm talking nonsense I'll just have to prove it to you.' He stood up and started undressing. He took off his white vest and threw it on to the rock. He checked to gauge her reaction, but the girl wasn't even looking in his direction. She was looking up at the sky. He felt cold. He took off his shorts, was left standing in a pair of red pants. 'It seems to me you need something to draw today,' he told her, his voice shaking a little. 'Draw me.' She rolled over on to her side, looked him over without embarrassment, her gaze direct. She didn't take her eyes off him, she was showing him how confident she was. She wanted to break him. And he stood staring at her, too. They waited to see who would lower their eyes first. Zitlawi drew in another breath and pulled his briefs clear in one go. 'Go on, draw me,' he said. 'I'll run through the fields if you tell me to.' She laughed. Really laughed. She had this sheepish gaze – at least that's the way Zitlawi described it – a sweet, innocent look, really cute. He claimed to have seen a twinkle deep down in her eyes. But she got up, gathered her belongings and mounted her bike. 'Get a life,' she told him, and rode off. He shouted after her – 'Hey, wait up!' – put on his underpants and his shorts, hung the shirt around his neck and set off after her on this child's bike. 'I was just trying to make you laugh,' he said. 'Talk to me.' She rode faster, and so did he. They sped along the deserted road, competing, cutting each other off, spinning in circles. She really had laughed, that little witch. Near the entrance to the village he ran into her – not too hard – and blocked her path. He said, 'Listen, sweetheart, it's not fair this way. Give me a chance. Just once. Come for a hike with me tomorrow, or the day after. I'll be a good boy.' She was so beautiful.

'You're staying with Menahem and Rivka?' she asked.

'Yes,' he replied.

'So we'll see each other,' she said, and she raced off into the village.

'Those were the purest moments of my life.' That is how Zitlawi, the arse, the pervert, described those few minutes. And every time he tells it he blushes, then he's quick to try to erase the romantic glow from his face and return to descriptions of his rising prick, in order to overcome his embarrassment. But on that day, when he returned to the house, he refused to tell them a word of what had happened. He sat in front of the computer and challenged Bayliss's little brothers to a car race, while River lay on the couch in the living room, gloomy and blank-faced, letting the television keep him occupied. Fatigue was a convincing excuse, which is why Zitlawi didn't sense that something was wrong. When Bayliss finished planning their trek and suggested the three of them drive out in the the ATV and watch the sunset over the Sea of Galilee, River declined. They tried to persuade him, but it was a lost cause.

He went upstairs; threw himself down on the mattress and tried to sleep. He could hear them revving the engine, having fun.

The sun was already orange. The ATV raced across the fields to a spot on the winding dirt road behind the southernmost homes of the Bnei Yehuda settlement. There, among the thistles on the cliff, you could see everything. Darkening red water, the hills. No drug in the world could compare with this serenity. Bayliss wondered whether to mention Hodaya, but decided against it. He didn't have the energy to get into a conversation like that. And mainly he just didn't want to know what had happened. They sat in silence, waiting for the sky to turn black, and then they returned to Nov, skipped dinner and went straight to bed. River heard them come in, but he kept his eyes shut. Zitlawi lay down on his mattress next to River's. They fell asleep together, each hoping that a good night's sleep would make the next day happier and more fun.

But sometime after midnight, the inconceivable happened, a moment that it seems will be for ever engraved in the annals of our company. River was the first to wake up at the sound of someone climbing up the drainpipe, and when the porch door opened the other two opened their eyes. Zitlawi, who was closest to the door, immediately recognized Hodaya inside a blue parka, and he jumped up to greet her. She looked into the room and whispered, 'I came,' with a pleased smile, glowing from the courage she'd mustered. He placed a finger over her mouth to keep her quiet. 'The boys are sleeping,' he said, and then he walked outside and pulled her after him. They closed the glass door. Hodaya leaned against a low stone railing. Bayliss turned his back to them at once, stayed all night with his face to the wall. River, on the other hand, insisted on torturing himself and watched them bleary-eyed in the dark. 'Don't think I'm just a little girl,' Hodaya said. 'I'm not shy, either.' Really, that's exactly what she said. The others heard her, there are witnesses. If River hadn't been there, if Bayliss hadn't been there, none of us would have believed Zitlawi. She opened her parka, then took it off, threw it to the ground. She stood facing him in a white sweatshirt and green skirt. He watched her as if he was dreaming, didn't react. Next she removed her skirt and dropped it to her feet, and in seconds she had removed her tights, too. She was left wearing only a pair of soft, tight, white underpants and a sweatshirt on the back porch of the house, which, luckily, faced a small grove of trees and not the neighbours' houses, although the two of them could still be seen by anyone walking along the path below. A lot of rabbis walked this way, she was taking a huge risk. Hodaya seemed to be waiting for Zitlawi to give her the signal to keep stripping, but he wasn't capable of batting an eyelid. He couldn't even blink. It's strange he didn't hug her, didn't grab her arse, didn't shove his hands under her top. The man was in shock. When she took the initiative and began removing her sweatshirt, he understood that the girl had no limits – she was crazed, a nymphomaniac – so he opened the door and pushed her inside, into the room. What else could he do? She sat down on his mattress and in seconds was wearing nothing but a thin white t-shirt, no bra. She had perfect breasts – everyone agrees on that – and that night they were hot and erect. Zitlawi, totally in shock now, struggled with what to do next, which is to say, how to deal with the fact that two other men were stuck there in the room with him pretending to sleep. He lay on his back, exhausted, confused, and hoping she would embrace him. She drew close, took hold of his underpants and pulled them right off, stripped him, not a bit shy. What a lunatic this girl was! Then she lay down next to him, shivering with cold, or excitement, and covered herself. They began to kiss, Zitlawi stuck his tongue as far in as it would go. He held her breasts through her t-shirt, mashed them. River watched. He heard the tiny sighs, the stifled giggles. For a second Hodaya's white backside flashed in front of his eyes with Zitlawi's large paw clasping it. He saw her – quivering, drugged. Her soft hair was wild, her sweet lips calling out, thirsty for as much contact as possible, biting Zitlawi's nipples, her hands kneading his arms, his face. And his hands, under the blanket, gripping her small, round arse. God, what was going on there?

This girl was mad for him, that much was clear. And above them, on the shelf, three volumes of holy writings by Rabbi Kook shone in the moonbeams filtering in from outside.

Early in the morning River took off. He caught a bus home, passed up on the trek.

10

That same evening I had a fight with Lila. She told me about a friend of hers, an army social worker, who had a boyfriend who was wounded while fighting with a Nahal army youth unit in Lebanon. He'd stepped on a landmine and lost a foot and his left eye. She stayed with him, held out for six months, but in private she would tell Lila how hard it was for her. 'I just want to go out and have a good time, but I can't,' she'd say. 'If he came with me, what exactly would he do? Watch from the side? He used to love dancing but now he's too embarrassed. And it kills him when I dance, you can see by his body language how hard it is for him.' Like an idiot, Lila asked her how their sex life was since the accident. Her friend told her it was non-existent. It had been six months since they'd done it. 'There have been a few kisses,' she said, 'but no heavy stuff.' Could you blame her? Of course not. It put her off, it was scary. The poor fellow probably looks like a monster: he's missing an eye, walks around with a black eye-patch. When he's at home and isn't feeling ashamed he takes off the patch and goes around with a glass eye. She admitted that he didn't really attract her any more. Then one day, after half a year, the guy tells her – on his own initiative – that they'd better split up. She pretended to be sad about it, told him that she'd be happy if they stayed together, but she didn't really insist. Everybody knew that she wanted to breathe, to get away. She wanted someone to go to the beach with, not a cripple. She wanted to walk down the street with her nose in the clouds thinking that everyone's talking about her and the stud she'd caught, the hunk, the male model. She was sick and tired of feeling embarrassed, sick and tired of that whole long period of crying and troubles. She wanted to muck around, be happy, smile. Smell a new body. She wanted someone to tear her to pieces so that she'd enjoy it. Lila told me the story and I said, 'That guy comes out of this a real man, a total stud. It's clear the bitch wouldn't have stayed with him in the long run, he beat her to it.' Lila was really pissed off. 'I would stay with you,' she said. 'No you wouldn't,' I told her. 'You all pack up and leave.' In the history of our company, in all of the neighbouring outposts, in every story of wounded soldiers I'd ever heard, the girlfriend always leaves, sooner or later. 'You would too,' I told her. 'No doubt about it. But don't worry, I've already thought about it, and if it happens to me I'm bailing out. I'd jump out of the rescue helicopter on the way to the hospital, or maybe shoot myself. No question.' She started to cry, then she screamed that I was being childish and stupid and that the army had messed with my head. We had a serious fight. That night we didn't even sleep together.

Lila had gone to the secondary school for nerds. I'd gone to the one for losers. A well-to-do girl and a boy from the slums, that was us. At school I had long, straight hair and a baby face and I was up to no good and went around with different girls and hit all the parties and barely even pissed in her direction. I guess that's why, when she was thirteen, she decided I'd be her husband. The first year we were on and off, the second we were together, fucking with each other's minds but not actually doing the deed. In the third year we kissed for the first time, at night we'd run off and mess around in the woods near her house, or in her mother's VW Beetle, or on the roof terrace of her grandmother's cottage. In the fourth year she would sit on her little bed, half nude, and play the guitar for me while I drooled. We slept together. Any time she wanted to set me on fire she'd play the guitar like that in her underpants. I would pounce on her, sniff her scent. Everyone's got a scent, and hers I like best. It's a matter of taste. If I don't like a girl's scent it doesn't mean she smells bad, it only means she's not for me. And if I love it so much that sometimes I go mad when I'm alone, can't concentrate on anything but trying to recapture that scent, it means that she's the girl most right for me in the whole world. Lila graduated with honours, while I didn't even sit my matric exams. Her father would say, 'The game's up. Another man doesn't stand a chance, Lila. Listen to what I'm telling you, I see how you look at him and I know it's for life.' That's what he said from the first day, and she would deny it, but she always knew he was right. And in the fifth year, for the first time, I put my head on hers instead of hers on mine. That said it all: that for me, too, it was life. I would come back from the army and curl up with her, spend whole days spooning with her, wrap myself around her, trying to maximize the contact between our two bodies. We would fall asleep at night embracing and I would think that it was impossible that I'd become that kind of man, the kind who keeps on holding his girlfriend rather than heading off to his own side of the bed, where it was peaceful, about six seconds after the loving was over and she closed her eyes. I wasn't shy around her, either, almost never. I said nearly everything that came into my mind without hesitation.

On Thursday, a week after Ziv was killed, Lila came back from lunch at her parents' house and opened the door to my room. I was still sleeping. Bitter, who was hiding between my legs, jumped on her, yelping, and licked her face from every angle and direction. The two of them sat next to me on the bed and Lila took hold of my hand. I woke up and told her I was breaking up with her. Just like that. Boom. I was totally dazed, my brain was working slowly, my eyes were half shut, but I knew what I was doing. There was no turning back. I took one look at her and I knew it was over. I sat up, stroked her cheek for a second, gave her a quick kiss and went to have a shower. She didn't cry, which was strange. She didn't shout at me. When I came out of the bathroom she was gone. Maybe I'd hurt her too much, or maybe she just remembered that I'm too much of a dumb fuck for her, finally realized she'd been running around with a jerk, a boring arsehole with no future. Why should she care? Well if that was it, then she could go fuck herself because there was no place for her in my life. I needed to concentrate on carrying out my job without the burden of a girl-friend. She was so preoccupied with totally unimportant things. She could spend ages trying to pick out the colours of sheets and blankets, or where to hang pictures. She'd organize her winter and summer clothes and expect me to give my opinion on pairs of socks that she didn't like any more, or on desserts in the fridge – which were good, which were fattening – or she'd spend hours telling me all about the plot of some television programme. And about her friends, how she was angry with one of them. What a lot of thought she put into being angry! But I was sick of being a part of her petty thoughts about the simple life. In another place, at that very second, someone was torturing himself with a life or death deci-sion. She would laugh, all happy with that bullshit, wouldn't lay off when I needed to be alone sometimes. She didn't understand that I had to be. But how could she? How could she reach out and talk to me in my own language when she wasn't up there at Beaufort, couldn't know how it felt? From the window of my room I could see her walking away – slowly, without looking back. Maybe this would be my last glimpse of her for the rest of my life, or maybe it was only for a while – who knew? She probably didn't understand why I'd done it, thought that I was a complete arsehole. But what choice did I have?

On Saturday night we got ready to return to Beaufort. We gath-ered at the meeting point – training grounds near Kiryat Shmona – where we carried out a counter-ambush exercise. Forty minutes before we were due to set out we got a message from Command cancelling the convoy. We were told there were red alerts from Intelligence. 'We're setting out tomorrow,' I told the squad. 'In the meantime we'll take over a few rooms at the Soldiers' Hotel. Anyone who wants to visit wounded soldiers at Rambam Hospital in Haifa is welcome to.' A lot of soldiers did, and so did I.

Almost every time we went into or out of Lebanon we'd spend some time at the Soldiers' Hotel. It's an old building, six beds or more to a room with thin and tattered green and white sheets like a hospital, but to us it was a five star hotel. Sometimes we managed to get our girlfriends up there and they'd lie in our arms and sleep with us. Other times we'd just watch cable TV and take hot showers that lasted an hour or two. That was part of the experience: to sit nursing a cappuccino in the lobby, where there were shelves of stained and faded donated books, an old television facing the long army benches, a small pool table and metal armchairs with thin foam cushions. We could sprawl out, relax, or shoot the breeze on the beds in our underwear or naked, no flak jackets or boots, without worrying about coming under attack. When we got there that evening, I sent the boys to bed and Oshri and I sat down over a couple of pints of beer and a bucket of black coffee in a makeshift pub sponsored by the servicemen's welfare association in the basement of the hotel. We sat alone in a corner, trying to take it all in: we only had six days left together. This was our last stay together at the Soldiers' Hotel, the last convoy into Lebanon, the first day of our last week. And then that would be it. On Saturday night he'd catch a lift home and plunge into his discharge furlough, while I'd continue with routine, barely able to pick up the phone and talk to him. Soon he'd have a completely different life. New friends. How would I manage? He was the silent king of the company, that Oshri, the number one administrator: he knew better than anyone how to get his hands on food, petrol, clothing, ammunition. The number one fighter, too: reserved, patient, fearless. A real man. And of course, my number one friend: modest, concerned about everyone being happy, never thinking about his own needs. Someone unique. When he asked, 'What's up?' it wasn't just any old 'What's up?' with a fake smile like everyone else. It was a true

'What's up?' As in, 'Tell me what's happening with you, brother, I really want to know.' Oshri's skin is super dark and his heart is hot as fire. I'm crazy about him, love him to pieces. So we toasted each other '*L'haim*,' and shared some company gossip and I brought him up to date on the crisis with Lila. He was pissed off with me. 'You'll regret it your whole life,' he said. I couldn't believe how angry he was. 'You are one mad arsehole. She's the only person who can make something out of you. You think you're going to spend your whole life in the army, in this stinking mud hole? What are you going to do without her, when it's all over up here? You're a jerk. That's what you are.'

'I can't think about that right now. Who am I, you? Off to fuck girls in South America two days from now? I'm stuck here in the mud, and that's that. Nothing I can do about it.'

'Aren't you afraid,' he asked, 'of being on your own? If your arm gets blown off you'll never find anybody to fall in love with you and look after you. You'll die all by yourself, a disgusting, miserable old man. Aren't you afraid of being alone?'

What? Where did that come from? Fucking unbelievable! God must have put him up to it. I mean, only two days earlier Lila and I had argued about this very thing and now suddenly, out of nowhere, he hits me with this question, looks at me so strangely. How could this happen?

But the truth is, this wasn't new. A long time earlier, we'd agreed, Oshri and me, that losing a limb was worse than anything, worse than death. We weren't the only ones who thought that way, either. All the boys in the brigade said so, it's a known fact. When you lose a limb no girl will want you any more. And you can't play football any more, or swim. No treks. You're going to get bumped around your whole life, so it's better to die, no doubt about it. When I finished officers' academy I said to Oshri, 'If I get blown up and lose a part of my body just shoot me. Kill me on the spot.' He asked if I was sure about it, and I answered that I was. I made him swear he'd do it. When you die, I explained to him, you have maybe two or three seconds of pain and then you lose consciousness and you're in the world to come. The people who die don't go through long-term suffering. On the other hand, when you lose a limb you're assured of life-long misery. Decades of it. Oshri thought for a few minutes and told me I was right and suggested we should promise the same for each other, that if one of us lost a part of his body the other would finish him off, fire a bullet into him. Ever since then, each time before we went into Lebanon, we would promise each other again and swear an oath. And that night, too, on the eve of his discharge, I demanded he do it again. I didn't care if he had to come from the other side of the world to do it, I wanted him to grab a weapon, sneak into my hospital room without leaving tracks or traces and do the job. He swore to it and then we went to bed.

Before I fell asleep I thought about how lonely I'd be in another week when Oshri turned into a regular citizen and forgot it all. I also thought about that soldier from the Nahal unit who doesn't have a clue how to find another girlfriend. Best he could do would be a girl in a wheelchair. Or worse. Probably better off not finding anyone. And why didn't I feel anything when I thought about Lila? Only a big relief.

The next day we entered Lebanon.

Oshri's farewell party was scheduled for Wednesday. That's part of the ritual when a member of the senior staff leaves: you take his soldiers out for a morning of fun in the ancient fortress that sits next to our outpost. The Arabs call it *Qalaat A-Shakif*. It stands three storeys high, and there are seven storeys or more built down into the hill. Legend has it that the fortress reaches all the way down to the Litani River, to the place where they would draw water, like as endless underground bunker. But we stop two floors below ground level, because rumour has it that the fortress was booby-trapped by terrorists, Palestinians, during the time of the Lebanese War eighteen years earlier. No point in taking chances.

We leave our secure area, climb the rusty metal ladder at the back of the outpost, step over the ruins of the outer stone wall and find ourselves in the courtyard of the fortress. Thistles reach as high as your chest and scratch the shit out of you. We squeeze through the narrow opening one by one, sucked inside. We crawl through tunnels, descend ropes, cram into a dark and narrow stairwell and come out into a wide hall that looks like a place where kings might have paced back and forth at night when they couldn't sleep. What an empire they created here: suddenly huge arched windows come into sight and long, tall firing slits through which narrow sunbeams shine. Whoever planned the lighting for this place was a genius. If you look through the windows you catch sight of the clear water flowing down below, at an angle you can't see from anywhere else on the hill. Trees with thick, green crowns hang over into the water, where there are dark, slippery stones. This is one of my favourite places, somewhere you can see how everything was, once: back as far as the time of the Bible and the Middle Ages and the world wars and the Lebanese civil war. No matter when you were to pass through here – on a caravan of elephants, on a camel, in a French tank or in a parachute, dropped from the sky by a warplane – no surprise would greet you. Everything's as it was. Same view. The only change is the flag – blue and white for the moment.

But now it's time for the Argentine video camera.

Is that thing filming, brother? Come on, push the button! Pay attention, folks, this is Zitlawi, your presenter. Good morning, brothers. Beautiful, eh? The most romantic place in the country. We're here like tourists. Like tourists. That man – what's his name? – the one who does those travel shows all around the world – he'd kill to be here, yeah? But he can't. Not allowed. Too bad six million Israelis can't make it up here. On second thoughts, maybe it's not too bad. They don't deserve it. Let them keep on drinking cappuccinos with whipped cream. Now to the point: Erez, fucking hell, buddy, they've got to get some girls up here to us fast. Even Lebanese girls, I don't care. Sixteen years old. Tell me the truth, you'd go for it, wouldn't you? Of course you would. This place makes me really turned on. It's the perfect place for asking a girl to marry you, believe me. River, man, you bring a girl up here at sunset, and whoa! You can already start ordering the catering. What is that? What did you find over there? Holy shit, something really fine: an indoor garden. Look at this, look at the defence system they built themselves. These firing slits are much more sophisticated than anything we've got. I'm going to blow this guy away! *Ratatat, ratatat*! And what about these huge rocks? How'd they get them up here a thousand years ago, can you tell me that? I'm starting to get tired, I'm not bullshitting you, they've got so many fucking rooms. Emilio, baby, why don't you trip and fall and we'll get on *Candid Camera* and you'll win a car for sure. Hey, look at this. You filming? These must be their torture chambers. What do you think, Bayliss? Look at the graffiti. Terrorists. Wonder what it says. They've destroyed the walls. Let's put our names up there, too. What do you say? The Ugly Israeli, the Ugly Arab, it's all the same. Come on you fat fuck, Itamar, get a move on, we're trying to move forward here. What are you waiting for, someone to massage your arse? Move! Bloody hell, it must have been a fucking nightmare to conquer this place. I can't even imagine it. All the shit we've been through up here in Lebanon has been worth it, just to get into this place. See the sheep down in the field? Man, wouldn't you like to ride the shit out of one of those babies? A flying sheep, now why haven't they invented one of those yet? You know, this spot is perfect for tossing people out. Yeah, like that, from this window. Just pitch them out. Go on, throw me out. I'd really like it. Come on, let's go down another level. It's like Rome. So what if I've never been to Rome?

We ran around the passageways for a while and then made our way back down to the main hall. There was an indoor swimming pool, about a fourth of an Olympic-sized pool, empty, with carved stone pillars surrounding it. Zitlawi pulled out the gas burner and the lemon-flavoured wafers. Oshri lit a small fire and I skewered marshmallows on sticks for roasting. We brought out the cigarettes – even for the boys who don't smoke, it's part of the ritual. We threw our uniforms off to the side, lay naked in the sand. And we were silent. It's not every day you see the boys all quiet, but in that cold, mouldy, compressed air there was something stronger than all of us, something that made us feel strange, wore us out, made each of us focus on himself, speak in whispers, be quiet. We laid our heads on our flak jackets and helmets, we sank into the dreamy atmosphere. We were safe there, no terrorist would blow up the fortress. And if they did, they couldn't hit us way down deep inside. Maybe we were allowed to be there, maybe not – probably not, we hadn't checked the rulebooks – but it was tradition, and company tradition is more important than all those commands that change constantly. This was the way we took leave of a friend, with honour. I sat next to River. 'What's wrong?' I asked him. 'Why the long face?' But he brushed me off. 'Nothing,' he whispered. 'Liar,' I said. He looked so sad. He tried hard to change the subject, to find something to talk about, but our brains work slowly underground. 'The minute there's peace with Lebanon I'm coming up here to do some rock-climbing,' he said. 'Right from the bottom, from the wadi, up the steepest part of the hill, stone by stone, up to the cliff. I'm dying to do it.' Then he pretended to fall asleep, turned his back to me. The others drowsed, too. I lit a cigarette. Lila would kill me if she saw me smoking, she doesn't allow it, worries. She keeps me on a short leash. Then again, she doesn't any more. Another half a year until the new millennium, I thought. That big, round number. Weird. When it happens, on the first day of January in the year 2000, at zero-zero hours and zero-zero minutes, when the dials all go to zero at the zero-second, we may still be up here on the hill. What kind of a moment will that be? Quiet and regular, like now? Disappointing?

Just a moment like any other? Will we lie there in the submarine munching, say, sunflower seeds and pistachios, and looking at our watches? Or maybe it will be one of those unforgettable moments. We'll go crazy, throw a party the likes of which Lebanon has never seen before. Or maybe Hezbollah will decide to shake up the world at that very moment, zero hour, and light the skies up with orange? They can do it if they want to, and maybe if they do we'll run and hide like mice with our mouths hanging open, in shock, until we get our act together and fire back at them. Maybe it will be a real war, maybe even a world war if someone wants it, the kind that starts at zero hour. We'll have to be sober that night. And in another 700 years or so someone is going to stand here and ask, imagining, who was here right at the start of the new millennium, at that historic moment? They'll be thinking about us. Or not. Maybe I'll be on a furlough at the start of the new millennium, who knows? I'll hook up with Lila again, maybe, and we'll go to Tel Aviv. In the biggest square, hundreds of thousands of people will count backwards, watching huge screens and they'll kiss and the skies will be filled with colour by all the fireworks. Maybe. I'm not sure where I'd rather be on the first of January. With all the doomsday prophesies, the disasters people are predicting, and God making a big comeback, and legends and mysticism and miracle workers, tension will be high. I mean, our curiosity – even if in the end nothing happens and if we all believe nothing's going to happen – our curiosity is what will get us. If I could hug Lila and keep her safe, but spend that night with Oshri and everybody here, that would be the best. Not with the city jerks, the slick crowd, the ones stinking of pollution and asphalt, that bunch of fucking sheep, the atheist pacifists who look down their noses at anyone who doesn't worship their perverted sex and drugs and art. I'd rather be here, these biblical moments suit me best. When my grandchildren ask me, 'Where were you, Grandpa, at that moment?' I'll have a good answer for them: 'At war,' I'll say. 'At war.' The new millennium is almost here. Billions of people have been imagining it: spaceships, star wars, robots. But I'll be hiding out in a crusader fortress. How weird.

I fell asleep.

Rare footage. Our squad commander is sleeping like a puppy. Hey man, that thing's running, right? Look, Lana sweetheart, don't let the guy's dwarf-like height throw you off, we're talking about a well-oiled war machine here. He's a Rottweiler with the balls of a hippopotamus. The most gung-ho soldier in the Israeli army. He knows what he's doing, he knows what he's fighting for, he's as cool as a lemon ice lolly. You can count on him to shoot first. And here's River, our little mascot. Tell us, River, you little monkey, what haven't you managed to do yet in life? Yes, Lana's dying to hear, brother. Imagine that you get wasted up here: what would be the thing you'd most regret having missed, the thing you'd wish you'd had a chance to do? In that last moment before you pop off to heaven, or hell, what have you got to do? I'm asking you for real. What's with this 'Don't want to talk about death' business? Cut the bullshit, we're family. Toss something out, everyone's got something. Me, for example. I've never seen Tzvika Pick sing in Caesarea, something I've wanted to do for a long time. I know, it's pretty easy to make me happy, isn't it? Another thing: I've never killed anybody. Yet. What? What are you all looking at me like that for? I'm talking about a terrorist. Come on, River, your turn. Good. Yes. You haven't screwed a Brazilian girl yet. Excellent answer. Here's a tip from your big brother, Zitlawi: there's one on Ben Yehuda Street in Tel Aviv. Chez Jasmine. Know the place? What? What do you mean that doesn't cut it? It's got to be at Carnival? OK, I understand. Oh yeah, and you wouldn't mind trouncing your older brother at tennis, either. We'll try and set something up for you. Bayliss, what about you? Shoot. Really? You've never been overseas? That's a real fuck-up. Next. Spitzer. Spitz. How about you, my friend? Here, brother, talk into the microphone. It's your girlfriend we're talking to, not mine. Give her some drama, don't be afraid to show off a little, we all love you here, you little sweetie. Make it something from your heart, that's the best. What? You've never really made your parents proud? Come on, man, I'm going to puke in a minute. What's got into you?

And here's Oshri, our sergeant, the hero. The one who's leaving us. Say goodbye to him. Say something nice about modesty. You'll never get a word out of this quiet guy. He's real introvert. Notice how he's always got this peaceful expression on his face. Mister Cool. And, dark as he is, he's got the taste of an Ashkenazi, listens to worn out recordings of Israeli classics all day long on his Walkman. Teaches horseback riding, too, at this ranch for rich girls. I'll bet you didn't pick up on that at first glance, did you? He'll arrange some riding lessons for you if you want. But when there are no girls around and he isn't feeling shy, then the wild man inside him comes out, the vampire, the kind who picks fights for kicks – friendly fights, for fun, and he beats the shit out of all our sorry arses. He head-butts you, bites you, bear-hugs you. Loves a good fight, that's his favourite thing. Tell me, sergeant, sir, what made you join an infantry unit? What? What do you mean, the induction officer? You mean they just sent you here? You're supposed to say that you had a role model, some bloke from the neighbourhood, older than you, someone you looked up to who was killed in an accident, and his death gave you the drive for revenge, or that your father was a commander and he brought you up to believe in continuity and excellence and the pioneering spirit and Zionism. What? No? How could that be? So why'd you stay on? You've been here so long.

A heavy fog descended on the hill without warning. Zero visibility. I remember Oshri waking me up, suggesting we get out of there and back into the secure area fast. A thick white cloud surrounded the fortress, and then the fog started to come inside through the firing slits in waves. It's not a good idea to walk around outside in weather like that. Terrorists love it, they come out of their holes and move around under the cover of the fog. The loudspeakers were already warning against potential incoming launches while we were climbing up to the exit. Up there, on the highest point of the whole mountain range, the sky was clear and blue. We looked down, to the ring of clouds that seemed like a white ocean flowing to the horizon, a heavy mass of cloud that only we and the ruined fortress were floating above. In the midst of all that euphoria, that pastoral landscape, our ears were already attuned to the sound of the first shots that would be fired. We had no choice but to get down inside the cloud to the outpost. We felt our way to the ladder, dived down. I was first, Oshri was last, and the boys were in the middle. Like blind men we felt our way.

The first explosion hit just as my feet touched ground. It was a mortar shell. Seconds later there was another one. The loud-speakers hadn't announced launches, the sirens weren't wailing. The bombs just fell. Boom, then silence. I shouted, 'Move it!' and the boys sped up, came down one after the other and ran like hell, disappearing into the white whirlpool as they tried to find their way to the buildings. I stood next to the ladder, catching them as they hit the ground and pushing them in the right direction. Until I got hold of Oshri. 'It's me, that's it,' he said. 'Last one.' I grabbed his hand and we started running together. We couldn't see a thing. Another hit, right on the outpost. Another, the closest yet. A yellow flash and then thick grey smoke. I lost Oshri's hand for a minute, then a second later I heard him screaming. But I couldn't see him. I went looking, started shouting 'Where are you?' I could hear his voice but I didn't know where he was. It didn't make any sense – he was a few feet away from me, no more than that. 'Oshri! Talk to me!' Then I heard him moaning, saw him running in the opposite direction. I could tell he didn't know what to do, that he was confused. 'Where are you going?' I shouted. 'Oshri, talk to me. You're going the wrong way!' I kept shouting. A strong arm took hold of me. It was Furman.

'Get inside,' he hollered, pulling me in. 'Not without Oshri,' I said. He pulled me in hard, shoved me. 'Settle down, we're bringing him in, too,' he said.

Even inside we were in a kind of fog. The boys were standing around, we were all waiting. River dashed in covered in blood – Oshri's blood. He was pulling him by his left arm, dragging him inside. 'Wounded soldier, I've got a wounded soldier!' he shouted. The smell of gunpowder trailed in after them. Oshri was conscious but completely dazed. And his arm was shredded. It was totally shredded. He was holding it tight. He'd taken a direct hit from a big piece of shrapnel and his right arm had been sliced, one of his bones was fractured and hanging out. Another piece of shrapnel had hit his leg and he was limping. He stood facing me and began to cry. He came close to me, his arm had been ripped out of place, mangled. He looked me in the eye and shouted, 'Help me! Help me!' I froze. 'Help me, Erez!' he pleaded. He stood in front of me, terrified, waiting, but I had frozen. I didn't do anything. I wasn't functioning. We'd talked about what we'd do in this situation so many times, but I just stood there while time passed and kept on moving. 'What do you want me to do?' I asked, like I was angry with him; that's the way it came out. 'There's nothing I can do.' I stood there looking at him, powerless, and then I lowered my gaze. I couldn't understand why he wasn't running to someone else for help, but then his legs gave way and he dropped to a sitting position. River tried laying him out flat but he put up a fight. Why fight? And then he passed out. Everyone just stood there watching. Dave stood at the door to make sure nobody lost it and ran outside to get hit. It happens. Furman went back outside to make sure there were no other wounded out there. Why? Why did I freeze up?

It wasn't some penny that dropped all of a sudden, it was a blinding explosion in my brain. That's when I started to cry, too. Without meaning to. It was the first time I had cried. When Ziv got hit I didn't cry. And Ziv's injuries were fatal, he was stone dead. Oshri was lying there on the cold floor. When I pulled myself together I held him for a while in my arms, I tried pushing his flesh back inside so it wouldn't spill out, but I didn't really know what I was doing. I felt like it was eating me up, I was crashing, all my limbs were collapsing, and under my skin there was nothing but tiny slivers of glass. What skin, what am I talking about? I didn't have any skin, I was suddenly just a big bundle of exposed nerves without a bit of skin for cover, burned up and burning with every touch and every word. I was in pain, horrified, everything was sharp, knocking me off my feet. My muscles were constricting, I was having trouble breathing, trying to draw air into my lungs, as much air as possible, but I couldn't breathe. And I felt so embarrassed. Then the doctor showed up with his equipment and started setting the arm, gave Oshri morphine. Pressure dressings to stop the bleeding, an infusion, all that stuff – he didn't feel a thing. The morphine was flowing through his blood, and he woke and shouted, 'Erez, come here!' He didn't notice that I was already right there next to him, sitting by the stretcher. 'Light a Marlboro for me,' he said. We stared at him, stunned. Did he know what had happened to him? Didn't he understand? Maybe they'd drugged him too much. It didn't make sense for him to be talking like that. I asked the doctor what was going on and he told me, 'Keep him busy, that's good, we don't want him to lose consciousness again.'

'Light a Marlboro for me,' Oshri said again.

'Forget about cigarettes for the time being, it's not good for you,' I told him.

'Why, what's going on? Did I give up smoking?' he asked, his eyes closed.

I didn't know what to say, what to talk about.

'Hang on,' Zitlawi said, jumping in from the side, 'you nicked my lighter, didn't you, Oshri?' Oshri said yes and stuck his left hand into the pocket of his trousers and pulled out Zitlawi's lighter. It was scary. 'Keep him busy!' the doctor ordered us, agitated now.

But how? River noticed that the patch had fallen off his mutilated right arm and his tattoo was exposed for the first time. 'Hey, look,' he said. 'You got rid of the tattoo, and without having a painful operation.' He looked at Zitlawi. If Zitlawi couldn't talk, who could? 'I met a girl once who had a tattoo of a mouse running away from her arse,' he said, feeling his way. 'Yup, it's true. And another one with a tattoo of a hand holding her tits. I even heard about some chick that had the name of her boyfriend tattooed on her pussy. I swear it. And then they broke up.'

We strapped Oshri on to the stretcher. I stepped aside because I'd started crying again. Everyone was staring at me, as much as they were staring at the mangled arm and the pool of blood. Oshri looked dazed, but he kept talking. 'What are you crying for?' he asked me. 'What? Am I dead or something?' There was a long silence. Then the rescue team landed and loaded him into the helicopter. 'That's it, Lebanon's all over for me,' Oshri said, and we were separated. He took off. I didn't put a bullet in his head, he didn't jump off the helicopter.

What a world this is. Just a week earlier, on our furlough, we'd gone together to Rambam Hospital in Haifa to visit Gulo, a sniper from the Dlaat outpost. In the middle of a battle he was hit by friendly fire, a bullet fired at close range from a Negev light machine-gun. The soldier who hit him was apparently shooting too wide. It happens. It was a real mess – fire, grenades. While we were at the hospital Oshri came out with something really weird. He said, 'Don't worry, pretty soon I'll be joining you. I'll be lying right there in the bed next to you.' And now, a week later, there he'd be – maybe lying in the next bed. How could it be? Yeah, I know, I don't believe it either when someone tries to sell me tales about weird fate and tragic coincidences. Like the soldier who tells his mother which song he wants played at his funeral, and then the next day he gets killed. Or the mother who jumps out of bed in the middle of the night, certain that something terrible has happened. It comes to her through a nightmare or a premonition.

She goes out on to the porch to wait for the car bringing army personnel who will deliver the news. And they come. What are the chances? Almost nil. Or the friend who talks to you about his fear of losing an arm and then loses it four days later. Believe it, brother, believe it. I swear it. If that had been part of a movie I wouldn't have accepted the string of coincidences either. But that's reality. I swear it on my mother's life.

Even today, when I'm alone, I can sometimes picture Oshri coming through the door in slow motion. His arm is hanging there, behind him everything's smoke, and he's screaming, 'Help me!' They lie him out on the floor, trying to reattach the severed arm, there's blood everywhere. All in slow motion. I close my eyes and I can see him. When people talk to me about 'Cursed Lebanon' that's the picture that comes to mind, those are the horrors. Me pushing his flesh back inside like he's a wounded animal, trying not to lose any pieces, the doctor applying a stomach bandage and River a sterilized field dressing, the helicopter arriving . . . that's Lebanon, you're totally smeared with blood and the soldier lying there is your best friend. So why is it that you don't stop for a minute to reflect? And what about that last Saturday night we spent together before going back into Lebanon – I see that, too, when I close my eyes. To this very day. We travelled from his village, Arugot, down to the Besor district, to the huge reservoir between Re'im and Be'eri. There in the darkness, on the edge of the water, we made plans, eating ripe bananas and mandarin oranges. We promised ourselves we'd be the best commanders Beaufort had ever seen. We decided to make it through alive, in one piece. We swore it. We'd go in and out of Lebanon this last time without a scratch – not on us, not on the boys. We swore it. And when you take an oath on something, we thought, there's no chance God will let it get messed up.

I swear on my mother's life that every word of this story is true.

11

Depressing letters always begin with 'Dear Sweetie,' which is usually followed by a line or two from some song by Shlomo Artzi. And then the real stuff pours out.

Dear Sweetie, how are you? *These days are full of rage, that's what they say. These days are of an age* . . . How am I? I don't know who to rage at first: you, my parents, my commanders, the soldiers. God, for putting me in this shitty situation. Most of all, myself. In my darkest moments I feel as though I don't even have any anger left, and that makes me even sadder.

This isn't just another letter about how much I miss you, this time it's bottom-of-the-barrel stuff, total demoralization. Read it and try to understand. Just try. I've had it. I know that's a stupid statement to make these days, so banal and unoriginal, but I swear it: I've had it. I don't know what to do with myself. Oshri's been my friend for three years, the best friend a man can have. For three years we've been dealing with all kinds of bullshit, asking each other for help with dumb things. Simple stuff, like carrying a jerrycan from one place to another. I always lent a hand, I was careful to be the perfect friend, the best there is. That's what I know how to do – be a friend – I'm really good at that. But then, when the moment of truth arrived, when he came running in with his arm hanging in the air, shouting and crying, 'Help me, Erez!' – when he really and truly needed me, that's when I didn't help him. I stood there like some pencil-pushing arse-hole. I saw how much he needed me and I froze. It's not that I didn't know where to apply pressure, how to take care of his injury. I did. I've done tons of training, so that should have come naturally, without me even thinking. But I just stood there, paralysed. Why? If someone else hadn't taken charge Oshri might not even be with us any more, he might have lost too much blood and wasted on us. 'Wasted,' sweetie, that's our way of saying 'died'.

Something held me back, and I didn't even have the balls to say to myself, 'You loser! Why aren't you helping?' Maybe I didn't want it enough. No, that's not it. I know the reason. I was scared shitless. He didn't deserve that, Oshri. He didn't deserve for me to be scared shitless. I shouldn't even be saying these things, shouldn't even be thinking them. I can't allow myself to be afraid, or soft, or overly sensitive. This is a cruel place and you've got to be tough. And no, it seems that there's no room for love up here: *All love comes to an end. It's just that this end seems cursed to me.*

I hope you'll miss me.

Love, Erez.

I started writing depressing letters when Ziv was killed. Short ones, every night. Lila was the logical – and only – candidate for receiving my outpourings. When all is said and done, a woman's a woman. She may be utterly idiotic when it comes to army matters, may not understand a single thing, but she cares about me. And even though she was always trying to get me to turn in my uniform, never understood what the hell it was I was doing up at Beaufort, why I was looking for trouble, she would listen to me with this really sweet look on her face and react lovingly, between one scolding and the next. When I broke up with her I had to find a new addressee for my letters. In a way I was happy about it, at last it was a chance to find someone who might really understand. I made a thorough study of everyone who knows me – parents, brothers, friends – and gave some thought to who might want to hear it all. But I came up with no one. There was no replacement for Lila. Then Oshri was wounded and the letters got longer. I would go back to bed, find once again that he wasn't there, and I wouldn't be able to fall asleep. So I wrote. To her, for the time being, her name floated there at the top of each page. Maybe I'm more in love with her than somebody should be, and maybe I'll go back to her when it's all over, like nothing happened, pick up right where we left off, like we're back on the roof of her grandmother's cottage during our third year together. We'd be great together when I come back, if I ever come back. Some of the letters, the toughest of them, she's never seen. They're between me and God. I wrote them and tore them up later, or shoved them way down deep in my knapsack. That happens sometimes, after you've written the first four lines or so you realize that you can't send the letter. That if your girlfriend reads it you'll lose her, she'll stop loving you. It's too depressing, too horrible, too extreme, too scary. A letter that exposes you to be someone other than the boy she knows from home. You're more cruel, for example, and a lot less funny. While writing a letter like that, you discover who you really are. And then one day you write that you've had enough. Enough of shooting, enough of soldiering, enough of yourself. You write that you're worn out, exhausted, that you've discovered they're all a bunch of liars. Me too, I'm a liar, because I'm not really here to protect the residents of northern Israel but because I have this urge to kill. I enjoy it. And my commander is a liar because he stands beside me and says he's there for me, but the minute the bullets start flying he's looking out for his own arse – at least that's the way it seems to me these days. In the end, we're all liars. Everything here is a matter of chance. That's all, only chance: nothing else. Whether you die or whether you live, it's just your fate. Doesn't matter how many exercises you've taken part in, what a good fighter you are, how careful and alert you are: if you're standing at the wrong place at the wrong time you're wasted. And the enemy? We have one, but I've never ever seen his face. Every rocket is just a ball of fire that soars through the air and falls on you. They drop from the sky, launched from places you can't see, but they've got your name on them. Have the blood and filth and noise made me indifferent? Coarser? I don't know.

I see a few of the other soldiers with notepads, scribbling lines and looking around all the time to make sure no one sees them. I wonder – I really do – if their letters are saner than mine. Once I yanked a letter out of Itamar's hands, just out of curiosity. He shouted and begged me to give it back but I just had to read it. 'I feel like I can't go on,' he'd written to his girlfriend. 'I dream at night about lox on toast or a good steak, but here at the outpost they've got me on a dog's diet. The cook decided I'm too fat and keeps stuffing me with salads all the time. I'm shattered, falling apart, don't feel well. They can all go fuck themselves.' That's what his letter said.

Those were the last days of winter at Beaufort in 1999, the first days of hot sun; the snow on the surrounding mountain peaks had melted long before. These were joyless days, days without the security of knowing Lila was waiting for me. Soon, on 3 June, we would leave the outpost and go down to a training base in the Golan Heights. We'd be getting back into shape, going home from time to time – that's what was awaiting us. There'd be girls, too: army secretaries and social workers and personnel managers and training course leaders. The boys would flourish. In the meantime, our sector was quiet. No purple rain had fallen on us for the last few days, and in the mornings we'd go out to open roads feeling free and relaxed because our gut instinct inexplicably told us there were no ambushes waiting for us along the road. And it was true. There was a kind of ceasefire – maybe we'd paid enough of a price already. Most of the time I was quiet and businesslike. Sometimes I was sad, sometimes just detached. Closed up, introverted. I'd think about Lila mostly in the mornings. I'd wake up with a hard-on like the barrel of a Merkava tank, only thicker. I'd rub myself a little, gently rock the bed, imagine her scent. But then after a minute or two I'd be overcome with fatigue, by thoughts about the missions ahead, and by the realization that it was best not to remember. At other times, during really bad bouts of depression, I'd catch myself imagining Lila with someone else, maybe a soldier – even a non-combat soldier, a pencil pusher – someone who might be with her at that very moment. Maybe I even knew the fellow. I'd torture myself with all kinds of scenarios, then I'd pull myself together, focus, convince myself she wouldn't get it on with anyone else, we'd been together for so long. She'd only ever slept with me. So there was no way it would happen. She didn't know how to kiss other guys. I'd put her out of my mind and keep on working.

The boys were fine, I think. But as far as I was concerned this was the end. I decided I wouldn't do another tour at Beaufort. It was time to put an end to it, to get out. I was determined: I had nothing more to do there. My parents were pushing me, too. At every opportunity, even during short phone calls, they brought up the fact that my brother had been wounded in Lebanon and that they couldn't deal with that again. They liked to say that our family had contributed enough. It was the end of Beaufort for me.

SECOND TOUR
OF DUTY

12

Next year they won't be calling me River. Naor, either.

Maybe Shanti, Master Shanti. Or Santosh or Yogi. Or Dharma, Rajesh, Rakesh, Asao, Bhajan, Ashutosh. Who knows what they'll call me, there's no end to the possibilities. Maybe they'll make up a completely new name for me. They'll find one for you, too, Lana. Something from nature. That is, if you'll come with us, you and Spitzer. There are Israelis out there – Kothumi and Kareem – all of them Israelis, but they've had enough of Israel so they've taken off for a while. That's OK. Why not? They're happy now.

Have you heard about Pacha Mama? That's 'Mother Earth,' a commune – the most famous one. That suits me, a commune. Heard of Costa Rica? Sure you have: the 'rich coast'. And how about Kundalini yoga? Means 'twisted'. It's based on the idea that there's a kind of serpent living dormant at the base of your spine and you have to wake it up. If it wakes up inside you then you bring on liberation – I'm not bullshitting you: you nourish the soul, merge with the flow of creative energy, invigorate the psyche and boom! You've reached enlightenment. I swear it. It calms your soul, puts the pieces of your heart back together. A totally spiritual life. OK, I'm going to show you. First stage: stand with your knees bent and move your body around, easy, earth to sky, shake it out, breathe deep, flow, slowly. Second stage: dance, put on some good music – Spitzer will play something for you – close your eyes, let the dance come from inside you, be natural. Don't force it, just let yourself get caught up in it, carried away. Third stage: sit down, your eyes still closed, then, when you're ready to chill out, lie down on your back – that's the fourth stage – completely peaceful. In a minute or two the Kundalini serpent will wake up. You'll see. 'Snake' and 'Messiah' have the same numerological value in Hebrew, I'm not kidding you: 358. You think that's a coincidence? Not according to the guru who came up with this Kundalini thing, a Jewish guy from New York called Swami Rudrananda, who everybody called Rudi. He lived like a king until his plane crashed into a hill during a flight from New Jersey. Poor bloke.

No? What do you mean, no? You didn't like it? Well, there are lots of options: Kundalini yoga, Bikram yoga, Hatha yoga, a workshop in spiritual cleansing; whatever you're into. We'll be happy, and aware – awareness, that's the most important thing. And there'll be workshops on the dimension of time, and on the creation of worlds according to Kabbalah. Yeah, even in Costa Rica people are crazy about Kabbalah. About channelling, too. And reincarnation, and healing. And of course intimacy, because everything is connected to intimacy in a commune. So how could we not be happy?

December 1999. While an entire nation was demanding we get out of Lebanon that winter, all I wanted to do was get in. Well, at first I didn't. I'd decided to become a regular citizen. I went to Tel Aviv to breathe a little. I sat alone, watching from the side, trying to work out how to connect with it all, to life outside the army, in the Tel Aviv bubble, on the beachfront promenade, in the cafés. At home. An entire nation was there, drinking mango and banana smoothies, having a great time. I really hoped I'd feel part of it, flow with the new rules, play along, get used to it. But it didn't happen. I know, I know, those army pencil pushers have a different girl every night – that's what I was thinking – but they don't have a clue what friendship is, what it is to feel so close to somebody. I watched them come into a pub together, arguing with each other about money. In our company all the money belonged to everybody. That's what I was used to, that's how I liked it. Those shallow non-combat soldiers didn't know what a red laser sighting is, or a Madonna set, or the guard booths we call 'hedgehogs', or what it feels like to complete a fifty-five mile beret march. They didn't know what it is to go on the attack, to take a bullet, to apply pressure to a part of your best friend's body while he's lying there half dead. They disgusted me.

Maybe the truth is that I had a lot more fun going on deadly missions than drinking mango smoothies. A lot. So who was I kidding? What was I moaning about? I liked it. I liked painting my face up and crawling in the fog. I liked the darkness, the cold nights, the sweat on my forehead from so much stress, how the drops would trickle on to my cheeks. A person who hasn't been there will never understand. And every time I had really bad frost-bite I liked to discover all over again that I still hadn't gone too far, that I still hadn't reached the height of pain. I was curious to get there, to see how much further I could push my luck, prove to myself that I could stand each new level of intensity – a lot of pain, a lot of fun. I believed that if I gave in to myself I would keep giving in for the rest of my life. I'd marry some dull woman and have dull friends. I'd give in to my son when he did badly in English. Everything in my life would be mediocre, and mediocrity is scary. It's shitty. I decided never to give in. My soldiers – I was prepared to die for them, I swear it: I really was ready to die for them. That's not just some slogan; I felt good about it. It seemed to me they were willing to die for me, too, and that's an incredible feeling.

On the way north the roads were full of homemade signs: BRING OUR BOYS HOME. The car I was catching a ride in barely made it through Golani junction because a small group of women were trying to block the traffic. It happened again further north, at the Mahanaim junction, where people had made a human chain across the road. They were holding torches, and policemen were standing by, restrained; instead of whipping out their clubs and knocking a few of those women on the head, they were asleep on their feet. One big Ashkenazi cow stuck her face up against the window of the car. Her eyes looked right into mine for a few seconds, just inches away. She pressed her hands to the windshield and screamed, 'Cannon fodder!' She was hysterical. It was a pity they couldn't see the whole picture, the way we can. Up there, in Lebanon, the war looked a whole lot better.

On the door of the sergeants' room at our training base in the Golan heights there was a sign that said WAKE IN CASE OF WAR, but nobody had ever dared to wake them up. On the door of the staff sergeants' room a sign read IN CASE OF WAR WAKE THE SERGEANTS: WE WON'T WAKE UP ANYWAY and over the entrance to the showers was some blood-red graffiti: ENTRY FORBIDDEN TO DOGS AND INFORMERS. The bloke who wrote that – and I'm not naming names here – was referring to soldiers who run crying to Carmela Menashe, the Israel Radio correspondent for army affairs, whenever we try to make men out of them. That's a problem. During the months we spent in training, close to civilization, there was suddenly access to mobile phones and TV news and newspapers. When those broadcasters started wailing about soldiers being afraid to cross the border, and the whole country was flooded with protest marches by women in black, then the boys started asking questions, it was only natural.

Zitlawi was the first of them. His wiring got screwed up. He sat down next to me in the canteen about a month before our second tour of duty at the front and told me about his doubts. 'Ehud Barak is prime minister, right?' he asked. 'And he says he's pulling the IDF out of Lebanon, right? What do you mean, you don't know? He said so on television and ever since then everyone's been talking about it.'

'OK, let's say that's true,' I said.

'So what are we going up there for now? Explain it to me.'

'What's that supposed to mean?' I asked, fixing him with a threatening look. It didn't throw him off a bit. He kept at it. Zitlawi, the last soldier I'd expect this from.

'If the prime minister promised to pull the IDF out of Lebanon in another eight months,' he continued, 'then why not do it now? Yeah, right now. This morning. We're just going to draw fire up there for nothing. We'll be targets. Next week River'll take a hit and get wasted, two days later it'll be Zion and Boaz, a week after that I'll wind up in a wheelchair and then everybody will say, "Wow, that's right, we should've pulled out of there a long time ago, before this big wave of casualties." I'm telling you straight: I don't understand the logic of it.'

That blew my fuse. I roared, 'Nobody's getting out of anywhere!' because I couldn't think of anything better to say. 'Do you really believe they're going to abandon the security zone? Forget it. Who would let Hezbollah get that close, pressed up against the Good Fence, as we call the border with Lebanon, making mincemeat out of the little kids in the kibbutzim along the border? The IDF is not pulling out of Lebanon in defeat, you can bet this army wouldn't dare to. Beaufort is the army's eyes. You'd better get that into your head.'

What else could I have said?

In discussions with the officers, Furman would tell us that Barak was no fool, that the man was leading our nation strategically, that there'd been no fatalities in Lebanon for several months and that the annual number of IDF casualties had fallen by nearly half. Now they were just trying to hang on to that achievement, stall for time, make the other side understand it was losing and then make a political settlement in which Israel had the upper hand. Army Intelligence and the Mossad would know exactly when we should pull out – that's what Furman said, expecting us to agree. 'Shit, why doesn't Barak stick his daughter up there with us on Beaufort,' I would say, just to piss him off. 'Let all the government ministers put their stinking children up there, if that's their strategy, and explain to them that it's a lofty goal to sacrifice your own life in order to stall for time. If they trust us so well, let them leave their children in our hands, then they're welcome to stall for as long as they want.'

Furman's explanation didn't make sense to me. If this was true, that there was such a strategy, that we were there as pawns in a political game, part of the tactics, and that they would be pulling us out anyway, then our situation was much worse than I'd thought. I couldn't believe it.

That night, when I went to the officers' showers, River ducked inside and sat down on the bench. 'Do you have answers?' he asked. 'Real answers, I'm only interested in real answers.' I shouted at him to get out of there.

'I think it's important, you should have answers,' he said, not budging. 'It sounds bad, as though the government has no emotional involvement, like they couldn't care less. Zitlawi's right: our boys are going to get knocked off one after the other and it'll all be for nothing, because they're pulling us out anyway. That much is clear. Some of us will leave Lebanon in coffins, and it would be a shame to die without understanding why. That's sad.'

River. What a disappointment. That's what he said. I'd never heard a soldier get carried away in such a dangerous direction. 'Someone's been brainwashing you,' I told him. 'Soldiers shouldn't be asking these questions, shouldn't even be talking like this. If those ideas seep into your brain you'll become a lousy fighter. Doubt is the thing that'll kill you, the only thing, and it'll kill your friends, too. You'd better bury those doubts and cool off, fast.'

He did. The next afternoon he announced that he'd decided not to go to officers' academy. He passed up the place that had been allotted to him and signed a waiver. He was the second to do so, after Bayliss, who'd turned down the academy when there were the first tangible signs that Israel would make an agreement with Syria to pull out of the Golan Heights and evacuate the settlements there. That hurt, but I accepted it, tried to understand. River, on the other hand, the soldier closest to me in our squad – well, there was just no way this boy wasn't going to be an officer. River, who'd saved Oshri; River, who dashed into the cloud of fire that had consumed Ziv, while I was still hesitating; River, who knew no boundaries: how could he not be an officer? He refused to explain. I tried threatening him, bribing him, appealing to him personally. Nothing helped. I was powerless.

That evening I gathered the squad on the parade grounds and put it as plainly as possible: 'Anyone who doesn't want to go back into Lebanon, raise your hand, now.' There was total silence. I waited a minute, then another, and another. They looked from one to the other, each waiting to see how their friends would react. 'Whoever wants out, let him go now or keep quiet until discharge.' No one came forward, no one left. 'From this moment on,' I announced, 'anyone who dares question our mission will be booted out, sent home, with a stopover in military prison.'

That was how we returned to the Land of Cedars, to a different Beaufort: with cracks in our faith and a strong echo at our backs telling us, 'You don't even need to be fighting now.' You hear it, and you still have to put that heavy pack on your back and march into the cold, and you're asking yourself, 'Why should I?' And the nation was divided: some were carrying the burden, others simply didn't care, others were chasing after your very soul, hounding you, not giving up, shouting END THE OCCUPATION, that it was sheer madness. And you as a commander try to make peace with the knowledge that you will end this tour of duty with casualties, or at the very least with wounded men. Those are realistic scenarios you can't help playing in your head, along with the soldiers' names. There were other rumours floating around at the time, too, they were coming at us from everywhere. For example, that fighters had been caught in outposts in the security zone smoking dope on duty. It was bad enough that they were jerking off on duty, I'd already heard about that. More than once there had been soldiers who had bragged about it or been caught, and even that was too much for me, to think about them lowering their guns and jerking off during such a volatile period, right while they're on guard duty and the lives of all their friends depend on them and all around mortar shells are exploding and terrorists are trying to infiltrate. When I had my suspicions I would make my way through the trenches to pay a visit, sneaking up on them in the middle of the night. I even forbade them from taking a piss during guard duty to make sure there were no misunderstandings, no excuses, no temptations. If you stick a dish of cream under a hungry cat's nose, don't be surprised if it eats the plate along with the cream. If I don't rub my dick for thirty-five days, even after watching Sharon Stone open her legs in *Basic Instinct*, then the boys can hold off for a little while, at least until they're in their sleeping bags at night. But drugs? Drugs at the guard posts? It couldn't be. 'I promise to fire a bullet into the head of anyone I catch smoking,' I told them when we first heard the stories. I had friends who lit up at home, in their free time. But at the outpost? I couldn't even imagine it. What a disgrace. I forced myself to believe that in my squad this had never happened.

That was another time Zitlawi the big mouth defused the tension. He agreed that was pretty serious, but said the blame shouldn't be placed on the soldiers. 'If something like that happens,' he explained, 'it's because somebody has pushed those soldiers into a corner, put them in an impossible situation, so they fall apart. Drugs become their only way out, their only way to forget their troubles for a few hours.' Bayliss said that was bullshit, that ours was just a hopeless generation. 'That's the face we present to the world, every home has somebody smoking dope. I've heard of parents who light up with their children around, and children who smoke with their parents.' But Zitlawi wasn't giving up. He stood on a chair. 'If we had even slightly better conditions here,' he said, 'for example, if we didn't have to walk through sewage twice a day to brush our teeth, maybe morale among the soldiers would be a little higher.' What do you want? That's the IDF, that's what we have to offer. 'And how is it that they manage to get us up here any way possible,' he continued, 'but they can't get the packages that people send from home here? They can't send a helicopter or a convoy for that? We get crap treatment here.' It was all coming out now. This is going to be one hell of a tour of duty, I thought to myself.

As if the business with the drugs wasn't enough to put a damper on our return to the front, Amos, the battalion commander, arrived a few hours before we set out, just to make our misery complete. He announced that there would be no further ambushes staged from Beaufort. While it was true that we'd been going out on ambushes every night for years, a new division commander had been appointed, and he had made some innovative conclusions about the situation. Ambushes were unnecessary, he said. Ineffectual. The outpost could be secured from within, there was no need to lie in a bush a half-mile away for that, and there was no need for opening roads, or for 'grass widow' operations (the code name for ambushes carried out from inside a house), or for playing cat-and-mouse games with terrorists between nearby villages. In other words, there was no need to endanger soldiers' lives with operational activity outside the safety of the outpost except in urgent cases where there was some clear imperative. That was what the division commander had decreed and that would be policy until the IDF pulled out of Lebanon. 'You've decided to ruin us!' I shouted at Amos, furious. I was really pissed off. 'There are terrorists out there and we need them dead. Let us go into some village and fuck them over, give us something, just don't make us sit there in the outpost scratching our balls on guard duty day and night. The soldiers have to get outside the gates now and again, they need to walk, feel the territory under their feet. You people are going to bleed us dry, you'll destroy the unit. It's like bringing in the most elite squad and asking them to do kitchen duty all day long.'

When Oshri and I finished officer training, our company commander had told us that the best part of serving at Beaufort was the knowledge that maybe tonight, maybe tomorrow night, and certainly by the night after that you would take down the terrorists who had hurt your friend, you'd wipe out that specific cell. It was the big dream we all shared, a fantasy of sorts that began with a face-to-face encounter, the kind that comes off perfect, the best there is: I see suspicious activity in the distance, coming closer, about seventy yards away, a body facing me straight on but not seeing me at all, and I pump a good number of bullets into him and then I storm, come closer, I'm on top of him, I perform a death verification, right in his face. After that I open River's stretcher and bring the body up to the outpost. And when he's lying there dead, a stinking terrorist, a pile of shit, in the exact spot where all our dead and wounded have been brought in at their worst moments, I wrap him in our company flag, sit him upright, spit a giant glob of phlegm into his face and have my picture taken with my arm around him. Maybe even put a beret on the corpse and smile for another photo. Then a last round of pictures with the entire squad before I announce a long furlough, at the very least, for everyone. I would spend time imagining the moment – after all, your imagination is the key survival tool of a tour of duty in Lebanon. You linger over every second of the story. And not just me, everybody was like that, taking part in the special ambience, an entire folklore of revenge. That's the food chain, the chain of life.

In those early years, they would send us out on real missions at every opportunity, the kind that made a fighter feel he hadn't been stuck on the hill for nothing. He might carry out a 'grass widow' operation on the home of the local collaborator, for example. Anyone who served at Beaufort knows the house, the fanciest building in the village of Arnoun: five storeys, who knows how many levels, full of leather couches, terraced gardens with fountains, luxury windows, expensive paintings on all the walls: Hollywood. It wasn't the collaborator himself who lived there, it was his brother; the brother of a collaborator deserves to live like a king. He was the only resident of the village given permission by the IDF to bring his car inside the village, while everyone else had to park outside at a distance and walk in. That's the way it was until one day, back when I was still pretty new at Beaufort, something went wrong. A soldier lying in ambush under the house spotted a pair of eyes peering out from a shuttered window every few minutes, keeping watch on him. It aroused the suspicions of the squad commander, set alarm bells ringing. He reported it to the outpost. In the morning a force entered the house and conducted a search. They found maps, binoculars and a mobile phone. The stash was sent to Army Intelligence and from there to the Shin Bet and after a few days we were informed that the confiscated items indeed raised questions about the man. They said that the number of a suspected Hezbollah operative was stored in the memory of his mobile phone. It turned out that the brother was collaborating with the terrorists. He'd double-crossed us. The IDF announced that the collaborator's house was to be sealed off. The residents of the house were expelled that same day, the contents of the house were parcelled out to SLA soldiers in the area and an IDF force showed up with a D9 bulldozer to knock down a few walls and neutralize the target. Shortly after that we began to use what was left of the mansion as a starting point for ambushes. Sometimes we would hide inside it during daylight hours, leaving only at night on operational activities, and sometimes we would spend days there, using the house as an observation point from which we could see the approach roads.

When we received intelligence information about terrorists who were going to be using a certain access road, we'd set out on a 'grass widow' operation, finding a house that abutted the road – preferably abandoned, of course, but that wasn't essential – with good visibility, the kind that overlooked intersecting roads or places that couldn't be seen from the outpost guard posts, and we would occupy it. The problem with grass widows is that they can backfire: if you had mud on your boots when you entered the house, or you sprayed a little when you took a leak on the floor, the whole squad was in danger. One of the locals could come in later, notice that the IDF had left tracks, and run to report to Hezbollah. When you came back there'd be an explosive device waiting for you.

And then there were the lying-down ambushes. When I was a young soldier we were out every night on one of those. A 'banana ambush' was the regular on-your-stomach kind. On a more interesting day there'd be a 'warn and strike' ambush, in which the squad was divided into two: one carried out an observation using marksmen while the other carried out an attack on a target. Then there was the 'thermometer ambush' which involved the use of an anti-tank grenade launcher for larger scale destruction. Use of a tank made it an 'artichoke ambush'. And then there was the 'assimilation ambush' which was really fun: you'd put on a disguise and blend in with the landscape. One day you were a rock, another day you were a bush, on the third you were a tree. You reached the site of the operation with a large camouflage kit – latex covered with rubber – which had been perfectly adapted to disappear into the surroundings. Getting ready for an assimilation ambush took a long time. First you made a quick trip out to the site and took pictures from every angle, and you collected rock samples and sent all the material back to Israel. A little while later this perfect kit was sent to the outpost, and all you needed to do was slip into it and hide. For example, three fighters could fit into every fake rock. In an average ambush there would be five such rocks, one next to the other. The last soldier in covered the rocks with mud and a few branches, secured them to the ground, got inside and sealed up the entrance. We were completely hidden. You'd lie in there for seventy-two hours, sometimes even a lot longer. Every once in a while you opened the zipper of the firing slit, took in some air, and then went back inside your rock, where you hummed the top hits from the army entertainment corps, the ones everyone loved. On a mission like that you really felt like you were James Bond.

But now it was all over. Our operational activities schedule had been wiped out. The battalion commander made his announcement and it spread quickly among the squads as they hung out, killing time, waiting for the green light to enter Lebanon. Most of them, like me, went nuts. These fighters, my boys, were not made for sitting around with nothing to do. They weren't afraid, they weren't looking to run away from the battlefield. They wanted to do their part, contribute something to the nation. They went to Amos and asked him straight out if what they were hearing was true. He understood that the situation was explosive and called them together, in formation, lined up in threes, to explain that there was no choice, that the IDF guidelines had changed and that the operational activities were no longer considered effective.

'What exactly are you saying?' they asked him. 'That everything we worked for and endangered our lives for till today is worth shit? Unimportant?'

'No,' he answered, 'but we've reached the decision that there is no point at the moment in taking unnecessary chances.' They asked him what was going to happen with the approach roads to Beaufort – after all, Hezbollah would be planting landmines and explosive devices. Amos told them there was no choice, that it was indeed a risk, that we would have to be on the lookout from the outpost, that we'd stop using the roads and make use of helicopters to get in and out instead. I think he even let slip the following words, probably without meaning to: 'The IDF can't afford any more casualties right now.'

Maybe the army heads were right, maybe our methods had been stupid. Out on ambushes, we would draw fire for no good reason and without any operational gain. Lying out there, at the foot of the outpost, for nights on end in the rain when there was a tank sitting parked inside the outpost, with night-vision equipment that enabled observation at a distance of three miles, and a grenade launcher and a missile launcher and ten MAG machine-guns – with all that, perhaps it was senseless to lie outside exposed and in danger of getting hit. But if that was the case, then what the fuck had we been doing all this time? In fact, without operational activity our whole army service seemed meaningless. I'd gone into Lebanon like Rambo, urging my soldiers to be 'murderers'. I told them the story of the early Zionist Joseph Trumpeldor, how he took a bullet and fell to the ground and still had the strength to push his guts back inside his stomach and say, 'It's good to die for our country.' I wanted to push forward with all of that pioneering spirit. And now, suddenly, for what?

We returned to a different Lebanon. Army Intelligence reported on a new addition to the Hezbollah death arsenal: the TOW, a rocket-launched, optically-tracked, wire-guided anti-tank missile, which had been airlifted into Damascus from Tehran and from there smuggled by convoy in vegetable trucks and cement mixers to our battle grounds. This missile was particularly efficient, and deadly. It could be fired at a distance of 2.3 miles, had a warhead of about thirteen pounds, was capable of penetrating two and a half feet of armoured vehicle and was characterized by its precision. It could be fired from a collapsible tripod or even from a vehicle. Up until then, we were told, the terrorists had been equipped solely with old Russian-made missiles. Now these new state-of-the-art models – originally American – had fallen into their hands via Iran. 'They're going to try and set our sector ablaze,' Amos told us at an intelligence briefing. 'They're going to make a bigger effort than ever before, they want to make sure that Israel's last year in Lebanon will go down in the history books as one big bloodbath, so that we'll be seen as having retreated under fire, in panic and in tears.'

Half an hour before midnight a fat Yasur helicopter dropped down from the darkness to pick us up. A few minutes before lift-off, an embarrassed but determined River took out a small laminated card he'd brought from home and read The Traveller's Prayer over the radio. His voice boomed to every corner of the base, and from the vehicles parked in the area, surrounding us and silencing the squads gathered near the helicopter pad. My boys stood around listening to him: *'May it be your will, our God and God of our fore-fathers, that you head us towards peace, guide our feet towards peace, lead us to peace, and bring us . . .'*

'. . . *make us reach*,' Bayliss interrupted, correcting him.

'What?' River asked, confused.

'*Make us reach*, you loser, not *bring us . . .*'

'. . . *make us reach*,' Bayliss continued, '*our desired destination for life, gladness and peace. May you rescue us from the hand of every foe, ambush, bandit and evil animal along the way, and from all manner of punishments that gather on earth. May you send blessings to all our handiwork and grant us grace, kindness and mercy in your eyes and in the eyes of all who look upon us. May you hear the sound of our supplications, because you are God, who hears prayer and supplications. Blessed are you, God, who hears prayer.*'

'Amen!' they answered, and the helicopter took off, rising sharply. We squashed pieces of yellow foam and shoved them into our ears for plugs, which did nothing to stop the high-pitched whistle and the rumble of the engines from piercing our eardrums, causing each of us to turn inward for a few last moments of quality time with himself. I was feeling pretty good, surprisingly. I felt really good, strong, excited. I was thinking about my bed waiting out there for me, half a year later, how I'd missed it. I'd nearly forgotten it all: the long, narrow corridors, the scary darkness, the dim red and blue lighting, the view, the feel of the wind up there, the taste of schnitzel and the smell of Lysol and piss and five-foot-tall wet thistles that bury you, and all of it together. And no, I wasn't afraid any more that I would die curious, without knowing what was written on that little scrap of paper that Lila had shoved inside the cloth pouch that held my dog tags. I would read it on the day of my discharge and not a second sooner. And I wouldn't think about her. For half a year I hadn't breathed her smell, hadn't put my head on her small belly. More than once I'd considered it, nearly broken down and gone to her to see about getting back together – once I even talked to her sister – but I knew that the time wasn't right. It was partly a test of resolve and stamina. In times like these, my happiness couldn't be dependent on love or physical contact. My concerns couldn't be with the little woman back home: if she was worried, that was bad and painful; if she wasn't, that was far worse, it meant I would have to live with the fear that she'd be out the door any minute. Even if it was written somewhere that we were meant for each other, I knew I had to be focused at this point, precise. In spite of all the regulations and bad news and tough decisions, this was, for me, a welcome return to Lebanon.

Fifty-nine seconds and no more: this was the amount of time that the pilot was permitted to stay on the landing pad at Beaufort. We had to hold our packs tight and jump to the ground in record time, before he lifted off again. Whoever got off was off. Whoever got on was on. And if anyone didn't manage – it was his tough luck. It didn't matter if you were hanging from the landing skids, the helicopter would hurry to disappear into the horizon. Every additional second added danger. A direct hit on a stationary target like that – by missile or shell – would be Hezbollah's biggest achievement of all time.

That night, six minutes elapsed from our feet touching the dirt to the first salvoes of mortar shells spraying the concrete roofs and the parking area and the guard posts. The enemy had taken note of the soldier rotation and wanted to catch us in those moments of disorganization. It was a way of letting us know what to expect on this tour of duty. Launch! Launch! Helmets in place on our heads, flak jackets, too. The onslaught lasted thirty minutes, and when it was over we – the officers – ran the length of the trenches to make sure we hadn't been attacked on foot and that none of our soldiers had been taken hostage under cover of the barrage. After that I got myself set up in the submarine. Oshri's bed was now occupied by Levanoni, the new sergeant. That's right: the Turks had expelled his grandfather from Palestine and sent him to Lebanon, thinking he'd spied for the British. The grandfather lived for a few years near Beirut, which is how he'd got the nickname that later became his family name, a kind of commemoration of the incident. Some of the family had even remained there. One cousin had been rescued by the Mossad and smuggled into Israel in 1982, at the time of the invasion. Two others had refused to leave, and there was practically no contact between them and the family back in Israel. They were living well there among the Muslims, they owned a luxury suit business and travelled once a month to the presidential palace in Damascus to custom-tailor suits for Assad. This Levanoni who was now serving with us was no less mad than his family stories, a frustrated kibbutznik from the Jordan Valley, a real loner who never smiled. Every once in a while he'd glare at you, skewer you with this killer look without warning or reason. Even I was afraid of the guy, and knew it wasn't a good idea to piss him off. He was the serial-killer type. Within seconds he would shut down, close off the outside world. Kind of robot-like. He'd give himself Israeli history lessons while we'd be watching *Die Hard* on video. What a weirdo! I'm pretty into patriotism and all that stuff, but why go to extremes? And he didn't put me to sleep with all kinds of bullshit talk, or heart-to-hearts either. He'd say, 'Goodnight,' like he was being polite or something. Who at the outpost ever said, 'Goodnight?' This was going to be tough.

We came back to Beaufort in style: Eldad, that man of rosy dreams, brought seedlings from miniature citrus trees and stuck them in a makeshift planter at the entrance to the submarine, promising the boys a private garden. River installed a metal bar across the doorway for pull-ups. He would hang there and everyone would punch his stomach muscles to strengthen his abdominals. Spitzer brought an electric keyboard. It was small and crappy but it worked. A new toaster oven, too. He and Zitlawi set up a little baking corner on a small cabinet. They would cook some *malawakh* dough then smear it with a red concoction made from four different sauces and add slices of hard cheese. There was always a bowl of cherry tomatoes on hand as well. Emilio was given the task of collecting the parcels from home that had been trickling in for the Hanukkah holiday. They were sergeants now, so they made sure that these rare treats made their way to them. Boxes of different sizes with colourful wrapping buried the dusty knapsacks in the narrow spaces between the beds. Emilio gathered them between his legs, pulled out a letter and read it out loud to the boys: 'Tami, age seven, from Bnei Zion.' Zitlawi asked if seven was considered a minor. 'To the soldier guarding us,' she wrote, 'Happy Hanukkah. I really hope you won't die in Lebanon and a missile won't fall on you.' She didn't leave a phone number or include a photo. Just some junk food and a pair of underpants and a package of liquorice in the shape of snakes. And beef jerky as though there was no beef jerky in Lebanon. No Marlboros, though. Stingy.

That week we inaugurated our own movie theatre, called 'Cinema Miriam and Shushu' in honour of Pinchuk's mother, who donated the equipment – she sent it from Chicago – and his parrot, who was killed by a mortar shell when we left him outside next to the kennels during an attack. It's possible that it wasn't actually a mortar shell that got him, but one of the dogs, who went mad from the noise of the explosions and swallowed him. The bottom line is, he got wasted, so we honoured him. Why not? Getting your name on that cinema was one fucking excellent honour because we had it running all day long, always some full-length movie showing. *Independence Day*, for example was a blockbuster hit, a damn good movie about aliens who try to take over the earth. Afternoons were for episodes of *Xena: Warrior Princess*, and last of all, every night, at three in the morning, the big finale, the most popular screening, that nobody missed: romance films. We had some good ones, lots of them, and we'd sit there watching, and there'd be refreshments and cocktails. The house special was a homemade concoction of mint leaves, verbena and lemon grass with milk and honey and a chocolate-covered wafer all mixed together. It was out of this world.

For spiritual balance and the purification of negative energy, Zitlawi brought incense and a candle from home. He was quick to make himself at home in the Signal Corps Company Club, Beaufort's improvised fighters' club, now that he was a sergeant and allowed to enter. The club was a dark and gloomy concrete shelter for the veterans of Beaufort. Three of its walls were painted grey and the fourth was light-coloured with white splotches and a wobbly Golani Brigade Signal Corps insignia painted in on it. In the centre of the wall were the words: IN MEMORY OF OUR

FRIENDS IN THE ALON SQUAD — THE BEST AND BRIGHTEST — WHO FELL IN THE HELICOPTER TRAGEDY, FEBRUARY 1997. Twenty names were inscribed there, the boys who'd been killed on their way to Beaufort. On the opposite wall was the face of the Sephardic Chief Rabbi Ovadiah Yosef pasted on to the body of a girl with tits the size of tanks, and another of the miracle-working Rabbi Baba Barukh surrounded by twenty-five gorgeous girls each with a speech bubble coming out of her mouth with some wise-crack or saying stuck up there over the years by different squads. There was a ping-pong table, too, and a few Indian cloths to give the place the feeling of an ashram, and, lying on the floor, a guide to making cocktails. In that little kingdom, shirts weren't tucked into trousers and there were no commanders to worry about. Everything was laid back, people sprawled out on the floor on shabby pillows, smoking cigarettes. They called it the Council Room, home of the alternative leadership, the men who got things done at the outpost. They would gather around a portable burner where Bayliss boiled spicy, bitter coffee and Zitlawi would crush ice cubes in plastic bags, hurling them over and over again at the list of names on the wall, with apologies to the Signal Corps. In those days we shitted coffee and our blood ran black from it.

On the fifth night after we'd arrived back at Beaufort, Zitlawi taught the boys how to hold a séance. He made everyone sit cross-legged, had them meditate, lit four scented candles on the floor – yellow, blue, green, red – and then he pulled out cloves and rose-mary from a cloth army satchel. 'Cloves are a good luck charm,' he explained. 'They evoke positive spirits.' In the middle of the room he set down a rectangular board made of white plywood with letters of the alphabet burnt into it in a circle, and little symbols and numbers and the words YES and NO and four stars in the corners, and on top of the board he placed a thin piece of wood carved in the shape of a heart with a hole in the centre. 'You should know that there's nothing simpler than getting advice from the souls of relatives and friends,' he informed the room. Then he demonstrated how it worked by placing the three middle fingers of each hand on the wooden heart so that the dead could move his fingers to form words. He'd clearly done this before. 'Is someone there?' he called out. 'I am summoning the pure souls.' You weren't allowed to be rude or insistent with a spirit, you had to say 'thank you' and 'excuse me' so they wouldn't get angry. 'One little mistake and something terrible will happen here,' he warned everyone. He asked Emilio to dribble lemon juice on to the candles in order to ward off evil guests. The boys thumped the *darbuka* drums and got to work. 'Who do you want to call?' Zitlawi asked. Spitzer suggested Maimon. Who the hell was that? Maimon was a soldier he'd been together with in training who'd been killed at the Reichan outpost. 'What's Maimon going to be able to do for you? Who's interested in Maimon?' Eldad retorted. 'How about Zohar?' Yes, yes, everyone agreed that Zohar was a great idea. 'Which Zohar?' Emilio asked. 'Which Zohar?! Which Zohar?! Zohar Argov, you retard! The king! The greatest Israeli singer of all time.' However, Zitlawi put a damper on their excitement: 'You're not allowed to summon suicides,' he said.

'When did you make that one up?' Eldad and Pinchuk demanded.

'Are you calling me an amateur?' Zitlawi asked, clearly pissed off.

Bayliss suggested asking for Menahem Begin. 'You jerk, Begin's still alive!' Zitlawi exclaimed, and everyone cracked up. 'What are you talking about, still alive? He's been dead for at least twenty years. What about Ziv? Ziv Farran?' River vetoed the idea, said they should just go for Maimon. They concentrated, closed their eyes, positioned their hands, but Maimon did not show up that evening.

Shortly after midnight they came back to the submarine. Zitlawi asked Spitzer to play a lullaby on his electric piano, an old favourite like 'Ammunition Hill'. Spitzer refused. They started without him – Zitlawi on the drums, Boaz and River banging the metal beds, and even Bayliss singing along under his breath: *We descended to the trenches, returning to our holes/Back to certain death, awaiting us like trolls.* Spitzer pulled out a wad of photocopied pages, which turned out to be the play *Henry V.* The curious among them took note, sat up, demanded an explanation. He told them he was going to audition at the Beit Zvi Acting School, which surprised everyone. He would be performing in front of five judges, which was scary as hell, and only a select few got in. He would do a piece from classical theatre and then a song of his choice.

'Want a tip from your brother?' Zitlawi asked. 'Only homos get in. Take that into consideration.'

'What are you going to sing?' Emilio asked.

'Homo songs,' Zitlawi interjected.

'What the fuck, will you give him a little credit?' River butted in. 'The man's making a stab at achieving his dreams and aspirations.'

'Listen, bitch,' Zitlawi said, clearly offended, 'what are you trying to tell me? That I don't aspire to anything?'

'I'm not worried about the song,' Spitzer said. 'Shakespeare's my problem right now.'

River grabbed the pages and started reading aloud, hesitant and unsure of himself. '*You have witchcraft in your lips, Kate: there is more eloquence in a sugar touch of them than in the tongues of the French council.*'

'*And they should sooner persuade Harry of England,*' Spitzer continued, having memorized the words, '*than a general petition of monarchs.*'

'*Come,*' River continued, getting carried away, '*your answer in broken music; for thy voice is music and thy English broken; therefore, queen of all, Katharine, break thy mind to me in broken English; wilt thou have me?*'

'What is this crap, for crying out loud?' Zitlawi wailed. 'You have to cut it out, now!' Spitzer suggested war, there was war in the play, too. He knelt in the narrow space between the beds, took hold of a broom and, leaning on it, declaimed, full of pathos, '*O God of battles! Steel my soldiers' hearts; possess them not with fear.*'

'It's a prayer,' Bayliss said, cutting him off. 'Make it softer.'

River asked, 'Does he win in the end?'

'*And take from them now the sense of reckoning, if the opposed numbers pluck their hearts from them. Not to-day, O Lord, O, not to-day!*' Spitzer carried on while everyone watched, at first amused, then gradually more absorbed. '*In peace there's nothing so becomes a man as modest stillness and humility: but when the blast of war blows in our ears, then imitate the action of the tiger; stiffen the sinews, summon up the blood, disguise fair nature with hard-favour'd rage; then lend the eye a terrible aspect; let it pry through the portage of the head like the brass cannon; let the brow o'erwhelm it as fearfully as doth a galled rock o'erhang and jutty his confounded base, swill'd with the wild and wasteful ocean. Now set the teeth and stretch the nostril wide, hold hard the breath and bend up every spirit to his full height.*' Spitzer paused, breathing heavily, then concluded. '*Fathers that, like so many Alexanders, have in these parts from morn till even fought and sheathed their swords for lack of argument. Dishonour not your mothers; now attest that those whom you call'd fathers did beget you!*'

'Wow!' Zitlawi shouted, 'the man took the prayer right out of my mouth! A war like that wouldn't be bad for us right now, a real good one to wake us all up. The kind of war they used to have back when people really knew how to make war. Why shouldn't we? If old English fairies in wigs could do it then why wouldn't we be able to? Lions, tigers, foxes – a reason to wake up in the morning. Bring it on, I swear that's what I want. Freeze my blood. If I'm wounded in battle just leave me there to fall into enemy hands. That's an order. Don't come back to get me, be men, for God's sake, all of you, be more manly than that. A little cruelty will do us good. It'll give people hope. They don't give us a chance to fight, they don't give us targets. They don't let us see the enemy. Anybody seen an enemy around here lately? I've never seen a single one. What's the matter, we don't have enough courage? We're not gung-ho enough? Come on, Kate, do a little witchcraft on me and I'll free the Western Wall for you.'

They all applauded him and whistled until they'd had enough of it and got ready for bed.

During that period of increased tension a new rule came into effect: half of the fighters at the outpost would sleep each night with their army boots on. The squads were divided into pairs so that every fighter could sleep one out of two nights barefoot. That Thursday night Zitlawi and River, the two best friends in the unit, twin souls, nearly killed each other when they couldn't agree on whose turn it was to sleep without boots, to give his feet the chance to breathe the fresh mountain air. Before they'd managed to count the days backwards and make a simple calculation, civil war had broken out between them, their basest impulses exposed. Neither one was willing to get into bed with weights on his feet. 'What's going on with you two,' Spitzer shouted at them, trying to separate them. 'You think you're in the Holocaust or something? Look what you're arguing about! How low can you get?' But it was too late. They were no longer speaking.

At three in the morning, River and Zitlawi reported for duty at the Green guard post, which was furthest from the outpost. River settled in to the trench that was the external part of the post. He leaned on the sandbags and used his night-vision equipment to look for cats and boar in the bush. Martens and weasels were all over the place, too. When he got tired of that he started counting the girls he'd messed around with – anything not to fall asleep, or, worse yet, to get into a conversation with Zitlawi. The two hadn't spoken since the boot incident some days back, and there was no reason for them to make up that night. Even River's innocence had its limits. He felt that everyone was trying to hide Zitlawi's regular meetings with Hodaya from him, which had gone on all through the months they were in training in the Golan Heights. Everyone avoided mentioning it to him; they all knew how Zitlawi would take almost every opportunity, even weeknights, to slip out of the base and hitch a ride (once he went as far as stealing an army van, that is to say, he borrowed one) to spend a few hours with her. On weekends they would go hiking together, falling asleep in the pastures overlooking the Sea of Galilee or at the Umm-el-Kanatier lookout point or above Eagle Falls. Everyone knew and no one mentioned it; but River knew it was happening, and convinced himself he was disgusted. Mostly, he refused to forgive.

Zitlawi moved the radio dial to the Sayas network. 'Good evening to the girls at Command headquarters. Allow me to entertain you,' he said to Corporal Julie in the war room, 'with a joke about the guy who meets a blonde in a bar and fucks her brains out without a condom. Have you heard this one? No? Well, the next day she phones him up, asks him if he has AIDS. "No," he says, "why do you ask?" "Because I already got it once," she tells him, "and I don't want it again." What? You don't think that's funny? OK, how about this one: An ant is walking through the woods when she comes to a river. She thinks and thinks about how she's going to cross it when suddenly she sees an elephant. "Elephant, elephant," she says to him, "be a man and get me across this river." So he does. When they get to the other side she gets off his back and says, "Thank you very much, elephant." So the elephant says, "What do you mean thank you? Take your clothes off." What, that's not funny either? You're just bullshitting me now, making fun of me. Who says ants can't talk? It's called personification. Anyway, this ant is from Tiberias, you haven't seen the ants we've got there.'

Christ, what an arse, that Zitlawi. Next he tried drawing Julie into a conversation about drugs. That's right, he didn't understand that those radio transmissions are all recorded. 'No, sweetheart, not me. I don't do drugs. Maybe just poppers. You know what poppers are? Let's say you're having fun with a guy and when you're getting close to orgasm you take a whiff, and it enhances your orgasm. Comes in a little bottle, you get it at sex shops. It's not a hard drug, it's legal, I think. I use it mostly when I'm tripping. I put the poppers on the tabs, you get it? What, you don't know about

LSD tabs? Shit, you really missed the most important lectures at school, didn't you? It's this thing that makes you hallucinate, makes you laugh, smile. You'll be looking at the view and it'll start coming at you in waves, like *The Matrix* or something, and you'll be trying to focus and your eyes will go haywire, as though you're seeing these mini video games. It's great, really. And then there's ecstasy. You know what ecstasy does to you? They call it the love drug because it puts all your emotions in action, like, let's say we're sitting there, alone, feeling good, and I take one, then we feel like we're in love, I swear it, and we've got to touch each other and stuff, and it's such a great feeling, like someone loves you. It lasts for maybe two and a half hours, you feel like you're loved for that whole time. Want to try it? You're not going to report me to the police or anything, are you?

'Holy shit, Julie, I've been staring at the same thing for an hour and a half already. Makes you mental. Fucking hell, if they don't change channels soon I'm going to do something really fucked up.'

Just before dawn their replacements still hadn't climbed up from below. There's nothing more demoralizing than the feeling that your replacement on guard duty isn't going to show up. Someone may have woken the fucker up but he's still asleep. Or, the war room runner, who goes around every night and shakes the next shift awake, thinks the bloke is on his way but doesn't notice when he isn't. There you are at your post, counting the minutes, slowly realizing you won't have time to catch a short sleep before morning duty, and that throws you off for the whole day.

At 4.35 a.m. Zion and Tom emerged from the secure area walking in a sleepy daze. They crossed the lot where the armoured personnel carriers were parked, and the kennels, where our predators were still sleeping. It was the silence of that seam between night and day. The only sound was the soft click of the generator. They approached the stairs, and then there was this popping noise, dull, from far off, followed by the sound of flight along with a slight whistling. It wasn't a mortar shell; they knew the sound of mortar shells. It was a missile, you could tell by the sound it made as it soared. But not a Sagger missile, either. Strange. The loudspeakers didn't announce a launch, or incoming missiles. Not even a siren. Zion and Tom froze in place because there was no way of knowing where it was going to hit and whether it was better to run forward or backward. And anyway, who could possibly run at all at that time of the morning? A few more seconds passed, and then an enormous blast shook the hill, and earth flew into the air and sandbags burst open and sprayed in every direction. A gigantic flame burned fast and bright a few yards away from the hedgehog guard post at Green and turned quickly into thick smoke that covered everything. River, who had been thrown backward by the blast, picked himself up and marched right into the grey cloud, as usual without hesitation. Zitlawi's cries of pain led him through the trench, and when Zitlawi shouted, 'I'm hit!' Tom and Zion followed on his trail, grabbing fire extinguishers and spraying like mad. I had just jumped out of bed and was putting on my helmet and flak jacket. I raced outside.

We got down on our knees in the soot-covered guard post, choking on the smoke. He was lying there, wounded. Pieces of the destroyed radio, binoculars and gun were lying nearby. Furman showed up with the doctor and two medics, who brought their equipment and a stretcher. They started a transfusion and we pulled him out of there carefully. They stopped the blood flow, bandaged him up. I asked who was supposed to replace him at Green. Bayliss? Wake him up, get him up here, and have him bring a MAG machine-gun and two crates of ammo. We had to have a guard there. What was Zitlawi's condition? Bleeding like crazy, shrapnel in his gut. Maybe his lung was punctured, or his intestines. The doctor was consulting with himself, aloud. What was his condition, damn it? Just don't let him go into shock. He was OK. Furman got Amos on the radio, explained what was happening – kind of hysterical, only faking a cool act – how there were hits, shit going down, even a 'poppy'. 'I'm not a poppy,' Zitlawi said, correcting him. What a man! He tried to shout so that Furman would hear. 'I'm not a "poppy", I'm a "flower",' he said. Not a dead body but a live one, just wounded. Even the doctor said he was OK. He'd be all right, he just had to keep breathing. The smoke was starting to clear. Zitlawi tried to call me, I think, to tell me something. I came near. He seemed to get a syllable or two out but he was having trouble. I patted his forehead, held his hand. You're OK, man. We all worked like soldiers, real professionals.

The rescue helicopter landed thirty minutes later. Levanoni ordered the boys to phone home, reassure their families that everything was fine, no problem, let them know they were alive and well and that the bad news they'd be hearing had nothing to do with our company. There was no reason to worry them and get rumours started. The boys all stood in line for the phone. It was a weird sight: their eyes were full of tears but they'd altered their voices to sound happy. They told their parents there was no trouble, that all was well. When asked why they sounded strange they answered that they'd been shouting more than usual, singing, and now they were hoarse. The report from the operating room in Haifa came in an hour later. The doctors were encouraged. The soldier was suffering from internal bleeding, but he was strong. Two hours later we were already back to routine, even ate lunch. Spitzer packed Zitlawi's belongings in his knapsack, folded his clothes and sheets, his towel. He tried to squeeze in Zitlawi's *darbuka* drum and his flip-flops. And his half-eaten bag of potato chips. Then the SLA guys came to repair the guard post. They mixed cement, poured concrete, added another layer of protection. Only Zitlawi's blood remained where it was on the walls, blackening the post. When the sun went down it was the first night of Hanukkah, but we didn't light candles. How the hell were we supposed to recite '*Blessed are you who has kept us in life, sustained us, and enabled us to reach this joyous occasion,*' giving thanks for miracles and wonders at a time like that, only hours after Zitlawi had been wounded?

A little later we gathered in the briefing room to watch the news.

The reception was crappy, noisy. I was leaning on the wall, off to the side. The correspondent for military affairs was going on about something to do with army intelligence and how Hezbollah's strategy was to portray the Israeli army as fleeing, hurt and trounced. Suddenly the newsreader cut in. 'We are now authorized to release for publication,' she said, 'the name of another casualty of the Hezbollah attack today. He is Sergeant Tomer Zitlawi, nineteen years old, from Tiberias, an IDF fighter serving at Beaufort. May his memory be blessed.' For a moment we all thought there was no connection to our Zitlawi. How could there be? We stood watching the screen, nobody could believe it. We'd sent him off alive and breathing, we'd given everything we had so that he would live.

I looked at the boys, at their immobile faces, their open mouths, all of them staring off into space. The doctor, too. Spitzer kicked the television cabinet and left the room. I left too, ran straight for Furman's office. 'Zitlawi's dead?! One of my soldiers is dead and the whole country knows it before us?' I shouted at Furman. I threw chairs around, pulled binders from shelves on to the floor, kicked the telephone equipment. 'Has the army lost its mind? This is really the end,' I said. 'These things destroy the soldiers, crush them. And as usual there's not going to be any retaliation, is there? We're not going to march into Arnoun and fuck them up good. We'll sit up here on the hill like bitches on the rag and take it all.' Furman remained sitting, listening, restrained and expressionless.

'I thought you'd grown up,' was his response.

13

Zitlawi won't be able to fantasize about heaven any more. 'Soldiers don't get sent to hell. Ever.' That was something he would always say, and even I would admit there was something encouraging in that.

You know this game that everyone plays, right? When a friend of theirs dies, I mean. Zitlawi won't say 'Life is beautiful, but I'm *more* beautiful' any more. He won't whisper to Spitzer 'Come on, little monkey, let's make love all night long' any more, and he won't hear us laughing any more, and he won't kiss Spitzer on the lips so that Spitzer spits on the floor of the submarine, and he won't roll around with him between the beds any more and hit his head on the metal legs.

Zitlawi won't make up new words for us any more, he won't smoke Marlboros through his nose or in the rain, he won't eat the cream from Oreo biscuits, and throw the rest away or buy Mars bars from the canteen. He won't make fun of the fat non-commissioned education officer who thinks she's hot. He won't shout at her any more, 'Ilanit, you're like a five-shekel coin: worth something, but not much.' He won't need Miri any more, the ugly bitch he phones when he's sick of jerking off, and he certainly won't need to lie to her and swear that he loves her and call her 'my pine cone' the way she insists. Zitlawi won't come in a girl's mouth or on her face. He'd never come on a girl's face, but he'd planned to.

Zitlawi won't take Hodaya to a film in Tel Aviv any more – he promised her he would – and he won't bring Spitzer's dad's jeep and let her drive in the sand at Gaash beach and he won't go down on her in the car, just as the sun sets. He said he would, but he didn't. He won't buy her a bathing suit either, she'll continue to wait for ever.

He won't mash our faces in the pitch dark any more, trying to guess which one of us it is and always getting it right. He won't ask every night, 'Hey, what did they say about us on the news?' And we won't laugh at him any more, and he won't get offended any more and ask 'Are you making fun of the way I talk?' And he won't stick his special words into every sentence any more. Wild guy. An arse with a cigarette behind his ear. But as far as *chakras* are concerned, he's the man. Sunbeams shone out of the guy and watched out for all of us.

Zitlawi won't play the only song he knew – 'London Bridge is Falling Down' – on the electric keyboard any more. He won't get tickets to be in the audience of the Dudu Topaz television programme and he won't get to see Tzvika Pick in the Caesarea amphitheatre. He won't buy a black Mercedes, the convertible he swore he'd buy, with black leather seats and a wooden dashboard and everything electric – the windows, the seats, the steering wheel, the girl. Because he won't be opening a stand in the *shuk* in Tiberias any more, and he won't be selling watermelon seeds (roasted and unroasted) or olives – lots of them in green and purple, big and small, with and without pits, pickled in vinegar or brine or sugar for that matter. He really wanted to do that.

He won't wake up on Saturday afternoons any more to the smell of his mother's *khamin* meat stew. He won't spy on his aunt in the shower any more. One sweet pussy, that aunt of his. Li-or-a. Sounds like someone who'd play the violin. I'll bet she does. Now we can fantasize about her whenever we want, because Zitlawi isn't around any more, isn't anywhere any more, and certainly not out with us on ambushes. And when someone brings an empty juice bottle into the submarine for pissing in, he won't say any more; 'Didn't your mother tell you my dick is too big for that?'

Zitlawi won't tell Herzl the homeless man back in his village any more, 'May you live long and prosperate.' Fucking hell, prosperate! What an idiot. But so good-hearted. He won't buy two *shwarmas* for Herzl any more, one after the other, both smeared with hot sauce and stuffed with gherkins. He won't pick his nose at traffic lights any more, he won't run a red light any more just when there's a traffic cop right behind him. Always had shitty luck, right up to the end. Maybe because of that he won't be an old-timer in the army, or a father, or a grandfather, and he won't learn to sky dive. Did you know that fuck-up wanted to be a paratrooper? It's true, he actually tried to get in, but he lasted about fifteen minutes. Lucky thing. Or maybe not.

Zitlawi won't know that we weren't at his funeral because they wouldn't let us go. Because it was impossible for us to leave the outpost. They sent other squads from the brigade in our place so there'd be a lot of berets there, all crowded, and the parents would be proud.

Zitlawi won't any more. That's the way the game is played. Then his name is erased from the duty roster. His bed becomes the submarine's storage area and you try not to talk too much about death. You get back to routine. But at night you fall asleep curled up, filled with a kind of tense anxiety that comes from the split second that awaits on the other side, when your eyes open and the news hits you again, suddenly, so that morning after morning you have to get used to it once more. If only we didn't have to sleep, it would all have been much easier.

14

A new word: Eaten. The eaten. Eatenness. That's it, in all its conjugations. It replaced the word a-f-r-a-i-d, which was not allowed to be used at the outpost. Occasionally, an entire squad was eaten, temporarily or chronically. But mostly the eaten ones were individuals – one here, one there – who tried to hide their condition, to blend into the crowd. A soldier who's eaten will never, ever say so – it's others who will point him out. If they recognize it.

There were identifying signs. The eaten, for example, wrote wills. At the time, whole squads went around with wills in their flak jackets. They bequeathed the car to Mum, the stereo to River, the dog to their little brother. The eaten either talked about death obsessively or they refused to mention the word at all, going mental if someone steered the conversation in that direction. The eaten attached good luck charms from miracle-working rabbis to their jackets or put laminated cards from the Lubavitcher rabbi under their pillows or carried ancient Chinese coins in their trouser pockets or had an angel tattooed on their stomachs or built little altars and danced around them with their mates before heading out under the open skies, to danger. They latched on to portents, to superstitions, to ancient and ornate Iraqi good luck sticks capped with gilded eagles, their expressions cruel and demented.

They kept a distance between one another when their pictures were taken, so there would be space for the 'death circle', the red outline used by the newspapers with the caption FINAL PHOTOGRAPH. A pornography of grief. Naturally, they tried to disguise their eatenness beneath humour. They would laugh with embarrassment. They were only pretending to laugh, the eaten, because in fact they were dead serious. Even reading The Traveller's Prayer out over the outpost intercom indicated a certain kind of eatenness.

This isn't the time to fall apart, I would tell them. It's a time to be strong. And they all made an effort – apart from a few exceptions. Emilio, for example, announced that he wasn't capable of taking part in guard duty any more, wasn't willing to go up into a guard post. He became completely cold, blank, stayed away from people, listened to Spanish discs alone in his bed, went to eat when everyone else had finished. I asked if he wanted to leave the outpost. He refused. 'I'll never leave my friends here, just don't put me out in a guard post,' he said. I told him that someone had to guard the outpost, and that I had no intention of filling in for him during the next few months. He didn't respond. I tried to keep him moving as much as possible, gave him tasks to carry out, keeping him busy rearranging the storeroom, preparing the duty roster – you could call it a kind of occupational therapy – but I couldn't get him to open up or talk to me directly. We all tried to sound him out. He remained silent. That's how it is with the eaten: it's all stuck inside them, stuck, stuck, stuck, until suddenly it comes bursting out. I guessed that the trick was to make it burst out. One night I asked him to guard the door of the war room. No one had ever stood guard there: it didn't make sense to guard it, there was no need to, and no fear involved because there was no chance of anything dangerous happening. Emilio made a face but agreed. A few minutes after he reported to his post I went up to join him, with two cups of hot tea. I stood next to him but kept quiet, on purpose. Just like that, waiting. He didn't say a word. I muttered at one point that Beaufort had become the pits, and then I fell silent for a long time. Out of the corner of my eye, I could see how the wheels in his brain were spinning wildly. Now and then he mumbled a word or two, which I ignored, as though I wasn't listening, not even paying attention to the fact he was there. And then it happened.

'That's it! I can't take it any more!' he shouted suddenly. 'I can't take it any more, I can't take it any more! I don't get what's going on here: We've got wounded all over the place: at Karkum and Reichan, Ishiye, Galgalit. What the fuck are we doing here?' He fell silent, before erupting once more. 'I'm sick of everyone pretending they don't think I'm *afraid*.' There it was, the forbidden word. He'd managed to say it. 'I'm sick of everyone trying to find solutions that are supposed to make it easier for me. I know it, I know all of you think I'm afraid. I know I *am* afraid. I don't need your pity: I'm afraid! But tell me this, please, I want to know: why the fuck are we in this hell-hole anyway?'

I tried to explain that there was a certain operational logic to our remaining here, but he didn't give me the impression I'd convinced him or even that he was really listening. Then I tried moving the conversation to girls, to home, to his family in Argentina. 'Tell me something, would you set me up with your sister, Ariella?' I asked. 'I'm serious. Would you? If the answer's no, hey, it's no problem, forget I asked. Mistake! Never mind.' I told him lots about myself, got carried away. About the break-up with Lila and how I was trying to decide if I should get back together with her. 'No communication,' I told him. 'Not a word between us. Well, I did go to her house once during the summer. To check up on her. She wasn't there. She'd already been discharged from the army and headed down to Eilat, where she was working in security at the airport. She hadn't even let me know.' I told him about money troubles at home, too, things I never should have talked to him about. It was a long conversation. He talked a lot too, kept grabbing my shirt, pulling at it while he talked. 'Look what's going on here,' he kept saying. It was clear to me that he was not OK, that he was deeply troubled. 'You've got to get this fear of yours under control,' I told him. 'Because fear is contagious. If you don't manage it, it'll spread like a plague through the outpost and knock everyone down, every last man. I've been afraid, too, a lot of times. I've even almost fallen apart, but I've stopped myself. Listen, Emilio, listen up: You can't be afraid.' When I finally said goodbye he wouldn't let me go. He said, 'Stay here with me,' even though there was nothing more for us to say.

The next morning at breakfast I found it hard to look straight at him. I was embarrassed. I'm an officer, and he's one of the boys, and I'd told him things I shouldn't have. He knew I thought the place was a hell-hole, too, and how bad matters were between me and Lila. He knew too many personal things about me.

Three days later I saw in his eyes how fear had turned into complete indifference, another known phenomenon. At first he'd been afraid to leave his bed in the secure area, but now we'd find him running around the parking area without a care, exposed. He would say, 'Screw it, fuck Hezbollah.' His eyes looked more worried than ever, but he didn't seem to register what was happening around him. Nothing interested him, he wasn't afraid of mortar shells or missiles. He started doing guard duty again.

In the meantime, I declared war on black humour. Humour can be a vehicle for expressing distress, and nearly the whole squad was guilty of using it in this way. 'OK, man, go get wasted on guard duty. We'll meet in heaven, later. I'll be an hour and a half behind you getting wasted,' they'd say and crack up laughing. They'd tell jokes about dead people, too, and ghosts, and they'd make up songs. 'I've been hearing wisecracks I don't like at all,' I informed them. 'Some people up here are sensitive and you don't notice it. It has a bad effect on them, weakens them. I don't like the mood around here. Get this bullshit out of your heads.' I kept them busy, arranged sports activities for them in the evenings, exercise, sprints, group competitions. I tried to keep them away from the radio and television, and if they did watch the news I wanted it to be in my presence.

'The surveillance point at the Galgalit outpost took a direct and devastating hit,' explained the correspondent for military affairs. The boys were mesmerized, didn't open their mouths. 'The casualties are Captain Eyal Koppel, twenty-two, from Ashdod, and Staff Sergeant Yair Harari, twenty, from Tivon. Six other soldiers were wounded, one critically. The cabinet will hold a special session this evening to discuss the recent escalation along the Lebanese border. IDF chief of staff Lieutenant General Shaul Mofaz will present the cabinet with plans for the withdrawal from Lebanon, which is supposed to take place this coming July.' The correspondent for political affairs added that 'The government again today approved 7 July as the day for IDF withdrawal from Lebanon.' The picture skipped and faded, the broadcast was cut short. When the commercials came on the boys' mouths watered. This was their connection to the world, where they learned about life on the outside.

And then there was a report of a funeral taking place at the Kiryat Shaul cemetery: 'The government is abandoning our best soldiers,' a father shouted. 'Something needs to be done, this can't go on. The best among us are going like lambs to the slaughter. Poor soldiers, they're willing to fight but they can't even defend themselves and keep safe. After all, this isn't really a war. This is absurd and primitive! And how long is it going to last? The people of this country are flayed to the bone.'

Then the faces of the fallen soldiers, handsome, with wide smiles, their last photos from their final tours of duty. And a street poll, a wandering microphone, parents relating how they no longer sleep at night.

* * *

One day someone hung an interview with a paratrooper who had refused to fight that had appeared in an Israeli newspaper on the wall of the dining room. And not just any paratrooper, but a member of the elite commando squad. His company commander had been killed, and his squad commander, and an Engineering Corps officer, and five others were wounded, sensitive weaponry had been stolen from them, including night-vision equipment and a radio, and he had watched it all without storming, stayed behind a boulder, hiding. 'I didn't want to die for no good reason,' he'd explained to the journalist. That piece of shit said he was afraid, said it without any shame. The thought that we didn't even need to be in Lebanon had overcome him right in the middle of battle.

Not only was this interview hanging next to the cabinet where our prayer books were stored but SUPERSTAR! had been scrawled on it with a thick marker. That same evening at a briefing, Furman called on the soldier who hung it there to turn himself in. We all looked around, trying to guess who had dared to take that traitor and raise him to the status of a hero and then prove to be a chicken himself by not admitting to doing it. No one claimed responsibility. We waited five minutes. Furman asked who among them thought the paratrooper had been right. From every corner of the room the men shouted, 'He's scum!' 'A soldier who doesn't go on the attack is a loser!' The briefing ended. I yanked the interview from the wall and tore it up. Just before dumping the pieces into the rubbish that night in the submarine, I had a look.

What the hell would cause a man not to storm? What would make him lie there doing nothing while he watched his friends dodging bullets, shooting and taking hits while his commander shouted. 'After me'? That evening, and every evening after that for the next few weeks, I was constantly on the lookout, monitoring the outpost soldiers in search of the ones who might possibly, at a crucial moment, fail to follow me in an attack. If something like that could happen in an elite commando squad – a squad that takes itself very seriously and commands a lot of respect – then it could happen here, too. I knew which of the boys would make the sacrifice for me: the arses, the losers, the stupid ones – they'd definitely do it. They may not be smart, but they know what friendship is, that's just how they are. Take a soldier like that and tell him, 'Brother, it's good to bang your head against the wall,' and he'll say, 'Oh yeah? So let's do it,' and he'll bang his head against the wall, he'll split his skull open if he needs to. If he loves you then he'll take a bullet for you, too. That's how it is with the arses, the losers. The smart ones, on the other hand, don't always stand behind you and charge when you need them to. The smart ones will wonder each time about the benefit of everything they're asked to do, ask themselves if this or that is worth it, or the cost is too high, or they might want to know who made the decision, they're just generally pre-occupied with all kinds of questions that have no connection to warfare. At the Sujud outpost there were paratroopers like that, so that when a terrorist penetrated and planted a flag they didn't even chase after him, they let him escape. The chief of staff himself dismissed them, and the unit never recovered from their humiliation. They walk down the street and everyone looks at them, the unit that had a flag planted on them. Yeah, that's what happens when you ask too many questions.

Personally, I'm on the side of the fools. I always march at the front of the squad, knowing that the head is where the casualties are. And when, here and there, I'm afraid, I'm glad. I tell myself that it's healthy to be afraid, it makes you do everything by the book.

I put the pieces of the torn-up article on my blanket, riveted. What a disgrace, leaving your friends in the lurch. He hadn't gone on the attack with them, he'd buried himself in a hole. And then, when he'd returned home, instead of hiding away, he'd gone on the attack. Sent letters to politicians, put up a fight, written that they were sending us out to get killed without a second thought, that they weren't thinking about us, the fighters, or about managing this war. They didn't worry about those things, only about their own campaign wars.

What an arrogant bastard, the homo. What was he trying to say? At Sujud, the paper said, a wounded paratrooper had fought with his bare hands against an armed terrorist who'd infiltrated the outpost, a crazed, six-foot-two Hezbollah operative wearing a camouflage uniform and planning to wipe them out with an M-72 LAW missile, a Kalashnikov machine-gun and two hand grenades. The *tznef* – that's what we called the young, green para-troopers – attacked the terrorist, nearly fell captive, but managed in the end to wrestle the ape to the ground, get his weapons off him and chase him away. For a day he was called a hero. Then the chief of staff dismissed him for failing to continue the chase. Why hadn't he gone after him? 'A disgrace,' the paper called it. 'The soldier went back into his hole.' I was hankering for a little action up there at the outpost to get morale up and remind all the soldiers why we were there. We'd come to fight.

River entered carrying two cups of hot chocolate. When River brought hot chocolate you knew he wanted to talk. I tossed the torn pieces of newspaper in the rubbish bit. 'What do you think?' I asked him.

'I don't know,' he answered.

'What's there to know?'

'It's complicated.'

'It's not complicated at all, believe me, River. I read the article. He admits it, the poor fuck. His mother's a left-wing activist who drilled the stuff into his brain every time he was home on leave. That's what happened. Excellent proof that home visits affect your ability to function.'

'It's not that simple, Erez.'

'Go on,' I said, pressing him. 'Let it out.'

'How can you argue with his position? Everyone around him who stood up got shot. He understood it was a lost cause, hope-less, that he was in a completely impossible situation and at an insurmountable disadvantage. He knew that if he stuck his head out of his hiding place he was wasted, no doubt about it. What was he supposed to do, commit suicide? Aren't three casualties better than five or six? Was he supposed to die just so it could be said that he'd engaged in combat?'

Levanoni jumped down from the upper bunk bed – we'd thought he was sleeping. He had that killer look in his eyes, and he grabbed River around the neck. 'You're going rotten, Naor River,' he told him, quiet but threatening. 'Rotten apples need to be taken out of the barrel.' River and I stood there, stunned; we couldn't understand what the lunatic wanted. River muttered, 'Never mind,' and ran out of the submarine. I shouted at Levanoni: 'Are you out of your fucking mind? Let the boy talk!' I raced after River and found him in the hall by the stretchers and pushed him up against the wall. His eyes were red and he had the look of a wounded puppy. 'It might just be, he said, 'that the IDF prefers its heroes dead.'

'We're all here in the same boat,' I told him. I was holding him tight, by the arms. 'If something happens to me it'll happen to you, too, to all of us, and there won't be anyone to rescue you. If something happens to Bayliss, or to you, or to Spitzer, it's because one of us didn't lend him a hand. You all have to understand that if one of you doesn't go on the attack it'll be selling out your friends. It's no longer a matter of carrying out an operation or defending the settlements along Israel's northern border. It's between all of us, between friends.'

River nodded, he understood. I went into the submarine with him and gathered everyone. 'Listen up,' I told them. 'Engaging in combat, camaraderie, bravery, leadership, personal example. Remember those things? That's what we're doing here, and that's what will protect us and how we'll protect each other. I'm giving you one more chance, your second and last – a parachute, an ejector seat that will float you right out of here to a mediocre life at home. If there's anyone who feels he doesn't have the balls for it, who doesn't love the squad enough, who isn't prepared for sacrifice, let him speak up now. That sort of person doesn't need to be here.'

No one made a sound. Silence, again.

'Who thinks we shouldn't be here?' I asked. 'Raise your hand.' Boaz and Itamar put their hands in the air. A few seconds later Emilio and Koka did, too. It was clear from his eyes that River was dying to raise his hand as well but he was afraid of disappointing me, again, in front of everyone. 'So why are you here?' I asked. They said nothing. 'Answer me!' I shouted.

'We're being betrayed by Israel,' Boaz erupted, agitated. 'We're here and nobody could care less about getting us radiators when we're freezing from the cold, and nobody gives a shit about getting supplies here on time or refilling the empty water tanks or giving us a lift when we're standing at an intersection in Kiryat Shmona trying to get home. So what are we doing it for? Nobody in Israel respects us any more.'

'Are you listening to yourself, you big fucking whiner?' I asked. I pulled out my Zionist speech about Israel's eyes trained on Nabatiye and guarding Metullah: I didn't have any better ideas. 'There's a well-known rule of war,' I told them. 'The line of contact can never be broken. If there's a chain of people and I run at them, they'll repel me the first time, maybe the second, too. But eventually I'll break through. If two of us run at the enemy, one will manage to jump over their heads. The IDF set up the security zone to ensure that if a terrorist gets past the first outpost he'll run into the second, and if he gets past that one he'll get snagged on the third. The point is that he'll never make it to the border fence itself. And it's a fact that thanks to the security zone there haven't been any infiltrations over the border. Don't listen to a lot of nonsense. The IDF thinks it's crucial for us to be here and so we'll stay.'

'Cut the officer speak now,' River interrupted. 'You're one of us. Put your hand on your heart and, as a citizen of Israel, tell me that you believe we should be here.'

'Forget it,' I said, silencing him. 'There's an army order and we have to carry it out.'

As a soldier I'd never dared to ask what we were doing in Lebanon. My older brothers, who were in Lebanon before me, never asked. Neither did my father. When I was a common soldier no one questioned the authority of their commanding officers; back then the prevailing mood was completely different. Suddenly, over the last two months, everyone was arguing and asking questions that undermined authority. 'What's the purpose?' they would ask. Every time they were sent outside the secure area, out from under the outpost's reinforced concrete roof, they said, 'You want to send us to our deaths?' I'll admit, it wasn't easy to command soldiers during this wave of funerals and thirty rocket attacks a day. That's no way to wage a war. But really, the breakdown in morale was the fault of that band of old women who didn't understand shit about the army. They were the ones responsible for creating the fucked-up situation in the country. Them and Carmela Menashe from Israel Radio. And the pictures broadcast on television, which weakened morale: of weeping soldiers, of fighters telling everyone they were targets, close-ups of bleeding, wounded soldiers getting medical attention after a battle. The IDF was guilty, too. Guilty of failing to carry out a deadly retaliation when a division commander, Brigadier General Erez Gerstein, was killed. None of the soldiers could believe it. 'No retaliation?' they asked. 'They murder the biggest hero in the IDF, they humiliate us, and we don't react? We're not even going to raze a village somewhere?' All these things, combined with the public debate, were affecting our ability to engage in combat. There was frustration hitting us from every angle. It killed the boys to hear on the radio that people didn't believe in what they were doing. Yes, something had changed, had seeped in, you could feel it. Suddenly people in your neighbourhood were shouting, 'Sucker! You're getting wasted in Lebanon for nothing!' They didn't give you the respect they'd given you once.

And the fear that your friend wouldn't go on the attack for you

– it wasn't only me who was worried that there might be frightened soldiers hiding among us. All of them were suspicious of each other, of their comrades. I could see it in their eyes.

And how were the boys supposed to feel when a cartoon of Beaufort appeared in a weekend paper, its guard posts manned by dogs instead of soldiers? That happened, too, just after Zitlawi died. Bayliss saw the picture, held his head in his hands and ran from room to room shouting. 'What is this?! What is this?!' They all walked around completely crushed. They came to me wanting answers – I was the establishment, as far as they were concerned – but I could offer them no explanation.

15

One morning we received a shipment of mannequins. Twenty-five of them, made of wax, the kind you see in shop windows with little noses and big ears and a man's face and broad chest and open mouth, with eyelashes and hair painted on black. They had nice physiques and flexible hands that could swivel 360 degrees. The only thing missing was their privates. They were unloaded from a military truck driven by an SLA soldier, one of our regulars, a guy named Kabuk.

We asked Kabuk, 'What are they bringing us these big dolls for now? We haven't heard anything about it.'

'How should I know?' he answered, claiming he was only the messenger. He shrugged as if he didn't have a clue. But Kabuk always had a clue, he was always up to date on everything. When pressed, he winked and told us. 'It's a "thickening procedure" but make sure that stays between us, OK?'

'What's a "thickening procedure"?' I wanted to know.

'It's new, comes from way up high in Command. You thicken your guard posts,' he explained in a whisper. 'A mannequin in every guard post, every trench. Confuse those sons of bitches. Someone'll tell you how it's done. Don't worry, the order's on its way.'

We laid them out on the tables in the dining room and dressed them in uniforms, complete with flak jackets, helmets, dog tags – the works. We didn't have enough boots, though, so we gave them our own flip-flops, which we didn't need any more. When we'd finished making soldiers out of them we dispatched them everywhere. We put them where they'd stick out, where the enemy could see them. Every few hours we'd move their arms so the enemy wouldn't catch on. During the day they'd guard from inside the hedgehogs while the real soldiers hid behind sandbags in the trenches – one would watch with a pair of binoculars, scanning the sector, while the other patrolled. At night it was the real soldiers who guarded from inside the hedgehogs with the mannequins out between the sandbags. For the time being, that was procedure. Furman would walk around checking to make sure everything was carried out properly, that the arm positions were shifted and the heads moved. We took good care of them, made sure they weren't cold. We gave them names – men's names, African-American names. We wrote their names on their jackets and helmets so we could tell them apart, since they were all from the same mould: same face, same overly broad shoulders. The boys stood further back or off to the side on guard duty, watching, better protected. If a missile fell they'd be injured by the blast, but that's all; the mannequins would absorb the direct hits. That was the logic.

From the start, the whole business with our new guys was conducted in English. There were conversations late into the night, pre-duty briefings. The boys would entertain them, get advice from them, bring food for them, make them salute officers and sergeants so they knew who to respect, who was senior. They volunteered them for operations, saddled them with heavy loads, sent them on errands. They carried them from place to place so they wouldn't get bored from staring at the same view all the time. Everywhere you looked you'd see a soldier walking around holding a big doll like it was nothing, normal. They'd bring them to bed at night in the submarine, fall asleep with their arms around Snoop Dogg or Magic Johnson or both of them together.

Beaufort in those days turned into something different, entrenched. Under the code name *Shawshank Redemption*, Christian Lebanese labourers – collaborators from the surrounding villages – took part in a fortification process the likes of which had never been seen, in an attempt at dealing with the new missile threat. Fifty cement trucks climbed the hill to the outpost, construction crews erected walls, concrete roofs were strengthened, huge nets were stretched above the guards posts so that incoming missiles would be detonated from contact with the nets and explode in the air rather than on the ground, where they would do more damage. The labourers built and poured and excavated, giant walls of concrete sprang up as though we were never leaving. Secret electronic scrambling devices were installed as well. 'Forty million shekels are being spent to reinforce the outposts,' Furman informed us. Things went on like that for a month. But we already knew that the innovations, the treats, always arrived too late.

16

And then the new millennium arrived, on a Friday night. At the exact moment, the first second of the first day of the first month of the year 2000, I was in the kitchen of the Beaufort outpost baking a lemon cake. Chili was sitting next to me giving advice and stuffing down some cheese lasagna while working on a crossword puzzle. 'The star of *Gone With the Wind*, eleven letters. What are you talking about, "Sharon Stone"!? Are you crazy? You're as stupid as a Lebanese whore! Next. The code name the Americans gave to the bombing of Hiroshima. Nagasaki? I don't think so. That's the other city they bombed.' Dave dashed in just then, called us, told us not to miss the fireworks from the celebrations at Tibnit, which we did – by choice – and in the end, nothing happened at that moment. The gates of heaven did not open and did not spit cascades of fire, the weather didn't go bonkers, the sea didn't rise and flood, the Litani River didn't dry up. Hezbollah didn't even attack. It was an utterly boring moment, the kind that'll be forgotten. When my grandchildren ask about it, I won't be able to tell them 'I was with Grandma,' or 'I was dead drunk, drunk with joy,' or 'I was engaged in momentous events.' I heard the boys gathering at the entrance to the secure area, counting backwards. Seven, six, five. A shortwave radio was tuned in to a broadcast from Tel Aviv. The broadcaster was shrieking like she was having a fucking orgasm, counting down with people at a big party at the Tel Aviv port where everyone was shouting 'four, three, two!' I wondered what Lila was doing at that moment. No way of knowing. I shouldn't have been thinking about it, about her. Then again . . . maybe she was just coming, at that very moment, in perfect synchronization. Some German guy was giving it to her in a five star hotel. Or a security guard from the airport. I couldn't believe she wasn't with me. 'One, zero!' Everyone was whistling, cheering. Where's Oshri? I thought. I'd have planted a big fat one right on his lips if he'd been there. I even missed his scent. And where was Zitlawi? He would have pulled out a bottle of whisky from who knows where and got everyone going. I put the baking tin in the oven, filled a thermos with strong tea steeped with mountains of sugar and went out to tour the guard posts.

Two mannequins and Spitzer were guarding Green. I could hear him in the dark, practising *Henry V* inside the hedgehog. *'If we are mark'd to die, we are enow to do our country loss; and if to live, the fewer men, the greater share of honour.'* I went in. If he hadn't been blue with cold he would have blushed with embarrassment. I stood next to him, asked him to go on. I told him it was interesting, I enjoyed it. *'O, do not wish one more,'* he mumbled, by heart, not glancing at the pages poking from his trouser pocket. *'He which hath no stomach to this fight, let him depart; his passport shall be made and crowns for convoy put into his purse: we would not die in that man's company that fears his fellowship to die with us.'*

'War, huh?' I said. 'There's nothing like a show about war.'

'We few, we happy few, we band of brothers,' he said, raising his voice as he gained confidence and put on a real performance. *'For he to-day that sheds his blood with me shall be my brother; be he ne'er so vile, this day shall gentle his condition: And gentlemen in England now a-bed shall think themselves accursed they were not here, and hold their manhoods cheap whiles any speaks that fought with us upon Saint Crispin's day.'*

'You think they'll make a show about us one day?' I asked.

'A play?' he said, correcting me. 'No, I don't think so.'

'No? Really? What about Goni Harnick, the man who conquered Beaufort? He was a real hero, every soldier knows about him. Don't you think he'd be great for a Hollywood flick?'

'No, I don't,' Spitzer answered.

He drank his tea. 'They weren't even supposed to conquer this hill, they didn't mean to. Did you know that?' he asked me. 'To this very day nobody knows how it happened. It was a mistake – there was no military significance in conquering Beaufort. IDF convoys had already surrounded the whole range of hills on the first morning of the war and our troops were much deeper in Lebanese territory, on their way to Beirut. They'd left Beaufort behind and the fortress itself didn't bother anyone. It was just a little enclave. The terrorists weren't firing from there, they'd have taken off, disappeared within a day or two out of boredom, since nothing was happening here. Command gave the order to call off the operation, told them not to attack, but the order got lost on the way, fell between the cracks somewhere between Command and division officers: someone forgot to pass it on. So the reconnaissance unit came up here. On foot.'

'What the fuck are you talking about?' I asked, furious. 'Who put this bullshit in your head? You're profaning the dead.'

'No really, it's the truth,' he said. 'It was a senseless battle, Goni's battle. The next morning Ariel Sharon arrived – he was minister of defence then – and he stood right here facing the guard post, on what's known as French Hill, wearing a windbreaker, with a whole entourage and a TV crew. There were still puddles of blood on the ground. He proclaimed it as a historic achievement, boasted about how they'd taken the fortress so smoothly, without any casualties or wounded. One of the young soldiers, named Tamir, corrected him. "Six men were killed," he said. "I saw them, I helped evacuate them. The head of the reconnaissance unit was killed." But the minister of defence said, "I think you are mistaken. No one was wounded here. You've had a difficult night, I believe you don't really understand what happened here." Menahem Begin, the prime minister at the time, didn't get it either. He was mad about the air up here in the mountains, proclaimed the place "godlike" and asked if the terrorists had machine-guns.'

'Bullshit,' I said. 'You're totally fucking wrong, you jerk.'

He persisted. 'The radio reported no injuries. They said it was an instance of "supreme heroism and daring enterprise" and that there were no casualties. But in the war room and at Command headquarters nobody could understand how it was that the reconnaissance unit had taken control of Beaufort against orders.'

'Somebody's been fucking with you, brother, they've been telling you stories.'

'Begin was overheard talking to his wife on the phone when the war broke out, told her it would all be over in two days.'

'For fuck's sake, Spitzer, cut it out.'

We were quiet for a few moments, both of us smiling but for different reasons. 'For your information,' he said, 'I've never had a friend that I loved like Zitlawi. And I won't ever again. I spend hours up here every night and the only thing I think about is him, nothing else. I try to picture his last few seconds up here, what they were like. I stand here reciting Shakespeare, waiting for him to make fun of me. For him to call me a sperm-sucking piece of shit and whisper in my ear: "When you win an Oscar you say a big thank you to Zitlawi into the microphone and tell everybody, 'This is for the guy who made me a great actor and loved me to death,' and if you don't, I'm going to open up a second hole in your arse."'

They were that close? I had no idea.

'Tell me a secret,' I said. 'Toss me a bone. Something top secret and sensitive, something personal that nobody else knows.'

He thought, took his time, tried to dodge the question. I wouldn't let him off the hook. I wanted him to feel close to me. 'Lana,' he said. 'She makes me listen to The Cranberries whenever we do it. Exclusively, The Cranberries. That's my only secret, I think.'

'Always?' I asked.

'Fifth song on the first album. Always. She can't do it without it. Same song, playing over and over again.'

'What the fuck? How can you concentrate?' I said, dead serious. 'She's really warped. But cute, too.'

'I'm willing to listen to her Cranberries album until I'm a hundred,' Spitzer said, smiling.

River was guarding in the hedgehog at Blue. 'Happy Millennium,' I said when I saw him. I shook his hand, held it for a while. At Beaufort we didn't have the luxury of staying angry with someone, especially on a festive night. 'Everything OK between us?' I asked. He nodded. 'I'm sending you boys home to squeeze some quality time out of Mummy next week,' I told him.

'The Sons-Shall-Return-to-their-Borders Procedure,' he said with a grin.

'River, I'm giving you two additional missions. I think both are waiting for you on the Golan Heights.'

'Missions?' he asked, pretending not to know what I was talking about.

'First, the Reconciliation Mission, otherwise known by its code name, Bayliss's Boots. You've got to make up with him. That's an order. It's not open for discussion. Second, the Holy Vagina Mission, whose code name is River Grows Up and Goes To Talk to the Girl Who Has Turned His Brain to Mush for an Entire Year.'

One of the basic tenets of our division – the black Ten Commandments – was an iron rule that everyone swore to wholeheartedly: never, ever, covet the bereaved girlfriend of a friend who's been wasted. Do not drool over her, do not seduce her, do not cop a feel under her shirt. She might undress when it's not even warm out, ply you with hot coffee, stroke you all over, and you might be seduced. But you will be strong, you will not cheat on your brother. When a fighter goes into battle he must be tranquil and lucid, must focus on the goal without suspecting that if, God forbid, he bites it, his friends will take turns doing his girl. If this kind of suspicion takes hold of him, if he can't be sure they won't make her forget him, he won't be worth shit in battle. Shlomo Artzi screwed a girl who was in mourning for her boyfriend and wrote a song about it. That just tore me up when I learned about it. How could he? But that Shlomo, he's a king, so just once I forgave the unforgivable. It made me feel better to know that he tortured himself over it, never got this friend of his out of his head: the dead man would visit him in his dreams, crying and afraid and getting hit by a bullet and dying. Shlomo realized what a mistake it was. With us, that couldn't happen. But in River's case, Hodaya was his from the first moment, back behind Rabbi Elifaz's cowshed in the Golan Heights. Old Zitlawi had bypassed him, got in there first and staked out the territory. River had to go to her.

'Not possible,' he said.

I wasn't giving in. 'Somebody has to tell her about Zitlawi,' I told him. 'She may not know. Or maybe she does, maybe she saw it on television, if they let religious girls watch TV, and now she hasn't got anybody to confide in or anybody she can lean on, and she's a complete mess.'

River dismissed the idea.

'I'm giving you three days from the time we land in Israel,' I told him. 'If you don't do it, I'm going there myself.'

He had a sad smile on his face, or maybe it was resignation. It was hard to tell. The flames that had blazed in the eyes of the River I loved were not there. 'What's happened to us?' I asked him. 'Why have you given up? You should have been an officer by now, not wasting your time here as a common soldier. What's going on with you? Is it fear that's been eating you up inside and smashing your faith to bits? Is that it?'

'I'm not afraid of the fear,' he said. 'On the contrary, Erez: the best thing is not to be afraid of the fear.'

'Good,' I said. 'Excellent. Don't be afraid of the fear.'

'I'm not afraid to give in to it sometimes, too,' he said. 'It's not going to turn me into a failure if I give in to it sometimes. Or you, either.'

'Yes it will,' I responded. 'And you'll be pissed off with yourself. You won't forgive yourself for years.'

Meanwhile, up in White, Emilio was crying. That's what he can tell his grandchildren about the first hour of the new millennium: that he spent it crying. He didn't stop, either. It came in waves, came and went, all the way to morning. His video recorder – which was his alone until it became a tour guide for Lana – seared his face on that morning into all of our memories, biting his lips as if trying to stop, and looking exhausted.

Come on, that's enough. Enough. Stop filming, Spitzer. Leave me alone. Isn't it enough that you brought us bad luck with all your bullshit? You and Zitlawi. You shouldn't have started all this filming, believe me. Now look what's happened to us, everything's gone sour. No, I'm not crying. Come on, leave me alone. All of you. It's enough.

Do you feel it, Spitzer? Shut up a minute, turn the camera off and try to feel it. I'm telling you, I feel it, in the air. Something bad's about to happen. You'd think we've had enough bad stuff already, but no. It's going to get worse. Much. I was beginning to think the bad shit was behind us, but now I don't think so any more. Do you feel it? My heart's already booming on its own, like exploding missiles. All our drills and exercises aren't worth shit. A big hoax. How can I possibly dodge a missile that takes two and a half seconds to reach here? Why am I standing here guarding the place? I can feel it coming. I'm done for, believe me. Done for.

Enough.

17

What are you going to do when you get home? First thing for me: beach. I need to smell the beach, stop there on the way home just to breathe. Next: a bath. A six-hour bath. And then, cruising in the car. Man, you've got to see how many virgins there are walking around this country. Soft, smooth skin, cropped t-shirts, huge tits full of milk – I'd go wild if I weren't so shy. Just drive around for an hour, slip on down to the highway without even planning to, tear it up, alone, quiet music on the radio, no plans, no navigating, no map, going places there's no chance of knowing how to get back from. End of the world. To think. To float. That's what I feel like doing. And I'll blow my money on a strawberry-banana smoothie and lots of beer, get drunk. Really drunk, blind drunk and then, when my head clears, I'll spend some quality time with my sister, Vicky, make sure none of the boys in the neighbourhood have been groping her, God forbid. Elias and Motke, friends from the street, they'll get their hands on a jeep and a camping stove and we'll check out the desert, go crazy, act like juvenile delinquents, nut cases, the kind you'd never in your life trust for a second.

Good evening. Outpost briefing. New rule: no removing of boots, by order. Not even every two days, or every week for that matter. No discussion. Maybe just three minutes to air the feet, a quickie, in the secure area – but no more than that. No showers, either.

From this minute on the showers will be locked shut. They're too dangerous, not a place you can take off your flak jacket and helmet. Bathe at home. Anyway, it's risky to waste water, since there's no way of knowing when the supply trucks can come out to refill them. In an emergency you can rinse off in the room behind the kitchen over the drainage hole using gallon jugs, but only with special permission and under the supervision of Furman. And that's exclusively for life and death rinsing. And, since the sewage system is blocked and the shit has overflowed on to the toilet floors, a sign has been posted saying BY ORDER: CLOSED FOR REPAIRS until a combat plumbing unit can be brought in to fix it. In the meantime we're going to shit into our helmets lined with plastic bags. There's an emergency supply of shit bags, enough for everybody. Anybody who wants to can take anti-diarrohea pills.

Is everything clear so far? OK. Intelligence update: Hezbollah have a sniper. That's to say, they have a terrorist cell with an anti-tank missile sniper. The real thing, imported from Russia. He never misses. He gets IDF guard posts in his sights and hits the bull's eye every time. Yeah, it's insane, inhuman, Olympian, to have a 100 per cent success rate, like shooting with a pistol from 500 yards and hitting somebody between the eyes. What are the chances of that? By the time the fourth missile hit us we worked out what was going on. The intelligence officers put the maps on the table and worked out their movements. They killed our boys at Rotem in the western sector, then Galgalit, then here at Beaufort and at Dlaat, moving straight across the security zone, very neat, from west to east, outpost to outpost. The next few targets are already prepared for attack: Sujud, Ishiye, Reichan. They're next in line, if the pattern holds. And what's going to happen when they finish? Will they start a new round? From beginning to end? From end to beginning? In the same order? They're not stupid, Hezbollah. It took them a little while, but in the end they figured out that the IDF is barely letting its soldiers stick a big toe out of the outposts, so that to mow a few down they'd have to get inside. And that's exactly what they're doing. Command has issued orders effective immediately to change operational procedures, security methods and guard duty. Note that in the event of mortar shells being fired, fighters are now to close all openings of the hedgehog. On the other hand, if it's missiles being fired then you need to leave the door open so you can get out into the trench, take a step backwards and hide behind the concrete walls. You've got to keep your eyes peeled on the sky at all times, use a minimum of lights, never raise your voice. We're talking total concentration. And sprint every time you're outside the secure area, even for a second. That's all for now.

A heavy snow, soft and airy and pleasant, covered our hill. It fell slowly, hovering in the air. Long rows of bare, skeletal apple trees stood draped in white in the valley below us, while black and brown cows sank into the ice on the slopes, pawing at the ground but not finding a single speck of green. Everything looked friendlier, with little Arabs building fat *kaffiyeh*-wearing snowmen and the old lady in Arnoun opening the red door to her black stone cottage and stepping out into the alley wrapped in a *galabia* and leaning on her cane. Her eyes peered out from between layers of cloth; she'd spent seventy winters there, maybe more, but I'm sure every year the snow still fascinated her, made her head spin all over again. At the pastoral little kiosk by the Litani River, under the Khardaleh bridge where the oleander stood frozen, members of the UN forces were wrestling like children, cracking up with laughter, really happy. It's more beautiful than our own Hatzbani River, I swear it, more beautiful than anywhere else in the world. You can be really happy there until nightfall, when a cold wind makes you moody and depressed. And lonely. Even the old lady seemed to feel it. The faraway clusters of light, from home, tickle your imagination and torture you.

Twenty minutes after the winter sun had set on the second day of the first week of the new millennium, a Yasur helicopter landed and took us back to Israel. By 9.30 a.m. we – my squad and Levanoni and I – were already at Grandma's, a pub in the town of Katzrin in the Golan Heights. It's a small place, intimate, an old Syrian house, and it's kosher, closed on the Sabbath. We were there for group building, a kind of off-the-base social activity that was supposed to make us closer. We ate grilled feta cheese sandwiches and drank beer. The whole thing felt pretty forced and strange. We were dying to laugh but couldn't find anything or anyone to laugh at. We spread out across the room: Boaz and Zion tried entertaining the waitresses, Tom took care of the background music on the stereo system over the bar, Spitzer sat at the piano, attempting to keep up with the music. Bayliss was swallowed up by the locals, burly moshavnik types in old-style sandals and kibbutz girls with wet hair wearing fleece jackets and dripping with the scent of sweet bath oils. River sat in thoughtful silence, observing us all from the corner of the room. Emilio told him that his falling out with Bayliss was a shame. 'One of you will get wasted,' he said, 'and the other one will feel so bad for not making up that he'll kill himself.' I leaned over to Emilio and whispered into his ear: 'Listen up, my friend. From this moment on, no more talk about death, no more whining, no more hysterics. Enough of this bullshit. It just brings us all bad luck and puts us in a shitty mood.' Emilio fell silent. River and Koka didn't say anything either. They were dying to get out of there and go home, praying the evening would end, but they knew it wouldn't be nice to just get up and leave for no good reason.

I went to the bar for a refill. 'Can I talk to you for a minute outside?' a girl whispered in my ear. She was small and dark-skinned, with big, puffy, heart-shaped lips and no tits. I said, 'What?' and she persisted: 'I want to talk to you for a minute outside.'

'What about?'

'Are you afraid?' she asked.

So I agreed to go outside with her. When the door slammed behind us she offered me her hand and pulled me along, leading the way. When we reached the car park, she stopped and stood facing me, fixing me with a gaze that said it all.

'So?' I said.

'Do you have a girlfriend?'

'Yeah,' I answered. I don't know why. I still felt like I did.

'Ah,' she said. Truth is, she looked the opposite of disappointed. This was confusing.

'Was that your question? That's it?' I asked.

'No,' she said.

'It's cold out here. Let's go back inside.'

'How about my car?' she asked. 'It's parked over there.'

'OK,' I said.

We got inside. She sat at the wheel, I sat next to her. She closed the door, pushed the seat back and brought her lips close to mine. 'Excuse me,' she said, and started kissing me. At first the kisses were slow and gentle and then they weren't any more, and she started opening the belt of my uniform and the buttons on my shirt. She stroked my stomach, it was hot. She drew her hand across my trousers.

'How long's it been since he came?' she asked.

Whoa. I was disgusted all of a sudden. I grimaced. You slut, you loser, why are you talking about my dick in the third person? What do you want? You want it, you want it here in the car? You're sick in the head! And with my soldiers a few feet away, they can come out at any minute. Who are you, anyway? You don't know me, but the thought that I have a girlfriend turns you on, doesn't it? What a nymphomaniac! I opened the door, said, 'This isn't for me,' and got out of the car. I wasn't even polite about it. On the way back inside to my boys I buttoned myself back into shape, but in the few quiet seconds it took to reach the door I understood that I should be worried – very – because what I'd just done was fucked up. It was unnatural behaviour. If anyone found out about it they would be disgusted by me, not her. What was going on with me? Was I a homo? Why didn't she turn me on? If I'd had, say, in theory, a good reason not to fuck her, hadn't wanted to 'duplicate the key inside her', as Zitlawi called screwing, then at the very least I should have said, 'Baby, you're more than welcome to suck me off.' I should have pulled her knickers down to her feet in one swift motion and sucked the living daylights out of her clit. There were lots of things I should have done, but I didn't even have a hard-on. Now that's sick. I was tired and didn't feel anything at all when I got out of there. I felt extinguished, and wondered if I wasn't still bound to Lila, who'd probably been bound to somebody else for ages already by now.

Inside I found Levanoni holding forth with everybody gathered around him. 'The fear of humiliation is greater than the fear of death,' he was saying, explaining his motto and why it was suitable for every situation. What humiliation? The humiliation of the soldier who is afraid, has a panic attack, fails his mission, lets his friends down. And also the humiliation of the pathetic image people are forming of us, all of us, as long as we continue to sit up there on the receiving end, never going out on operations or doing anything useful or having a chance to succeed at anything, at killing terrorists. He told them we were good at spouting slogans – 'We won't rest until we've made sure they're dead,' or 'That which does not kill you, strengthens you; that which kills you, strengthens your mother,' or 'The pencil pusher's prick is a combat soldier, the combat soldier's prick is a pencil pusher.' I didn't like his slogan about humiliation, and I was hearing it at totally the wrong moment. 'Get over here, fast,' I signalled to him. Levanoni left the boys and followed me to the toilets. 'You'd better shut your mouth, I'm warning you,' I told him. If I hear something like that one more time, I'm going to push your head into the toilet.'

'You didn't like what I was saying?' he asked in a cynical tone, his eyes narrowed and his expression mocking. 'I'm turning them into fighters. Do have you a problem with that?'

Without a second of forethought my hands flew forward and pushed him hard in the chest, smashing him against the door. He was all fired up immediately, crazed and flushed with hatred, a real hothead, no less than me. A wild beast. But he bit his lip, threw a punch and stopped himself in mid air. 'I'd finish you off right here, Erez, I swear it,' he whispered. 'But I'm not stupid like you. I'm not getting myself thrown in jail.' And before I could even digest this or react, he was out the door, back into the main room, while I stayed behind alone, not knowing what to do with myself. Maybe kick the door, maybe ram an elbow into the window or a wall. I'm telling you, I felt completely powerless. I didn't know what was happening to me. I felt like a pear whose insides have been gutted by a worm and there's just the skin left, but it refuses to fall from the tree. What was happening to me?

Early the next morning, River made his way back up to the Golan Heights from a suburb of Tel Aviv in his older brother's little Fiat. He went back to the Bajurya pool. It seemed incredible that a year had passed since they'd stripped there and chased after the ATV, waving their hands like wounded animals and cursing like Palestinian policemen. Even the road itself seemed to have grown older, its three layers of asphalt were cracked and greying, but at least the smell was the same, a healthy green, and the ground was wet just like it had been back then, when he'd first seen Hodaya's shy smile and stolen her bicycle, her blonde hair was so smooth that he'd wanted to reach out and caress it, even then, and since then he'd tried endlessly to recall the contours of her face, and her smell, and that brief moment when her eyes met his. He didn't know if she'd really taken him in, that is to say, what exactly she saw and how much she'd focused on him, or what exactly she thought of him. He was desperate to know. Now, a year later, he rested on a small boulder looking at the pool of water, alone, wearing a white v-neck shirt and a choker of red beads his brother had brought him back from Costa Rica. He hated this place intensely without knowing why – simply hated it. Maybe it was the eucalyptus trees. There was nothing he despised more than cheap eucalyptuses, they reminded him of army bases. And how the hell was he supposed to find the girl? He wondered if he'd have the balls to talk to her if he did, to tell her everything he'd planned to. He'd even practised in front of broken mirrors at the outpost – I'm willing to swear on it – because he wanted to make sure he used the right words, to prove he was after her heart, that love was his intention, since maybe she'd lost her faith in men after what that horny bastard Zitlawi had dragged her into. And what had Zitlawi told her about him, anyway? There was no way of knowing. Maybe he'd made fun of him, filled her head with bullshit about him. River was tormented, but decisive. He would take her up to the wind turbines at Alonei Habashan and hold her in his arms as strong gusts of air swirled around them, making them freeze up there on the hill. If they connected, then they'd use the sleeping bags waiting in the boot of the Fiat. They could go to the Odem Forest and fall asleep among the trees and the anemones, among the deer and the small, ruined Syrian stone buildings. Maybe they'd visit the shores of the Sea of Galilee, sleep at Naftali's beach, where the sunrise would wake them up. Whatever she wanted he'd give her – anything but letting her return to the reign of terror of her religious girls' school. That he couldn't bring himself to do.

River drove the length of the road that led to the cowsheds, towards the fields belonging to Kibbutz Natur: maybe she was there, walking around like she had been a year earlier. He rolled along slowly, scouring the landscape, praying she'd pop into view. Black and brown cows with white faces were walking around there, too, just like they did on our side of the fence, in Lebanon. Carefree, they could fuck each other whenever they felt like it, mounting one another and taking a ride. No pressure, no accountability. She didn't appear. An hour later he parked by the bus stop at the entrance to Nov, thinking maybe she'd come out, then after a little while he gave up and drove in through the metal gate, parking the Fiat in the centre of town, in front of the synagogue, between two idle tractors. He decided not to move from that spot until she turned up. A while later he took off on foot to the playground,

which he thought should be checked out. When he failed to find
her on one of the swings there, he set out to find the girls' school,
going so far as to ask directions from a lady riding a large tricycle
along one of the paths. When he found the school he sat down
on the wet grass facing the entrance and waited for her to walk
out, or at least peer through a window. But she didn't, not for two
hours. Then out of nowhere, at three o'clock in the afternoon,
Bayliss turned up. All of a sudden he was there, sitting to River's
right – he'd come up from behind in silence. He didn't say a word,
just sat there on the grass. At first, River was taken aback, averted
his eyes, thought for a few moments. After a while he asked, 'How
did it happen?' and Bayliss squeezed his hand and said, 'I'm sorry.'
'Me too,' River said. And that was the end of their big, stupid,
senseless falling out. It was gone, as though it had never existed,
and it left no scars. They didn't even try to argue about the facts
or blame one another. They talked for a while, catching up on
things and swapping stories.

Bayliss went inside the school to get Hodaya. She came out
wearing a blue skirt and a white shirt. Her hair was in a ponytail,
and in River's eyes she was more beautiful than ever. He stood
there barely breathing. She said hello but didn't seem at all surprised
to see him. Bayliss left them alone.

'Did you hear about Zitlawi?' River asked.

'Yes,' she said.

'Oh. I wanted to know that you'd heard. Who told you?'

'I saw. I mean, in the paper.'

'Nobody told us, either, we learned from the news that he was
dead,' River explained. He asked if it was hard for her.

'I'm sure it's harder for you soldiers,' she said nonchalantly, which
seemed to River pretty strange. 'I'm sorry,' she said in a cold, calm
voice.

River hesitated, trying to decide whether to continue. She smiled.
'I can tell you're a pretty sensitive person,' she said. He didn't know
if that was good or bad, because in any other situation it would be

bad but in this one it might just, logically, be good. There was no way of knowing. She laughed, maybe he was making a funny face: tortured, focused, intense. He had so many questions he wanted to ask her, but once again she got there first: 'They're waiting for me inside,' she said. 'Thanks for thinking of me. I'm really all right.' What a cold-hearted bitch. When he didn't respond – he barely managed a nod – she took a few steps backwards and said, 'Take care.' Then she turned her back to him and walked away. So did he, to Bayliss's house. That was how it ended. Like nothing. Stupid. Senseless.

That night they sat at the observation point above the El-Al creek, Bayliss and River along with a few friends from Nov. They lit coloured fluorescent stick lights from the hidden weapons stash of a neighbour. You bend the stick light in the middle, making a little slit, then you shake it and the stuff inside shines like the sun, a radioactive pool of light. Stick lights last for eight hours, and they paint the night and the world in different colours. They borrowed Bayliss's father's mobile phone and got updates from all the squad members about what they were doing. It made no difference that nobody had anything interesting to report – nobody had gone to the sea, nobody had been cruising around Israel in search of virgins. But there was always something to tell. Late at night, sprawled out side by side on mattresses in Bayliss's bedroom, they tried to guess what each of them would be like as adults, at a reunion – a barbecue party next to Eldad the rich boy's private pool, he'd already be stinking rich by then. He'd take his father's millions and turn them into billions, that slick, manipulative little white boy. Spitzer would be famous, a well-known actor. The whole neighbourhood would go crazy whenever he showed up with some fancy car and a girl, maybe even Lana, since he loved stability. Then there was Boaz, who hated stability. He'd come for a short visit to show off to the boys, between an operation with guerilla rebels in Angola and commando training in Chile, or maybe even with the Shi'ites in Iran. If someone was willing to pay, Boaz would sell himself: for excitement, he'd give his all. He'd circle the globe with suitcases full of cash, train assassins, fall in love with local girls, the daughters of cannibal chieftains in remote places. He'd continue to think of himself as a killer, running around with a khaki-coloured piece of cloth protecting his watch and his hair cropped like a Marine's. Totally juvenile. He'd wear Timberland mountain boots and drive around in a slick jeep filled with men with little pricks: he'd never stop being a member of Erez's squad. In the end, when nobody needed the services of an aging mercenary any more, he'd rot, alone, but not before trying to set up, say, an auto-theft protection business. He'd convince himself that car theft was the scourge of Israeli society and that he was going to find himself among the rich bastards of the world thanks to some special gadget: a steering wheel that electrocutes the thief, or an air-conditioning system that poisons him. But nobody would buy it. Pathetic. Then there was Pinchuk: he'd be a homo. You could see it in his eyes, the pervert. He'd end up teaching P.E. to children, get himself in trouble with some sexual harassment case, then he'd leave Israel, in fact he wouldn't even make the reunion, they wouldn't manage to find him. Zion, on the other hand, would be there, driving a 1986 red Subaru. He'd bring his wife, a fat nursery school teacher who'd started growing to the size of a gorilla the day after their wedding. She'd shout at him all the time, too, totally disgusting. Girls always kept that bloke on a short leash. He'd be employed by the Egged bus company, arranging holiday packages for the bus co-operative's employees. Koka would be a lifeguard at a city pool, the first Ethiopian lifeguard. Itamar would be fat. River would be a doctor. Bayliss, a reporter. Barnoy would be a vet, or else he'd own a shoe shop in Jaffa. Tom would get special permission from the psychiatric hospital he'd be in to attend the reunion. They'd take off the strips of brown cloth that tied him to his bed and shoot him up with sedatives before they sent him to us. He had the look of a psychotic and the eyes of a murderer, and he wrote poetry, lines and lines of it that were disjointed and made no sense. He was definitely going to wind up in a nuthouse. And Emilio? No way of knowing. It was hard to imagine him grown up. And then there was Zitlawi, who wasn't any more. This group wasn't going to produce a chief of staff like we'd thought once, or a prime minister, either. Weird. How could that be? And me? They reckoned I'd still be living in Afula, a little man with a big opinion of himself, a Shin Bet operative who interrogated Arabs and handled agents. A family man and a government man who sometimes took his children fishing. They didn't have any doubts when they talked about my future, it was clear to them.

The next morning we visited Zitlawi's grave, all of us. The military cemetery in Tiberias is very small – two parcels of land, seventy graves and two huge grassy plots waiting for more bodies. It takes up a lot less space than you'd think. On the path that leads to the civilian cemetery there are old gravestones, farmers from among the early Zionist settlers and a learned rabbi's wife who died in 1906, back when it was still possible to skinny dip in the Sea of Galilee in the middle of the day, or walk on the water, and everything was deserted and pristine and there weren't a thousand picnickers grilling meat and choking you to death. Attached to the fence was an official IDF black-bordered announcement that Sergeant Tomer Zitlawi, may he rest in peace, son of Abraham and Aliza, had gone to his eternal resting place. From his grave, which was covered with flowers, you could see the Sea of Galilee between the Israeli flag and a tall palm tree. At the head of the grave was a black basalt memorial plaque engraved with a verse from Jeremiah: *'For whenever I speak of him, I earnestly remember him still.'* The Hebrew was difficult, though, and none of us – even Bayliss – had any idea what it meant. Three Arab workers were paving the pathway between the graves and watching us with curiosity. We stood there for twenty minutes or so. Every once in a while someone would imitate that pet of ours whom we'd lost. 'Cocksucker!' someone would say in that deep, happy bass of his. 'What's up, cocksucker? Coming to eat, cocksucker?' He'd shout, 'Hold your horses!' when he meant 'Calm down,' all proud of the new expression he'd coined, and we'd tell him, 'You jerk, that's a translation from English. You didn't make it up.' That would drive him nuts. Birds of every kind gathered there, in the military cemetery.

After that we found a little spot of shade under some cypress trees and we sat down there, on the dirt, in a circle, like a group of boy scouts. 'What would you be willing to die for?' I asked, opening up the discussion. 'This land,' Koka answered. I grabbed a handful of earth and tossed it. 'For that?' I asked. 'Who'd be willing to die for that?' They looked at one another, nobody raised a hand. Even Koka lowered his eyes. 'So then,' I said. 'Nobody at all?' They all looked to Bayliss, thinking that as the squad's right-winger he'd be willing to sacrifice himself for the homeland – even if he had stopped wearing his *kippa*. He said, 'I'd be willing to die for the boys.' They all nodded, every one of them, and raised their hands – they'd be willing to die for their friends. 'The trouble with dying,' I explained, 'is the feeling of missing out on something. Most people die with the feeling that they've missed out because they die for no good reason. But if you and the people who love you know that you weren't wasted for nothing, that you saved someone's life, that you wiped out a terrorist, that you did something that'll go down in the history books, it makes dealing with it a lot easier. Being buried here in this cemetery – in this well-tended plot, with Israeli flags and grass and benches – means the nation salutes you, honours your memory for having given your life in the line of duty. That's not like smashing into a truck and getting thrown into a pit along-side all the people who died in vain without any glory. When you're afraid, ask yourself why you're endangering your life and it gets easier.'

Something caught their attention, and all at once they were all staring at the path, stunned. Nothing could have prepared me for that moment. I turned my head, too, and there was Oshri walking towards us. He was with his mother, an iron rod fixed to his arm. It looked like a spaceship, with metal rings held from the sides by nuts and bolts. He saw me and gazed straight in my direction. Eight months without him, and what did I have to say?

The boys raced to him, crowded around him in a circle of hugs and kisses. I stood up too, walked towards him, but stopped a little way back. I took my time. When he'd finished petting them, one by one, with his left hand, he came over to me. His timid Yemenite face had remained soft and smooth and his skin was like a baby's. But it was thinner than before, more mature, really mature, like he was looking at me from some other world, the world to come, that I hadn't yet reached. I was a memory, one of those soldiers stuck in the past, not maturing, someone still inside the bubble who hadn't learned all the things that Oshri knew and maybe even had had time to forget. That's what he was thinking. 'What are you doing here?' I asked him, idiot that I am.

'River told me you'd be here,' he answered. 'So I came. I was at the funeral, too.'

'You look good,' I told him. 'Really good, like you've been on holiday. Tanned and shaven.' Hemda, his mother, was watching us from the side, pretty emotional – maybe happy for him, but worried, protective, like she was standing by waiting to pounce if he got hurt. Why would he get hurt?

'How are things up there? The usual?' Oshri asked.

'Like always,' I said. 'It's not as though I haven't thought about leaving. I thought it over, before the winter. In the end I decided to stay on, for the time being.'

'Of course,' he said. 'They need you there, right?'

He pulled a black wrist band with a red bead from his pocket. 'I made it,' he said. 'Want it?' I put it around my right wrist and tied it. We went down to the benches that look out over the sea. I wanted to ask, but didn't, how exactly that metal thing on his arm worked and what exactly it was there for, and what Oshri couldn't do any more. He said, 'It's easier for you there than at home. At home you'd sit around staring at the ceiling and going over the newspapers again and again.'

'Yeah. At least up there they need me,' I said.

'But down here they'll need you, too,' he said. 'When you have the guts to give it up and start something new.'

'Life in Israel is boring,' I told him. 'You know me, I'm afraid of being bored. Boredom makes a person do stupid things. It's like a drug, and it makes you depressed.'

'I'm your brother,' he said. 'Still. We'll watch out for you when you come home, when it's all over.'

18

Spitzer had this smile that winked at you and whispered in your ear, 'I've got it all figured out, but I'm not telling you.' And I would say to him, 'Come on, out with it,' and he'd laugh and say, 'It's nothing. Forget about it,' and he'd shut up. He was an introvert.

When I returned to the Soldiers' Hotel at the end of our furlough, his smile was the first to greet me. All Yasur helicopter flights had been cancelled and the convoys weren't going out since there was a high alert on attacks, so we were staying in Kiryat Shmona, waiting to be called. The entrance to the hotel and the lobby were crawling with reporters on the prowl for clichés, after a soldier who'd say, 'I only wanted to make it home safe,' and after blood, too. There were microphones, cameras, tape recorders, soundmen on cigarette breaks – all ordinary citizens invading the world of the simple soldier, no senior officers to speak with, no representatives of the IDF to give briefings. 'Don't you feel like cannon fodder?' the reporters clamoured. But the combat soldiers, acting like combat soldiers do – finding everything funny – shouted, 'Take my picture for the paper!' and smothered every reporter in the vicinity. Spitzer was sitting on a couch, surrounded by soldiers I didn't recognize, with Carmela Menashe standing over him. Yup, *the* Carmela from the radio: mouthpiece for the Four Mothers and the whiners and the faggots. I knew it was her, it couldn't have been anyone but her. I came close, recognized the voice from the radio, and all the blood rushed to my head. I wanted to say something, chuck the truth in her face – the damage she was doing to the Israeli army, to all of us. 'How do you boys feel?' she asked, sticking a microphone into the face of a burly Golani brigade sergeant sitting on a table. 'Carmela, I'm telling you: after the withdrawal everyone's going to say, "Wow, too bad we didn't get out of there a few years earlier, what a waste." I have a message for Prime Minister Barak: man, get us out *now*, what are you waiting till July for? The sooner the better.'

'What about you?' she asked, turning to Spitzer. 'Why are you so quiet?'

'I don't have anything special to say,' he answered with a smile.

'So what is it that you feel? Afraid?'

'If anyone here tells you he's not afraid, he's a liar,' he said.

The fat little Golani teddy bear grabbed the microphone back, asking to send a message to the protesters preventing us from getting our tough job done. What exactly was it that he wanted? It was hard to know. I took advantage of the distraction to whisper into Spitzer's ear, 'Come on, buy me a cappuccino.' He was surprised, really and truly surprised. He followed me out of the room. 'Don't get mixed up with them,' I told him. 'Journalists will fuck with you, believe me.' He asked me if he'd made a mistake by answering the question about being afraid and I told him no, he hadn't. 'Brother, you were cool,' I said. 'It was fine. Talking straight is important. Just remember to be careful.'

Fear is catchy, I know that, and when someone admits it suddenly it's a thing that exists, a legitimate emotion, and it knocks everyone over, one by one. There's nothing more dangerous.

'So what you're saying is that I did blow it,' Spitzer said.

'Next time use the word "tense", don't talk about being afraid. Save being afraid for the really big stuff, when there's no choice. That's what I do. Just don't spend too much time worrying, that's the most important thing.'

The cafeteria was swarming with soldiers waiting in a long line for candy bars and chocolate milk. 'We're from Galgalit, the Outpost of Death,' three young soldiers told the cashier, all proud of themselves, trying to impress her, shouting, nearly coming to blows. Who the hell had decided they were the Outpost of Death? Who was to say it shouldn't have been Ishiye or Karkum? Everyone wanted to be the Outpost of Death. I asked Spitzer if he'd taken the key to his room yet. 'Top floor,' he said, 'great view of the Katyusha rockets.' I suggested we get away from the crowds, and asked if it was OK to go to his room until Levanoni came back with my room key and the squad returned from ten pin bowling. Again Spitzer looked surprised. He pulled his knapsack from a huge pile in the lobby, along with a new guitar. 'I'm going to have a shower,' I told him, 'and when I finish you'll be waiting with a mug of cappuccino, and MTV on the television, but with the volume turned down, just the picture, the way I like it, and you can play me one fucking great solo on your guitar. Go crazy: rip the shit out of the strings, break the wood, make the building shake.'

When I came out of the steamy bathroom wrapped in a towel, to the hot mug of coffee waiting for me, Spitzer didn't go wild on the guitar. He strummed quietly, sang softly and prettily, almost in a whisper, a well-known psalm, but to a new, Middle Eastern tune I didn't know: *A Song of Ascents. I will lift up my eyes unto the mountains: from whence shall my help come? My help comes from the Lord, who made heaven and earth. He will not suffer your foot to be moved; He that keeps you will not slumber. Behold, He that keeps Israel does neither slumber nor sleep. The Lord is your keeper; the Lord is the shade upon your right hand. The sun shall not smite thee by day, nor the moon*

by night. The Lord shall keep you from all evil; He shall keep your soul.
The Lord shall guard your going out and your coming in, from this time
forth and for ever.'

We sat there feeling awkward, embarrassed, when he'd finished.
There wasn't much to say. We kept switching channels looking for
film clips, especially girls in bikinis, and happened on the news.
'It appears that something has changed, a landmark in the history
of the war in Lebanon,' the correspondent was saying. 'Now it is
no longer the parents demanding immediate withdrawal, it is the
soldiers themselves. "Bring us home", that is the new motto
spreading from unit to unit. They are saying in a clear, direct voice,
"None of us wants to be the last casualty in Lebanon. None of us
wants to die for no reason."' A young Armoured Corps soldier
looked at the camera and said, 'You have the power to help us.
Help us get out of there. Anyone who serves in Lebanon knows
we have no way of winning there.' And as if that wasn't enough,
an Engineering Corps fighter added, 'We've gone from being the
hunters to the hunted. We're just targets that draw fire and never
return it, targets waiting to be hit. Six of our men were killed in
ten days. What are we still doing there?'

Then the chief of staff came on and tried to calm things down.
'We are defeating Hezbollah,' he said. He was right, I decided: in
this war there was no such thing as a knockout, it was all a matter
of adding up the points. He'd visited the Reichan outpost and
called the fighters who'd opened their mouths 'whining rags', and
forbidden entry to journalists and photographers. It wasn't the time
for talk, for the media. What a mess, what a noisy fucking blitz.
The commander of an elite unit told a reporter that it was the
public at large that needed therapy, not the soldiers.

'What do you think?' I asked Spitzer. He told me about some
Irish playwright named George Bernard Shaw who once said that
commanders never expect their soldiers to think. 'Maybe that's the
problem,' Spitzer said. I didn't get angry. I was glad that he could
talk honestly, that he wasn't afraid of me. 'I thought you were the

type that never asks questions,' I said. He laughed, looked happy. As always, he had it all figured out.

'You still with the Russian girl?' I asked.

'Yes,' he answered, with that innocent look in his eyes.

'Don't worry, she'll drop you soon enough,' I said, laughing. 'They all do.'

He pulled a few lemon-flavoured wafers from his knapsack and had trouble opening them, did it like a nice Ashkenazi boy with his delicate hands. I thought how nice the peace and quiet was. We ate. 'I'm OK,' he said. 'Don't worry about me. But Emilio? He's a mess. Can't pull himself out of it, sees war everywhere he looks.' He waited for me to react. I kept silent. 'What we're going through,' he said, 'it isn't like a movie, is it? I keep telling myself it's not like a movie, where you know the good guys are going to win. This time the good guys could lose.'

How was I supposed to answer that? 'The good guys will win,' I reassured him. I stood up to get dressed. He caught sight of my wallet, with my army ID sitting on top of it, on the dresser. He looked at the picture, read what was written there. 'What is it?' I asked him with a smile. I knew.

'Nothing,' he answered. 'Nothing at all.'

'The name?' I asked.

'It says, "Liraz Liberti",' he said.

The squad hadn't known until then, didn't have a clue. Everywhere – signatures, lists, documents – I was Erez. 'When I enlisted I was still called Liraz,' I told him. He was stunned, I think, but he played it cool, afraid of offending me or asking too many questions. 'Yeah, that makes sense,' he said. 'I have a friend named Jaime, but all the losers in the army couldn't say his name so he changed it to Hebrew: Jimmy.' Jimmy? What kind of Hebrew name was that? I didn't get the connection. 'My girlfriend might change hers to a Hebrew name, too,' Spitzer said. 'She doesn't like her name. Lana. She hardly even has an accent. It's true.'

They'd met on a beach at the Sea of Galilee, he told me. 'What are you ashamed of, you jerk? She's fucking beautiful, right? You love her, right? She doesn't need to change her name. You convince her to stay as she is. Trust me, it's a great name. And, next furlough, we're all going to meet her. It's time. We're all going to love her, I can tell.'

'Can I say one more word about fear, or is it infectious?' he asked.

'Fire away.'

'Ever since I've been with her I'm afraid. To die, that is.'

'What's that supposed to mean? That before you met her you couldn't care less?' I asked him, idiot that I am.

'I don't remember. I don't think so. Less, for sure. Now it's really strong.'

A dark-coloured plastic bag was sticking out from one of the knapsacks on the floor. He pulled it out, opened it, and took out a black t-shirt. It had our unit's insignia on it, with the words 'There is love inside us, and it will conquer.' He handed it to me, said he'd had them printed for all of us. 'What's going on?' I asked him. 'Are you turning into a fag?' 'No,' he answered. 'It's a man thing. Remember how Zitlawi's favourite soccer team was Hapoel Jerusalem? Well their star player said it, and Zitlawi used to quote him. He'd tell us, "This love is going to send us up to Lebanon safely and bring us back safely."'

I turned the t-shirt around. A silhouette of Zitlawi in white – smiling, his hair wild – took up the whole back side. 'Kind of sick, isn't it?' I said.

'A memorial,' Spitzer answered.

On the TV screen, a mother who had only just lost her son was talking about how the whole thing had slammed her in the face. 'I phoned his mobile, I wanted to play the song "Forever Young" for him, it was his birthday. I left a message. I didn't know he was already dead.' Spitzer watched her, mesmerized. There were tears in his eyes. I'm not kidding, what a good boy, so sensitive. One minute he had the resilient look of a real man; the next minute he looked like a child, tender and fragile. Zitlawi used to call him the Little Prince. He was thin, tall, with huge eyes and tiny ears. And that winning, beautiful smile. The face of a genius, of a rich boy – but the quality kind – the kind who worked in fancy Tel Aviv suburbs as a DJ when he was aged twelve, his hair gelled. He was considered one of the rising stars, right from the time he enlisted, destined for great things. He was quiet, but a leader, with great stamina and a positive attitude. He was always singing. Everyone knew him. I actually hadn't thought much of him at the beginning. In training, and during the first tour of duty in Lebanon, he hadn't seemed enough of a killer, wasn't hot-blooded enough. He was about as different from me as possible. 'So tell me,' I said to him that evening in the hotel. 'What would you think about being sent to officers' academy?'

'Are you serious?' he asked.

'No, the question is, are *you* serious,' I answered. 'Are you willing to postpone your audition for another year or two?'

His eyes sparkled. 'Why me?' he asked, and then answered immediately: 'I think so. I mean,' he added, beaming and confused, 'Yes. Yes I am. I'm willing.' And he played his guitar.

The next morning the whole squad had coffee together at Yedidya's Place in the central bus station, then we filled out lottery cards and had an early lunch at Bomba Burger. It was a fun day. Kiryat Shmona was filled with khaki: tank convoys, equipment trucks and legions of fighters were crammed into the town, waiting for clearance into Lebanon. There were two doors with long lines outside them: one was a tiny synagogue that had never had so much business. Or maybe it had, during the 1982 war or one of the big military operations of '93 and '96. The other was a shop called The Blue Dragon, Kiryat Shmona's tattooist. A Chinese dragon for luck, angels of death, the black cougar that was Golani's mascot – 'A little good luck charm can't hurt,' Boaz explained, all worked up and excited after a visit there. 'When a missile might fall on your head at any moment, any kind of amulet is welcome,' he said. 'Piercing, too. People want to feel the pain.' I announced a ban on The Blue Dragon. 'There's even a rule about it,' I warned them. 'You're desecrating IDF property by scarring your skin like that. The next soldier caught is going to be sent home.'

And they were afraid of being sent home. They didn't want to drop out. It's a fact: everyone showed up when it was time to pull out, just after sunset. During the last furlough, mothers had been more hysterical than ever and fathers begged their sons not to go back and girlfriends threatened to leave them; the pressure was intense. Shit, what stupid, hypocritical parents: they try to convince their children not to serve with us, then they give them the keys to the car on Friday night so they can go drinking at a pub, as if twenty times more people didn't get killed on the roads than in the army. Those parents didn't understand that fighting a war is good for their sons, makes them grow up, teaches them, toughens them up, makes them good citizens. And in the end, the boys themselves are happy. You can take my word for it. My men weren't stupid like their parents, they showed up. Eldad, Boaz, Tom, Itamar. Zion, Koka, River, Bayliss. Pinchuk. Barnoy. Spitzer. It was good for them. Status report, iron numbers. Where was Emilio? Emilio wasn't there. He'd disappeared, vanished. No army officials – the social worker, the adjutant – had heard from him. We phoned his kibbutz, talked to his adoptive parents. They said he'd taken off. They called it a holiday, said he'd gone to see his parents in Argentina, but he hadn't left a message or phone number for us. They would tell him we'd been looking for him, would send our regards if he called. That was that: he stepped on to a plane without a word, and no one had heard from him since. No, the earth didn't swallow him up, but Argentina is a big place, there's no way of finding him. Every once in a while we'd mention his name or imitate him and bust up laughing, all nostalgic. He was a nice fellow, a bit spaced out. He'd walked out of our lives without even saying goodbye.

This time we didn't fly in. Another turning point: according to intelligence reports, the terrorists were planning to knock out a helicopter and the arithmetic was simple: one to fifteen casualties sustained during a Hezbollah attack on a convoy going into Lebanon by road was preferable to forty in a downed helicopter. After all, there's no escaping a burning helicopter. No miracles, no wounded. So we were back to Safari trucks like the good old days. Iron numbers, count off. Mission confirmed, move out. Everyone was fingering something: with me it was the cloth pouch containing my dog tags with Lila's message inside, and Oshri's wrist band; Spitzer had a medallion imprinted with the image of a golden dove that his mother gave him for luck. For Levanoni it was his own face. He kneaded his cheeks. We rolled along fast enough to get there as quickly as possible and slow enough not to overturn and fall into the dark abyss. Any vehicle parked at the side of the road might blow us to smithereens. I concentrated on being tense, not afraid. The gate to the outpost opened and we ran like mad for the secure area. Everything was a big puddle of mud and water, and like always, the whole place was covered in dust and dirt. When you came back from a furlough it choked you.

Just inside, in the middle of the open area, was a dense pile nearly as tall as the room itself. It was all there: our toaster oven, the deep fryer, the mini fridge and the microwave from the war room, the squad's sweet cabinet, the senior staff coffee machine, all the televisions and videos and the projector – the Miriam and Shushu Cinema had been shut down – even the electric kettle. 'What's going on?' we asked, stunned. 'Shutting up shop,' we were told. 'New decrees. They want to see how we'll manage without all this stuff.'

I went to Furman's office. 'What's the story?' I asked.

'They're starting to move equipment out of the outposts,' he answered, 'in stages, in preparation for the withdrawal.'

'Withdrawal? There's not going to be any withdrawal! What are they fucking with our minds for?'

'They're starting with personal belongings. They don't want anything to remain here that isn't essential.'

245

'What's the problem with leaving us a television set?'

'Those are the orders,' he said.

At 2.15 a.m., three empty Mercedes trucks passed through the gate with an armed escort. They were painted black and had local licence plates. They parked with their backs to the entrance of the secure area. The boys loaded the trucks, and twenty minutes later all our refuges of sanity, every connection we had with the outside world, made its way down the hill, back to Israel. We watched with an air of farewell as the trucks grew distant, as though stretchers carrying our friends under blankets were in there. Even Spitzer's guitar was confiscated and sent down. It had only just arrived, hadn't even had time to breathe the Lebanese air. 'Orders,' Furman insisted. 'Explicit and detailed.' All we managed to salvage was Spitzer's electric keyboard and the little video camera, both of which had been stashed under the sofa in the Signal Corps Company Club.

Dave stuck his head out of the war room and called to me. 'Good thing you're back,' he said, 'because I'm not making this list by myself.' He pointed to the left-hand column of the duty roster: the Green guard post. 'Don't tell me you've started with that bullshit, too!' I shouted. In seconds I had randomly filled in the names, one after the other, in whatever order they popped into my head. 'Sorry,' Dave said, 'but I'm not willing to place people there.' He watched everything I did and copied it all down, like an old lady on bingo night, on to a big pink poster, and asked me to hang it on the message board next to the kitchen. 'I don't want to have anything to do with it!' he wailed. I gave him a resounding slap on the back and asked him when he was going to grow up, then I went to hang the thing. A few seconds later a crowd of curious soldiers had emerged from their holes to see who'd landed on the highest, most exposed guard post, the one the sniper was familiar with and was expected to visit again. They looked, digested the information, and went back to the Company Club for a smoke, carrying leftover cartons of juice. They sealed the door closed and threw themselves down on pillows and wicker mats. 'Hey man, who wrote *Sherlock Holmes*?' A crossword puzzle. 'And what's the capital of Vietnam? Five letters.' They got stuck. There was no longer a stereo system hooked up there, so Spitzer took over the keyboard, which was kind of a replacement for the stereo, and played a slow dance under the dim lights. River pulled Pinchuk to his feet for a waltz. One, two, three, one two three. They danced gently but it still came out clumsy, and just like in a ballroom, the others joined in, one couple at a time, five couples in khaki dancing to love songs. Itamar the gorilla squashed Bayliss, Zion the beast made Tom swoon, grabbed his little arse and swung him around. The gloomy atmosphere was banished. Who says we didn't have it good? Eldad lit some memorial candles he found in an old cabinet in the war room (scented candles that had lost their scent) and asked where Zitlawi was when we needed him, remembering the yellow, the blue, the green and the red he'd lit in that very same place when they'd held the séance, on the floor; there were drops of wax still there that squished under their feet, small cold drops that had turned black with mud. Eldad suggested they hold a séance and bring back Zitlawi himself. A group channelling meeting with departed souls. After all, Zitlawi's professional equipment was lying there, orphaned. River pulled out the board. For the record, Dave expressed his dissent, but he stayed to watch.

They started with a short meditation ceremony for spiritual cleansing and balancing energies, their eyes closed: the flow of a river, a waterfall, tranquillity. A plant was placed in the middle, and a bowl of water. Three middle fingers on the wood waiting to be moved. 'I call upon the pure soul of our brother Zitlawi, may he rest in peace,' Eldad proclaimed. 'Are you with us? Are you here, friend?' The fingers moved, all by themselves, over the words on the board. Yes. Yes, he was with them. Silence. Could it be? 'Thank you, thank you for coming,' Spitzer said. You have to be polite, remember to say thank you, as Zitlawi had taught them. It was important to honour the spirit's will.

'Zitlawi, did you see the missile coming at you?' Tom asked.

'Yes,' the fingers answered.

'Did it hurt?' Spitzer asked.

'No.'

'Were you afraid?' Koka asked.

'Yes.'

'What should we do?' Pinchuk shouted hysterically. 'Tell us what we should do!' Eldad grabbed his face, shook him, made him calm down. 'He can't answer questions like that, you idiot!' he shouted.

'Can you see us from up there?' Bayliss asked.

'No.'

'Is there sex in heaven?' Zion asked.

'Yes.'

'Are any more of us going to die here?' Barnoy asked.

'Cut it out,' Eldad said, angry. 'It's not the kind of question to ask him. That's determined by the head honcho of the world. And the prime minister.' After all, if one of them was to die, why should they know about it, and why should they put Zitlawi in such an unpleasant position, asking him to tell them? It wasn't fair. But Barnoy persisted. 'Is anyone else going to die?' he shouted. 'Let him answer! It's the only thing that's worth knowing!' And the fingers moved.

'No,' the board told them.

Towards morning a missile landed on the Tziporen outpost. The boys saw it fly across and explode. They waited at the doorway to the war room for updates, for the names of the wounded, because they all had friends there and rumours flew around in the wake of attacks like those. Soldiers walked around crying. I finally gave up trying to get some sleep and went to Furman's office. 'How close is he?' I asked.

'The sniper?'

'Yeah. When's our turn?'

'He's back in our sector,' Furman told me. 'It's Galgalit or Dlaat or us next in line.'

I sat down. He offered me chocolates and a bottle of orange soda but I couldn't have swallowed a grain of rice. 'What's the plan?' I asked. He pushed a big, thick book across the desk. At least 600 pages, more even, freshly printed, the Northern Command insignia on the cover. *'Back to the Future'*, was the title. *'Command Deployment'*. Classified.

'It's for the withdrawal,' Furman said. 'Procedures for evacuating the outposts.'

I leafed through it. Charts, maps, instructions. Everything was there.

'They're serious,' he said.

'Directions for *shikhluf*,' one of the headings read. *'Shikhluf?'* I asked. 'What's that?'

'It's a new word,' he explained. 'There are loads of them.'

Slowly, choppily, I read, trying to understand the jumble of words: *'All means for carrying out a quick shikhluf must be co-ordinated upon arrival at the site.'*

'It's a procedure for moving equipment between trucks to keep it from getting ruined in the chaos. They even give details about taking out the screws from the beds and wrapping them in plastic.'

'I'm not fucking going to wrap screws for them,' I said. 'You're making this *shikhluf* stuff up!'

'And,' Furman continued, 'you have to know whether to unscrew them left to right or right to left. I can't remember.'

A small radio stood on the desk, playing Israeli songs. Periodically, the songs would be interrupted when the enemy's *Nur* station overtook the frequency. We could hear the news broadcast in poor Hebrew, and the Lebanese jingle we heard all the time and knew by heart: *'You'll go down, you'll go down, get it now: you'll go down. To us war is a dream and peace is a nightmare. That's why we'll win. Get it now: you're going down.'*

We looked at each other, deadly serious and worried, for a few seconds, then, with no warning, we both burst out laughing. For no reason, at the same time, we found ourselves roaring, totally out of control. Smiling from ear to ear I said, 'This situation is totally fucked!' and smashed my head on the table once or twice. 'Completely!' Furman answered, practically choking with laughter. It came in waves, this laughter; when one of us tried to settle down the other would start up all over again. It took us a few long, hard minutes to regain our self-control. We were still smiling, but now we were quieter, more self-conscious. 'What the hell was that supposed to be?' I asked. Neither one of us had an answer.

I went back to bed. Levanoni was lying there like a sphinx with his eyes wide open, not moving. I didn't even try talking to him. There wasn't any point. I prayed I would fall asleep, but it didn't help. Hi Sweetie, I wrote on my yellow legal pad. The situation here sucks. No, that's not a line from a Shlomo Artzi song; Shlomo doesn't have songs that fit our situation any more. I am so tired. Missiles whizz by my ear, but even that doesn't rouse me. No energy left. You could put the body of a dead terrorist on the ground, between my legs, and I would still be tired. Even a soldier's body, maybe. I'm not so gung-ho any more. No fire in me, no tension, only exhaustion. I met this journalist when we were waiting to be shipped back into Lebanon. Haimovitch is his name, a white-haired guy, very experienced. He got in to the base somehow, came up to me as I was sitting alone while Levanoni was handing out the iron numbers. He said to me, 'Sad?' and offered me a cigarette. Then he sat down next to me in the sand. Everything is fantastic, couldn't be better, I told him, and anyway, I don't talk to reporters. I say, 'You people, all you want to do is catch us crying, you push your cameras in our faces so you've got shots of us weak, at funerals. And that makes us weaker. Pictures of soldiers crying – that's a disgrace. Brings everyone down, weakens our fighting abilities, affects our parents.' 'I've been to a lot of funerals this year,' Haimovitch told me. 'Lots of really sad memorial services. I watched your friends hugging each other, kissing, crying, and I learned a few things about myself. I'm an old paratrooper, Class of '65. Your boys dare to do what we saved for the depths of our sleeping bags.

Late at night – and only late at night – you could hear the sound of stifled crying in our tents. In our company there was a sign that read: IF YOU DON'T HANG TOGETHER YOU'LL BE HANGED TOGETHER. You soldiers don't need signs. You believe in tears. So who, exactly, is stronger? Who's more of a paratrooper, more of fighter? I don't have the answer.' I answered, 'If you fought in the Six Day War in '67 then I have a lot of respect for you. Really. But I was taught that we're a country of strong people who know how to keep things to themselves. That's how we won. And that's the reason we're going to lose now.' I took a cigarette from him.

After that, sweetie, I came back here, leaned on the wall and looked at my squad and I realized that they're just high school students at break. Boys. Standing in front of the message board, horsing around, punching each other for attention, smiling all the time. Not one of them has come through adolescence yet. They're puppies. Human puppies.

What, was I becoming a poet all of a sudden? The pompous, whining, absolutely honest thought that some of these soldiers were the walking dead was what did it to me. I've started thinking about that recently. I don't like thinking that way, but that's what came to me: the walking dead are among us, with death cards in their hands. You know what's really sick about this? If one of my soldiers had said that to me, I would have chucked him right out of there, no questions asked, and without a trial. And yet here I was with this thought, this realization, and this knowledge drove me nuts, because without some way of suppressing it, how could I be a fighter? I wasn't who I thought I was any more, I'd lost my peace of mind. And what incredible peace of mind a fighter or a sniper or a gunner needs, no matter how experienced he is, in order to make a direct hit on a soldier standing inside a hedgehog or a trench, barely any part of him sticking out. I don't have that kind of peace of mind any more.

I can't help myself, baby, but the time is drawing near for me to read your note, the one inside the pouch around my neck. I don't have the strength to wait any more. I'll try to hold out. Just for you. I love you.

I wrote until sunrise. When the loudspeakers announced Dawn Alert I ripped the pages out and destroyed them, then I put on a flak jacket and went upstairs. I stood for an hour and a half like a zombie in the corner of the secure area, along with everyone else, staring at the sky and waiting for an attack on the outpost. By 6.45 a.m. I was back in bed. I lay there reading old graffiti, drawn on the walls of the submarine in thin coloured markers: 'You'll never walk alone' and 'Men of Golani, August '88', and this one, dated March '94:

> Here we are a bunch of jocks
> Hiding out between the Lebanese rocks
> We'll fight this war for Sharon the fox
> And come back home inside a box

Just before seven o'clock there was a boom, and shouting. 'Missiles! Missiles! Missiles!' Someone broke in over the loudspeakers: 'Carmel One to positions' – that's the emergency alert force – then somebody ran through the hall shouting, 'Wounded in Green!' I was already on my way, running like a madman up the endless stairs that lead to the guard post, no helmet on my head, panting; all that mattered was getting up there. It's only about 150 yards, but I could barely breathe, it seemed more than I could handle, too much, and I felt so heavy. I told myself it was possible that the boys up there had done what we'd trained for, managed to jump from the guard post and broken a shoulder, and that we wouldn't even need the lifesaving equipment this morning. But a missile like that – what were the chances of dodging it? It was in the air two-and-a-half seconds, six at the most. How could you possibly jump back behind the reinforced concrete? All the procedures were bullshit. But maybe, just maybe, it was only a broken leg, I muttered to myself, or maybe just the mannequins that had been wasted. There was a sharp smell of burnt chicken, really, really strong, nothing like you've ever smelled in your life. Heavy smoke rose from the fighting trench and debris was scattered everywhere. Eldad was lying on the ground, blood covering both eyes. A crescent-shaped piece of shrapnel had sliced open his ankle and more shrapnel was littered across his face, but he appeared to be whole and alive. He'd managed to drag himself to the radio, I could see the trail of blood. I went over to him. 'I can't see anything,' he said. 'My eyes, I can't see.' 'It's OK,' I told him. 'It's only sand, it's covering your eyes. Just stay calm.' I stroked his forehead. His hand was cut wide open, I could see the tendons, the bones.

'Talk to me,' I said to him. 'Talk to me, I'm here, I'm with you.'

'I can't see,' he said.

River and the evacuation team opened stretchers, began treatment. 'Forget about me,' Eldad shouted. 'What about Yonatan? What about Yonatan Spitzer?' An axe blow hit my soul, a knockout punch slammed my heart. My whole body began to shake. How had I forgotten him? Something had suppressed it, kept me from reviewing in my mind the duty roster, prevented me from asking questions. I ran inside, feeling through that black cloud and trying to find my way down the tunnel. I got down on my hands and knees, groped the air, the ground. I shouted to him: 'Spitzer? Yonatan?' but he didn't answer. A few seconds later I saw a body in front of me, through the haze, a pair of legs. He was lying on his back. I leaned towards him, trying to see. I grabbed his vest and pulled with both arms. In a split second the thought entered my mind that he was too light, that there was no counterweight to my pulling, and that this was strange. But before I could begin to grasp why, I saw the terrible thing. His entire head, from shoulder to shoulder, was missing. His arms were dangling there. Everything was scorched inside. There was no blood, it had all been burnt away. I let go, sprang backwards. I couldn't bring myself to get close to him. Furman was there beside me. 'Go back down,' he said. 'Give a report and prepare the Nakpadon for rescue.' But I couldn't move, I felt I was collapsing like a house of cards. River came in, too. Took hold of the body, screamed. He leaned over Spitzer, his forehead on his stomach, and held on tight. Furman and I tried to pull him off, get him outside. It was impossible. I don't remember what we did next, there are a few long moments that have been wiped from my memory. But we were there, inside, until I decided I'd better start acting like an officer, a professional.

Furman shouted, 'Everyone on all fours, crawling, I don't want any part of you sticking out above the tunnel.' We didn't want to get hit by another missile. We got River out of there, then we crawled back inside, me and Furman, to bring Spitzer's body down. I held his upper body, Furman took his legs. We got him to the stairs that way. Two soldiers were waiting there with an open stretcher. We put him on it and covered him up right away with a blanket.

There was no head to be found. We went back to look for it. From all that stress I was in need of air, lots of it, but inside the cloud it was impossible to breathe. I could feel myself choking, getting dizzy. I shouted, 'Where's the head?' The only thing I didn't want was for the boys to find it first. We searched for it. 'We've got to look around the hedgehog, between the rocks, near the fence,' Furman said. 'Maybe it flew out, hit a boulder and bounced back.'

We made our way through the entire tunnel. Nothing. We came out empty-handed. We didn't find a head, only a mannequin, in one piece, lying on the ground. 'Shit, Erez, it must have flown down to the river,' Furman said. I told him that couldn't be. 'Maybe it just went up in smoke,' I suggested. Furman dashed off to the war room to talk to Command, get instructions. On the way there he sent Tom and Barnoy, the next on the list, to man the post.

I went to the stairs. River, Bayliss, Zion and Koka were waiting there. They asked me where Spitzer's head was. I told them we hadn't found it. Yet. 'Maybe it rolled down the slope, there's nothing we can do about it.'

'Let's go and look for it,' River said with determination. I told him it was too dangerous and against the rules, forbidden by command – there was no crossing the barbed-wire fence surrounding the outpost. I said we were waiting for instructions. 'If we wait, the head will disappear, it'll be carried off in the Litani,' River said. 'I'm going out to look for it, I don't care.' 'Stop!' I shouted at him. But he took off at a run, jumped over the trench, climbed the small fence. I saw him cut his hand. I raced after him, to stop him by force, but I didn't make it in time. He kept going. I stopped at the edge. 'River! Stop!' I shouted. 'Now! You're exposed! Stop!' Bayliss gave me an apologetic look and he jumped over the fence and out too, followed by Zion and Koka, down the slope. I stood there, powerless, pressed up against the fence, commanding them to come back, shouting about breaking orders. But I wasn't really fighting them, wasn't really threatening them like I know how to, wasn't blocking them with my body. My brain was working slowly. I could see them making their way down the slope, then I jumped over and ran after them. I got the war room over my radio and said to Dave: 'We're looking for the head, send out whoever you can to help.' In minutes, they were all there, the whole squad, all the boys. They were running between the boulders, scanning the ground. We worked together as a team – organized and fast.

There were so many times I'd wanted to disobey orders since I'd become an officer. I'd bitten my tongue on so many operations and before so many senior officers talking bullshit when I knew more than they did, because I knew the lie of the land and had the full picture. I had sworn to myself that I wasn't going back to jail, that I would be an exemplary military man – and so orders had to be obeyed. Never again would someone shout at me, 'Erez, you psycho! Stay where you are. That's an order! Erez, you're in violation of an order!' I'd kept my mouth shut so many times, but not again, not now. It wasn't because there was some terrorist on the slope outside the outpost that I was hungry to kill. I was disobeying orders so I could bring Spitzer's head back to his mother.

Furman showed up, caught sight of us overturning stones on the slope, and joined in. Even he was outside the fence now. He gave me a look that said 'You're OK, you took the right action,' or maybe even 'I'm proud of you.' But we didn't find the head. We searched for it until four that afternoon. It was a lost cause. 'There's no choice, we've got to go back inside,' Furman said finally, and everyone returned, resigned, to the secure area. He came to me and said, 'I've got a fucking awful job for you. Go and pick up the little pieces of him left behind. Take a pair of gloves. We don't want the boys to see the mess.' So I went, carrying a black bag. I walked the length of the tunnel collecting burnt clothes, pieces of flesh, his weapon and magazine, everything spattered with blood. The walls were covered with it too, red and black, and shiny. Bayliss packed up Spitzer's personal belongings to send to his mother. What would you find in the knapsack of a dead guy? A few books, some underwear, linen and discs and snacks, a toothbrush and shaving cream, and the kind of pyjamas only a little rich boy would own, folded neatly and smelling fresh; which he never wore. River took over his video recorder, asked to hang on to it for the time being with the cassette inside, *A Guide for Lana*, his Russian girl-friend. He wanted to finish the film, turn it into a commemor-ation, and I approved his request on condition that he write to the family. I wanted him to get their permission. At five o'clock, another attack on the outpost began.

It wasn't really an attack on the outpost, it was just some nut case running up the hill and shooting in our direction. Maybe he was on drugs, maybe he was retarded. We watched him dashing back and forth and shooting, out of control. We had a field day: the whole outpost started shooting at him at the same time. Everyone. But not only at him. Grenade-launchers, MAG 58s and M24s, tanks: a real Firebox Procedure. We called for combat heli-copters which fired as well. I climbed a rampart and emptied ammo like crazy, like Rambo, another round and another and another. You have no idea who you're shooting at, or where, but you've got your outlet, you can vent. The air is dark and full of dust, there's no visibility, all you care about is shooting. It was a total loss of control, we were running wild, one big, bad party. All the tension that had been in the air just burst at once. The boys in the White guard post kept shouting, 'Die you fucker, die!' It wouldn't bring Spitzer back, but at least we'd killed a terrorist. At last. How long had we been waiting to do that? We were so trigger-happy, so worked up. All we were praying for was for them to keep coming, more of them, up close. We didn't care if they threw grenades at us, just so long as they acted like men and came close, so we could kill them with blows. Someone shouted, 'Suspicious movement!' and we opened fire again, turning everything into fog. I couldn't see a thing. They were firing the MAGs like madmen, not even aiming. Spitzer was dead! If we didn't take down at least three terrorists that night the outpost would become another Massada! Suddenly, somebody said they'd heard a noise from one of the unmanned tank positions near Yukhmur. I shouted, 'Position 11! Position 11!' and before I'd even finished the command we were firing two phosphorus bombs and a round of grenades and massive tank fire in that direction. The whole outpost was shooting at the spot. And then it ended. Everything was a blur: you couldn't remember what you were doing there or why you were being attacked or who was attacking or even what was going on. All you knew was that they hated us and we hated them. All you knew was that they had killed Spitzer. We waited fifteen minutes and watched as an ambulance entered Yukhmur. It left with casualties. Only then did we close up shop.

Days went by, and I could still smell that sharp burnt smell in the air. It came in waves, every day, as if it would never go away, and Green guard post itself remained black. In the dining room we had to face the table we'd put Eldad on before he was evacuated. Nobody would eat there, only the youngest soldiers during Shabbat meals did, when the place was full to capacity and they had no choice. The sniper had let up; he'd been silent for two weeks. Surveillance cameras were installed on top of the sandbags lining the trenches, and were operated by joysticks. Soldiers on duty could watch the screen from a seated, protected position without exposing themselves. Cement mixers came up the hill to us every day and made walls of reinforced concrete, and convoys brought more protective equipment and took back all non-essential items, breaking down the outpost week by week. And us – we didn't poke our noses out of the place the whole time. Sometimes we received permission to perform a preventive bombardment and our weapons would fill up the night with noise as we riddled the wadis, those lush hothouses perfect for hiding terrorist cells, with bullets and rockets. Every night I would imagine that the whistling of the wind was actually the sound of propellers coming to take us out of there. But on we stayed, shut inside and waiting. And we played *What Yonatan Spitzer Can't Do Any More*, sometimes for hours: Yonatan won't know the feeling of renting a flat with his girlfriend. He won't take a piss with us from the highest peak in South America, he won't ski in Chacaltaya, he won't screw the hottest Peruvian chick in Casa Fistuk any more. He'll never cheat, he'll never be in pain, he'll never understand, he'll never know what's happening with us any more.

One morning I was standing in the trench, looking through my binoculars. Everything was quiet, when suddenly I spotted two strange civilian trucks, a kind I wasn't familiar with – Mustangs or something – that looked like huge refrigeration vehicles. They approached Arnoun, then turned on to the road leading up to Beaufort and began their climb. A few minutes later they entered the gate and their doors were opened. I came out to see what was inside. It was totally unexpected: towers of hundreds of landmines piled one on top of the other filled the interior 'M15 and M29 anti-tank landmines,' Furman explained. 'There are 980 of them, six and a half tons.' They were round, with a cake of TNT in the centre top of each one. 'It's our job to take possession of them and store them safely,' he said. 'We'll put them in the storeroom next to the gym.' Dave gathered twenty or thirty soldiers he found lounging in the submarine and had them form a human chain. The mines were taken off the trucks and piled in the storeroom, filling it entirely, then Furman put a lock on the door and that was the end of that. They were out of sight, as if they didn't exist. From that night on we slept on top of those landmines, which were a kind of hourglass, it was as though your mind sensed the sand pouring through all the time. We walked back and forth past that locked door all day, every day, knowing, even understanding, but trying not to think about it.

19

Even if we thought about it, we didn't talk about it. There was no withdrawal. None whatsoever. It was business as usual, that was the tactic we'd chosen. Too dangerous to dig around in these matters, the boys would ask too many unhealthy questions. If you mentioned withdrawal once then it would happen. If you set it out on the table it would hover around for ever. Keeping quiet was best. It was hard enough as a commander to keep them in suspense for such a long period. They were curious, stuck their noses in places they didn't belong, understood even when nothing was explained to them – there was no hiding anything from them. Especially when we started thinning out the place, getting rid of the non-essentials: the gym was dismantled and we received new orders every day. So we made an effort to suppress it, to play dumb, and from the time Spitzer was killed the word itself was never mentioned. From our point of view there was no withdrawal.

That is, until Brigadier General Kaplan joined us for the Passover Seder. We read the Hagaddah, held the ceremony like usual. We were waiting for someone to ram a chicken leg down the military rabbi's throat for going into such great detail, explaining every ramification of every word of the story of Passover. It seemed as though he'd go on for ever, until Furman, thank God, cut him off and asked if he might speak. He tapped his wine glass and said, 'Brigadier General Kaplan, the commander of our division, took part in the historic battle in 1982 in which Beaufort was captured. Back then this place was a breeding ground for Palestinian terrorists. They would fire on Israel from this spot, until a small band of brave young fighters cleaned out the place and set up our presence here, on the first day of the war. Kaplan commanded those fighters, the reconnaissance unit. He himself was injured.'

Fucking hell, what a man this General Kaplan was! We gave him a big, noisy round of applause. He smiled, kind of embarrassed, and sank down in his chair. 'We've prepared a little surprise for you,' Furman said as he produced a framed parchment that had a silhouette of the Beaufort fortress along with the text of the communication log from the big battle. He read out Kaplan's last commands before he was wounded: 'Commander here, all armoured personnel carriers in a single line. Over. Commander here, shine a light so we can see you. Over.' Then he got hit, and when he fell backwards a voice came over the radio: 'Kaplan, have you been hit? Kaplan, are you wounded?' Then it was quiet. It was quiet, too, in our dining room just then. 'Kaplan, you're hit!' Furman said, as he turned to him. 'I'm sorry I took you by surprise like this, commander. But we'd like to hear about that battle, especially since the commandment on this holiday is to "tell the story to your sons".' We waited for Kaplan to speak.

When he stood up, tears were pouring down his face. We all saw it, a brigadier general crying. Zitlawi would have been on the floor laughing if he'd been with us. He'd have bitten his lips, tried to stop himself, really made an effort, but in the end his big laugh would have come bursting out and pulled half the room along with him, or at least a quarter of us, spreading through the benches. If he'd been with us. But he wasn't. Good thing. Without him, the place was silent and serious.

'I've come full circle this evening,' Kaplan said. 'Most of my adult life has been connected to this piece of earth, my entire military service has had something to do with it. My friends – my best friends – remained here, most of them, and they'll stay behind when we pull out. Tonight I'm here at Beaufort for the last time. To say goodbye to it. You men will be the ones who evacuate it.'

So that was that.

That's when it happened, when it was all over. There was no going back. We'd taken it all in, understood. The IDF was serious about this, we'd really be leaving. With one, matter-of-fact statement, the story ended. It was over. Even Kaplan had given up. All I could think about was how incredibly stupid I had been. And how it could be that this place, an entire world, a real city, an empire, our own, our whole lives – how could it suddenly just disappear? How could we abandon it? Blow it up, so that it ceased to exist, so that nobody would live here again, would sleep here any more, guard the place? It was our own patch of heaven and we were going to be moved somewhere else? There wasn't a single drop of logic in it.

Kaplan took a look at the parchment, read the words to himself, and looked out over the expectant faces of the crowded rows of soldiers sitting in silence. 'No,' he said. 'I wasn't in command of the battle. I didn't have a chance, I was wounded before it began. While my friends were being killed, one after the other, I was lying wounded in a field down below, on the slope. I was doped up with painkillers, sometimes alert and sometimes not, lying there waiting to be evacuated with an injured lung, trying to follow what I was hearing on the radio.

'I'd been given this mission back in 1980,' he said as he moved away from the head table and crossed the room to squeeze in between two startled Russian soldiers, the youngest among us. 'They told us that taking control of Beaufort meant taking control of the entire region. It can be seen from everywhere, and everywhere is visible from it. A fortress, with walls that look out for miles and miles. Even the Syrians used to dispatch observers to Beaufort. Back then I was an operations officer. I took my men up to Kalaat Nimrod, the Crusader fortress on the Golan Heights, to train. After that I took a year off to study, and when I came back – a week before the war – Goni Harnick handed over command of the unit to me. His discharge party was planned for Saturday night. Two days earlier terrorists had attacked the Israeli ambassador in London, who sustained severe injuries. All furloughs were cancelled, we got orders, the party was cancelled and we were sent up to the launching area, preparing to enter Lebanon.

'We moved out at two o'clock on a Sunday afternoon. We crossed into Lebanon in armoured personnel carriers, passed by Mount Shomriyah and the Akia bridge, and started climbing. The trip took four hours. We watched an evacuation helicopter fall, killing five soldiers, and saw huge numbers of troops streaming in, and long columns of armoured vehicles. We made it in without incident, were barely even shot at once. Beaufort was being constantly bombarded by IDF artillery, we could see the smoke all along the way. My boys shouted, "Stop firing! Come on, leave something for us! What are you doing?" They were afraid there'd be nothing left for them to do. They laughed, had a good time.

'It was 6 June. We entered the village of Arnoun from the south so that we wouldn't pass through the main street. The attack, with tanks, was supposed to start between three and four in the afternoon so that it would still be light, but we got stuck in a long traffic jam and it was getting dark. It was there, in the grove between Arnoun and Beaufort that you men are all familiar with, that we came under fire for the first time. I took a bullet in the upper back. They dragged me to an open field at the edge of the mountain and put me on a stretcher.

'Goni, who could never let himself give up and had volunteered to join the forces at the front, heard what had happened and asked to take my place. He jumped in an armoured personnel carrier and raced towards the mountain. On the way up he overturned on one of the curves and was thrown out of the vehicle, injured, but he kept on, on foot. In the meantime, the tanks had stopped working – they were a mechanical mess, they never even reached us. The track on the last of them fell off on its way out of the village. So we had no cover. Goni ordered the men to storm Beaufort on foot. He came over the radio. "Commander here, all men off vehicles, meet at the house with the arched windows." He briefed them. "OK, men, we're going up to take Beaufort. We've waited years for this moment and we're going to pull it off as best we can. Erez to the right, Avikam to the left, Yuval in front, Tzvika in back." And they started up the steep path in the moonlight, hoping the terrorists had bailed out because it was quiet at the top of the hill, and we'd been told that the terrorists always ran off at night, and if they didn't always run off, then surely they would when they saw armoured convoys and troops coming at them from every direction? They had every reason to run off. I was lying there, listening – the connection was poor – without being able to take in the fact that my men were being mowed down one after the other. Yaron Zamir, my signaller, was killed at a run, at the entrance. Yossi Eliel, on the day of his discharge, was downed by a round of gunfire on the road. The squads continued up the hill, I heard them as they discovered that the fighting trenches were too narrow because of reinforced concrete, and they couldn't fit inside them. The terrorists hadn't run away, were entrenched inside reinforced positions where no grenades could reach them. Gil Ben-Akiva fell, too, and then Avikam Sherf – Abu we called him – whose brother had also fallen in battle. And Razi Guterman. Erez was wounded. Morris, too, who injected himself with morphine. They all lay in pools of blood and tried to treat themselves. To tell you the truth, we'd thought we'd get out of there without a single injury. The boys had agreed to meet in the national stadium in Beirut. And then Goni was hit by a single bullet to the chest, right inside the target, and died. Goni Harnick.

'I've been moving around inside Lebanon for years now,' Kaplan continued, 'and as I go from village to village I look up at the hill. I send troops up here, make visits. In the meantime, Beaufort has become famous, every child in Israel has heard of it. The men who gave their lives to this place have become symbols. Goni. Erez, too. You all know that our division commander, Brigadier General Erez Gerstein, the Erez who was wounded with us, was killed last year. I keep asking myself what Erez would say if he were here, what he would do. And Amir. And Hussein. All the men I loved. Whenever I brief soldiers before a mission I tell about them, how each one was killed. You men are already experienced, you know how hard it is to lose a friend and also how you have to go on. You bite the bullet and carry on. Personally, I've continued in their path, it's my way of making up for their deaths, it's how I cope.'

'And was it worth it?' River asked. It came out suddenly, and so loud that everyone heard him. 'Do you feel it was worth it?' River persisted. Shit, what courage. I shot him a look that said, 'Just you wait, I'm going to rip you to shreds the minute Kaplan's helicopter takes off.' Kaplan searched the crowd to see who'd spoken, waited a moment, then pulled himself together and said, 'I've always asked that question: was it worth it, or not? I hope it was. I remind myself how many lives we've saved. How hard we've tried to protect the sanctity of each and every one of your lives. More than that, I can't answer.'

'I'm sorry,' River said very quietly, though each and every one of us could hear him. 'I've been trying to convince myself that what we lost was worth it. I haven't succeeded.' Kaplan stood up. His face had a consoling look to it, and he was smiling thinly, but you could see a deep sadness in his eyes. He said, 'Imagine it's the European league basketball championships, one second to the finish. The other team is leading by a point and our own Katash is at the foul line. You know the situation? Well, that's where we are now. All that's left for you men is to be strong, focused, and to make sure that we end this campaign ahead of the other men.'

'Hey, wait a minute,' everyone shouted. 'A second to the finish? Really? When?' They wanted a date.

'This summer,' Kaplan told them. 'Three months from now, more or less. There's a lot to prepare. It'll be the biggest battle this division has seen since that war, the battle of two divisions waging a withdrawal. And in this kind of battle you need heroism. There's no room for people to fall apart.'

Spitzer wasn't there to sing and Zitlawi wasn't there to play the *darbuka* drums, so we ate. When it was over, Kaplan took Furman for a chat in the office. On the way there he caught sight of me leaning on the doorpost of the war room, watching nothing happen out there, a steaming cup of black coffee in my hand. He asked if there was any more where that came from. I offered to make him a cup, and he invited me to join them, so I did. We sat there, the three of us, tired, talking about what had happened in the dining room. 'It's a different era,' Kaplan said, with a smile. 'You're a different generation, a generation that asks questions. And we are obliged to give you answers. That's good.' I was hoping to hear him say, 'Between us, this withdrawal business is bad shit, dangerous, and the country's sick in the head.'

'Yes,' he said, 'I'm one of the squares who thinks that the only way to protect Israel's northern settlements from the growing threat that is Hezbollah is by maintaining a security zone in southern Lebanon. And control of Beaufort, with its topographical superiority, is exactly what makes the difference. We weren't lying to you when we told you we believed our presence here has prevented terrorists from reaching Kiryat Shmona, and we weren't lying when we said that the attacks on Beaufort – instead of on the Good Fence at Metullah – are saving civilian lives. We believe it. Or at least I do. And I'm frightened. I don't know what's going to happen the day after we leave.' That's what he said. 'But who knows? Maybe afterwards, when this whole thing is over, we'll ask ourselves why we didn't withdraw a few years earlier, why we were sunk so deep in tactics, without strategies. It isn't simple. Not at all.'

I felt drunk. I sucked in some coffee. Furman seemed pretty agitated. Kaplan cut us each a piece of cake. 'Tell me something,' I asked him. 'Is there a chance that it all happened by accident?' He didn't exactly understand what I meant. 'This whole mess,' I explained. 'Is there a chance that you weren't even supposed to conquer Beaufort that day, but you stormed anyway?' Kaplan took a deep breath, and his small, sad smile nearly disappeared. 'Yes, there is,' he answered. 'There was apparently some sort of order like that – not to attack – but it never reached us. To this very day it's not clear where exactly it got stopped.'

So, it turned out I was the real jerk: Spitzer had been telling the truth. 'You have to know this: it's the history,' Kaplan continued. 'Everything began here. Not only the heroes and the symbols, but the public rift, too, and the protest demonstrations, and the Peace Now movement. Here, for the first time, was where thoughts of the futility of our position first began. I don't think that feeling has ever been stronger among our troops than it is here and now. It's only natural when you're dealing with withdrawal, and that's our mission at the moment: to clamp down on the torment, not to broadcast it – or the doubts, either – to the outside world. Simply to strengthen the soldiers. That's what we need to do, for the time being.'

That was what happened on the night of the Passover Seder, 19 April.

20

Friday night, 19 May. Hezbollah likes to strike on Friday nights. As many as 300 missiles, shells and rockets landed on IDF positions in the security zone during one twenty-four hour period. The Reichan outpost went up in flames and three soldiers were critically injured before the fire extinguishers could cover the area in a blanket of white. Terrorists tried to capture another outpost, Rotem, on foot – and failed. And at the SLA's Armata outpost, a local minibus loaded with nearly ten pounds of explosives blew the gates open and caused the buildings to tumble one after the other, killing scores of people. The Israeli air force responded by shelling Sujud and Yaatar, destroying cannons and vehicles with rocket launchers and a pick-up truck carrying heavy machine-guns. That hell was the background music to our Friday night prayers and Sabbath meal.

On Saturday night Amos landed at Beaufort. 'It's going down faster than we thought,' he said as he jumped out of the helicopter. 'Maybe even within the month. We're closing up shop. And from now on everything's going to be tougher, more dangerous.' He called the officers together and talked straight, put his cards on the table. 'Intelligence has been issuing warnings about what we're likely to be in for on the night of the pull out,' he said. 'Hezbollah is looking for a bloodbath. They want to make sure this withdrawal is etched on our collective memories as a bloody retreat. The terrorists have been co-ordinating code names for the "big surprises" they've got planned for us. They're stashing ammunition and loading their arsenal with new types of explosives and preparing operational plans for attacking our convoys. Not an easy situation.' He asked us to believe him when he told us that the entire IDF was working day and night on this, and that the army was spending big money to thwart enemy plans and provide as much protection as possible. But as for us, he said, we were going to have to be mentally and physically prepared for what was ahead, because it was about to happen.

'You've got to get out of here tonight,' I whispered to Furman. 'Go home. It's going to be your last chance before the grand finale. We'll manage.' He lifted off with Amos and I settled into his chair and got River to quiz me on withdrawal procedures from *Back to the Future*. With no video and no toaster there was nothing to do at the outpost but test each other from the book. All of us were walking around with the thing, learning it by heart and making up quizzes. It became a kind of sport. River made fun of it all. 'The most important thing,' he said, 'is not to let that stupid book fall on your foot, because that's the only really dangerous thing that might happen to you during the pull out.'

Procedures for burning secret documents, the gathering of equipment for destruction, how to dismantle a generator, when to disconnect the secure radio, which foods from Chili's pantry to pack and which to leave behind. How much ammunition to stock up on, when to open fire, status reports on the area of operation, land and aerial support, the time frame, dozens of code names. River read out the situations and I gave the responses.

Early on Sunday morning a convoy carrying limited supplies managed to reach us. There were packages from home, newspapers, uniforms, laundry. A little food. The SLA drivers who unloaded the large plastic containers were in a hurry to take off. We offered them coffee but they just wanted to leave – no laughing, no cigarettes. I went off to get some sleep.

Dave shook me awake at 10.20 a.m. 'The Taibe outpost has fallen!' he shouted. 'It's a real mess!' He said that from the Green and Red guard posts, facing south, you could see hundreds of women and children climbing up towards it. The main area of our own outpost was its usual Sunday busy, the way it was at the beginning of each week, with everyone doing outpost chores, disinfecting the kitchen, polishing equipment. At a run we pushed through the crowd until we reached the war room and I grabbed a pair of electronic binoculars and looked to the far left. It was hard to see, but I could just make out a long, long line – endless, in fact – of people heading towards the SLA outpost in the south of our sector. The imams in the mosques in the village below had urged them to march on the outpost, and now they were. 'Shit!' I shouted. 'Why aren't those fucking SLA soldiers firing on them? They should keep them at bay by shooting at them!'

'The SLA isn't there any more,' I was told by the officer on duty in the war room, a Russian.

'What do you mean?' I asked.

'They've abandoned the outpost. It's deserted. At ten o'clock the gate opened and they left: five Mercedes, a jeep and an old tank. They took off like madmen.'

At 10.45 a.m. we watched as the yellow flag of the enemy was raised. Green flags of Islam covered the guard posts. From that moment, Hezbollah was in possession of an outpost, its first ever, and it was obtained without a battle. Our helicopters took off and circled the outpost as a deterrent, but it was too late. Fucking bad news, we all said. I sent Dave to redo the guard duty roster, to provide more cover for Blue so that four soldiers would be on duty there at all times. If a procession of marchers headed towards us, too, the boys in Blue would be the first to know it. I ran to the office and contacted Amos on the secure radio. 'We're completely exposed from the south,' I told him. He already knew about it. 'Not only you men,' he said. 'There are processions like that marching in every district. Listen in to the radio. We're trying to block them.' What we were hearing on the division's operational network was stuff we'd never heard before: 'They're jumping ship from Shayareen, too,' came the report from Galgalit. And from Olesh: 'Randuriye, too. There's a long line of citizens marching. In another five minutes they'll be across the Litani.' A river of people – Lebanese locals, simple folk – flowed to the Kanetra outpost and captured it without warning. It was war. Our allies the Christians had run away without warning Northern Command. The Gamba outpost was about to fall: a country that had been living for years in hiding was suddenly showing its face, by the thousands. It was a popular revolution carried out on a bad morning for popular revolutions, since the visibility on that foggy day was so poor.

Half an hour before lunch, the teleprinter spat out a cable and

I told Dave to call everyone to the briefing room immediately. The entire outpost squeezed in, abandoning dirty pots and pans and buckets of ammonia and sewing machines. I didn't even have a chance to get worked up. When you get a cable like this you let your soldiers know about it right away – it's procedure, they teach it in officers' academy. And so I did: 'There's a good chance we're leaving here soon,' I told them. 'Very soon. Maybe even tomorrow.' Never will you see the dropped jaws and the popping eyes that those who were there with me saw. Let's hear some whistling, some applause! Nothing: they were paralysed, in shock. 'There's a lot to do and we're starting now, so concentrate,' I said. 'First stage: strip the submarine bare, empty out the rooms. In the next fifteen minutes I want all personal belongings upstairs. That means knapsacks, sleeping bags, walkmans, souvenirs, narghiles. Whoever feels the need should take a second to slip on his lucky underwear. Second stage: take down all the maps, collect all the secret documents, fold up the flags, whitewash the graffiti. The kitchen will be closed down, the phone and transmission lines cut. We're not leaving a pin behind when we go, not a single can of paint with the IDF logo on it. That's our mission now, and we're all going to help pull it off. Third stage: prepare the buildings for explosion. We have 980 mines to hook up. My squad will start placing them. Furman will be arriving this evening and he'll have more information. He'll let us know exactly how we're going to be carrying this out.'

I told them, in short, that we were going to leave Beaufort in the most dignified way possible. Like gung-ho beasts of prey, they attacked the outpost, ripping eighteen years from the walls. River put himself in charge of forming a human chain to remove the fat, round cakes of TNT from the storeroom and stack them like towers at the medical bay. Levanoni and I took two wooden crates – the withdrawal kit, which contained equipment necessary for breaking down a base – from the cabinet in the office. We found five nail guns and the outpost construction plan. 'We have to scatter the mines,' I explained to the crew. 'Two mines every two yards or so. The first one will be attached to the wall about two-thirds of the way up from the floor and held in place by three nails, one above and two below the mine. The next will be placed on a chair or stool or box or table; ideally it should be off the ground. Next, place a mine above and below the beds in the submarine. And of course they must surround the buildings and be placed inside the trenches, except for those on the eastern wall because it abuts the ancient fortress.'

I phoned Amos. 'We don't have enough trucks to carry all the equipment,' I told him. 'We'll need at least another five. And we need a crane to load the generator. It's specified in the book.'

'Listen,' he said, cutting me off. 'No trucks, no cranes. Load whatever you can into your vehicles. Burn classified documents. That's all you can do. Everything else goes up in smoke with the mines. And one more thing: Furman won't make it back into Lebanon before the withdrawal. There's no way of getting anyone in this evening. You men are on your own. I have full confidence that you'll manage.'

Yes, sir. Roger. Over and out.

I went to gather my own personal belongings. I packed my bag, removed the pair of my grandfather's *tefillin* from the small cabinet, along with the yellow legal pad filled with letters I never sent, and a photo of me and Oshri, both of us looking so young, arms around each other, on our way into Lebanon in the winter of '97. And the big flag of Israel that had been hanging on the wall since our first night at Beaufort. I packed it all in and tossed my knapsack on to the pile that nearly reached the ceiling.

At about 9 p.m. I was up on the roof with six soldiers, preparing to pull down the main antenna, which would leave us without phone contact. Only the secure radio was left. I pushed the iron rods one way while they tugged from the other side using a rope, and Itamar stood ready to saw off the metal legs. We started the countdown. 'Hold on,' I shouted. 'Wait for me, just two minutes.'

I ran to the ladder, climbed halfway down then jumped the rest of the way. I ran to the war room and phoned Israel from the hotline. Furman happened to be in the Command war room at the time, just back from a brief visit home, and he told me how the whole country was flooded with rumours, people were talking in the streets, word was spreading from person to person.

'How about you?' Furman asked. 'Stressed out?'

'No, not at all. We're pulling it off, no big problems.'

'It'll be fine,' he told me.

I hesitated for a moment. I didn't answer.

'What's the matter, little girl? Are you afraid?' he asked. He was making fun of me. After all, that stupid question about being afraid was stolen from my own repertoire. I didn't laugh.

'Furman,' I said. 'Get your hands on a Nakpadon and get yourself up here, on the double.'

'I wish I could,' he answered. 'Border's closed. They're not letting anyone in. We're on high alert.'

'Listen,' I said, giving myself a few seconds. I swallowed. 'I'm being serious now. I need you here for this thing. There's no way you can leave me here alone with the boys. I don't care how – grab a motor scooter and get yourself here.'

'No chance,' he said, making himself clear. 'I'm sorry.'

Minutes later the antenna came down. We spent the whole night like a conveyor belt, sticking mines to the walls. Every once in a while I'd send some of the boys off for a quick nap on their cold mattresses. 'Tomorrow's going to be a really tough day,' I told them. But within seconds they'd slip outside again. Who could possibly sleep at a time like that?

An order came in from Command, suspending all ambushes being carried out by special and elite units across the various sectors, and the squads were told to return to their bases immediately. All operations were halted at once, the fighters gathered up the newspapers they'd been shitting into and the bottles they'd been filling with piss and moved back to base in the dark. Meanwhile, River,

Bayliss and I placed mines in the kennel and on top of the generator and the diesel oil tank.

'Can I ask you a question?' River said. 'Well, actually, two questions. A kind of a test.'

'General knowledge?' I asked. 'What, do you want to humiliate me at a time like this?'

'If you're wasted, who would you want to be remembered as being like? Give me a name. Somebody, you know, famous. Say it fast, don't think first.'

'I don't know. Nobody. I'm not interested in that kind of bullshit.'

'Try anyway,' he pleaded. 'Who would it be?'

'How about you? You go first,' I insisted.

'Buddha, I suppose,' River answered. 'A little Indian prince, fed up with life, bored, sitting under a tree and suddenly he attains enlightenment. Or maybe Gandhi.'

'So what's the second question?' I asked him.

'If you had only two weeks left to live,' River said, 'what would you do?'

'How about you?' I asked.

'I'd fly to Fiji,' he answered.

'For fuck's sake, River, cut it out,' I said. 'What's with all these stupid questions?' He told me he couldn't stop thinking about the gap, the chasm between the life you live and the life you'd want to be remembered for. People live, mistakenly, the life they want to be remembered for, he said. They live that life instead of the life that would make them feel good. The smaller the gap between the two, the happier the person. Wanting to be remembered as being like Ariel Sharon, for example, or David Ben Gurion, or even Bill Gates, just doesn't go together with dreaming of spending the final two weeks of your life in the arms of someone you love on a Red Sea beach. The two aren't compatible. Then, when River pushed me again to tell him what my choice would be, my mind went blank. I couldn't think of a single person. Who would I want to be remembered as being like? A decorated soldier? A famous general? That would be too obvious, under the circumstances. Maybe Michael Jordan? Everyone says he's a god, a really great guy. And a good businessman, too. Not a bad way to be remembered. But kind of juvenile on my part. No ideas, none at all. And what would I do with the last two weeks of my life? Nothing. Nada. Home? Friends? A trek? It all seemed to miss the point.

'I would sit and write,' Bayliss said. 'I would spend the last two weeks of my life writing.'

'What good would that do?' River said, angrily. 'A waste of time. Barely even enough words to remember you by.'

I still hadn't come up with anything. I was empty of ideas. What did that say about me? By 4.30 a.m. we could barely see straight. I fell asleep on Dave's mattress beneath the mines I'd hung. I figured I'd catch fifteen minutes to relax the muscles. In a fraction of a second I was already dreaming, a dream I can remember: It was a geometry lesson, we were learning about triangles for an exam and I didn't know a thing. My friends started whistling from outside, Jojo was there with a car, calling me to come out for a spin, shouting that they'd leave without me. The teacher, a real bitch, was staring at me like she hated me. A second later I found myself back on my feet at Beaufort, with huge explosions shaking the cement floor and a fresh round of mortar shells pounding us. From that time on they didn't let up: half an hour of bombing followed by fifteen minutes of quiet. Again and again and again. The terrorists had guessed that something big was happening. River came in as I was standing there, half asleep, with tears streaming down my face. 'It's just fatigue,' I told him. 'I swear it, I'm just tired.' I pulled myself together with difficulty.

'We've got visitors on their way up here,' he said.

'Who?' I asked.

'A Nakpadon and a Safari,' he answered. 'They're on their way. But how the hell are we going to get them in, with all this shelling?'

We went to the entrance of the secure area and looked outside, trying to count the seconds of quiet between one explosion and the next, to learn the rhythm. When we thought we'd figured it out we took a deep breath and River shouted, 'Run for it!' and we hightailed it to the war room. We stood there in front of the display screens watching as two vehicles roared along the dark, narrow road not far from Manzurieh. They were driving like madmen. I told the tank to fire in all directions and then I requested that explosive artillery be launched at the sources of the attacks from back in Israel, in the hope of keeping the enemy busy for a while. I asked for a smokescreen, too, on the road leading up to Beaufort. And so it was that they navigated the curves through a thick, grey cloud of smoke, hidden from Hezbollah observers.

At about 5.30 a.m. the vehicles entered the compound and stopped. The Safari was empty, and Furman popped out of the Nakpadon. 'You missed me, huh?' he whispered into my ear. The commander of an Engineering Corps company – Meir Koffler, the 'bomb doctor' – had come with him. 'Hezbollah's placed seven huge, roadside bombs along our access road,' Furman reported. 'They're waiting for us, for the withdrawal. That's what Intelligence is saying.' I brought him up to date with our work in progress, and then he divided up assignments between us.

'What's happening with the SLA?' I asked him.

'The collapse has been stopped,' he answered. 'Their leaders have informed us that everything is under control, that they'll keep fighting for a long time, as long as it takes. Command wants us to calm everyone down here, keep everybody from believing all the rumours.'

By 9.15 a.m. on Monday, two SLA battalions in the western sector had laid down their arms, and in their wake, the Druze battalion had deserted. At 10.15 a.m. in the tiny stronghold of Arnoun, directly below us, the old T55 tank aimed its barrel towards the gate and stood waiting. Lined up behind it stood a diesel half track, a black Mercedes and a few military jeeps. The SLA soldiers jumped into the vehicles and came hurtling out in a crazy race to reach the Israeli border. In Manzurieh, the cannons were abandoned. We heard via radio that everyone there had taken off at a run. From Tibnit, too. Hezbollah had captured the security zone without firing a single shot. By midday the territory still under control of our good Christian partners commanded by General Antoine Lahad had been reduced to a single enclave near Marjayoun and two small outposts near us at Beaufort, on the mountain range. An entire army had disappeared.

At 10.35 we were, for the first time, in the sights of the mob. It was reported that dozens of vehicles with Hezbollah flags were making their way towards Tibnit, just a mile and a half from us, and that a huge procession of local residents was heading in our direction. Furman requested artillery fire from Israel, but his request was denied. Cover would be provided when the procession got close. We were ordered to prepare for incoming terrorists. The snipers took their positions. I watched from White guard post, with Bayliss and Itamar. An orange van suddenly appeared out of nowhere on the road and stopped less than a mile from our gates. 'If they get any closer we're opening fire,' I told Bayliss. He positioned his weapon. The van moved forward at a crawl, just a few yards, then stopped. Bayliss was waiting for me to give the word. I waited. The van lurched forward again, braked again. We didn't shoot. The van zigzagged in spurts on our winding road, as if it was testing the limits of our patience. The driver came as close as 700 yards away from the gates to Beaufort.

'Maybe we should seek clearance from Command?' Bayliss said.

'No,' I answered. 'There's no question here. Another step and we pump them with bullets.'

After a few long moments of suspense, the doors of the van opened. What the fuck was he doing? Out came a woman, a child and a young guy on crutches, out here in the middle of a closed military zone.

'Should I shoot?' Bayliss asked.

'Wait,' I answered.

'Let me shoot,' he said. 'We'll take one down and they'll get out of here.'

'Wait,' I insisted.

'It's a ruse!' he shouted. 'In another second they'll pull a missile launcher out of the van and send us all sky high. Let me finish them off!'

They stood erect in a row in front of the van, looking at us. They did not move. 'What are they planning?' Itamar asked. Truth is, I didn't know what to answer. I got on the radio. 'Cheetah to Deputy One,' I said, calling Furman. I asked him to join us at White. 'How old do you think the boy is?' Itamar asked. Bayliss pulled his eye away from his sight and took a good look at the pudgy little redheaded Arab boy standing there in a khaki shirt and blue tie that looked like a boy scout uniform.

'Eight,' he said.

'No,' Itamar insisted. 'I have an eight year old cousin who's twice as big as him.'

'Arabs develop more slowly,' Bayliss answered. 'This boy is eight. Seven at the least.'

They argued about the boy's age, about whether or not boy scout ties were the same colour internationally, but I wasn't listening. I was trying to gather my thoughts together, work out how Furman would react. When he showed up he issued an order for every guard post to open fire. 'Shoot 200 yards away from them,' he instructed. He was holding a weapon, too. 'You have to show them you're aggressive enough,' he explained. We fired shells and rounds of ammunition and the boy looked scared. But he was disciplined, and the three of them stood without moving. A few seconds later they began marching together, up towards us. This was fucking unbelievable. 'Sniper,' Furman called out to Bayliss, 'push them back. No more playing around.' Bayliss took a deep breath and said, 'These people have no limits, they're not afraid of anything.' A few more long seconds passed. We waited. 'At least eight years old,' he whispered and then he fired, hitting the passenger seat and shattering the front windshield. Before he could fire another bullet, the van turned around and the three of them jumped inside and disappeared. The whole scene was totally surreal. The mortar shells began exploding on us in greater force again and we had to take shelter. And that was how the day passed: once an hour or so a few citizens would approach – sometimes riding motorbikes, sometimes driving vans or ice cream trucks – and Bayliss would shoot at them until they turned around and went back, and then the shelling would increase. Furman and I went running between the guard posts with Madonna sets on, waiting for instructions from Israel.

At 3.30 p.m. we dragged four five-gallon jerrycans of diesel fuel and petrol outside. Crates of ammunition, too. Everything had to go up in flames. Dave told us about soldiers from the Golani brigade who'd abandoned an outpost close to the border with Israel. They'd gone home on their own, on foot. He also said Hezbollah was plundering equipment and uniforms in each place that had been evacuated. No, the soldiers were walking around saying, it must just be a rumour. Couldn't be true. Over the radio we could hear a military correspondent broadcasting from Narkis. 'Beaufort is behind enemy lines,' he announced. 'Hezbollah has the outpost surrounded. At present, IDF soldiers cannot leave there. Beaufort has been cut off.' Our parents were probably shitting themselves.

Furman gave the command and the squads began unravelling white detonating fuses. The fuses were composed of TNT and lead covered in burlap cloth and wrapped in white plastic. Each fuse is only about 400 feet long, so we had to knot dozens of them together in order to cover the entire outpost. It was a job that would take at least four hours, we had to move from one mine to the next, pulling tripwires out, inserting detonating fuses into the hole, and filling them with TNT. From that moment on, we knew that we were in danger of blowing ourselves up.

When the job was done Furman gathered us for a briefing. He

was businesslike, no play for emotions. 'In exactly one hour from now we're sending out two Safari trucks, an equipment truck and an APC,' he informed them. 'Nearly all of you will return to Israel with this convoy. You'll be taking all the remaining equipment and the soldiers' personal belongings. Anything we don't manage to load will be destroyed here. The only people staying on with me here will be Erez and Levanoni, thirteen fighters, the tank squad, and Meir Koffler, the Engineering Corps officer. The last men here will hook up the fuses, and then we'll turn out the lights. Three hours after the rest of you have left we'll blow the place up and get out of here, fast. We'll meet up in Israel at midnight.'

That night there were something like eighty men at the outpost: fighters, surveillance officers, soldiers from the Signal Corps, the Ordnance Corps, the Armoured Corps, and two D9 bulldozer operators. Furman read out the list of who was assigned to which vehicle. 'These are the fighters who will be here to the end,' he announced. 'Erez's squad: Tom, Itamar, Zion, Koka, Boaz, Pinchuk, Barnoy, River and Bayliss. And four more: Murphy, Koby, Shauly and Sela.' He didn't wait for questions, and left everyone to go mad without him. All the soldiers scheduled to leave in the first group went mental, threw furniture around. 'We're not taking part in the big pull out?' they hollered. 'It can't be!' It was such a historic operation, who wouldn't want to be part of it? 'I'm not leaving!' was the cry heard from several soldiers. I tried to calm them down: 'You're all part of the pull out. It's only a three-hour difference.'

When I left them, Dave ran after me. He was among the first evacuees. 'It's important to me,' he said. 'I've got to stay here with you. Got to be here to the end.' I told him there was nothing I could do about it, it was a matter of priorities and professional considerations. He removed the black *kippa* from his thick, red hair and crumpled it in his hand, waving it in front of my face. 'You've got to understand how important it is to me,' he pleaded. 'Tell Furman he has to let me stay.'

'What's the *kippa* got to do with anything?' Levanoni said with a mean laugh. 'You think God ordained that you should be part of the withdrawal? Or maybe you think we need divine protection? A miracle worker?'

'Erez understands,' he said. 'Erez understands.'

'Not a chance,' I told him coldly. This wasn't the time for drama. 'You've got to go. And that's an order.' He started to cry. When he turned to walk away I called after him, 'Wait for me at the fence, OK?'

Running quickly back and forth under the open sky, exposed, we loaded the trucks with sensitive equipment: surveillance apparatus, radios and even missiles, along with all the personal belongings of all the soldiers, even those of us staying on to the end. Everything but the little video camera, because Furman wanted to film the mushroom cloud from the explosion. We wrapped up operations in a kind of pandemonium, everything happening at a run, and then, under the tall flagpole at the fortress, River and Boaz and Pinchuk and a bunch of younger soldiers pushed and cursed each other and nearly got into a brawl over who was going to climb up to lower the flag and fold it. There was only room for one man on the flagpole. 'Chili!' I shouted from the parking area. 'Everyone take a step back,' I commanded them. 'Let Chili do it.' So, to calls of encouragement from below, our cook climbed to the top and undid the knots and slipped back down wrapped in the old, stained and faded cloth.

Just before eight o'clock the first evacuees stood in two long lines in the secure area facing the exit like paratroopers preparing to jump. The first truck had backed up to the exit. Furman passed among the soldiers and gave them iron numbers for the count off and a tap on the shoulder. The rest of us – the select few staying on to the end – made the rounds for farewell hugs. 'Don't worry, we'll meet at midnight,' we said. 'Watch our bags for us.' Then the order came and they were sent out. There was heavy shelling all around. The Armoured Corps outpost below Marjayoun responded, trying to hit the sources of their fire, and the sky glowed like a lightning storm. The gates were opened and the convoy left, and, just before slamming the iron door shut, we glimpsed the yellow trail of dust from the trucks lighting up the darkness. We stood there in reduced numbers, trying to get used to the silence. We looked around at each other.

'Kind of alone, aren't we?' River said. A barrage of mortar shells fell on the roof but there was no one to announce, 'Hit! Hit!' since there was no longer a war room. There were only six soldiers left manning the guard posts and without proper equipment, so they were half blind out there. I joined Bayliss, who had lit a fire in a large metal rubbish bin in the corner of the room and was burning classified documents. 'Kind of sick, don't you think?' he asked. 'Everybody wanted desperately to stay on, even though they knew there could be a slaughter here. What people won't do for glory. All so they can walk around their neighbourhood like big shots.'

'Action, that's what people love,' I told him. 'Action. And fear. Fear's pretty addictive.'

'The longer you serve out here,' Bayliss said, 'the more your survival instinct gets messed up, dulled. It really affects you. They tell us that carrying out your mission at all costs is the first of the eleven IDF basic principles, even above the preservation of human life. The mission before human life. Does that make sense to you?'

I was ripping pages from *Back to the Future*, and slowly dropping them in bunches into the bin so the flames would remain under control and wouldn't set the building on fire. All of a sudden, in a flash, fire leapt from the bin and took hold of me. Maybe I'd put my hand in too far, because it started to burn. My right hand. Bayliss jumped on me, knocked me to the ground and sprayed me with an extinguisher. I lay there on my arm, then I ran to stick it in cold water. River showed up with the medic's kit. 'These burns look pretty bad,' he said. But there wasn't any chance of being evacuated. There were no helicopters. He would have to treat me right there with wet bandages and some morphine for the pain. 'There you go,' Bayliss whispered to me. 'At the very last moment you've managed to get yourself a scar from this place. It's actually pretty strange you never had one before.' In fact, I did. Two. Once I'd split my head open when I got into a fight with a soldier named Twina while we were waiting in a queue to lift weights. Another time I fell on a piece of rusty metal during an ambush, back when we stormed the Abu-Jabai terrorist cell. There was still a line running from my calf to my foot where they'd sewed up the deep gash. After River finished with me I went back to work with everyone else.

Another few minutes and the whole thing should have been over, the end of Beaufort. It was 10.35 p.m. Bayliss was already sitting in the seat of the Nakpadon and had asked River for his small, laminated copy of the Traveller's Prayer. He attached it in the front, to the spot where in a normal car you'd find the rear-view mirror. Pinchuk, who'd tucked his shirt into his trousers and tidied himself, was standing in the doorway with his helmet and his flak jacket and his gun slung from his shoulder, waiting for a green light. But a female voice came over the radio with a brief message: 'Mission postponed,' she announced. 'We'll get back to you with more information later.' Postponed? Till when? 'No way of knowing,' the voice answered.

Furman went off at a run to the White guard post. He pulled a mobile phone he'd brought from home out of his trousers pocket. It was only out there, at one certain angle between the third and fourth sandbags that there was mobile-phone reception at the outpost, and only sporadically and with luck. No soldier had ever dared try to phone, even though generations of fighters were in on the secret. Furman phoned Amos. 'We can't postpone,' he said. Amos apologized, told Furman everything was chaotic and he couldn't get answers. It turned out there were still a few differences of opinion, something to do with the prime minister, so we'd have to stay on in Lebanon another few days. They were stalling while political negotiations could be completed. But it was still likely the withdrawal would take place that week, he guessed, because the politicians understood that the situation was dire. 'Hang on,' Amos concluded, and the line went dead.

21

On Tuesday morning, a few minutes before sunrise, River started shouting that the flagpole was bare. There was no flag on it! Shit! We'd taken it down when we thought we were on our way out, but now we were staying and Hezbollah would soon be rolling out of bed and looking up at Beaufort, where they would see a bare flagpole and conclude that we'd abandoned the outpost – and up they'd come to capture the place. A huge wave of people would make their way here with pickaxes while a group of armed terrorists in black commando uniforms provided cover for them. And what exactly would we do in the face of all this? We had to get the flag back up there, and fast, because in just a few minutes, when the skies lightened, it would be too dangerous to send a soldier on a ladder up the wall of the fortress, and from there up the flagpole, exposed.

I was lying on the kitchen floor wrapped in one of the blue tablecloths Chili saved for special occasions, trying to relax my muscles. River and Furman ran in, kicked me, and pulled me to my feet. Where was the flag? We went hunting for it, looking everywhere: the office, the medical bay, inside crates, under beds. Where could Chili have tossed it before he caught his ride home? Wait a minute. Was it possible? Yes, it was. Likely, even: the flag was probably back in Israel. Chili might have wrapped himself in it in the Safari. Yeah, it had to be. We were seriously fucked. In that whole goddamned outpost there wasn't a single flag, not even one of the little ones from Independence Day, not the plastic kind lined up on a string that until the night before had been draped over breasts and bikinis on the wall and around the framed pledge to defend Israel's northern border, not even a single piece of cloth a flag could be drawn on. What were we supposed to do? Draw a flag on a piece of cardboard? Wood? Bayliss suggested that someone – especially someone fat, like Itamar – should take off his white t-shirt for us to use. And that's when it hit me. I ran to the submarine and overturned the rusted iron cabinet in the corner. I was right, it was still there, stuffed behind the cabinet. Unbelievable. An entire year of cleaning duty and they hadn't once moved the cabinet and pulled it out. I had stuffed it in there myself. It was grey and covered in dust, but it was still there, Ziv Farran's Four Mothers t-shirt. I cut the cloth with a penknife. Furman found a tube of green camouflage paint and squirted out two stripes, added a lopsided Star of David and we ran outside with it. Bayliss, the skinniest and fastest of us, climbed the pole and hung it. 'This is totally surreal,' he called down from above. 'Totally fucking surreal,' I answered him. The sky was already orange. River was humming the national anthem and busting up laughing. Furman filmed us saluting.

A new day was dawning. It would be a tough one. The soldiers spent it doing non-stop guard duty. Furman and I went from one post to the next, oblivious to the mortar shells falling like crazy all around us. A little after nine in the morning the SLA soldiers at Hadar and Valencia waved goodbye to the nearby Dlaat outpost, which they were supposed to be guarding, and took off. We watched as their half-track stalled about 200 yards from the gate and they jumped out of it – two of them barefoot even – and ran away on the hot asphalt. A few minutes later, while dozens of local citizens were climbing on top of the half-track, a tow truck showed up and the mechanic started to fix the engine and do a little body work. Children were fighting over the steering wheel, and suddenly the thing started moving. 'It's all over,' I said to Furman. 'There's no such thing as the Ali Taher mountain range battalion any more.' We were surrounded by terrorists. There were three combat helicopters circling over our heads, keeping us safe from above by driving off anyone who came near. By this time there were processions streaming out of every village – with flags, without weapons – marching slowly in our direction. I watched them from Blue, trying to make out their faces through the binoculars and waiting for them to reach our shooting zone. Each time someone got too near the helicopters would open fire and push them back. That morning word had also come from Israel that they could use the artillery, live ammunition. At our request they fired 200 shells in order to scare off anyone approaching and to convince Hezbollah to stay in their foxholes. 'Don't trust anyone,' Furman said. 'Anyone coming close gets shot.' He ordered the tank outside the gates to shoot at Arnoun so they'd get the message down there. If Hezbollah entered the village and settled in there, at the foot of Beaufort, we wouldn't be able to get out. They'd be waiting for us around the bend.

At two in the afternoon the order came: we'd pull out that night at eleven. Supposedly. Bayliss climbed on to the D9 bulldozer and we went out and tore up the asphalt, pulled down the sheds and crushed the rubbish bins. Hezbollah wasn't going to get anything from us. We whitewashed the unit insignias that were painted on a concrete wall. Just before nightfall we started laying the detonating fuses outside, in the trenches and at the guard posts, to be sure they would burn down, too. From then on, a direct hit by a shell would kill us all on the spot. We'd be vaporized, because the mines would blow up in a chain reaction. There wouldn't even be any remains of bodies left behind. We understood this, but nobody complained. There was no choice.

At nine o'clock we received bad news that was really hard to swallow: Amos explained to us that the Lebanese government had registered an urgent complaint with the UN that Israel was planning to blow up an historic site. 'Dismantle the mines,' he told us. 'You're going to hand over the outpost undamaged to the UN.' 'We don't have time,' Furman told him over the radio. 'There's no way we can manage it. And we can't leave behind six and a half tons of TNT as a gift for the terrorists, which will come back at us in the form of bombings along the northern border towns. All the fuses are already attached and in place. We spent three days setting it up, a real work of art. And what about the equipment we didn't manage to load on to the trucks? What are we supposed to do with that? We've got TOW missiles that didn't make it back to Israel. How can we leave those behind? I can't bear the thought of watching the Lebanese messing around with our uniforms and weapons, on television tomorrow. And what am I supposed to tell the soldiers? That we did all this work for nothing?' Over the earphones the fighters could hear Amos, helpless, and Furman exploding, barely in control, his voice trembling. When he understood it was a lost cause he ripped the earphone from his ear, went into his office and slammed the door.

The boys roared, releasing all their built-up tension. I did, too, swore like a maniac. All of a sudden they're playing dumb? I mean, it never bothered those bastards before – the UN, the Lebanese government – that Hezbollah was bombarding the fortress with mortar shells day and night. Damaging the landscape? Destroying historic ruins? My arse! They'd never shown the slightest interest, so what was all this theatre for now, this pretending to be bleeding hearts?

I opened the door and went in to talk to Furman. 'This is fucked, isn't it?' I said as I sat down on the edge of his desk.

'Royally,' he answered.

'So tell them we're not leaving.' My voice was suddenly full of confidence.

'What?' he said, grimacing.

'Let's inform them that we're not leaving this outpost without blowing it up,' I suggested. 'We blow it up or we don't leave. We stay here.'

'You're really insane, aren't you?'

'What do you have to lose?' I asked. 'You believe it's the right thing to do, don't you? We're right, aren't we? So do the right thing and go all the way with it.'

'You want us to disobey an order? In the middle of the withdrawal?'

'You did it before, when we went looking for Spitzer's head. You'll get used to it little by little. It'll turn you into a nicer person.'

'It's actually been a while since you've disobeyed an order,' he said with a smile.

'I've never stopped missing those days,' I told him.

'It'll be the end for both of us, you know that.'

'Short prison term, nothing too bad. After that I'm inviting you to Fiji. The trip's on me!'

He put on his headset and contacted Command. We were happy. It gave us great satisfaction to do something important, to make a brave decision. 'We cannot carry out this mission,' he told them. The operations sergeant on the other side didn't understand, she asked him to repeat himself three times. Then she got off the line. Everything was quiet. We sat and waited. 'Tell me about prison,' Furman said. He didn't even look especially tense. I mean, less tense than he did at any other time during that last day. I told him that officers' prison was a country club, a Garden of Eden without the swimming pool and the girls. He just had to make sure he brought suntan lotion and sunglasses and he'd be fine.

We spent a long time alone in his office together. In the meantime, Levanoni, on his own initiative, was keeping the boys busy with a little vehicle maintenance in preparation for withdrawal. We joined them, sat with them in the dirt. Zion handed out cigarettes, River gave us the last of the apple juice. And we waited. At 10.20 p.m., Barnoy, who was guarding at the furthest guard post, White, suddenly thought it was too quiet. If it was that quiet, he reasoned, we must have left already without calling him. He figured we might have forgotten him in all the chaos. After all, the count offs don't always work, there are mistakes. Maybe in another second or two he was going to be blown up with the outpost. So he started making weird animal noises and shouting 'Hello!' to see if anyone could hear him. Nobody answered. He ran into the war room and found no soldiers, only mines and detonating fuses. He panicked. He was desperate to run down and look for us, but he knew that if we hadn't left and we caught him running around, his post abandoned, he'd be court-martialled and thrown in jail (and we weren't talking about officers' prison for him). It was dangerous, too, to abandon the guard post like that. He climbed back up, continued to guard. But fear was eating him up inside. Five minutes later he took his chances and made a mad dash to the secure area. The entrance, which was usually as busy as a shopping centre on a Saturday night, was dead quiet. Barnoy was sure it was all over for him, that we were already back in Israel. He decided that it was better for him to get away from the explosion on foot and spend the rest of his life under a new identity with some Lebanese woman in the village below. He started running again, this time in the direction of the front gate. It was only then that he saw the Nakpadons, and Levanoni. And us. He calmed down. And then he panicked again, because he realized that the White guard post was standing empty. He grimaced and sprinted back up to his post. It was three months before he told us exactly what had happened, because he was afraid he'd be court-martialled, or worse – that he'd be a laughing stock for generations of soldiers to come, until his dying day. In fact, we were completely sympathetic, because even I had the thought that we might forget somebody up there on the hill, some spaced out young soldier. It wasn't such a mad idea, and it was scarier than the threat of being attacked by terrorists or sustaining a direct missile hit on one of the mines.

At 10.25 p.m. we heard Kaplan's warm voice over the radio. He wanted Furman. I silenced the boys so we could listen in. 'You are authorized to detonate,' Kaplan said, and we cheered, threw our arms around each other. You wouldn't believe it, it was as intense as when the hostages were freed at Entebbe. 'Go on, get out of there,' Kaplan ordered. 'You have clearance to leave.'

From then on, everything happened in a whirlwind. Levanoni ran from guard post to guard post, relieving the last guards of their duty. Just like that, you were allowed to abandon your post, desert the holy shrine. The hedgehogs were empty and the skies didn't fall. Furman and Meir Koffler checked the mines to make sure no wires had come loose. I gave an order to 'man your vehicles like you're going to war, because there's going to be combat involved. I want four MAGs on each Nakpadon.' At eleven p.m. we stood ready at the gate for our last briefing.

In officer training you learn to prepare yourself for briefings that last an hour and include maps, manoeuvres and diagrams. But here was Furman holding one crumpled sheet of paper and making the shortest speech we'd ever heard, about the biggest mission we'd ever carry out, the mission of a lifetime. 'You know what to do,' he said. 'There's no time. Just operate the way you did today and good luck.' Someone from Command was shouting at us down the radio: 'Get out of there now, get out as fast as you can.' We got the boys into the two Nakpadons. The tank and the bulldozer were first in line.

'River,' I said, 'adjust the frequencies in the Nakpadon.'

'I'm not a signaller,' he answered.

'You won't believe this but you just got qualified. You're the signaller for the withdrawal.'

I asked Furman to wait sixty seconds for me. 'There's no time,' he shouted from behind. 'You fuck-up! *Now* you need to take a piss?' I didn't answer. I went back into the secure area for one last look, to sear it into my memory. The kitchen, for example, an image that will stay with me for the rest of my life: a tray of schnitzels pulled out of the oven that no one took a single bite of, and the salads and French fries that Chili left on the aluminium counter before he left. We hadn't had time to eat any of it, hadn't had the inclination either, so it was all left behind, those schnitzels all lined up and waiting to be blown up. I went to the Signal Corps Company Club, too, and stood in front of the memorial wall and read what was written there: IN MEMORY OF OUR FRIENDS IN THE ALON SQUAD – THE BEST AND BRIGHTEST – WHO FELL IN THE HELICOPTER TRAGEDY, FEBRUARY 1997. Who were we, anyway, compared to them? Who were we to cry over what we'd lost, when they'd lost twenty comrades in a single blow? One minute they were here, twenty men, the next they were no longer alive. How do you lose dozens of men in a moment and keep on going, surviving, like nothing happened? When all of a sudden you don't have anyone to fight with or sleep with mattress-to-mattress any more? This soldier's laugh and that one's eyes, they all hound your memory, and all you want to do is forget, and sometimes all you want to do is *not* forget. Thirty-three men bound for Beaufort died that night, including the district commander, Lieutenant Colonel Moshe Muallem. And the squad leader, Lieutenant Alon Babiyan. I wondered in what ways that man was like me. And who I was compared to him, a man who'd given everything.

I didn't notice Furman come in behind me until he put his hand on my shoulder. I thought about saying something about how I felt, but I was afraid of sounding pompous. Neither of us said a word. All of a sudden he pulled me close and hugged me. 'You little shithead,' he said. 'Come on, let's get you home to Mummy.'

We turned off the main light switch and left the building. 'Command to Cheetah,' Kaplan came in over the radio, 'take my friends out of there with you, will you?' We raced over to the low whitewashed wall and set to work taking down the metal plaque hanging from it by chains. THE BEAUFORT WAS CAPTURED BY THE SOLDIERS AND COMMANDERS OF THE GOLANI RECON-NAISSANCE UNIT ... WHERE DO YOU FIND MEN LIKE THESE ... This was just where Menahem Begin had stood. When Ariel Sharon bragged about it being one of our greatest achievements, Begin said, 'It was an open wound. An open wound.'

'Did you fight the whole night long?' Begin asked that soldier, Tamir. 'What kind of resistance had they set up there?'

'There weren't a lot of them,' Tamir explained, 'but they were really entrenched.'

'Were there many who surrendered?' Begin asked.

'No, sir, no one,' Tamir told him. 'Everyone was killed.'

At Beaufort, no one surrenders. There's been no grey area, only black and white, for hundreds of years. This time it was us. I wondered who the next boys to be sent up here would be, and what reason there would be for spilling their blood. We pulled the plaque free and loaded it on to the Nakpadon. We pronounced the outpost empty.

At the gate, Meir Koffler connected an electric detonator to the first detonating fuse and, using a wire cable, spooled it all the way to the Nakpadon, which was parked thirty yards down the hill. The tank had already set out down the road and stopped at the bend, where they could maintain eye contact. 'Come on, Meir, sweetheart,' I shouted. 'Enough pissing about. Blow that baby sky high.' At that very moment another huge round of mortar shells began falling, dozens of them one after another, from every direction, from all the surrounding villages and towns. We could see the launches, it was like a hailstorm on the hill. 'Take off!' they shouted at us from Command. 'Go, now, leave everything, don't even detonate.'

Thirteen flares went up in the air and night turned into day: Hezbollah knew something was up and they were trying to light the darkness. When the enemy uses flares the procedure is to get out of the place immediately, as fast as possible, like a blue streak, and not in a straight line. But we had nowhere to escape to for the moment. Furman ordered explosives and a smokescreen, the tank fired, and Bayliss never stopped screaming, 'Missiles! Missiles! Missiles!' Flames surged over the Dlaat outpost. That was our friends closing up shop, on their way out. The people at Command kept yelling at us over the radio. 'We're fine, don't worry,' Furman answered, and he told them we needed several more minutes before he went off to help with the landmines. 'We feel great. Give us a little time, be patient, it's about to happen.' In fact it took another seventeen minutes, which felt to us a lot longer than eternity. The boys sat hunched up and crowded in the belly of the armoured cars. Nobody said a word. There was only the sound of the engines, and the exploding shells. 'Get out of there,' Kaplan said. 'And that's an order. Now.'

Meir Koffler finished his work. 'Thirty seconds to explosion,' he shouted. 'Thirty seconds to explosion,' Furman repeated into the radio. 'Take a last look around for me,' Kaplan responded. 'You're cleared to detonate.'

River pressed the little PTT button and his voice came over the radio, just like he'd done when we came up for the boys' first tour of duty, only happy this time. He was just as scared as then, but strong: *'May it be your will, our God and God of our forefathers, that you head us towards peace, guide our feet towards peace, lead us to peace.'* Bayliss flashed him a look, a look that only the two of them understood, and River left off, just like that, in the middle of the prayer. Everything was quiet for a few moments, then Bayliss took over: *'And make us reach,'* he intoned, so that everyone could hear him, even back in Israel, *'and make us reach our desired destination for life, gladness and peace. May you rescue us.'* We all said, 'Amen.' Furman came over and handed me the wires, the fuse that would set off the explosion. 'All yours,' he said simply, passing up on doing the honours himself. 'Good luck,' he said. To everyone he shouted, 'Close all hatches!' and he climbed into one of the Nakpadons. They all battened down: there were only thirty yards between us and the gate, according to the rules barely a safe distance even for detonating a half-pound explosive brick, while we were about to ignite six and a half tons of dynamite, and not a single one of us – including the professor from the Engineering Corps – had any idea what the force of the flames and the blast would be, or whether the fortress would collapse, and what would happen to us. We knew there was a chance we'd go up in flames, too. But there's this moment when you don't care, you're indifferent. You say to yourself, Maybe I'll die, turn into ashes, and maybe not, let's just get it over with. You're so exhausted, so full of emotion. Meir Koffler sat down next to me. He nodded, waiting for me to activate the fuse. My hands were paralysed. I relaxed my fingers a bit, took a deep breath. 'Come on, bro, set it off,' he said to me, going through the motions with his hands. 'Do it. Do it.'

'You do it,' I said, handing it over to him. 'I'll watch.'

22

And so, we were the ones who pressed the button and sent the Beaufort outpost up in smoke. Actually, it was Meir Koffler who pressed the button, while the rest of us covered our ears tight. Everyone was closed up inside the vehicles; only I couldn't stand it, I had to stick my head out to watch 980 mines blow Beaufort to smithereens. Fucking hell, what an explosion that was! There was a huge red flame in the sky, an orange mushroom cloud, a wave of fire, light and bright as day, and then everything just fell apart, crumbled, and the earth shook. We were jolted five yards forward by the force of the blast, sixty-three tons of Nakpadon tossed into the air. I fell inside the vehicle. 'Done! Exploded!' I shouted into the radio. All around us, mortar shells continued falling. 'Move out. Over!' Furman shouted over the radio. 'Move out. Over!' We could barely hear him, the explosions continued to come in waves. 'Eighty-two, forward!' he commanded the tank. 'Aim, adjust and shoot while moving in the direction of Tibnit.' 'Come on, sweethearts,' I said to the soldiers, 'let's get the engines rolling. We're taking you home.' And off we went. It must have been crap for the boys listening to us back in Israel, at Command headquarters on the other side of the fence, not out here with us.

And for all those people drinking lemonade through a straw at a café on Sheinkin Street. I stuck my head out again. Our air force was striking at a distance. On the darkened horizon I could see the Reichan outpost going up in flames. Christ, what a wild night. Slabs of cement were flying in every direction, pieces of the outpost were falling from the clouds, concrete was coming down like rain. Boom! A concrete wall had fallen on our vehicle, nearly crushing it. 'Eighty-two, get your heads inside!' Furman was shouting over the radio, but I couldn't do it, I kept watching. All of a sudden I noticed him, Furman, behind me, his body also half exposed as he stared, too. His Nakpadon slowed down and mine did as well, and we watched, half blind, lit up in yellow, wanting to make sure with our own eyes that nothing would be left intact. Huge, shocked smiles were drawn across our faces. And no, you'll be surprised to hear that you don't think about home at a time like that, and you don't think about your mother, or girls, and you don't see your life flashing before your eyes like in the movies. All I could think about was uncertainty, about the seven roadside bombs awaiting us on our trip home, how maybe they'd be set off and maybe not, about the operation. And about the strength inside me – I suddenly had so much strength in me – and how I felt revived, and focused.

Four whistling bombs landed right in front of us, to the right of the tank. The tank was quick to fire white phosphorus shells, the kind that are supposed to misguide missiles and prevent them from reaching their targets. But the shells hit us instead, and we rolled around coughing, practically puking our lungs out because we couldn't breathe. 'Don't shoot any more of those!' Furman ordered over the radio. 'Even if they're firing missiles at you, don't shoot. They just hit us.' In the meantime, an unmanned plane circling overhead was sending thermal photos back to Israel showing the damage done by the white phosphorus shells. They thought we were goners. 'Keep cool,' we told them. More shots were being fired over the border in order to set up a smokescreen for us. 'Not so close!' I shouted. 'We can't see a thing.' But we weren't afraid,

I swear. We crossed the bend in the road, where Ziv had fallen, and we got our last look at Beaufort while Cobra helicopters flew in formation above us, escorting us home. 'OK,' I shouted to River. 'Make a sharp left here,' and we popped the Nakpadon on to the main road.

Like magic, everything suddenly cleared. On the road we seemed to be inside a ring of peace and quiet. Off in the distance everything was still burning, and an orange storm lit up the sky like some virtual war, and here and there the radio clicked to life and gave worrying reports about a lone tank stuck way off near Hatzbiyeh with ten soldiers inside, or about an overturned armoured personnel carrier. But with us, it was like we were in a tunnel, on a yellow brick road, and everything was quiet and calm. Near the Khardaleh bridge, just before one o'clock in the morning, we met up with convoys on their way down from Ishiye and Reichan. A group of Golani troops laid tracks and we crossed the river. We saw the convoy from Dlaat, too, moving along ahead of us. I sat down, it was pretty cold. Pinchuk pulled our homemade flag from his trouser pocket, the one we'd made out of Ziv's torn shirt. 'When did you boys manage to lower that thing?' I asked with a smile. He handed it to me, put it around my neck. And that's how I remained for the next forty minutes: wrapped inside it, silent like everyone else, trying to think about what I should be thinking about and actually thinking about nothing at all. I could hear Furman shouting, 'Man, Beaufort is burning! Beaufort is burning!'

At 1.43 a.m. Gate 93 was opened for us. We entered Israel, and nobody said anything like 'the nightmare's over', and nobody shouted at us that we'd 'run away'. We left with dignity, with pride. We climbed out of our vehicles, everyone was hugging, even Kaplan and Amos. They were saying what a great thing it had been, historic, a glorious event. People were kissing and slapping each other's backs and handing out compliments about a job well done. Furman was telling everyone he loved them, and tears of joy were flowing, and they all piled on top of each other in a huge human heap.

They danced and went mad with happiness. But not me. I took off my flak jacket and equipment, removed my helmet, and sat down on a rock. Alone. To this day, I believe that then and there was the saddest moment of my life.

We stayed there, next to the fence, until sunrise. Soldiers from Northern Command prepared a lousy breakfast for us and a doctor and medic treated my hand, changed the bandages. When Bayliss took off his helmet there was a *kippa* on his head. Everyone asked him about it, and he told them he'd gone back to being religious, and that's the way he was going to stay. Turns out he really still did want to be part of the clan. A person has to believe in something, hold on to something, he explained with a smile. And when the sun rose we looked towards Lebanon together, at the pillars of smoke still climbing skyward. I heard Amos telling someone about the soldiers from the Ishiye outpost, how they'd got into trouble on their way down, and something strong inside me wanted to go up to him and request to go back in to help rescue them. I felt I needed another short, quick breath of that piece of earth. Of that action. But I didn't have the strength to get up. At 6.42 a.m. the town of Kiryat Shmona was still under curfew, on high alert due to the threat of Katyusha rocket attacks. The gate to Lebanon was sealed. 'And so it has ended,' the military correspondent reported. 'Eighteen years after they crossed the border into Lebanon, IDF troops moved last night in the opposite direction – inbound. One after the other they blew up the outposts: Shani and Karkum, Ishiye and Reichan, Dlaat and Galgalit, names we've learned that have now been wiped from the map. And Beaufort, the most recognizable symbol of southern Lebanon.' The boys stood behind him, arms around each other, waving to the cameras, shouting and singing. 'Mother, Mother, embrace me/We'll never be separated.' I just sat there, still on my rock. I didn't even phone home, it never occurred to me that my family might be worried or that the whole country was going nuts. It never occurred to me that at six in the morning the whole country was preoccupied with us. And just then a red Mazda stopped on the road and the door opened. Out came Oshri, and his mother, and an officer from the Administrative Corps, and that space-age metal pole of an arm he had – all that suffering in store for him because of it, all of it avoidable, I thought. He came up to me and held me firm, while tears flowed from my eyes. I didn't try to hide them. 'If we'd only got out earlier . . .' I started to say, but he cut me off. 'No,' he said, kissing my forehead, his eyes shining, 'what's important is that it's over. Everything's going to be fine, now that it's over.'

23

Gaza, 2001. It's not over. Is that possible? Again? It doesn't make any sense. We've lost so much, while there are other squads who haven't lost a single man. What fucking bad luck. 'Live hammer!' a voice on the radio calls. That's the code name for an explosive device. There's a thick, black cloud of smoke and small flames and they're inside it, on the ground, unconscious. Two soldiers. There's muffled crying – I don't know whose it is – and a cry for help, and a few shouts and some coughing. A little mumbling and then everything goes silent, even the muezzin in the mosque at the refugee camp. All that's left is a ringing in the ears and the sound of burning, like a huge popcorn maker gone berserk. There's a strong smell of burnt rubber, like a basketball that slams you in the face, knocks you down and makes you dizzy. Burnt rubber and charred flesh, a fatal and asphyxiating mix of smells. I lose my balance.

I check myself. The body's whole, no blood, and I run over to them, bend down, grab hold of each of them in turn. Above the right hand there's a black wrist band with a red bead that is meant to be removed only on discharge day. Our squad's good luck charm. Oshri made them for all of us as gifts. I search for a pulse, verify death. These days I don't insist on pumping on the chest, going mental, screaming at the body like I used to: 'Breathe you mother fucker, please breathe,' or 'Hang in there, man, don't die on me now.' Once, even when they were dead I was convinced they wanted to tell me something, their dying words. Not any more. Dead is dead. Like now. And in the paper they'll call us the COMPANY OF DEATH once again. Only a little while longer to discharge.

That's the way it is here, brothers. It's just routine. In the first second a dark screen covers your eyes and snuffs out your breath. You go blind for a few moments, you freeze in your tracks, ball your fists. You don't breathe. In a flash your mind empties, erases all thoughts, like it's making space, and that's scary. Then the dam breaks, and within a second or two thousands of confused fragments of thought rush through you. And the words echo again and again in your brain: they're dead, they're dead, they're dead. You haven't even had a chance to take it all in, but grief washes through you from the inside like someone's pumping gallons of it into your veins – you feel it that strongly. Like it's the end of the world. I have become used to experiencing the end of the world on a regular basis, become used to crumbling at first, then pulling myself together within a matter of minutes and kissing a bloody forehead, a farewell of sorts. A last look into eyes that remain open. And then I go back to the base.

I'm used to going back to the base, to pairs of flip-flops next to army cots, and sunglasses lying on top of blankets. The book lying open on the pillow, with a title like *His Whole Life Ahead of Him*: that's irony pissing in our faces. The pastries Zion bought to get him through the Sabbath, the bag of potato chips we didn't finish, it's all still there. Pinchuk's green and white checked towel, the tattered one that's been unravelling in every hell-hole we've served in, hanging to dry on the rusted metal rack. A memory from that first week at the training base: that towel was there, faded and rough, so that it already felt like sandpaper. Zitlawi said, 'What gives? That's the best your mother can do for you, you stinking rich boy? She couldn't have made a little effort for her baby?' I remember how Pinchuk didn't say a word. You could see in his eyes that it hurt him, a lot, that he was a sensitive fellow, a mummy's boy. Wait a minute, his mother! Holy shit, she still doesn't know! They haven't reached her yet. She's probably smiling right now, ordering tickets to a movie this evening, has friends over sitting in the garden. Pretty soon her life is going to end, be devastated. Unlike us, she's not used to it. It's her first time. What a waste. If only she'd known that somebody had teased him that night at the training base she would have bought the most exclusive, the fanciest, the most glamorous towel ever for her little angel. He's the one who probably insisted on hanging on to that ratty piece of sandpaper because he didn't want to make his Mum feel bad. Poor Pinchuk. I sit on one of the beds holding tight to the blanket and trying to put the brakes on the confusion that's sucking me under. My head's banging around, going mad, but I'm used to it. Used to folding up personal belongings and packing them into knapsacks that aren't mine. The white t-shirt still has his smell. Hello, and welcome to the suppression stage. Because in our squad if somebody stands still he gets two slaps in the face, then he pulls himself together and snaps out of his shock.

Am I a cry baby? Absolutely not. Not a chicken either, or a faggot. I'm not the type that cries at funerals. I hug sometimes, real solid like, but just to lend support to others, hold them tight when the coffin is brought out, tuck their heads into my shoulder while the eulogy's being read. Sometimes, when things are really dire, I'll pat someone, stroke him. But I never cry. I go on. Two days later I'll be cracking jokes like anyone else, laughing about the situation. The usual.

When Barnoy was killed, Palestinian protestors crowded around the front gate of our outpost, put pictures of him cut from the morning papers on the ground and pissed on them. It was all still really raw, only twenty-four hours after it had happened, and there they were, pissing on Barnoy. I don't know how I managed not to open fire on them, put the gun on automatic and pump them full of holes. I was ready to riddle every last one of them with bullets, I swear it. I watched my own boys watching as these arseholes pissed on their friend. How did they manage not to fall apart then? How? I felt the need to boost their morale, so that afternoon, when we went out again to open up the roads, I was even more hotheaded than usual and I shot up the boilers on the rooftops as we passed by, firing rounds at 360 degrees into the refugee camp, into the filth. I got my hands on a local wagon driver, grabbed hold of his ears real hard and spat a big gob right between his eyes. I shouted at him like a maniac. I sensed that it was making my boys feel better, especially the younger ones. Partly I was getting it off my chest, partly I was hanging on to our dignity. Afterwards I felt bad about it, but I'm used to that, too.

It's fucking Saigon here, believe me, brother. Real fucking Saigon. Not as green, but the same shit. You enter Gaza through the Karni crossing, go to Rubbish Road, turn at Death Bend, continue straight till you get to the bridge where the paratroopers were killed, then on to Suicide Bomber Curve and in another four minutes you reach us, at the Netzarim junction. Mounds of metal junk line the road, the head of a dead donkey sticks out from a concrete slab, flies and mosquitoes fill the air like a plague of locusts, darkening the skies. And the stench, the stench. This place is an endless rubbish dump. After Beaufort, the Gaza landscape isn't going to win you over.

Our outpost at the Netzarim junction is called Samba, otherwise known as Magen Three. It's got thick barbed wire, rusted guard towers and a shed where the toilets are. Sometimes Palestinian police trucks show up outside the gate and unload dozens of children and a supply of large bricks. Local ambulances give rides to groups of teenagers carrying Molotov cocktails, and sometimes a slightly older crowd of men comes on the scene, armed Fatah members. They have a wild time out there. On bad days, at least a thousand people gather outside the gates of Samba. Inside there's only a handful of soldiers, about twenty of us, and we're besieged and worried about the day when the animals outside, the ones with murder in their eyes, will break the rules of the game without warning and storm the gate. Palestinian policemen wave wire cutters in the air shouting, 'Here we come, here we come,' like they're about to cut into the fence at any minute. They shout, 'You're not a soldier, you're a lady,' at me, promising to fuck me up my arse, slit my throat, in just another moment, really just a minute from now. But so far they haven't forced their way in. Maybe in the end they actually prefer to live.

On the horizon I can see a slow convoy crawling along the Gaza coastal road. Dozens of trucks and cars and donkeys, the flags of Hamas and Palestine, Islamic songs over the loudspeakers, Arab grandmothers with megaphones. Ten or twenty people are crowded on to the roof of every truck. The procession continues for an hour, coming from nowhere and leading nowhere. Where are they heading? It's the middle of a workday, a weekday, there's no funeral. What are they doing? We don't even bother to ask, we're too exhausted for that. Insane place, this Gaza.

All of a sudden two rounds are fired into the air. A Tanzim activist is firing from the east. We ready our guns while a battery of foreign photojournalists record us, Israeli soldiers with loaded weapons facing children who have come to protest against a cruel occupation. It looks bad. A wounded and battered man lying on a Red Crescent stretcher with a cigarette hanging from his mouth takes a drag, women shriek and moan all around us, and it doesn't let up for a minute. Great stuff for the newspapers. That's the way it is here, normal, what we're used to.

So what do you say, bro? How do you explain the fact that on these black nights in Gaza I dream of Lebanon? That the sadness I carry around inside me is linked to Lebanon? Beaufort is the only place I've ever been afraid. How can it be that I'm lying here in an ambush in the mud, or falling off my feet from fatigue on guard duty, or riding in an APC, or approaching an Arab vehicle that might blow me all the way to hell with the press of a single button, and it's only Lebanon I've got on my mind, all the time? When it's calm and when it's not, I can feel the Beaufort, smell its smells, sometimes I get the shivers just thinking about it. And how do you explain that the feeling is strongest when I'm enjoying myself? I'll be sitting with friends over a cold beer, having a great time, there's no mention of anything to do with Lebanon or the army, and then suddenly somebody laughs, and I laugh, and someone talks about a girl he's hooked up with, some new love interest, or a great party he was at. And right then, at that very moment, it hits me without warning, and it hurts, the worst pain there is. I can see green and it makes me feel bad. I think about the tulips and the poppies, the peanut fields, the laundry flapping in the gardens of the homes in Arnoun, and I'm all choked up. Nature doesn't calm me down, and quiet hurts my ears. The slamming of a door can send me flying. I'll be dancing and dead soldiers will be there, dancing along with me in my heart.

Remember the feeling of holding a dead man in your arms, how his body is completely slack? How he's warm from all the pooling blood? Sometimes I sense just that feeling in my fingers, all of a sudden, when I'm having a good time. I hear explosions from far away even when there aren't any, but they make me jump like the missile launches from Tibnit used to. I hear a lot of things, a lot of voices.

I'm sane, don't worry. I'm not shell-shocked. I'm certainly not the only Israeli twenty-one year old who's held the body of a friend missing a head. You could almost say it's the norm. And with a lot of pain and my hand on my heart, I must share this thought with you – and it's not exactly the most popular one at the moment: if peace doesn't come in the meantime, I want my own child to go through what I did. The challenges, the pain, the fear. They made me look at the world in a different way, find myself and what's truly important to me. My love for my family and my love of life, and how fragile they are. That's how it is when you're surrounded by people who have lost friends. Suddenly you're a lot more careful on the road, for example. Sounds stupid? That's how it is with me. I grew up in Lebanon, for better or worse, and I even enjoyed it there sometimes.

Sometimes, when we were lying in an ambush – Spitzer, Zitlawi, Eldad, all the boys – I would try and imagine what the last few moments would feel like: packing the bags, closing the gate, catching a ride home. Life without Beaufort. Then I'd dream about returning, there would be peace, and exactly where our outpost stood there'd be a fancy hotel. A hotel in that spot would rake in big bucks, the whole world would be talking about it. And Lila would be there with me, we'd walk hand in hand, and stone by stone I'd show her. 'Here, sweetheart, this is exactly where it happened.' That's the way I picture it, and I'm afraid I'll have tears in my eyes and she'll laugh at me and say, 'What's the big deal? This is the place where you broke down?' and she won't understand.

The truth is, I believe we'll return there, to Lebanon. There won't be a hotel on the hill, there'll be a Hezbollah command post we have to capture. What, you don't think we'll have to go back there? You don't think there will be another attack on Misgav Am, another attack in Maalot? You don't think Kiryat Shmona will be bombarded again? That we'll get slaughtered along the way? That's my opinion: it's all going to come back again, and if it's quiet up there for the time being that's only because the terrorists are gathering strength and weapons. They have lots of patience, it's a tactic of theirs, and eventually we'll be in deep shit again. They'll take a soldier hostage, commandeer a jeep at the border fence, bombard some northern settlement with mortar shells. And when it comes, anyone who thinks a flock of IAF fighter jets is capable of taking care of the job from the air is going to learn there's no replacing foot soldiers. We'll march in there, clean the place up, pass from house to house, overturn every stone. That's because for the time being, we're the losers in that war. We're the losers, no doubt about that. We didn't come away with a peace agreement, we didn't crush the terrorists before we left. We ran away, we left weapons behind, we left our partners – the SLA – high and dry. And that year, that last action-packed year the boys and I spent inside Lebanon, did it contribute anything? Did it help something, move something forward, change anything? I don't understand why our army waited, what they got out of remaining there so long. Why didn't they pull us out a long time earlier, when we weren't so weak? Why not a year earlier, when they'd decided to withdraw? Why were we there at all?

Yeah, my brother, my main man: it was all for nothing.

I Will Still.

Autumn 2005. I'm still going to find Oshri. He's hiding from us all. Maybe that's what he needs, to hide, but I'm going to pull him out of his hiding place and we'll tear up Africa on motorbikes. We'll find some sexy girl who'd like to wrestle with us and we'll do it with her, the two of us. We'll go all the way to the edge and look back. I'll be able to say to him, 'Yeah, man, it's fucking scary, no doubt about it.' Out loud, I mean. And I won't be afraid of the fear, and I won't be afraid to leave or to have things end and start something new. And I won't scare myself by saying things like, 'If you give in now, you'll always give in.' I'll still give in a lot, and I'll disengage loads of times.

I'll still see all of us growing ugly. We'll never be this handsome again, Spitzer was right. I'll still sit naked on the banks of the river, freezing, and I'll write. Lila wants me to write. All that stuff I destroyed, the stuff I was afraid to send, she wants it. And Bitter will wag his tail – the lion king – and I'll eat a flower and drink from the stem. Save me a bush or two, my friend, or at least a leaf. The time has come to rest.

I'll still wake up to my mother's meat stew, and I'll stick out my hands in the pitch black to feel faces and guess who's who, and I'll get it right every time. I won't get addicted, either. Mourning is addictive, not just fear, and the addiction drips in like poison. I'll still talk less about death, I'll try, because in contrast to an atmosphere of gloom, my situation is fantastic.

Five years have passed, so how could our wounds not heal? A few things have changed since those times, when we were such jerks. There's no more purple rain. They don't say over the radio 'Tapuz stations, confirm. Over and out' any more, and there's no reply, no 'Diesel, in order; Kfir, in order; Puma, in order; Venus, waiting for confirmation.' There's so much to make time for, and at the same time no pressure to finish anything. I'll still watch Hapoel bring home the trophy, I'll still take one of my little nephews to a movie, and my son, too, and maybe even my grandson, and we'll sit, just the two of us, on the grass. He'll be *chakras* and sunbeams, he'll smile that smile of his that whispers in your ear, 'I've got it all worked out, but I'm not telling you.' And he'll love me.

It seems like just yesterday that we were dancing a waltz in that fortress and lighting candles and we were glad to be there, together. 'Oshri won't any more . . .' River said to me when he saw me off to one side, gloomy and alone, on one of those sad days I remember only too well, when we couldn't see the end from up there. 'Oshri won't any more . . .' he said, waiting for me to continue the game. But I remained silent. Oshri won't be jerking off any more? Or maybe he can do it with his left hand, with effort? How about saluting? Playing an instrument? Changing the world? Oshri and I are still going to storm, to rebel. We'll still believe and dream, and dream and remember, and we'll ask questions, and we'll fall, together. We'll suck down vodka sours and drown ourselves in everything wet and hot and salty. And we'll make Mum proud, we'll piss from the highest mountain, maybe I'll still cheat on my woman and maybe I'll be sorry I did. The bottom line is that I'm lucky.

And in the garden of our new little house, on a hill that looks south, towards the Sea of Galilee, I gave Lila a ring this autumn. I have room for her now, lots of it, in my life and in my heart. And when I leave for work each morning, with my camera and my motorbike, I ask her if she'll let me open the cloth pouch containing my dog tags and read her note. She laughs, flustered, and says, 'No, not yet, Only at the end.' And of course I'm a jerk. I never learned to say no to her.

Afterword: Between Truth and Imagination

No, I wasn't familiar with the game that everyone plays when a friend is killed, 'What he can't do any more.' How could I be, when no friend of mine has been killed? I wasn't there, I didn't know what they were doing. On the radio there would be reports of exchanges of fire, even heavy ones, and for eighteen years people came and went and talked about outposts and ambushes. But I stayed in Israel.

I first met up with Lebanon in the heart of the Gaza Strip in the autumn of 2000. David Biri, a medic in the Givati Brigade Engineering Corps, was wounded by a bomb on the access road to the Netzarim settlement, and died. He was the first IDF soldier to be killed in this war. As a young reporter on the news desk at the *Yediot Ahronot* daily paper, I was assigned to cover the company in mourning. A Tel Aviv pencil pusher, I wasn't accustomed to the smells in the field, but there I was, taking down every curse and swear word in my notepad and trying, in vain, to peel back the armour of the company commander, who was tormented at having the media around.

Outside the mess hall, completely by accident, I met Rotem. Rotem Yair. Everyone called him Ronen, though, because Rotem was a girl's name. And there are no girls in the Givati brigade. He was the gung-ho type, but worn out, and sad. He was as dusty as if he'd been plucked right out of a chimney, but his spiked hair was shiny with gel. 'You know what?' he said to me. 'Wait an hour, I'm going out on an escort mission, I'll set off a bomb, lose a leg, come back and shower with you and tell you everything.' Later, he made me a cup of coffee and asked me what a newspaper reporter could possibly want to write about them. There's nothing interesting here, he insisted. It's all the usual stuff, and everybody back home knows it all, and if they don't then they don't want to. Towards morning, after we'd talked all night, he told me – on the grass, beneath the thunder of explosions and machine-gun fire from a nearby Palestinian town – about Lebanon.

We spent four days together. During daylight hours he would go out on the white dunes accompanying settlers who wished to cross the death road. When Gaza fell asleep and the lights went out, he would return to the barracks in the tiny enclave, lie down next to me and get blasted with my questions. He would compare Gaza to Beaufort, brag about it and miss it.

Three months later, on the day of his discharge, I was waiting for him at the gate of Givati headquarters. I offered him a ride. On the way we stopped off for a late lunch and I started asking him again about the Land of Cedars. I asked if he'd be willing to hole up with me in a hotel on the beach and cut himself off from life for a little while to sift through the details, fill in the gaps. He was hard put to understand my reason for wanting to hear his tale, took some convincing, but eventually he gave in to my insistence and agreed to come away with me and tell his story.

With time I came to know the others: Uri Glickman, signaller and Nakpadon driver; Idan Koris, medic. Eran Tzabari, sergeant. Guy Pozitzky, squad leader. At Beaufort they lost a fighter from the bomb disposal unit, Noam Barnea, and their squad member Tzakhi Itakh, who was the last IDF soldier killed in southern Lebanon. Tzakhi's good friend Roi Cohen, who was with him in his final moments, was severely injured. He managed to call for help, and when it arrived he insisted that Tzakhi be looked after, worrying only about his friend until the moment he lost consciousness. Roi lost sight in one of his eyes and underwent a number of operations. Today he works in business and is planning a trip to India. For the most part, he's happy.

I met Shai Khingali, too, the commander of Tzakhi and Roy's squad, who was the first one to reach the scorched guard post that had been hit by a missile. He looked at Tzakhi lying there, at peace, kissed him farewell and loaded his body on to a helicopter. Days later he received a citation for evacuating wounded soldiers under fire that morning. He never stops thinking about Tzakhi and Roi, even today, and about the terrible things he saw there. They come back to him, especially when he is happy.

The popular company sergeant major, Ran Yurman, was seriously injured when a piece of shrapnel hit his arm during a barrage of mortar shells that fell on the outpost. He's been rehabilitated and now lives in an agricultural village in the coastal region of Israel. He studied business administration, but he's pursuing a different dream now, in the kitchen, and rumour has it he's a promising chef.

Two months before the IDF withdrawal from Lebanon, the Givati engineering company completed a tour of duty and returned to Israel. They were replaced by an engineering unit from the Nahal brigade. At twenty-five, the company commander, Avi Dohan, became the last commander of the Beaufort outpost. His final mission was to peel eighteen years off the walls, blow the outpost up with 980 mines, and leave the hill. Today he is a lieutenant colonel and the commander of a Nahal brigade, alternating with his troops between Samaria and the outposts spread along Israel's northern border. He moves around with them and with the flag, the one he took down from the flagpole at Beaufort and which now hangs behind him in his office. He is troubled by the company's long list of bereaved families, an entire squad of which was killed in the helicopter disaster in February 1997. He makes himself available to them in his free time – on weekends and holidays and for late-night phone conversations.

How many commanders in history have had the privilege of giving a speech like the one Avi made minutes before the hill was blown up, or like the one Goni Harnick made minutes before the hill was captured? An exceedingly short speech that contains no pathos and no prophecy, only an ending and a beginning.

There are two more people I would like to mention from among the commanders of the outpost in that period: Gal Tamir and Boni Mazar. Also the commanders of the Ali Taher mountain range battalion, Oren Ebman – who remained on the hill to the very last moments – and Lior Lifshitz.

In the meantime, last year Rotem married Lipaz Azoulai, his girlfriend from the age of fourteen. She has never read the dozens of letters he wrote her from the hill because he destroyed them, afraid to send them, fearing she'd be disgusted and alarmed and that she'd leave him.

The plot of this novel was woven from the events that characterized the last years of the IDF presence in Lebanon, but it is not a work of historical documentation. Liraz (Erez) Liberti is not Rotem Yair. He's an invention. The soldiers he commands are also not based on real people. They are all creations of my imagination, and every last one of them, from the lowliest soldier to the highest brigade and battalion commanders, those alive as well as those dead, though inspired by real people, are the children of my invention. Only the commander of the division at the time, Major General Moshe Kaplinski (Kaplan), today the IDF's second in command, has been named among the story's heroes.

I originally published the diary of an officer at Beaufort in a much shorter version in the *Seven Days* magazine in May 2001. Since then the story has been hounding me, following me everywhere: the feeling of futility etched on to each of the victims, and the scars, the powerlessness in the knowledge that I knew nothing, the deep, personal feeling of having missed something by not having been there and experienced it, and the will, through the characters, to sear the force of their experience on to myself, and to understand – all these together are what brought me to write this book.

On the first day of the Lebanon War, 10 June 1982, my mother's brother, Colonel Haim Sela, was killed. Although from then on we became 'members' of the military cemetery at Kiryat Shaul, I remained – as a child and as a soldier – oblivious to what was going on on the other side of the border. The characters in the book opened the gate to Lebanon for me.

* * *

I am grateful to all those who assisted me in researching this book, who read the manuscript, commented, and gave advice.

With regard to the pain in dealing with this subject, I am indebted to the Itakh and Barnea families, and to Moran Khizki, Tzakhi's girlfriend for the last two years of his life. These people opened their doors and their hearts to me, as well as the depths of their pain.

I was never for a moment alone with the torments of this story, and I wish to thank from the bottom of my heart all those who were my partners in this endeavour:

Oren Ganor and Aviram Elad, who pored over the manuscript at every stage and gave so much advice that they seeped into it. Their voices can be heard in these pages.

Oren Griffin, Hanan Furman and Elad Katz, who made up words and created thoughts that no one else could have.

Nir Baram, who forced me to get to know my characters for real.

Joseph Cedar, who has been living Beaufort with me now for four years.

Professor Avi Oz who, from afar, provided me with a wonderful stash of translated quotes from Shakespeare's *Henry V*.

Noa Mannheim, the editor of this book and my refuge of sanity, who orchestrated this journey gently and firmly and made all the difference.

Shahar Alterman, Ruthie Yuval and the team at *Seven Days*, who first helped bring the story to life and courageously took it as far as possible. It never would have been, without them.

Amnon Dankner, editor in chief of *Yediot Ahronot*, who made me write and refused to be disappointed, and who continues to believe in me and instruct me and keep watch over me.

And finally, to Anat and to my parents who are all that, and more.

www.vintage-books.co.uk